# Night Driver

A novel by MARCELLE PERKS

## Urbane
PUBLICATIONS

urbanepublications.com

First published in Great Britain in 2018
by Urbane Publications Ltd
Suite 3, Brown Europe House, 33/34 Gleaming Wood Drive,
Chatham, Kent ME5 8RZ
Copyright © Marcelle Perks, 2018

The moral right of Marcelle Perks to be identified as the author of this work has been
asserted in accordance with the Copyright, Designs and Patents Act of 1988.

All characters in this book are fictitious, and any resemblance to
actual persons living or dead is purely coincidental.

A CIP catalogue record for this book is available
from the British Library.

ISBN 978-1-911583-96-7
MOBI 978-1-911583-97-4

Design and Typeset by Michelle Morgan

Cover by Mark Cox and Marcelle Perks

Printed and bound by 4edge Limited, UK

URBANE
urbanepublications.com

# Night Driver

A novel by MARCELLE PERKS

This book is dedicated to my aunts Carole Anderson
and Annie Smith who are no longer with us, but
as passionate readers they inspired me from my
childhood to read and write.

If only I could send them a copy of Night Driver...

You won't kill me; I'll be back – yes,
I shall be amongst you for all eternity.

Fritz Haarmann (1879–1925)

# Prologue

In the black and white photograph, he looks too cheerful to have killed anybody. But because of what he did he was the first serial killer to make newspaper headlines all over the world.

Look again and his expression is less benign, as though he's concentrating on something. The eyebrows are thick, like furry stripes, but his eyes are set too close together. Perhaps he is just frowning. The pre-war Hitler moustache he sports, with a bald stripe in the middle, makes him seem worse than he really is. His hat is broad and jaunty, with a light-coloured ribbon around the crown. It fails to hide his sticking-out ears. There's a flap of loose skin visible above his tight collar. The tie is a ridiculous miniature, in the dapper fashion of the time. Even all these years on, this middle-aged man is still trying to impress. He took so much, when he needed so little.

Every time Lars the lorry driver looks at his good-luck photo of Fritz, he feels a tingle of recognition.

When Lars picks someone up, they usually ask about the photo attached prominently on the dashboard.

'Who's that?'

'That's our Fritz,' he always says, zinging on the 'z' at the end. Usually he laughs then. If they know about the killer Haarmann already, it gets them thinking. He likes it better when they're scared.

Not that he knows who he will take and who he will just drop off at the next rest stop or wherever he's heading. That's *Schicksal*.

On the open road, anything's possible, especially after dark. Real life just seems to disappear under the wheels of his lorry. The only world that stretches out into infinity is the burning strip of *Autobahn* he is travelling on and the possibilities that it carries: boys wanting to hook up with drugs or danger. Or something else. And if Fritz were here right now, in this world, Lars knows that he would embrace it. Sometimes he wants to be Fritz; sometimes he is Fritz.

Such a force of nature could never be completely extinguished.

# Chapter One

What Francesca Snell disliked, she did badly. And when she tried her damnedest, *trotzdem*, to fight her inborn stubbornness, every part of her body sweated strife. At thirty-one it was hard adjusting to life in Germany. Until recently she'd worked for a dot. com company and travelled every month alone on business to amazing Caribbean islands. There'd been the unexpected thrill of the turquoise blue sea, and the warm balmy air that calmed her senses. She'd never even been with her parents on holiday before to a foreign country. After years of struggling to get a decent job with her English degree, of her parents being disappointed that their talented daughter only bounced from one lousy short-term contract to the next, suddenly she was an offshore B2B publishing consultant. She had a year-round glow and was always going off somewhere in a plane.

True, the job was more sales than creative, but she felt that her natural talent had been finally spotted. She could work anywhere and do anything as long as she had access to a laptop.

But then the recession came, and the publishing sector in which she'd worked was hit hard. With the rise of the internet, readers could search most things for free. She lost her fancy job and struggled to find a new one. She panicked and sold her East London three-bed terraced house rather than risk falling behind on the mortgage.

She'd had to struggle to find work in the creative industries, arts graduates were inevitably exploited, and it always irked her that the scientists and engineers who'd studied at university with her had it so much easier. Her parents didn't have much money to support her and resented the fact that she'd studied the soft option – arts rather than a profession. Her dad had hoped she would be a doctor or IT expert and never got tired of telling her so.

Of course, her husband was cut from another cloth. Not only was he an engineer, he was German. She'd met Kurt when he was testing a wind turbine project in the Cayman Islands. He'd been so relaxed then. He was naturally attractive, with wide-open features and deep blue eyes. His was the kind of face that made you think of old-fashioned movie stars in double-breasted suits. He hadn't tried to get her into bed instantly like the English guys she was used to. Instead he took her to dinner and showed her the best place for scuba-diving. He dated her, fastidiously, as if they were sixteen. Her every whim mattered to him. He wasn't a genius creative like her previous boyfriends, a crazy film director and a brash journalist, but his interest in her was overwhelming. And that was addictive. The only thing they had in common was mutual attraction, but at first that was enough.

That first week in the Cayman Islands they drank one Mudslider Sling after another as they watched the sun go down. After a year of commuting, seeing each other every three weeks, when she'd lost her job she'd taken the plunge and moved over to be with him. She'd sold her house at a good profit and thought she could always move back if things didn't work out. But then the property boom in London went crazy, and before she knew it she was priced out of the market.

Things were good with Kurt the first year or so but then they had got married and moved here, and after that their relationship had solidified in a direction she didn't like. What for Kurt was normality was, for her, oppression. After being an international jet-setter, suddenly she was stuck in the German suburbs with no driving licence. There was a bus once an hour. It was like living in the fifties. In their village there were no takeaways; you actually had to cook if you wanted to eat. If you went to the local pub, people only went there for nosh and were in bed by ten. Their house and garden were big – that was why they had chosen the village, and Kurt had grown up in the suburbs and was comfortable with it – and they had enough to live on, but every day was the same. Kurt worked, earned the money, but there was the unspoken assumption that she had to keep house. As a previously independent businesswoman, she was terrible at handling that. It upset her, having to live with her own clutter with no real job to pour her energies into. For the first time in her life, she felt as though she'd taken the wrong path. She just couldn't shake it off, a secret dread that her father had been right all along. All this time she had been wasting her talents.

A lot of the time she would throw herself into creative projects she could never bring to fruition. Two non-fiction books fell through. The never-ending cycle of housework deadened her, and she knew that her ambivalence, in her occasional phone calls, worried her parents. She was proud and stubborn and didn't like to reach out to anyone. A lot of her friends had distanced themselves now she was in Germany and not available to go down the pub.

Most of all she was frustrated with herself. She'd wanted security, a partner, to have children, but not this stilled life. She missed her old ways; the feeling of doing something with meaning and purpose.

When she had got pregnant accidentally, after a stomach upset made her pill ineffective, she hadn't known how to react. This had been part of her long-term plan, but she hadn't yet settled in Germany and had been secretly hoping to persuade Kurt to move back to the city and that she would find a job. Kurt had initially said he wanted her to keep the baby, but as her pregnancy had become visible, and her previously small breasts had become full and her flat stomach ballooned – and, she acknowledged, as getting heavier had made her more irritable – he'd started withdrawing from her. He wouldn't admit that, of course. Every time she tried to discuss it, he gave her a shopping list of her failings that she was supposed to improve. And they hadn't been intimate since the third month.

When they had first moved in, Kurt had convinced her that the key to coping with her new lifestyle was getting mobile, so she was taking daily driving lessons. But she hated the stupid driving rules. She had quickly realised she had a fear of driving; nothing else had the capacity to make her so anxious. She had persisted, but now it was even worse: it was hard to concentrate when you were hot and bloated and had to pee all the time.

The struggles with her driving instructor reinforced her view that living in Germany was miserable. But before she'd fallen pregnant she'd convinced herself that if she could just master this one mechanical skill, then she'd be able to drive to the local city, Hannover, and potentially find a new job and new friends. And if that was now out of reach, with the baby coming she would need to be able to drive just to buy baby supplies, to take the baby to its checkups, and so on. There was no corner shop and the doctor was three miles away.

Her driving instructor was laughably abrupt. His English was confined to a few words that he used inappropriately. Heinrich had been wearing drainpipe jeans since the eighties; he was fifty going on fifteen. There was no allowance made for the fact that she didn't really speak German. She had learned quite a lot, but Kurt's English was very good so they spoke English at home. Most of the vocabulary relating to cars, like 'windscreen wipers', was unknown to her, yet Heinrich would bark a command and expect her to instantly comply; he forced her to drive in that pushy style which was curiously German. Today was a typical lesson.

'Right,' he said, in his broken English, '*Nächste rechts*, go!'

Frannie squinted at the peculiar way the road snaked into the curve ahead. Could she make the turn? The car already seemed to be falling down the hill just moving into third gear. Her hand wavered on the gear stick. Should she change down to second gear already and risk the Mercedes behind going into her, or try and take the bend going at fifty? She fluttered with indecision.

'*RECHTS!*' Without warning Heinrich grabbed the steering wheel. The car dived sharply right. Through the windscreen, the road was a twisting blur. The wheel felt alien in Frannie's hands. It was a struggle not to instinctively brake to control her panic, because doing that annoyed her driving instructor more than anything else. And when he got angry, he shouted in German and forgot all his English.

*Shit.* There was another parked car blocking her side. The road was alive with dangers. The car screeched left, right. She was having a hard time being delicate with the wheel. She checked the mirrors. Thank God there was no one behind her. Other motorists terrified her. She could only drive comfortably when she had the road to herself.

Her face was screwed up in concentration. The car lurched suddenly forward, and the engine screamed with a grinding wrench. The speedometer topped seventy. She looked down, wondering if she'd pressed the accelerator by mistake. No, it was Heinrich again.

'Go! *Gehen!*' His foot was furiously working the parallel pedals. His face bristled with indignation. The car groaned as it responded to double commands. They sped abruptly left, forcing an oncoming vehicle to give them priority. Heinrich began to shout terse stuff in German she didn't understand.

'*Was machst du?*' He looked as if he was about to slap her. His startlingly green eyes, which once must have made him cute, didn't fit the rest of his face.

She flashed him a warning look. She was older than his teenage regulars, and they were both frustrated that it was taking her so long to master the basics. Not speaking each other's language didn't help. And the fact that she was heavily pregnant.

The first five months or so she'd almost ignored her pregnancy, telling herself not to stress about it. Then she'd hit the sixth month and woken up a crazy woman, consumed with the overwhelming desire to get everything ready for her baby, which she knew now was a boy – Kurt had insisted on finding out, and the evening of the scan had been almost as nice to her as when they'd first met, as if getting an heir was their singular reason for being together. He said he loved her but seemed to prefer the company of his mates. She had focused on getting the nursery just right, on having all the toiletries on hand (even the ones she might not even need). It all had to be perfect. And she'd booked a driving lesson every day so she'd be able to drive and look after her baby like a proper mother.

And now, alarmingly soon, tomorrow was her driving test, and if she didn't pass there wouldn't be another chance to do it again before the baby was born. She couldn't imagine how it would be once he was there, but she was sure it would be even harder to summon her energies.

Houses whooshed past. It was hard actually driving at the speed limit; Frannie always wanted to go much slower. She hated the constant pressure to concentrate on the road every second. She tried to sit straight, forget about her bump.

Suddenly, the road opened out, as a stream flows into a river, into a Schnellstrasse, the B6. The long, straight road thrummed with gleaming cars. Frannie's knees trembled. Now she'd have to somehow filter in and keep up with the flow of traffic that drove so close that if the windows were open you could smell their aftershave.

'*Gehen!*' shouted Heinrich. He flapped his little notebook at her. There was a dreadful screech, as if the car was driving over something broken. Frannie hadn't quite got into fifth gear. Heinrich shouted something. Frannie grimaced. Her white maternity dress was limp with sweat; it was an exceptionally hot June. Desperately, she looked for a gap in the traffic to get off the feeder road. The speeding cars ignored her frantic signals. Meanwhile, the entry lane was merging, but some idiot was behind her gunning for her tail-lights all the way.

*Shit.* Frannie went, pushing the car in front of her practically off the road. There was the whisper of a near-collision. Beside her, Heinrich gasped. Normally he had to tell her not to drive so slowly. Now, with the devil in her, she was belting down her side of the white line for all she was worth. When she really wanted something, she could surprise herself.

She was going to pass the driving test. She must.

# Chapter Two

When Lars was in his lorry it did not feel like work. Driving for him was nothing more than reflex. He was a tall man, but, inside his cab, the extra height of the lorry went to his head. He liked it best when he had all the weight of a full load hooked up to the gears. He used the truck's massive bulk to frighten other drivers and the berth of his cab to pick up men.

For a gay man, he was relatively old; already forty, with a beer belly. Still, Lars was good at attracting young'uns. His shaved head gave him a tough, odd-looking baby face. His deep brown eyes looked as though they were always misbehaving.

He could have done many jobs but driving suited him. When he was on the *Autobahn* he could cruise along on autopilot. It gave him hours of time to fantasise. And, when he was rolling on the road, there was only one thing on his mind.

Lars obsessed about young men's flesh the way other people salivated over cars. He saw people as falling into rough types. His favourite, Type I, was naturally fair and practically hairless (or at least on the chest and stomach). He liked their skin to have a rosy hue so that if you pushed at it with a fingernail it would flush. Type II was Irish-looking, with black hair and light eyes, but the skin tone was still milky with little hair. Then there were the rough-boned types from farming stock, and the lean, lanky Northern breeds. The dark, hairy ones he left. They were a turn-off, and if his little man couldn't get hard then there was no point.

The one he loved was Hans, a dark blond. He gave Hans every cent he earned while the good-for-nothing was out doing God knew what. Without him the boy would be nothing.

He was feeling lucky. He pulled into a rest stop. There was just a stand selling hot sausages, and a toilet. The bare basics for a hunting ground. He stepped out to take a cigarette, every part of him focused on the other patrons.

A couple were rowing outside their car. The girl, flabby, boringly dressed, was being loud about something. Lars drowned her out. Her boyfriend was about eighteen, far too good for her. Type II, slender. He was inhaling a cigarette as if he'd only just got the hang of it. Lars bought a sausage to get closer to them. He made his face look affable, as if he didn't have a care in the world. His sharp white teeth sank into the meat. Their voices got louder. Lars could hardly breathe; if anyone had looked, they would have seen that his knees were quivering.

'Get there yourself, then!' The girl flounced off and jumped into her red car, squealing out of the car park. The boy held his hands out in the air. Then he stumbled over in the direction of the booth, all big eyes and hunched shoulders.

Lars just gave him a friendly nod when he bought a beer. He didn't have to start anything; the boy took one look at his warm eyes and that was it. Some of them even called him *Onkel*.

'Second time she's done that,' the boy said, looking down at the floor. He carried on slugging at his beer.

'Mmm,' agreed Lars, affably, as if everywhere he went he saw the same thing happening.

'Are you going Hannover way, by any chance?' said the boy.

'Yeah, as it happens,' said Lars.

'Can I get a ride?'

Lars nodded his head. He enjoyed this bit: being the thoroughly normal guy doing another guy a favour. When they'd finished, he opened the door of the cab for the youngster.

'Thanks, I'm in a bit of a fix!' the boy said, pink in the face.

'I've got a drop-off at the Moonlights Club,' Lars said, casually wiping his mouth. 'You can jump out at Pferdeturmkreuzung or you can walk from the club to the train station.'

The young man blinked a lot. His face was mulling it all over.

'Fags are in there; beers under the seat in the cooler,' said Lars as if he'd been expecting company. His face was open, natural. He was neither handsome nor ugly, but he smiled so much that people opened up, especially when they wanted something.

'That's the third time Vera's left me,' said the boy.

'Oh,' said Lars, stroking the handle of his gear stick. 'And who might you be?'

'Peter,' the boy said, his cheeks still flushed a brilliant pink. He was a blusher. Lars loved to see blood suffusing under the skin.

'If you like, I can get you into the club. My mate is part-owner. There'll be plenty of Veras there,' said Lars. His tongue darted energetically over his lips. He had to push his body further down in the seat to hide his erection.

'Really?' said Peter, his young face caught in a half-smile.

'Sure, just say the word.' Lars beamed at Peter again. But his smile was clearly just a shade too eager…

'You know, I'll get out at Pferdeturmkreuzung,' Peter said, not so sure suddenly.

Lars laughed as if he didn't have a care in the world. '*Jawohl*.'

From then on, he drove like a crazy man. He jabbed his foot down and turned the lorry abruptly out of the slow lane into the middle one. A car had to shoot into the fast lane to avoid him. Lars knew the full spatial length of his vehicle and drove erratically in and out of lanes, scattering motorists like ants. It felt as if all the raw vibrations of the truck were being pounded through his inner thighs.

Peter's flush had spread to his neck. His lower lip shivered. For some reason he looked down at the gear stick and noticed Lars's hard-on. He squeezed his eyes shut. He shouldn't have got in the truck and he knew it.

The high pitch of a mobile phone broke the tension. Lars answered, taking both hands off the wheel to do so. Peter's face glowed crimson.

'Another one?' Lars said. 'Now, right this minute?' His voice wavered, like a child disappointed at not getting his favourite ice cream. 'If you could just give me half an hour.'

The person on the other end answered and Lars frowned at the response, his fat stomach flapped over his jeans. Whatever he was doing now, this looked like work.

Peter's expression was frozen like a wounded animal. Perhaps he thought that if he was quiet and still enough, the truck driver might forget he was there.

🚗

'KONZENTRIEREN!' shouted Heinrich directly in Frannie's face. She couldn't even look at him, dared not take her eyes off the busy road. The other vehicles continually changed lanes, slid off on slip lanes or overtook each other. She was terrified she would drive into the back of someone who had abruptly changed lane, or that someone would ram her from behind. The B6 had a speed limit of a hundred and twenty kilometres per hour. It was way quicker than her comfort zone of below seventy. Driving faster was both physically harder, and also mentally: she had to react quickly at this insane speed to the numerous traffic lights waiting to catch her out.

To make things worse, it started raining.

Heinrich shouted a word she didn't know. He must mean the bloody windscreen wipers. Her panicked fingers blindly pressed buttons, but she got the indicators instead. Shit! She hated fussing with any extras: lights, wipers, indicators; didn't even know where the horn was. Keeping the car in forward motion was hard enough. She was gripping the wheel so hard that it was hot. The rain pattered down remorselessly. Temperatures inside the car started to rise.

To Lars the truck was an extension of his personality. When he was calm he drove solidly. When his mind was torn up, everything became erratic. When Peter had said he didn't want to join him at the club, he had driven like a two-year-old. He rumbled up to the next traffic lights as if he didn't know what a red light was. He hit the brakes sharply at the last minute, working up a sweat. The smell of him crept into the cab. Peter looked as though, if he had to endure much more of this, he was going to be sick.

A little grey Volkswagen emblazoned with 'Heinrich's Driving School' was crawling in the slow lane in front of him. Lars grinned to himself. He pushed his foot down on the accelerator, feeling his body thrum to the extra vibrating movement of the truck. The learner driver was driving as slowly as she dared. He didn't have any tolerance for learners. He drove to within a few centimetres of her bumper. See how she found that! He laughed out loud. The car tried to speed out of danger and then was abruptly braked back.

The instructor was obviously insisting on the speed limit. From the frantic head movements of the passenger and driver, a row was in full swing.

The car signalled left and moved to the next lane. Lars did the same, squeezing in behind in hot pursuit. The instructor turned his head to look back at him and Lars nodded affably. Never look pissed off when you want to frighten somebody. If they're confused you scare 'em worse. The learner driver went back into the slow lane. Lars once again followed them, forcing two cars to hastily brake. A horn hooted. He was really playing them.

Lars laughed to himself. He went on tailgating the little car. Peter groaned. His mouth made lots of swallowing noises. The learner driver's movements were becoming more and more frantic. In a minute she was going to shoot through a red light. The cab echoed with the sound of Lars's maniacal laughter.

🚗

Frannie couldn't think straight. All she wanted was to get away from the goddamn truck. Her thick blonde hair kept falling into her eyes. This bloody truck driver was practically leaning on her bumper! She just wanted to put as much distance between them as possible. Shit. The light had just gone red. The car was already over the line; she had to go for it anyway.

'*Nein!*' There was a screech as Heinrich performed an emergency stop.

Frannie's head was jerked forward. She could feel the vibrations down into her solar plexus. She screamed. It was as if something deep inside her had been wrenched. *Oh, my God, the baby!* Frannie's hand immediately went to her stomach. Her middle had absorbed the jerking motion like a punch. She had to resist the urge to go and yank the driver out of his cab and give him what for. She couldn't believe this was happening. The car was clearly marked as a driving school vehicle. Everything started to get dark; she remembered what the nurse with the pink hair had said on her pre-natal course and tried to slow down her breathing. Her every thought was concentrated on keeping the baby safe.

Heinrich was too shocked to carry on shouting. He'd written down the licence number of the truck and looked as though he was thinking about what to do with it.

She pushed on the hazard lights and forced her way out of the door. 'I can't…' she said, oblivious to the honking cars that minded very much that she was holding up the traffic on the B6. She had to breathe. No longer cared what anyone thought. She took in huge gulps of fresh air as the rain battered down her fringe and stood there trying not to look eight months pregnant.

'I drive.' Heinrich leapt round into the driver's seat.

She got back in the car. The green traffic light had been on for some time and the car leapt forward to escape the angry motorists who were lining up and gesticulating.

'Baby OK?' He was trying to speak English.

'Not sure,' she said, waggling her head. Her stomach had swelled into a dull zone of discomfort.

As Heinrich drove, he kept glancing at her. Something warm trickled down her leg, soaking her dress. At first, she thought she had wet herself, but it was much worse. Heinrich saw the blood before she did. Her white dress showed up every trickle of it.

'Shall I take you to the hospital?' said Heinrich, pulling over, his face creased in concern. He had turned from adversary to support in minutes and it made Frannie want to weep with gratitude.

'No, they have no records for the pregnancy,' she said, her hand holding her stomach. 'My gynaecologist is just around the corner.'

She showed him her doctor's card for the address and Heinrich seemed to understand.

She tried to think positive, but it was hard to suppress the tears that kept forming, however hard she blinked. She *had* to learn to drive in order to function in the sticks, but she hadn't anticipated anything like this would happen. How often did your driving instructor forcibly perform an emergency stop? Her hand shook as she took her mobile out of her handbag to call Kurt.

'We go there, now,' Heinrich said, as concerned as if he were the baby's father. He put his foot down and drove as if he had a flashing blue light.

# Chapter
# Three

Lars drove on relentlessly for another kilometre, but the game was over. He'd gone too far. The driving instructor might call the police. And if he got pulled over they'd see the boy. Hans always said not to take chances. He had another one back at the club anyway.

Without warning he squealed into a lay-by. The truck teetered on its axle for a second before settling into place. Peter had pushed himself down into a little ball on the seat. He started trembling when the brakes stopped fizzing and the engine stilled.

'Pferdeturmkreuzung is just there,' Lars said, as if the ride had been perfectly normal. 'Now off you go, son – quicker than you expected, eh?' he added with a laugh.

The boy scuttled out of the van, barely able to believe his luck. Lars clamped his mouth tight. Now he'd see what Hans had for him.

The Moonlights Club was just outside Hannover, on the *Autobahn*. Lars actually owned thirty per cent of the club, which he had bought with an inheritance, but it was his lover, Hans Grans, who was the manager. The club had previously been the Niedersächsische bank vault. There were all kinds of brick-lined nooks and crannies that shimmered with candles. Red crushed satin drapes adorned the walls. Its clientele liked fast cars and wild women. There was a cavern-cum-hall where the punters could dance if they had drunk enough; the DJ was schizophrenic and did techno one night and goth rock the next. Other rooms offered more immediate pleasures. Hans loved all kinds of women, but especially strippers, hookers and lap-dancers. Sometimes Lars thought he'd only got the job of manager in the first place so he could staff his own exotic playground. There were girls of every type. If they flirted with him in the interview he hired them.

One thing Hans had got right was getting a guest chef from California. The club served the most authentic American food this side of the Atlantic. The perfect burger, a chilli that was spicy but flavoursome, some Mex-Tex dishes that the locals went crazy for. Despite its sexual licentiousness, it had a diverse clientele; the ex-chancellor was known to dine there.

Hans liked to walk around conspicuously, greeting guests personally as they sat at their little rickety cellar tables sipping their drinks. In America he'd have had his own TV show.

When Lars pulled into the club, Hans was waiting for him outside at the service entrance. As usual, he was impeccably dressed. Among his addictions compulsive shopping came high on the list, and the more he paid, the better he wore the garment. Today he was wearing a dusk-coloured skinny shirt and an ink and cobalt silk tie with his white Gucci suit. He could have been a model with his perfectly proportioned features. Although the good-for-nothing was dazzlingly corrupt, nobody wanted to dent their illusion of him.

Everybody knew that it was Lars's money that had been used to buy his share in the club. They could only guess at why he chose to deliver drinks instead of being up front with Hans.

There was something sexual between them, but their relationship was also more than that. Lars treated Hans like a son, and the younger man had been a willing pupil to all sorts of con schemes. But now Hans wanted to go his own way. Lars would often look hungrily at Hans for some sign of recognition of their intimacy, but he only looked away, his eyes little pebbles of nothingness.

'Can you give our guest the VIP treatment?' said Hans now as he approached. That was their code for eliminating someone. They had a very exclusive soundproofed room that served a variety of purposes. Normally they shared in the excitement. Lars yearned for the look they usually exchanged but was shrugged off. He said nothing. Hans was like Peter Pan, the perennial spoilt child. It was time the bloody kid grew up.

'OK, it's his lucky day,' said Lars in a tone of unconcern, walking with measured steps to the club entrance. Hans looked as if he wanted to say something, to call him back, but Lars could play games too. He strode to the club's entrance without a word. Weaving through throngs of people, he headed towards the main bar and slipped through the side door.

Not many people knew about the VIP room. Even fewer came out.

Although Hans had a feel for what Lars liked, Lars preferred to procure the boys on his own. It was unnatural not to hunt them down himself. His mouth went dry with expectation as he put his hand on the door. Sometimes he and whoever was waiting inside would do no more than touch. Occasionally, if he came in time, he let them go. He never really thought about the end point until he was in a frenzy. Thinking about it made his knees tremble. It was getting harder and harder to get to that point, though. He no longer dominated Hans, could not even control his own arousal. Everything was slipping through his fingers.

Even now he hesitated, but after he'd done it, he would be pumped full of confidence again. He needed this like the working girls needed their plastic bags of coke and wraps of smack.

He knocked smartly on the door. When it automatically whooshed open, he took a step back. Instead of some smart boy, it was that silly cow Anna.

Hans's latest hooker infatuation had caused ripples through the club. A network of casual sexual relationships only worked if they all had the same weight. Anna had come to mean too much. And now, she was standing there with a champagne bottle and a glass in her hand. Lars smarted from his own jealousy. The thing of it was that women just couldn't stop themselves being stupid with Hans. If he said no, they'd jump him anyway. Hans just accepted sexual favours. He was too bloody good-looking for his own good!

Lars's eyes bulged. So that was why the little blighter hadn't been able to look at him just now. *Schweinehund!* He had what Hans called his 'predilections', but he didn't kill women.

🚗

As Heinrich drove, Frannie slumped in the passenger seat. Her whole body radiated fear and self-loathing. She was too hot, and, when she swallowed, everything in her mouth tasted metallic. The good thing was that she could feel the baby kicking, but her stomach felt volatile. She felt angry with herself for not passing her driving test years ago when she was young and fearless; when being pregnant was just a stray thought. For any normal person driving was just a routine thing they didn't even need to think about, but in London it had always been easier to get on the tube than to try to drive somewhere.

She had sent Kurt frantic texts which had gone unanswered (it was his habit to turn his mobile off at work). She'd emailed him at his work address and left a message, but so far he hadn't replied. She felt as alone as ever. When she needed him, physically or emotionally, he was never available now.

When had it started to go wrong? This year, when she'd got pregnant, or the last one on their holiday when he'd paid too much attention (for her liking) to the other guys from the adjacent balcony that had drunk with them every night. In her darkest thoughts she imagined he might be having an affair. He'd had a powerful sex drive once. Maybe he was channelling it in some kind of romantic frisson with someone else. She'd heard about websites where you could hook up with like-minded people. There were things that he liked sexually that she was not into; maybe he was exploring that. He seemed to prefer the company of men. All she knew for certain was that she sure as hell wasn't the focus of his attention.

Heinrich squealed to a stop outside the gynaecologist's office. Frannie instinctively put a protective hand on her belly. She prayed that nothing bad had happened. She knew bleeding didn't necessarily mean anything: one of her friends had bled all through her pregnancy with no adverse affects. She went to the toilet and examined her underwear. The blood wasn't that extensive, no more than a period; it was just that her dress was so thin that it had seeped through easily. And of course she was wearing white, which made it show even worse!

She exited the bathroom and went back to the waiting room. Heinrich couldn't stop talking to the receptionist. Presumably he was feeling guilty about performing the emergency stop when the light had only just turned red. She didn't try to understand the German, had to save herself for Dr Kanton. She was almost instantly taken into a treatment room and hooked up to the ultrasound machine. She lay flat, afraid now of what her doctor might find. She twisted her hands into fists until her recently manicured finger nails dug into her skin.

In Frannie's view, Dr Kanton was an alarmist. For the past few months she had been coming here regularly and the gynaecologist had doggedly scanned her belly every chance she got, as if she wanted to find something wrong. As a doctor she was thorough and exact, but rather too plain-speaking. From a doctor Frannie wanted reassurance, not someone who played on her worst fears.

The bleeding was not extensive, but it clearly gave Dr Kanton the twitters. Her shoulders were so bony it was as if her white coat were stretched on wire. She never plucked her eyebrows and left her hair grey. As she did all the tests, she was ticking off a list on her fingers.

'Urine is OK, ECG reads fine, but the placenta has had a, how you say it, *Abbruch?*'

When she got deep into it, she talked in German, but the words were lost on Frannie. That was how the Germans always did it: even when they could speak English they preferred to make you feel small for not speaking perfect German.

'*Abbruch?*' Frannie said.

Dr Kanton tried to explain in another way. 'A tiny part has broken away from the plancenta,' she said.

Frannie frowned. 'Does that mean the baby is in danger?'

Bad question to ask. For Dr Kanton, babies were always in danger. Her face broke into a grimace. 'It could be. A lot of women bleed after such a trauma. Your car accident may have done some damage.' She looked at Frannie severely. 'So now you must be extra careful. You could give birth earlier or even lose the baby. We are still some weeks before full term.' Her eyes lingered on Frannie's bump.

'But driving can't normally hurt the pregnancy, right?' said Frannie.

'No,' conceded Doctor Kanton reluctantly. 'But you never know when you need to perform an emergency stop like today and that is the danger. It would be best not to drive any more.'

Frannie felt as if everything were about to go black. Her driving test was tomorrow. How could she function, with Kurt working such long hours and all his business trips, if she couldn't even get to the local supermarket? She clenched her fingers together. Surely nothing could happen to her baby: wasn't he protected by a lining of water in the womb?

She was about to ask her doctor for some ballpark figure of the chances of the placenta getting worse but bit her lip. Despite her heavily pregnant state, Frannie took pride in her appearance. She washed her hair every day, as she had her whole adult life, and continued to put on a full face of make-up. Dr Kanton, with her mannishness and disdain for all feminine frivolity, presumably thought she was vain and self-obsessed because she worked hard to look good. Photos of Dr Kanton's children were on display; she imagined the doctor had knitted and hand-carved toys out of wood when *she* had been pregnant.

She *had* to take the test, otherwise she'd have to walk everywhere on foot with her baby in tow.

She gave Heinrich a meaningful look and he nodded. He shuffled his feet and then spoke to Dr Kanton in a hard-sounding quick-fire German exchange. Thank God he was on her side now. He was evidently managing to persuade the doctor that he would see to it, personally, that Frannie would be safe during the test. She tried to stop the tears that squeezed out of the corner of her eyes.

'I know this test is important, but you really must keep out of cars afterwards until the baby is born,' said Dr Kanton, looking at the driving instructor pointedly.

When Frannie thought of the lorry driver who had caused this, anger bubbled up in her veins. That bastard! But this was ridiculous; on her test she didn't have to perform an emergency stop because of her pregnancy. In fact, they had never even practised one.

On the way home, with her hand laid flat on her stomach, she tried to pluck up the courage to dial Kurt. He should be home by now. She desperately needed comfort, but he'd be angry with her; he was always scratchy these days. When he failed to answer, she hung up. Better to let Heinrich do all the explanations. She was too tired to think any more.

'Annchen!' Lars said, going up to her with a fake bonhomie. Even though he rarely drank, he took a glass of champagne from the table. The room sat ten comfortably. Plush leather sofas provided a discreet play area in what was intended to be a VIP room for passing sports stars and actresses. It was stylish, excessively so.

A deep, royal-looking carpet softened the echoes of the room. Ornate glass shelves housed the most luxurious whiskies, cognacs and cigars the club had to offer. Lars had found it ideal on several occasions.

'Lars,' Anna drawled, in the affected style that very beautiful women often had. The minute she opened her mouth you could tell she was Polish; her bone structure was also characteristically bird-like. She was sitting in a nude chiffon dress, with spaghetti straps that gave him a fine view of her neck. She laughed, trying not to show her annoyance at seeing him.

'Have you hidden away Hans again?' she said.

He laughed. Tried to disguise the fact that his hands were shaking.

Anna had been annoying him for some time. She was a glamorous blonde who considered herself Hans Grans's main squeeze. Lars did not like women who wore too much make-up. Anna was so artificial, there was nothing true about her any more. And she had no taste. She wore cheap earrings with a real diamond bracelet and necklace. You could give her a four-thousand-euro dress, and she'd wear it with stupid shoes.

Although she had been irritating him about Hans, he didn't think he could do anything to her. She aroused his jealousy, but not his desire. Unlike Hans, who found flattery from either sex satisfying, Lars was gay. Nothing about her could get him going.

He didn't kill because he hated people or wanted to do them harm. It was simple *Lustmord*. When he got horny, shit happened. It was the frenzy of the experience he wanted: to bite and kill. But he didn't fuck women and he didn't kill them. Hans had no right putting her in this room with him at all.

All Lars could think was how small and child-like her hands were. She was a dainty creature, tiny, with barely-there breasts. If he put both hands around her neck he could have snapped it. He wanted very much not to have to kill her. He sighed. Hans was really taking the piss.

Anna sat and laughed at him. Not with her mouth but with her kohl-lined eyes. She turned and went to get herself a cigarette from a box on the ornate shelves. From the back, Lars noticed that, with her hair up, she became androgynous. His tongue darted furtively over his lips. Type I. Female, but still the right type. Try to think about her ethereal skin. He closed his eyes. Was Hans watching on the CCTV?

'Are we stuck in here, Lars-ey?' she said over her shoulder, mocking as usual. 'I don't mean to be rude, but I am actually waiting for Hans to take me to dinner.' She looked at him as if he was something under her stiletto. 'Why are you here?'

Even her hipbone pointed at him aggressively. She poked at a bowl of olives, wiggling the stick in annoyance. Her eyes were half-closed slits.

The little madam had been laughing about him for weeks, thinking she was better than him when she did nothing but turn tricks for Hans. She was trying to burrow into Hans's skin; thought she was so beautiful she had a right to know everything. He wrinkled his nose in disgust. She was such a turn-off. He tried to imagine the intense masculinity of the truck, the throb of its machine roar. Had somehow to get into the zone.

In two steps he was on her. He pushed her face down on to the wide sofa. She let out a shocked scream. He sat on her legs and made her lie prone, he wanted to avoid seeing her face. He ripped her dress off with one movement. Anna shouted and screamed and tried to push him off, but the arms that pinned her down might have been made of steel.

Underneath her body was practically androgynous. He pushed her long blonde hair over her head so he could concentrate on the nape of her neck. If he ignored the obvious, she could be an adolescent boy, all slim and nimble. Her young flesh coloured as he fondled it. He playfully squeezed her neck.

'Please, please don't,' she screamed. Her cries pierced the room. The more fiercely she struggled, the more right it felt to Lars. In his gay encounters he spent hours playing rough. His victims were usually exhausted from consensual play before he really started. If he just gazed at the back view of her naked body, perhaps he could convince himself he could get horny. He only ever killed in the throes of passion.

'Shut up!' Now her struggling was really annoying him. He

couldn't concentrate on his fantasies. It was taking all his effort just to keep her pushed down on the sofa. No, he was losing it. There was no tingle in his toes.

It was hard pushing her down when she was struggling so violently. His arms were aching. He looked up into the cameras and jerked no with his head. If Hans wanted this done, he was going to have to get out here and do it himself.

He threw her off the sofa.

'You bastard!' she screamed. Half-choked, she could do little more than mewl in fear.

Within a minute Hans was there. He came in smoking as if joining a dinner party and immediately turned on Lars.

'What kind of shit is going on here?' he said, grabbing Lars by his collar. Anna whimpered in his direction. She thought Hans was there to rescue her, but he quickly turned on her and slapped her. His face was reddened; he was angry with both of them and didn't want them to know it. Anna screamed harder. Her cute little world was seeping down her face in black streaks.

Hans went to Lars. He smiled at his much older lover and put his tongue in Lars's mouth. Lars instantly turned to putty in his hands.

'Oh, *Schatz,*' said Lars, his eyes rolling upwards in pure bliss.

Anna started screaming even louder. Somehow this show of tenderness disturbed her more than the violence. Her eyes widened in shock as Hans picked up one of the huge leather sofa cushions and advanced menacingly towards her. Roughly he shoved it over her face. She kicked and screamed all the louder. The bits of words she uttered were savage. Pure terror gave her a vicious energy.

'Fuck it, I don't believe this!' said Hans, his voice for once rough and hard. He didn't normally get his hands dirty, and he tried to actually touch Anna as little as possible, using the cushion as a third party. When her struggles got more frantic he actually sat on her and used his legs to keep her flattened.

'Get over here, will you?' he snapped.

Lars just sat smoking in the corner, not wanting any more part in it. His brain was not letting him register what he was seeing.

Anna let out an agonized cry and then went quiet.

Hans Grans got up gingerly, as if he'd sat in something that had stained his trousers. He put the cushion back neatly and smoothed it down. Anna was tipped callously on to the floor. Blood started to trickle from the nose. She must have broken it in the fall.

Watching the slow trail of red ease out onto the floor changed everything for Lars. He let out a groan. Hans's sharp eyes noticed everything, although he said and did nothing.

'Over to you, then; she's all yours. Can you drive her to the body farm when you're finished?' His face wore the look of a manager who had just taken care of some pressing task. He patted down his white suit trousers. Not a smudge on him. 'The paperwork's ready,' he added in a normal voice as if he was just referring to a drinks order. Lars just looked at him, aghast. It was as if he was seeing him for the first time. Hans left the room, looking like he'd just stepped out of *Vogue* after a very satisfactory lunch and would just like a little Cognac to settle his stomach.

Anna lay on the floor, dead to the world.

# Chapter Four

As Heinrich was parking in the street, Frannie spotted Kurt's car in the drive. She was so nervous about him finding out her news that she could barely swallow. She checked her phone. He hadn't answered one text or email. Yesterday he'd been in a foul mood just because his football team had lost. She was beginning to think she didn't really know him any more. He was always staying up late surfing on the net and getting lots of mysterious texts on his phone, but any time she sneaked a look it was always some guy from his ex-military service days.

She stood outside the front door hesitantly. The bright blue paint of the door had worn away, and the flowers in the pot next to it were wilting. The other houses in the smart suburban street had over-attentive owners. Their house from the outside looked out of place. Each house was individually built with a large garden. Lawns you could hold magazine shoots on, with windows that glistened in the sunlight. But everyone else was too busy to enjoy a glass of wine. Kurt had once loved her carefree ways, but his mother and his friends were constantly belittling her efforts to keep everything neat. *Ordnung.* She prided herself on being spirited and creative. Who wanted to be a Stepford wife? She hadn't gained two degrees to competitively keep house.

It was Heinrich who finally rang the doorbell. There was a sound of something heavy being put down (Kurt must be doing his weight training). After a minute, Kurt stood there, his muscles protruding out of his tight sports clothes. His dark blond hair was tousled, as if someone had just run their hands through it. Her heart lurched as she saw him, still as handsome as the first day they had met. But that face that had once focused completely on getting her attention was now sullen. Whatever they'd once had, it was gone now.

Kurt took a step back when he saw Frannie's bloodstained dress. He stood there blinking. She shrank into herself. Couldn't he show some emotion? As usual, she had no idea what he was thinking. They went inside into the living room. Heinrich looked distinctly nervous. Their lesson should have ended two hours ago. He started to explain what had happened in such quick German that Frannie couldn't do more than get the gist of it. This must be the first time for Heinrich that a pregnant learner had come a cropper.

She longed more than anything for Kurt to hold her and tell her everything would be fine. When he learned that part of her placenta had broken away, she saw the anger in his eyes turn to fear. He looked at her as if he just couldn't believe it.

Even though it had been his idea that she should learn to drive, still Kurt was furious that the baby's safety had been compromised. He kept saying she shouldn't drive under any circumstances, until she wanted to smack him. Heinrich tried to calm him down. Their voices could be heard all down the street; it was embarrassing. She pushed past them and ran to the loo; she couldn't understand when they spoke so fast anyway.

There was still a bit of blood, and she felt nauseous, but the baby was staying put, for now. She could hear the guttural 'ge-ugh' of the story being told in the past tense. One day she hoped she would be able to understand a hundred percent of a German conversation. Right now she had to be content with getting the gist of it. Every time she wrestled with the language she felt the familiar stab of failure. It was another one of those things that didn't come naturally to her.

But why had that mad lorry driver pursued her? He'd gone for her like a man possessed. It didn't make sense.

Kurt called her as soon as she came out of the bathroom. 'Heinrich wants to call the police,' he said. 'He's got the number plate and they should be able to check his tachograph.'

'His what?' she said. All she wanted was to lie down and fall asleep, but Kurt would have none of it.

'His tachograph. It shows how fast he was going. Lorry drivers are not allowed to go over eighty kilometres, so the police can check it and it'll show that he was driving too fast. Heinrich will meet us at the police station.'

Kurt went to find his shoes. It was typical of him that he was obsessing over details rather than engaging with her feelings. Why couldn't he just hold her the way he used to? She sighed and went to her room to change out of her bloodstained clothes. She really felt that Kurt didn't love her any more. His obsessive weight-training while she was pregnant made her feel physically more inadequate. What was she going to do? This was one of the thoughts she tried not to let herself dwell on. Was it living in this godforsaken country that had turned things bad, or was it the relationship itself?

On the way to the police station, Kurt drove badly. When he suggested for the second time that she had somehow made the lorry driver angry, Frannie could have strangled him.

'This driver did everything to provoke me,' she said. 'Ask Heinrich if you don't believe me! He practically pushed me off the road.'

His neck got redder. 'You shouldn't have let it get to the point where you had to learn to drive so late.' He banged the wheel with one hand. 'If you were properly organised, if you took the time to think ahead, you would have passed your test long ago, and now you won't be able to,' he said.

'Huh?' she said, pressing down her foot as if she was driving. 'It was your idea that I get mobile – and how do you know I'm going to fail? I haven't even taken the bloody test yet.'

'You can't...' said Kurt, too surprised to finish the sentence. 'Didn't Dr Kanton say...'

She almost stood up in the car to make her point. 'It's just *one more drive*,' she said, pushing her fringe out of her eyes. 'After everything I've gone through...'

'Calm down, it's not good for the baby.'

Frannie was tired of that one. Stress was bad, coffee was bad; anything remotely exciting was not allowed.

'KURT!' she shouted. 'I'm trying to learn German, and how to drive. You should try learning something new in a totally foreign language. It's not easy.' Her face was flushed with rage. Her hand continued to strike the dashboard in little slaps. 'Every day it's like climbing a mountain; it just never ends.'

Kurt looked as if he'd been stepped on. 'I've made a lot of sacrifices as well, you know,' he said. 'I could have stayed freelance and hung out in the Caribbean living the dream. The reason why we're back here is so that we have stability and a nice house to live in.'

'No, it's because you can't stay away from your family!' said Frannie. 'And you couldn't live abroad where they don't have a *football stadium*.' Kurt tutted. She bit her lip.

'Well, if you want to drive when you're pregnant and the doctor's dead against it, then don't expect me to help you,' said Kurt. His voice was hard and tight as if he couldn't breathe properly.

Frannie squirmed in her seat. Kurt was surprised at how motivated she had become, learning to drive. Because she was pretty and feminine, men were always taken aback when she revealed her determination. For too long since she had been in his country, Kurt had played the role of helper. In truth, she suspected that he enjoyed the fact that as a foreigner here she could only operate at half-strength.

The flat, monotonous countryside through the window depressed her further. Everything was pine trees and long straight roads. It was like waking up in the wrong house, every day. Often she had to quell an irresistible urge to run. Was it just her pregnancy hormones creating havoc? Or had she had enough?

The police station was, like everything else in Germany, spacious and clean. It gave the impression that it didn't matter if crimes were solved; the important thing was that the place was properly swept and mopped. An immaculately dressed policeman was waiting to hear their complaint. His eyes lit up when they walked in. He was young and dark, even taller than Kurt. He looked suspiciously at Frannie as soon as he realised she was an *Ausländer*.

Heinrich began to explain everything, and the policeman was murmuring sympathetically. From time to time he looked at Frannie and took a peek at her *Mutterpass*, where Dr Kanton had noted the latest problems. He looked Frannie up and down and inspected her passport. Then Heinrich theatrically produced the truck driver's numberplate. It was typed into a computer.

'So, we have a Lars Stiglegger,' he said, frowning, 'Lorry driver... Ah.' His face changed. He picked up a phone and shouted something to a colleague. Another policeman ran down some stairs; there were more shouts. Kurt shuffled his feet. So far he'd said nothing. Frannie couldn't understand what all the commotion was about.

The policeman now looked at them as if they were the criminals. 'You can't report someone just for bad driving,' he said, his voice suddenly sharp.

Heinrich looked as if he had been slapped. 'You mean you don't want to do anything?' he said, letting his stare bore into the policeman's eyes.

The officer glared back and looked at Frannie with undisguised contempt. 'He did not actually hit your car?'

Frannie shook her head. Kurt stood sulkily but Heinrich almost jumped on the policeman. 'But we had to perform an emergency stop because my student was made so nervous. And her pregnancy was affected. Never have I seen such driving.'

The policeman ignored him and stared at Frannie accusingly. 'Perhaps you don't know our German traffic regulations? This man is a professional lorry driver.' He cleared his throat and looked at Frannie's wide eyes.

Heinrich was about to burst. 'Surely you need to at least caution him?' he said in his most polite German.

Another policeman came up and whispered something in his colleague's ear. He nodded. 'Yes. We will speak to Herr Stiglegger,' he said, closing his report book with a neat little snap.

Frannie couldn't believe that no one was taking her seriously. She sat clutching her stomach, terrified that the baby had been affected. A migraine was starting behind her ears, all the tension of the day hitting its mark. From this morning, it had been one big balls-up, and, with all the tension riding on her performance tomorrow, it looked as if she was in for a rough night.

From deep inside her womb, the baby kicked. Frannie had the familiar feeling that she was sliding into nothingness. And now she was so pregnant they wouldn't even allow her on a plane back home.

# Chapter Five

When she was still, Lars could overlook the fact that she was female. It didn't matter. She was out of it. Her body turned into one expanse of flesh: pure, beautiful, smooth. A canvas. He leant over her skin and fondled it, making little gasps as if it was he himself who was being touched.

There was nothing like young skin, especially when it was perfectly even and unmarked. He hated the current fashion for tattoos. Anna's body was scarless and was free of piercing, but although the veins in her arm were clear it was obvious she'd injected smack in between her toes and the veins in her legs.

He laughed. She was trying to get away with it, but her body was giving up its secrets to Onkel Fritz.

He kissed her neck. He got excited just leaning over her body, imagining. He tried to visualise the network of veins and muscles under the skin. He'd already moved her into the huge metal drinks crate that had once been used to import outlandishly expensive champagne. They'd decided the crate served admirably as a very adult toy box. There was room in there to hover, Nosferatu-like, over a corpse.

He'd got into the habit of putting them in there before he started his games. Then, after he opened them up, all the blood could seep out in the waterproof crate and it was *egal*. He'd hose it down once the body was removed.

Anna's nose was dripping bright red blood. Lars looked down and groaned as he stroked her neck. All his energy was focused on the flood of sensations as he got more and more aroused. He pushed her chin up so that the delicate neck was exposed and started kissing it aggressively, letting his teeth sink in to the place where the jugular vein lay. The real Fritz was said to have bitten through the Adam's apple to suck the blood, but he had always found this impossible. Instead, he found the major artery in her neck with a trembling finger and made a neat slit with a carpet knife that he always carried in his pocket.

The blood started to fall out and, caring for nothing but the release waiting to spring, he let himself suckle the wound, wallowing in its warmth. In this position, steeped literally in the lifeblood of another, he could achieve his most satisfying orgasms.

When he came, it was like the entire contents of an ocean had leapt up in one motion and hit his body in one whooshing smack. It was an orgasm so high that when it waned it was like falling off a huge building. He was huge, unassailable, godlike.

*Lustmord* – no one anywhere, could ever have had an orgasm like it.

Life made sense again.

🚗

There was a private bathroom within the room, where he kept fresh clothes so that he was prepared in the event of a kill. He'd barely finished cleaning himself up when one of the bar staff buzzed up to tell him the police were on their way. Browbeaten Inspector Koch came in, his thick, ungainly body panting in the heat. He was a rough-looking man on the wrong side of fifty but had the soul of an artist. He'd often told Lars he wanted to publish a little collection of poetry that he'd been writing over forty years.

They'd formed an odd, but loyal alliance.

Koch's eyes were drawn to the metal packing crate that took up most of the space in the room. It was silver-coloured and expensive-looking. His mind was probably thinking of potential freebies in it. Let him imagine.

Anna's corpse was now bleeding out in the crate. Lars imagined the blood thickening, forming a dark red angry crust and congealing. With a neck wound, the blood immediately rushed towards the head in a vain attempt to repair the damage, so extremities like the hands and feet would start to cool and stiffen first. When a body was partly drained of blood, what was left felt different, started to get a certain smell, although usually he didn't keep them that long. The dead smelt bad very quickly. The first fly was attracted within half an hour.

Fortunately, the packing crate was airtight.

Hans and he had it down pat. The corpses were still fresh when despatched to the body farm. No one questioned him when he needed help getting a wine crate in and out; it was a nightclub. They had all kinds of expensive stuff that customers forked out for. There was a special machine that you just hooked up to the crate and then it could be rolled along with one hand. It was dead easy. A typical Hans operation. He was as slippery as an eel and none of it could be traced back to him, he always made sure of that. The more money he earned, the greedier he got. He would not stop until he owned the club outright, and half of Hannover too.

Koch was agitated. The man was practically waltzing on the spot.

'Lars, we've had a complaint from a bloke who runs a driving school, a Heinrich Bostel. You caused him to do an emergency stop and his pregnant student could have lost her baby,' said Koch firing the words out. 'It was on the B6 today around noon, do you recall?'

'I drove like shit,' said Lars wearily. He had to put on the right expression. 'There was a problem with the orders, the traffic was all blocked up and this silly fucking wannabe driver was as slow as a snail.' He let out a sigh. He could see, said the sigh, that he'd put Koch in a difficult position. 'I'm sorry, I was an arsehole. I just had a bad day. Perhaps we can forget all about this with a drink?' His smile became cagey. 'Anyway, I've still got to let you know the latest on that drug deal over at Rüdiger's. They want to drop the hit on Friday. Frank told me.'

Koch knew how it was. Lars was a touch stupid, pushed a bit of the soft stuff and was not averse to letting things fall off the back of his lorry. But he was fucking useful. Still, he had to show a bit of boot.

'If we get any more complaints, I won't be able to bury them,' he said, trying to make it look as if he was doing Lars a favour. 'They'll have to investigate, and then there'll be nothing I can do. Get a motorbike if you want to drive like an eighteen-year-old.'

Lars laughed. He let his voice make the right noises. Koch had no idea. Once he'd done the deed he felt invincible, a superman come to earth. He reached for the most expensive whisky in the VIP room, enjoyed the thrill of pouring it out in glasses, using the crate as a makeshift table.

The body would start to stiffen as its basal temperature dropped. He knew the score. Whatever Anna had once meant to Hans, she'd never be able to turn him on again. If he wanted to get back in with Hans, now was his chance.

Frannie had gone to bed early but sleep eluded her. She had watched the clock tick by while downstairs Kurt watched something loud. She was going to bed these days much earlier than him but wished he could keep the sound down. Perhaps he had his phone in his hand and was using the time to openly text whoever he was getting messages from. It had been going on for some weeks now. She'd hear a muted beep and then he'd disappear to the toilet for half an hour with his phone. She never asked questions; she'd didn't want to appear jealous. Only weak people were jealous. And any time she took a sneak peek it was always some bloke. When he rolled into bed late stinking of beer, she'd pretended to be asleep. It was easier. He made no move to hold her the way he used to. She would lie in the dark, sick with worry, her hand cradling her pregnant belly.

Frannie had often been nauseous in her first trimester, but nothing could have prepared her for the sickness that struck her next morning, on the day of her driving test. Although she was hungry, nothing got past her lips. Heinrich was coming for her at nine sharp and in the half-hour before that she was constantly running to the bathroom. Even her shoes did not fit properly. She tried to calm herself; for the baby's sake she had to pass.

She went through the motions in the pre-test lesson. After yesterday, Heinrich was unusually gentle, but she could not parallel-park properly and held her breath at every red light.

'Are you sure you are up to this?' said Heinrich in an unusually quiet voice.

'Yes! After everything I've done, I just want the chance, you know?' said Frannie, although part of her wanted to crawl back to bed and stay there.

The test instructor was an elderly man whose grey hair was streaked with black. He instantly understood that she was heavily pregnant, and not German. Heinrich struck up an animated conversation with the examiner that went right over her head. She was instructed to drive down a little road away from the main drag while the two men laughed and joked as if they were having a beer. Almost casually, the examiner said, 'Can you parallel-park behind the green vehicle, please.'

Automatically Frannie clenched up. It was hard to control her legs and hands under pressure. When she pulled forward she overshot it, and one of the car's wheels actually climbed the kerb. Both men stopped talking. In her anxiety her foot hit the accelerator too hard. She shot in reverse and mounted the kerb a second time. The passengers were once more jerked around. The examiner exchanged a look with Heinrich.

Frannie was crushed. Her shoulders slumped, but she was might as well go for broke now, show them what she was made of. She forgot about everything and focused on the test.

It seemed to go on forever. She had to go not once but three times on the *Autobahn*. The examiner gave absolutely no indication of how she was doing.

'Take the next left,' he said, in between reminiscing with Heinrich.

'Now reverse back and go right.'

Again and again Frannie had to reverse, drive around a maze of streets and turn wherever the examiner instructed her to. She didn't think, just went through the motions. Her hand and eye co-ordination had never been better. She worked the clutch like a pro. The examiner's voice never changed in tone once. She didn't even think about needing the toilet. Her mind was a grey blank. She just did what they told her.

At the end she remembered to put on the handbrake, and just sat there waiting. At first she didn't understand the German. It was only when he put the driving licence in her hand that she realised that she'd passed.

'Do you want to know your mistakes?' said Heinrich.

'I know I mounted the pavement twice,' she said.

'Ah,' said the instructor. 'You also nearly went into a car on the *Autobahn* and did not give way on the Forster Strasse.' He smiled broadly.

'I didn't realise…' She had made more of a mess of it than she realised.

Heinrich drove her home.

'Why didn't I fail?' she asked him suddenly. Her mother had failed nine times in England. She was sure that she shouldn't really have got away with so many faults.

'I had a little word with Herr Löschner last week,' said Heinrich. 'I explained that you'd had so many lessons, had tried really hard, and that this was your only chance before the baby comes.'

'Does that mean I didn't really do it?'

'Whatever I say to him, he still has to do his job,' said Heinrich stiffly. 'Anyway, it's not just a question of getting your *Führerschein*.' He let out a hollow laugh and looked at her as if she was completely naive. 'It's one thing to drive with me, but then you must be able to do it by yourself, and it's even harder with a baby in the back.' He smiled and shook her hand. 'I wish you the best of luck,' he said.

Frannie felt her heart sink. She hadn't thought about that. With Kurt not willing to help her, how would she gain the confidence to drive alone?

🚗

Being in the truck made Lars feel powerful: he liked the chug chug of its energy and the squealing noises it made when he changed down a gear; the gasp of the brakes. It was even more exciting for him when he had a corpse to transport. Although no other drivers on the road knew what he had in his truck, still it was a solemn task. It took seconds to kill them and then there was all this stuff around it.

Hans had told him that the real Fritz had cut up his victims in a small upstairs bedroom and carried them down four flights of stairs in a covered bucket to throw in the river. He talked about Fritz a lot. That must have been back-breaking – and the mess! You couldn't do that these days. He'd seen it on TV in detective shows they had all kind of shit – DNA, fingerprinting, forensic whatsit. He was glad he didn't have to wear latex gloves to handle the bodies. The feeling of dead flesh was pleasurable to him. It had the cool assuredness of beauty. The fact that its state was so temporary, that it would spoil in just days, made it all the more precious.

After death, a body's state constantly changed. It was no longer a person. It became human Play-Doh. Hans always wanted him to drive the bodies as quickly as possible to the lab, but sometimes he kept them a few days longer. Then it got to a point when even he was tired of them. Not that he wanted to cut them up or eat them or anything silly like that. Hans encouraged him to be like Fritz, who was meant to have sold his victims' flesh as sausages on a meat-stall opposite the *Hauptbahnhof*. But he had his limits. He didn't murder for profit, but he didn't object to getting compensation from old Buttgereit. And he could indulge in all these things because Hans had set everything up for him. He was the only person in the world who understood him.

The Kaiser Medical Institute or body farm left a cut-off hand or parts of a leg out in fenced-off woodland. Trainee forensic anthropologists needed to study how the body looked on day one, day fifty and so on. It was a secret project, and desperately needed bodies: often the body parts would be scavenged by wild animals, so they constantly had to replenish the scenery. It was hard to get them through official means, so a corrupt bureaucrat there forged the death certificates and sorted out all the paperwork.

It was a joke. They got rid of the body, no questions asked, and got five thousand euros for their trouble. And with no corpse there was no crime. The Institute used only partial corpses, so no one could be identified. His victims might as well have vanished into thin air.

Funny to think that his urges were providing a useful service.

No, Hans was good to him: he allowed him to be what he was. And in return Lars treated Hans like a son, gave him everything, did everything. And although, he, Lars, didn't kill women, didn't even fancy them, he'd killed Anna when Hans had wanted it done. That was what they had. They were everything to each other. There was something so fine about Hans. Lars had shown him everything, the drug dealing, the killing.

But his boy, who had him like putty in his hands, was growing up.

When he pulled into the Institute, it was quiet. Herr Buttgereit was there as usual. He was the operational manager, had the key to everything, and all the paperwork at his fingertips. He walked with a stoop, as if it was all a terrible burden. Nobody could guess his age. Could have been sixty or eighty. White, smooth hair, and a slight bow to his knee, with every movement exaggerated, as if it cost something to use.

'Evening, Stiglegger,' he said, directing him to the morgue. He winced as he opened the casing and saw the wound on her neck, and the extensive bruising where she'd fallen on the floor. 'Can't you be a bit more careful with them?' he said. 'Gotta have something for the students to look at.'

Together they lifted Anna out and put her on to a gurney. Buttgereit cut away her clothes with a pair of scissors and wiped off some of the blood. He used rubbing alcohol and gauze. Despite his age, he was brisk and efficient. He always paid in cash. Lars didn't know how he got the money. But then he didn't ask the questions, that was Hans's job.

Still, Buttgereit's next remark threw him. 'It would be better for all of us if they weren't quite so dead,' he said. 'Just a little bit dead is better.'

Lars could only laugh. 'What else should I do with them? Your students want to do a bit of life painting? Where's the money in that?' He rubbed his hands nervously together.

Buttgereit frowned, went to say something and thought better of it. Perhaps he'd had a bit to drink. Not everybody had the balls to do what they did. It must be creepy for him sitting above a morgue. The old man handed over the usual envelope. Lars didn't have to count it; he knew he wouldn't be ripped off. What they were doing was so heinous that payment was the least of it.

# Chapter Six

When the very first bird in the garden began singing, it woke Frannie. Like a drunken man slapped out of a coma, she was forced to seek nourishment. Since about week twenty-two of her pregnancy it had been as though she was activated by remote control. Some primitive, profoundly annoying instinct forced her to get up around three a.m., leaving Kurt a duvet-covered blur. With her mouth sand and her mind fog, she hated the bewildering clarity of these dawn reveries. It was the only time she felt awake.

When she slipped out of bed, she instantly got dressed. It had been building up to this and now she had to do it. She was tired of not being able to drive to get groceries, of endless rows with Kurt. It had been a week since her driving test, and she wanted to get out there. Even though she'd had no further problems with her pregnancy, her husband was still refusing to sit in the car with her.

If she was going to do it, she had to do it alone. If she dared to go out now, there would be virtually no other cars. It was the inky realm of pre-dawn. Only the owls were out. She laughed. Kurt didn't know her as well as he thought he did.

It was easy to imagine it. But when she got outside she was trembling. She'd never even driven Kurt's car. It was an Audi A4, much bigger than Heinrich's worn-out Volkswagen. When she was actually sitting inside it, it was like being in a tank. It took ages to adjust the seat so her feet could reach the pedals. She blushed as she started the ignition and the car made its signature chugging noise as she reversed out of the drive.

The thrust of the car was even: you didn't have to press hard on the pedal to get a result. Inside the car, she couldn't be sure she wasn't driving with the parking light on, so she left the car running, handbrake on, and got out to check the lights. Everything was fine. She got back in, put her seatbelt around her big tummy, turned the car into the road and prowled into the night.

The headlights nosed the empty street and the freedom made her feel light-headed. Just the slightest depression on the accelerator and – boom – it went like a horse out to win a race. She felt all her angst about the baby and Kurt melt away. It was a joy to be able to go as slow as she liked. She took her time getting the feel of the car, groping for her confidence.

This was easy. She could drive the way she wanted to. No Heinrich to shout and intervene. There was even the temptation to ignore the usual road signs because there was no one to give way to. She pushed the car towards the next village, Frielingen, a dot of a place built on a bend. Normally she dreaded driving this bit, but the car snaked around the curve like a pro.

As none of the houses had lights on, it was effectively a blackout. The only thing to focus on was the shape and feel of the road itself, which seemed to become alive as she drove over it. She opened the windows slightly. The night air smelt of long-ago rain.

She drove in the direction of Garbsen, with open fields each side. The country road was flanked by trees. She was surprised how rough some of the country road stretches were. It was good that she was going slower than the legal limit.

Her house was close to the B6, one of the trunk roads that sped traffic to Hannover. She'd been on sections of it during her driving lessons, but in the daytime it was hectic and prone to snarls of stop-start traffic, so Heinrich always diverted her off after a few kilometres. It ran parallel to the road she was on now, and she could see the lights of occasional cars flickering by. She hadn't left civilisation after all. In the distance a Tamoil petrol station stood out in neon blue, as if a gateway to other temptations. It flickered. She felt as though she was eighteen again. She found the rock station Radio 21 and started singing to an old Metallica song.

Even though there was no one behind her, she indicated to go right and made her way to the traffic lights. If she went straight home she could drive home anonymously in pitch black. But if she turned right then she'd be in the thick of things.

Ah, what the hell... She moved into the right-hand lane. The traffic light turned green and she was off and away. The overhead orange lights seem to frame her as if she was in a gigantic computer game. In quick succession she blasted through three sets of traffic lights, green all the way.

This was easy. She dipped her foot down on the pedal and whooped with joy as the car went faster. It was still dark; a big eerie moon was watching. The speed was pure exhilaration. She felt weightless, as if she could drive forever, just eating up the road.

From the open window, the wind rushed in, making little gasps. Although she'd been the sole driver out, behind her now was the ominous white eye of an advancing headlight. It was going like the clappers. The glare stung her eyes. She tried to drive faster away from it, but the speedometer was already on one hundred and forty. Normally she drove at half that speed.

The car's motion was no longer fluid. Every little bump in the road got magnified. Still the driver behind her came nearer. She could hear the familiar *gggguughhh* whine of the motorcycle's engine. She moved into the slow lane. Let whoever it was speed off and leave her an open road.

In her wing mirror, the profile of an intimidating motorcyclist, all long handlebars and cocked legs, sailed into view. It was the biggest bike she'd ever seen. He sat hunched on the huge metal beast, like an angry wasp about to sting. There was something of the cowboy about the way he gripped the machine. The throbbing engine screamed of an aching sex drive. As he hovered next to her, in the fast lane, the wind began to bludgeon its way through the gap in the window.

At this speed, if she made one false move, the car would quickly career out of control. She expected him to zoom off into the distance, but he stayed steadfast like a police convoy. Even when she went slower, he kept pace. For about a kilometre they drove in tandem. She couldn't understand what he was doing. He kept glancing in her direction. The sound of his engine was driving her crazy.

She should have been scared, but her face was rapt, concentrated. A little smile played around her lips. She became wrapped up in his fury. The roar of his engine was like hunger. When he went faster, she pushed her foot down too. She tried to imagine what it would feel like to be him, exposed on the saddle, with all that wind and night clawing all over him. And underneath, what would he look like? Frannie giggled.

The motorcyclist looked at her again. It was as if he was trying to communicate, but what? He roared on ahead. The sight of his butt suspended in the air, waggling from side to side, spurred her on. Her foot was nearly down all the way on the accelerator, her whole body getting sucked back by the speed.

Signs flashed past at a frantic rate. Hannover city was coming up. Unexpectedly, over the next hill, a red traffic light sat waiting, goggle-eyed. Frannie slammed down the brake, but she was going much too fast. The car swerved in a horrendous skid. The stink of burned rubber filled the car. The screech of it hovered like an echo and snapped her out of her exhilaration. She just about kept control, but as she spun to a halt her hands and legs were shaking. How could she have been so insane?

The motorcyclist, who was already stationary, looked anxiously in her direction. He'd see she was a middle-aged woman and laugh at her folly. The spell was over. She took deep breaths.

*Tat, tat.* She jumped. It was the motorcyclist at her window. Through his raised visor she could see neat grey eyes smiling at her. He was young enough to ride recklessly. She wound the window down some.

'You OK?' he said in German worse than hers.

'Think so,' she said, rolling her eyes.

'Don't press brake so hard,' he said laughing. 'You make tyres unhappy!'

'Are they OK, do you think?' she said. She shuddered. What would Kurt say if she couldn't drive home?

'We go to the Tamoil there,' he said pointing to the garage up the street. 'I check.'

He leapt on his bike and sped off. She followed him more slowly, and within a few minutes they pulled into the petrol station.

The stink lingered. He was already on one leg examining the tyres before she could get out of the car. She peeked at him.

With his helmet off he had a young, angular face with solid cheekbones. His dark hair fell all about.

'Brake crusher! Go forward, a little,' he said, indicating a tiny gap with his hands. 'I must check the rubber...is it tyre?' She got out of the car to get a better look at him. His body was strong and lithe. He looked as if he could handle himself.

'Thanks for helping,' she said, wondering if she should offer to buy him coffee. 'I'm Frannie, from England. I just got my *Führerschein* and wanted to go out when it was quiet.'

He looked pointedly at her bump. 'You can drive like that in one year's time. Now…a little bit slower.' Again, his hands moved. 'But your wheels are OK.' He patted the car and stood up, staring at her as if he couldn't make her out. His hips stood out in sharp relief in his jeans. For a second he hesitated.

She just stared at him, caught off guard.

'You're not German?' she said. It was funny how it was easier to click with other foreigners.

'*Nein!* I am Tomek from Polski.' He found it funny she didn't know his nationality straight away.

'Poland? Are you here on holiday?' she asked, wondering what he was doing here.

He pushed a photo of a delicate-looking blonde into her hand. 'I look for my sister,' he said, his cute eyes looking desperate, 'Her name is Anna. She says she has good job here, but then I hear nothing. I come to find her.' They studied the photo together. 'Yeah. She says she work for club Moonlights. Do you know it?' He fixed her with a haunted look in his eyes.

'No.' Frannie just smiled. They both laughed.

'She has a friend, Dorcas, who works on the *Autobahn*.' The way he moved his hands to explain everything was touching.

'*Autobahn?*' What did he mean?

'In a minivan,' he said as if that explained everything. 'But I cannot find her. Nobody knows anything. When I see you, a woman alone, in the night, I think maybe you know people.'

His eyes looked lost. He stood there holding the photo as if it was the only thing he had. Frannie smiled. Although he had burst out of the night like a demon, he was alright.

'I hope you find her,' she said, and meant it. She hugged her arms. Little Susan Timberley in her class had gone missing when she was eight. Frannie knew what it did to families. She didn't want it to eat away at this young man from the inside. 'Look, can I help in some way?' she said pushing her head forward. 'My German's not that great, but I can research online, hand out flyers.'

A look passed between them. His prominent upper lip trembled.

'Thanks,' he said. She had to lean forward to catch the words. 'Perhaps you night-drive again tomorrow?' he said, handing her a hand-written scrap of paper with his mobile number on it. 'Maybe we can make plan to find my sister. I just have one week. Then my job…I must go back.' For a second he looked even younger, as if he'd been temporarily puffed up by the noise of his engine.

Something in his face caught her. She wanted to kick out of this inertia of waiting for the baby to be born. Why drive around aimlessly when she could be doing something useful for someone?

'I also don't have much time,' she said, smiling. 'My baby is due in July.'

An ugly flood of yolk-yellow streaked the sky. Dawn was rushing into the sky to meet them. It was time to get back before Kurt woke up. She looked at Tomek, at the way the eerie morning light knocked the tension out of his face. She wanted to help, but more than that: she longed to see him again.

'Do you know the Shell garage in Garbsen? The one that's open twenty-four hours, opposite Burger King on the Bremer Strasse?' she said carefully, gauging his reaction. 'I'll be there at three a.m. tomorrow.'

'OK, done,' he said, looking at her as if she'd just given him more money than he could ever spend. 'I have to get a magazine that might have some information. Tomorrow we talk. Thank you, crazy lady.' Theatrically, he put on his helmet and fastened up his jacket. 'Now I have to meet a woman who say she know something, maybe, or perhaps she just take my money. Will tell you tomorrow,' he said, forcing his engine into life.

The longer she spent with him, the more vivid he seemed. He jumped on to his bike and soared off into the night with an animal roar. Frannie was left standing there breathing in the smell of burnt tyres and petrol fumes. The new day was starting in a testosterone haze. It was hard to take it all in. She had to make sure Kurt didn't hear one word about this or the fact she'd driven his car.

It was easy driving home. She didn't even have to think about it.

# Chapter Seven

Through the window of her minivan, the sun sparkled. So far it had been a lush June filled with many days of hot weather. The heat suited Dorcas. It allowed her to sit in the van in a little silver bikini with the windows wound right down. She knew she was a pretty thing. It was the one thing she could rely on.

Just scenting the summer breeze put a smile on her face. She was parked up on a *Rastplatz*, a popular truck stop, although right at this moment she was not thinking about the cars that might contain customers. She was giving all her attention to the sight of the majestic golden corn that grew in abundance in the fields.

She liked it here at the service station. It opened up to fertile farmland. Being next to the *Autobahn* in the middle of nowhere was like being in two places at the same time. The men came in hard, fast cars, with all their angst seeping out of their veins. And she soothed. Whatever it was that itched, she took it away. And, in turn, Hans eased her needs. He gave her lines of coke. You needed something for the boredom, to cope with the smell.

One day, soon, always soon, he'd told her, he would own the club outright. He'd stop messing around with the other girls. More than anything she wanted to believe they had a future. That his thing for Anna was just a passing phase. Hope was all she had.

Hans, the manager at Moonlights, had all the girls at his fingertips. One look at his face and he made you believe in him. It was unreal what he could do.

Her mobile phone beeped. She was on the phone as much as she was working.

It was Elli again. In between clients, the girls called each other or sent funny texts.

'You know, Anna still hasn't turned up.' She stopped to give an excited little laugh. 'Isn't that like weird – I mean after what she said about Hans?'

'Oh?' said Dorcas trying to sound neutral. Anna had got too close to her lover. Technically Dorcas was engaged to him, although that didn't mean much when there were half-naked women running around the club day and night.

Dorcas could hear Elli carefully inhaling on a cigarette while she thought about what to say next. They could talk freely about any of the ridiculous things their punters wanted them to do, but they never betrayed any intimate details about Hans. Because he slept with everybody, nobody wanted to talk about it out loud.

'Yeah, he had some new business going down that she didn't like the sound of. He left his laptop in her gaff and she had a peek,' said Elli in high, excited tones. Gossip fuelled her.

'Was it new girls coming in?' said Dorcas, trying to push away the familiar feelings of jealousy.

'I don't know. She said she'd forwarded me one of his emails, but I never got it,' said Elli. 'Hey, I bet it was more Russian tarts! You remember Lassia from Kiev?'

They both laughed. Everybody knew Hans liked Russian women.

'Anna's probably become a gang-bang porn star,' said Dorcas with a laugh. 'She was always very picky about her punters!' Elli shrieked hysterically in her ear.

Dorcas sensed a potential customer coming towards her door and hastily rang off. A well-dressed middle-aged man came towards the open window.

'Business?' she said, raising her eyebrows.

'Full sex,' he said as if he were ordering a Chinese.

'Forty,' said Dorcas, and gestured him to go round to the back of the van.

She had used the theme of the Arabian nights to make the inside of her van welcoming. Antique tapestries hung on the walls. A thick maroon rug covered the floor space, which had a raised area for sex. The quicker she got them lying down with their pants off, the faster she got it over with.

Dorcas flaunted her young beautiful body. In her barely-there bikini she knew she looked good. Her tan was perfect. Her fingernails and toes were lacquered jet black. Her client was older but well-maintained. She liked a man who kept his pride. Then he opened the little bag he had with him and showed her what was inside.

He handed her a pair of handcuffs. 'I'd like you to put these on,' he said, without smiling. In the dim light his eyes had an animal look. He also had a latex basque that presumably he wanted her to wear too.

For now, Dorcas kept her smile. 'If you'd like an S&M session I can organise that for you, but we don't offer bondage out of our vans.'

The man just stared at her. 'I thought the customer was always right.'

'*I* can handcuff *you* if you like or we can play with them, but you can't actually put them on me here,' she said, trying to keep her voice light. There was something about this one that gave her the creeps.

'Well, that's what I want,' he said in a monotone. He took out his wallet and pulled out a hundred-euro note and held it to her face. 'Will this do?'

'Sorry, it's not the money. We just can't do that here. It's against company rules.'

Dorcas managed to push a button on a bleeper that was hidden behind a tapestry. It was the alarm signal they all had installed. She just hoped they would get there in time.

Meanwhile the client, despite her protests, had laid the note on the bed, as if paying for it meant he could do what he wanted. He didn't seem to understand that it was all meant to be consensual.

Dorcas stiffened involuntarily. She didn't want him to see her reaction, but it was hard when she was standing there practically naked. He seemed to sense her unease. A sick sweet look came over his eyes as if he'd been drugged.

Dorcas struggled to maintain her composure. If she could keep on talking to him, perhaps it would buy some time. 'I can't do bondage here, and full sex is just forty.'

'I've told you what I want,' he said with a contemptuous smile. Dorcas struggled to keep him talking whilst she explained for a third time, as politely as she could, that bondage was not a service they did out of the minivans. He wouldn't be told. With a sneer of contempt, he threw himself on her and started biting her lips as hard as he could. She let out a series of loud screams; it felt as though she had been stung and her mouth poured with blood.

'Do as I say!' he said, quietly but directly in her face, intoning every word as if he really meant it.

She was dragged down. The handcuffs were snapped into place and he made a rough gag out of a pair of tights he had with him. Her own blood had run down her neck like chocolate and was staining her lovely bikini.

Dorcas was too afraid to even move her eyes. Beads of sweat broke out on her forehead. Although he kept on talking, all she could hear was her own heartbeat, screaming.

Without warning, the front windscreen shattered. The back door burst open. Lars jumped in, threw himself at the punter. He planted an angry fist in his face. Dorcas cowered in the corner, trying not to step on any broken glass.

'*Was machst du hier?*' shouted Lars. Dorcas had almost never heard him shout, he was normally so jolly and generous. His hands had found their target. That must have been the army training he talked about. He was punching like a prize fighter. The john's face was being beaten to a pulp. If she didn't stop him there'd be a body on the floor.

She made a loud 'Mmmmmhh!' sound through her gag.

Lars looked at her normally lively face, dripping with blood, and the sight of it seemed to enrage him further. She could see him automatically stiffening his hand into another fist. Her customer was pretty much on his knees, groaning. In the next millisecond Lars had turned again into a beast. The man was dragged to his feet. 'And now you go!' shouted Lars, physically pushing him out of the van. The money had vanished.

Lars undid the gag and handcuffs, took a Kleenex out of his pocket and proceeded to wipe some of the blood off her chin. She took out a packet of baby wipes to do a proper job. He shut the door, held her tenderly in his arms. 'My poor Dörchen!' he said as if talking to a child. He'd often told her that she was the best, and that one day he'd marry her. She was the only one of Hans's girls that he cared for. She usually laughed and pushed him off. Although they talked nearly every day and often cooked together, she knew he only liked boys. 'You're alright,' he said to her over and over, stroking her hair. 'I'm sorry about the window, needed to divert his attention!'

When he was holding her, she noticed that he smelled odd, as if he'd had a wash but hadn't been able to get rid of the smell underneath.

'What's happened to Anna?' she said looking deep into his face. They were as close as brother and sister. If he knew something, he'd tell her, eventually. She knew he pretended to be stupider than he really was.

He didn't look at her directly. 'Let's just say she fell off the back of a lorry,' he said, hugging her and landing little kisses on her cheek. Dorcas said nothing, but she winced. Thinking about Anna sent a dull, deep pain running through her stomach. She needed to know, one way or another, what was going on.

Lars stroked her hair and patted her cheek.

'Did Anna leave? Or was she forced?' said Dorcas, hugging him tight to her chest.

He just smiled at her with a big stupid grin, rubbed his hand across her face. 'She's getting all the attention she ever wanted,' he said.

'And is it over with Hans?' she said, voicing her jealousy for the first time.

Lars gave her a sideways look. '*Everything's* over for her,' he said. Dorcas couldn't think straight. It was hard to stop herself thinking dark thoughts. Something funny was going on. And Hans was in the thick of it.

Deep in her belly she had an odd feeling, a foreboding she couldn't shake off. The last time with Hans had been a bit crazy. She always used condoms with clients, but not Hans. It was different with him. There was only a slight chance. But she could be. She closed her eyes and didn't let herself think.

If she *was* pregnant, she had to find out what Hans was really up to.

# Chapter Eight

After her first night drive, Frannie could think of nothing else. She hugged the secret to herself. Every spare minute, she drank in the sensation of speeding along a neon-lit open road. Night-driving had released her from the cares of her everyday boring chores. She thought about Tomek non-stop.

Kurt noticed her unusually bright eyes the next morning, but he didn't say anything. At this stage in her pregnancy they were merely polite to each other. They hadn't had sex since the first trimester. The last time she'd tried to initiate it, Kurt had looked pointedly at her bulging stomach and turned his head away.

'I just want to be careful,' he'd said, concentrating on something on his laptop.

'Is it the baby?' she'd said, almost tearful at his rejection. She'd got pregnant much too soon, hadn't she? Perhaps he was regretting it.

'We've got other things to think of now,' he'd said, trying to laugh it off.

She was uplifted by thoughts of Tomek. In her mind's eye he was a lone, lithe figure on a personal crusade. She wished Kurt had a bit of his drive. He'd been so sweet and attentive for the first couple of years, but now he took her for granted. She was tired of hearing him talk about what he was going to do. The baby's room was still not ready.

Although she was extra tired in the day, and could do little more than waddle about, she didn't mind. It was a relief to go to bed extra-early. She wanted to be ready for tonight.

In bed she fell into an exhausted sleep that as usual lasted until she needed to pee. Normally she would then float in a light sleep, something in between dreaming and insomnia that disturbed her more than it refreshed. This time, when she felt her consciousness hit shallow waters, she pulled herself out of it and slipped out of bed.

Before she could stop herself, she changed her knickers and put on a little make-up. She hadn't expected to meet anyone before. Despite her pregnant bulk, she wanted to look half-decent. She knew the tight-fitting black sweater looked good with her long blonde hair.

She drove on autopilot to the petrol station. The dark road was clear of other cars and she found she could go a little faster. She drove round the parked vehicles without a second glance. The fact that she was not completely awake somehow made it easier. Not worrying about every little manoeuvre allowed her to build up a synchronicity with the car. It was only five minutes to the Shell station, but she seemed to slide there in seconds.

She parked eagerly. It was a quarter to three. She was psyched: going to meet Tomek in the middle of the night was the most exciting thing she had done for years.

A short, fat guy was devouring a schnitzel with chips, but other than that the dimly lit restaurant was empty. It was a very small space, with film posters on the walls and cute hanging lanterns. It was the German idea of what a diner might be. It was one of the few twenty-four-hour places around, so they tried to cater for anybody that might come through the doors after midnight. The schnitzel-eater ignored her.

On impulse, Frannie got herself a real coffee. As she hadn't had it for so long, she got a little jittery from the caffeine kick. Would he really turn up to meet her? The clock slid to one minute past three and when she looked up, he was there.

Tomek strode up to her. His lean hips pumped from side to side like two pistons. When he saw her, he smiled. The hair was a touch wavy, mostly wild, his look casual but sexy, as if he didn't give a damn. He wore his faded blue denim jacket as if it was a uniform. There was an energy drink in his hand. She noticed he had faint dark circles underneath his eyes.

'Driving OK tonight?' he said, smiling again.

'No problem!' she said. 'Yep, it's easy when there's no one about.'

She pushed back her long hair nervously. He was the best thing she'd seen in the flesh for ages. She wanted to just sit and stare. Better to talk. Her suppressed sexual urges were rippling away like an invisible but lethal river current.

'So, have you heard from your sister?' she said.

His eyes turned dull. 'Nothing,' he said, tensing his knuckles. 'Nobody know nothing!'

'And the woman last night?' she asked.

'I gave her twenty euros and still she know nothing.' His eyes showed the bitterness of the encounter.

Frannie slipped him a little card with her address and mobile number on it. 'This is how you can contact me,' she said, wondering if she was betraying Kurt in some way. She'd left her home telephone number off.

'And Dorcas?' she asked.

He took an amateurish-looking porn magazine out of his pocket and opened it up on page four. 'It say here that a Dorcas is at the fifth junction west of Hannover. Later I will go, see if I find her,' he said.

Frannie couldn't hide her surprise. 'Is that a porno mag?' she said.

'*Natürlich!*' said Tomek, trying to hide his smile. 'What do you think women do who work out of vans? This is a magazine for truck drivers. It tells you where they all are.'

Frannie was gobsmacked. 'They have prostitutes on the *Autobahn*?' she asked, trying not to blush.

'Yeah, here in Germany it is legal and men seem to feel a little bit sexy when they drive fast, or so I hear!' he said, laughing again.

She sipped her hot coffee, tongue-tied. Was his sister working here as a prostitute too? She didn't want to ask.

He shrugged his shoulders, looked at her intently. 'You want to drive with me on the *Autobahn*?' he asked. Once again, he was a boy in trouble. 'If you come with me, maybe this Dorcas, if I find her, she speak better to you, a woman.'

Frannie gave him a look of horror. Drive on the *Autobahn* already! What she wanted was to stay in her little rat-run of familiar streets. But he was so young; that face tore her resolve in two. He took out a map and showed her the route.

'I'll follow you,' she said, trying not to give a shiver. She was always afraid of being trapped on the *Autobahn* and never finding the right exit off.

🚗

She was not frightened to actually drive on the *Autobahn*, not at night anyway. The sticky bit was getting on and off. In full traffic this was no mean feat; often the speeding cars would not pull over or ease off and make a space for incoming drivers. Exits were also tricky. Some of them twisted like something from a funfair, and in peak traffic other drivers forced her to race round them when she didn't have the experience to handle it.

Tomek had promised to go slow. It was no problem following him. He kept an intimate distance between them and took care to signal well before every turn so she wouldn't have to do anything in a hurry. He led her on to the A2. There were no other cars around at first, so it was dead easy. He let her get into her stride then started to increase speed. The signs rushed past and again her car was eating up the road. She just exhaled and went with the flow. It was not so easy driving fast, but she didn't want to lose sight of him. Not when she had a good view of his rear jacked up on the bike.

They roared up the central lane. The half-dark outside seemed to push down on them as if it didn't want them to go any further. A trickle of lorries rumbled along on the slow lane. She had to resist the urge to flinch when she passed them. Her foot pressed down and she zoomed past.

The thought of encountering again the Lars lorry driver who had caused her accident filled her with dread. The German roads were full of huge trucks that dragged down the traffic and terrified her with their proximity. Her hands gripped the steering wheel. Much more of this and she was going to freak out.

Another burning stretch of road and they were pulling up at the *Rastplatz*. There were some truckers parked out back and a man fuelling up. The bright lights made it seem as if it were day. Tomek pointed out a maroon-coloured minivan that was parked among the trucks. She wouldn't have looked at it twice, but a fluorescent light shone brightly to illuminate the driver's seat.

When they were closer they saw a dark-haired woman with a Louise Brooks bob sitting incongruously in a bikini. Her already large eyes were highlighted by carefully drawn eyebrows. Frannie thought she would have looked good on horseback in a full set of armour.

Tomek turned to her. 'We go together?' he said. The photo of his sister was already in his hand.

When Tomek knocked on her door and Dorcas, the prostitute saw Frannie, she frowned. She must be wondering what a heavily pregnant woman was doing with a client. Frannie felt a flicker of jealousy as she saw the way Tomek glanced at her.

Dorcas looked exquisite, but uncomfortable.

Tomek handed her a note and showed her the photograph. He kept his voice polite. 'This is my sister, Anna, perhaps you know her?'

Frannie saw a funny look come over the woman's face. It looked as though her lips were actually bleeding. She took the photograph in her hand and looked at it under the light. Her face changed. She said something, but Frannie couldn't understand her strong Berlin accent.

'You know her?' said Tomek, anxiously.

'An Anna I know worked for Hans at the club, but blondes all look the same to me,' said Dorcas, pointedly looking at Frannie.

'Really?' said Frannie, rising to the bait instantly. Her whole life, other women had resented her natural blonde hair and good looks. But Tomek looked forlorn under the glare of the neon light.

'Hans…?' he said.

'Hans Grans, at the Moonlights club. But she left just last week,' the woman said. She handed the photograph back abruptly, as if she couldn't stand to see it. 'She was shagging the boss, and I guess it didn't work out.' Her voice was uneven, as if she was unsure of herself. Frannie could imagine what sort of person Hans Grans might be, from her voice.

'She just go?' said Tomek, looking in surprise at both women.

'It's a nightclub. Girls come and go all the time,' said Dorcas, as if they were talking about the price of butter. When Frannie came nearer, she stuck her tongue out. 'And who is *she*?'

'This is my English friend. She wants to drive better,' replied Tomek, pointing at Frannie's bump.

Dorcas broke into a raucous laugh. She was probably sniggering at her bloated middle. Dorcas was gorgeous. It was a pity she was sitting in the middle of nowhere waiting for strangers. Meanwhile she continued to eyeball Frannie, lit a cigarette and blew the smoke near to her face. Did she see her as a competitor? Surely not. What did the silly cow think she was doing?

Dorcas feigned an interest in Tomek. They spoke for a few minutes so fast that Frannie couldn't comprehend it. She just got the last bit, when Dorcas hung out of the window and said with a coquettish smile to Tomek, 'You know, if you're ever this way again, just come on by.'

Frannie couldn't decide whether it was professional or genuine. Much to her annoyance, Dorcas and Tomek seemed to be getting on very well. They kept making big eyes at each other. Dorcas kept looking at her with obvious dislike. Frannie tried not to feel jealous. She was a married woman with a bump the size of a basketball, but the third time Dorcas blew smoke in her face, she decided to go.

'Mind you don't get scabby knees,' she said sourly, turning on her heel. Dorcas shouted something contemptuous back, but she was gone. Tomek ran to join her.

Outside her car, there was an awkward silence. She wanted to scratch that woman's eyes out!

'Same time tomorrow at the café?' said Tomek, the wind kinking his hair into waves. 'I will go to this Moonlights club first, then tell you everything.' He put his arms around her and gave her an affectionate hug. He could see Dorcas had rattled her. 'Please be there; you are the only friend I have in Germany.'

She gasped. Dorcas was probably staring their way from her van.

'Please come,' he said again. 'If anything happen to me, no one will be there for Anna. I will send a text when I am at the club.'

She felt dizzy, nodded. He was only here a few more days. She could do that much for him. She stared into his light, laughing eyes and breathed in the sultry night air. *Natürlich* nothing was going to happen between them – she didn't want it to, really, she was eight months pregnant for heaven's sake – but a little attention was good.

But when she looked at Tomek, all geared up on his bike, it was hard not to feel something. It would be nice to get on the back of that bike of his – and just run.

This night-driving lark was addictive. If Kurt knew about anything about her secret life, he'd go mad. She had to get back before the serious traffic started, make sure he didn't find out and put an end to it. She was rushing now, but, when the moon was lonely in the sky again, the world would be hers.

# Chapter Nine

The next day, Lars went to the club around ten. It was the breath-holding time before the rush, when the last diners were finishing off their schnapps and only the keenest punters were in action on the dance floor. He walked through scattered groups looking for Hans. When they'd first shacked up together in a poky flat they'd dreamed of having a place like this to call theirs. Now he couldn't find the swine in all the retro gloom.

He went to check the VIP room, but it was locked. They must have changed the keypad. Perhaps Hans was in there with a woman. Lars snorted. The boy was getting out of control. Even Dorcas was getting riled, and she looked the other way a lot. You wanted to give your partner the freedom to explore their desires, but Hans took it too far. Even though the room was soundproofed, he could have sworn that he heard something kicking off.

He leant his head closer to the door but could make nothing out. Probably shagging, the dirty git! Lars laughed. He was just about to light a cigarette when the door opened and Hans was right there in front of him.

'Are you spying on me, you mad bastard?' said Hans, looking shifty. He took care to shut the door with a quick slap so that Lars couldn't see inside. As usual, he looked like an animated mannequin in a fawn grey suit with a navy waistcoat. Hans was all flourish. He wore the extra money he was getting.

'Did you know Dorcas was attacked by a weird punter last night?' said Lars in a careful voice. He was desperate to gauge the younger man's reaction. Hans was in the middle of becoming someone else, and Lars didn't know yet which side he was on.

Hans looked as if the bar had stopped serving free drinks. 'Really?' he said, lifting a hand to his fake pocket. 'Is she, er, scarred or anything?'

'Just a broken heart,' said Lars in a tone more serious than he meant it to come out. Hans narrowed his eyes.

A look passed between them. Just for a millisecond, Lars saw Hans as the older, wilier tyrant he would become. They eyed each other guiltily. Hans looked at him with watchful eyes. Every day he was becoming more of a predator, thought Lars. The young 'un was coming into his own.

Lars took a step towards him, mock-aggressively. 'So what's going down in the kill room?' He was tired of being excluded. Hans had an iconic face all right but was a raving queen who slept with men and yet still didn't know he was gay.

'Oh, just a Z-movie actor who thinks he can drink the bar dry for free 'cos he showed his ass on *Tatort*,' said Hans in a mocking tone. He hated the fact that Germans didn't really do celebrity like the good old US of A.

Hans was a 'true crime' nut. He had books in his private office that none of the girls would go near – stuff on autopsy photos and shit. Hans wanted his hero, serial killer Fritz Haarmann, to get the breathy respect that American killers got. Hans had assumed the name of Haarmann's good-looking younger accomplice. Not that Lars could imagine him really getting his hands dirty. He was too obsessed with getting his end away to get into all that. He was a piece of work alright.

They made their way uneasily into Hans's manager's office. Lars spent a lot of time sitting on the leather sofa here. Even though the décor was traditional, Hans had all the gadgets. Push a button and the door automatically closed. Another and a TV camera ran a live feed of the VIP room. There was a clunky automatic ice machine that they used for their whiskies, and an endless supply of Cuban cigars. You could fuck, smoke or argue.

The thing Lars liked most about Hans was that he was nimble on his feet. Deftly, he passed Lars a Cohiba and cut it for him so it was ready to smoke.

'Buttgereit was a bit weird this time,' said Lars, lighting the cigar with a practised touch. 'Wants me to bring 'em in not quite so dead.' He started laughing. Hans just sat there, smoking his cigar carefully. His face was beguiling, he had an innocent snub nose, but he sat there alert, ready to rip your emotions to shreds at a weak moment.

'I've had an opportunity,' said Hans, without moving his eyes. He continued to watch Lars's reaction. 'There's this guy who knows a heart surgeon… You know there are people dying without a transplant.' He took another puff of his cigar. 'And they're very hard to come by.'

'You want us to cut 'em up?' said Lars incredulously.

'No, it's just, if they're brain dead, most of the organs can be taken out.' He flicked a hair from his collar. 'They call it organ harvesting. It saves lives. And if we did just one a year we could live like kings,' said Hans as if it was the first time he'd thought of the idea, although Lars guessed he'd been hatching it for some time. He was like that: wily.

Lars drank down his whisky in one fire-burning gulp. Killing, that was one thing, was what he did. But this – faffing around with the prey, not doing it in, leaving it in the hands of godforsaken medics? No, you could count him out.

Hans instantly needled him. He just sat there and carried on talking softly. Logical extension, fastest-growing business, blah blah blah. That was Hans. He didn't do anything crooked himself, but he orchestrated others to carry out every little detail for him. He was like a smooth-faced spider spinning a bloody web.

Lars's face was red. Alcohol always went straight to his head. He'd drunk too much and he needed sleep. Still he thought longingly of pulling away in the truck. He wanted to get the fuck out of here right now. Hans was looking at him intently, as if he wanted to monitor his every thought.

Yeah, he got everyone to lie on their backs, made them all believe in him, but he was heartless. There was a wall of steel where there should have been something pumping blood. This nonsense had to stop.

Lars stood up, a little unsteady on his feet. He drank the rest of his whisky in one gulp.

'There's two things I do,' he said, standing swaggering on his feet. 'I drive, and I kill. Don't get in the way of that.'

Hans just looked at him.

'D'ya hear me?' said Lars, almost at fever pitch. He badly wanted to put his hands on the wretch. Shake him up a bit.

Hans just continued smoking his cigar. *Smug-faced bastard.* Where did he get his cheek from? Lars took another step towards him and put the cigar stub in the ashtray.

Hans had a Mona Lisa smile that gave nothing away. It meant the person he was talking to had to project their emotion on to him. He stood up right next to Lars and started speaking in a mock-preacher voice. '*Fear not them which kill the body but are not able to kill the soul but rather fear Him which is able to destroy both body and soul in hell.*'

'What's that?' said Lars.

'Matthew 10, verse 28. It appears on the memorial of victim Fanny Adams, murdered August 24th, 1867,' said Hans, who knew every detail about every famous murder case by heart.

'So?' It was Lars who was being combative this time.

'The body's not what's important. It's the significance of it,' said Hans slowly, seductively. He leaned forward so that he was within kissing distance. 'Take one life, save thirty lives. It's a good trade-off.' He casually refilled Lars's glass. 'And then I could buy the club outright rather than just running it.'

Silence. Lars fought with himself. If he took the glass and sat down then invariably he'd go along with any little scheme the young 'un had cooked up. But if he just left and ran out into the night, then what?

Outside the window, the vastness of the inky night sky seemed to call him. In his mind's eye he saw the open road, its white lines winking at him, urging him to take it faster and faster like a ramshackle whore that couldn't say no. In some distant part of him Lars knew that his Hans, the one that had been young and naive, had crossed a line. He just didn't know how far this interloper was willing to go.

'Let me put it to you straight,' said Hans, stroking down the perfect crease of his suit trouser leg. 'It's become too risky to twat about with killings for the body farm. If you don't come on board, I'm going to have to put the kill room out of bounds.'

Lars looked at him like a man fresh out of a hundred-year sleep.

Hans was so far up his own arse, he'd turned himself inside out.

The third night she went out, Frannie felt as if she had a routine. She'd slept, but not so deeply that she needed to splash her face with cold water. She was wide awake but deeply relaxed. Her stomach rumbled; perhaps she should grab a burger at the gas station whilst she was waiting for Tomek.

She couldn't wait to see him. She had had a text at one a.m. to say he'd arrived at the club. Perhaps he'd found his sister already. She hoped he would still stay in Germany a few more days. It was so much more fun following his motorbike.

Her car made it to the petrol station at twenty to three; plenty of time for a snack. She had the place to herself tonight, with only the ticking of the clock on the wall to keep her company.

At ten past three, she pushed away her empty plate and tapped her heels on the floor. Was he going to turn up? Perhaps a strawberry milkshake might be a good idea. At half-past, she bought a Sudoku magazine and a pen. By four am she'd given up. She felt suddenly weary. Did he even care that she was sitting here waiting? She leaned back in her chair, remembering his embrace, the hard, muscular grip of him. No, something was up. He'd been so insistent that she come.

She imagined Tomek being hit by a car, or someone beating him up at the club. A dozen negative scenarios played out in her mind. She went to the public bathroom and emptied the contents of her stomach down the toilet.

She looked at her sad reflection in the mirror. Her pregnancy was beginning to add water tension to her face. The reflected light was harsh, uncompromising. Something was up, she just knew it. She shivered. As sure as she was pregnant, she knew that his plan to find his sister had gone badly wrong.

It was becoming a proper mystery, and, if she dared, she could get herself out there and drive to find him. She was the worst person for the job, and scared shitless just thinking about it. But she was it. The cavalry. The only friend Tomek had in the country.

# Chapter Ten

Once, when Tomek was little, he'd woken up to find the room in complete darkness. His trusted night-light inexplicably gone. In its absence the world was blank. No chink of light, no shadows, nothing. Only his fear pinning him to the bed. The world reduced to a claustrophobic space loud with his laboured breathing. Just existing filled the room.

He wasn't afraid of ghosts or monsters or Freddie Kruger coming to get him. It was not what could be in the dark, it was the dark itself. What he was afraid of, what kept him from falling soundly back to sleep, was the thought of this nothingness creeping all over his face and invading him. To be stilled in the terribly hungry dark was unthinkable.

When he reached his hand out, it was worse than he thought. He could feel something hard. This was no dream he could wake out of. Surely they hadn't buried him alive? His breaths got raggedy. Frantically, he touched the sides. No, there was air coming from near his head, so he couldn't be actually buried. But he was trapped and hurting.

With his feet and fists he desperately tried to push and flail out. But it was no good. There was a smell of something sweet and sticky, slightly rotten. He had come to the club but, before he had got to speak to this Hans, someone had got him from behind. Now he was lying trapped in the waiting dark. How long? Could be an hour, or a day. There was no time in this realm.

That could only mean one thing. Something bad must have happened to Anna. Terrible images flashed in his mind. Tears ran silently down his face. Anna had always been so wild and misunderstood, but she was his older sister. He couldn't imagine life without her.

He shivered. Although he wasn't a little boy any more, he was back there again: afraid, alone. There was only one person who could help him. He just prayed to God that, whatever Frannie was going to do, she would do it soon.

Hugo was getting louder. It was what happened when he drank. He was a great bear of a man with a rubbery belly and a shock of black hair like fur. Every time he moved, he sweated so much that the girls flinched when they had to lap-dance for him. Lars sniggered. The fat fuck!

About a month ago, Hugo had mysteriously appeared with Hans as if he was his best friend. Lars could hardly see Hans at the club without party-boy Hugo in tow. He didn't know what the mutual attraction was: Hugo was definitely straight, in fact he shagged everything that moved. And their dog.

The three of them were sitting right in the middle of the club, working it up. Three empty pitchers stood used in the middle of the table. A couple of lap-dancers were radiating around Hugo and Hans as if their lives depended on it.

'Harder, baby.' Hugo slapped a couple of twenties on to the lap-dancer's butt. She was gyrating on his knee. She had a grip that could kill, figure of a gymnast with tits. When he attempted to grab her flesh she flexed from his grip like an angry python.

Hans looked on, laughing. Elli was naked on his lap. Hans was trying to fit in. He was at his best when he was uncomfortable; Lars suspected that it was because the jarring unease he felt day-to-day then felt real. He tipped the last of his drink down in one go. Shit, the last pitcher was already dry.

'More, more, MORE!' shouted Hugo. He was getting out of control, shaking the lap-dancer as she tried to go through her moves. The girl – Candice, Lars thought it was – yelped and looked to Hans for assistance, but he was too busy mechanically fondling Elli's inner thigh to notice.

'Hey, you know touching is not allowed,' shrieked Candice, making a startling noise for someone so tiny. She looked like she was being mauled.

Hans paused in mid-kiss and rolled his eyes at her. He seemed to lap up her unease. He pushed Elli to the side so hard that she nearly fell. She cried out, a half-hearted, 'Hey, baby,' as if it he'd done it a million times before.

In a second Hans stood next to Hugo and grabbed Candice's arms. She started. Laughing, they held her together and forced her to perform on Hugo's knee. She looked like a dog dry-humping something not canine. She squealed but went through the motions jerkily.

Hans looked as if he was going to kiss her. He stared into her eyes. 'The man paid for a lap-dance. You gotta dance on his dime.'

Hugo broke into a huge guffaw of laughter. Candice started to shake. Her legs started buckling. Other patrons stared on, uneasily. One man stood up and opened and closed his mouth like a fish. Hans laughed.

Lars stepped in and swooped up Candice in his arms. Carefully, he set her down. She stood there, naked, trembling. 'Just go out back and take a break,' said Lars, as gently as he could. He reached out to pat her on the shoulder and slipped her a fifty. 'On second thoughts, take the rest of the night off.' She scuttled off in her clackity heels.

Lars glared at Hans. If the young 'un didn't know that look by now, it was time to give in. Hans just faced him down without smiling. Lars fidgeted with his long fingers.

'You know, it'd be easy to ruin what you've got,' said Lars. Still the eyes bored into his, just watching. Lars felt as though his head was going to burst.

Hugo stood up and whooped. He waved his arms at a passing waitress as if he was about to save a goal. 'Another two pitchers, sweetheart,' he shouted, 'And yer tits!' He grinned round as the other punters stared. Hans was sat down again, voraciously kneading Elli's left breast. All the time he looked Lars full in the face, as if it were a competition. Elli just sat there, trying to grin. Her smile was appeasing, as if she were on the wrong end of a gun.

'*A man's gotta do what a man's gotta do,*' said Hans evenly.

Hugo grinned as if they were discussing football. He moved obscenely close to Lars, made a face as if he knew some fabulous secret.

'Thing is, Lars, this is big.' His hands gestured wildly. 'It moves everything to a new level. The sky's the limit,' he said, rubbing his hands. 'If we don't do it, someone else will.'

Hans started laughing in agreement. Elli's breast started to redden under the onslaught.

Lars felt sick. His head was in a million pieces. He stared directly in Hans's face and jabbed his forehead with his finger. 'Stop fucking around so much. The girls are getting riled.' He looked particularly at Hugo. 'And just quit with this shit,' he said with a ferocity he didn't expect.

Hans just sniggered at Hugo. They were like a couple of girls talking themselves up. Hans could dream all the plans he wanted to, but he didn't have the lead in his pencil to get the serious stuff done. That was *his* niche.

The hidden CCTV camera caught him striding off, jaw set and fists clenched. Fight or flight, his system was awash with adrenaline. He couldn't just walk it off. What he really wanted was release: a sickly-sweet kill with more blood than he could drink.

🚗

After Lars left, Hans's shoulders slumped. He seemed to deflate. His fancy clothes made him look like a kid in his dad's jacket. His face looked utterly drained. Elli started to nibble his ear, but he pushed her hand away. Hugo looked on, worried.

But suddenly Hans seemed to become animated again. He stood up, almost falling, and roughly gestured for Hugo to come with him.

'I know what we need! Let's go test drive the two new girls I just hired,' he said. Elli was dismissed with a wave of his hand.

The two of them strutted upstairs to the infamous Blu Club, where the girls were completely nude. Hans strode through the fancy mirrors and smoke and signalled to a couple of girls who were on the floor, dancing. One was black, with a full ass like a beautiful peach, the other a redhead with unbelievable breasts. Hans smiled and chatted coyly to both girls then led them by the hand to a private room. Hugo followed.

A few minutes later the frenzy of Hans and Hugo going at the two girls could be heard across the whole floor. They whooped and shouted like kids with a box of fireworks. Boys who didn't want to grow up.

In Hans's office, the camera was trained on the crate in the kill room. The footage wasn't running live, but all the time it was recording something. Because it was pitch black in there, you couldn't make anything out. But you could hear something: a gasp, a moan.

For once, Hans could not clearly calculate the next move.

# Chapter Eleven

Outside on the garage forecourt, Frannie was confronted by a new dawn. The changeling grey of first light already saturated the sky. She felt out of sync. The food had slowed her down; her body wanted to curl up, digest. The baby was kicking. But she had to find Dorcas quickly or she wouldn't make it back before Kurt got up.

Frannie yawned. Another driver stared at her as he pulled in to fuel up. She knew she looked incongruous, a heavily pregnant woman at four a.m., but she had to do something. And, much as she hated it, her only contact to Tomek was Dorcas.

Frannie didn't do maps; there was a navigation system in the car, but she had no idea how to start it. She thought she could remember the way to where Dorcas's van was parked. If she just got on to the A2 and took the turning off after the airport, it should be just there. But of course, the thought of going on the *Autobahn* alone terrified her. It was a struggle to fasten her seatbelt. She felt awkward again in the car on the road on her own. Without Tomek as her guide, she shoved the gears around too much and the car fought her every move.

She kept on the middle lane on the *Autobahn*, pressing her foot down as hard as she dared. She was not looking forward to speaking to Dorcas, but she had to get it over with and get home fast before Kurt woke up, like a vampire needing to avoid the sun's first rays.

In the slow lane, to her alarm, a steady trickle of trucks started to come up on the right of her. A lot of them preferred to drive in this ghost time, when the roads were relatively calm. Frannie started to sweat. She was tired and worried, hoped she could manage the drive.

Before she knew it, she was on the turn-off that led to where Dorcas was parked. This garage had a twenty-four-hour service station and the car park was surprisingly full. She balked: driving was bad enough, but parking was another matter. She drove round the spaces too fast in first gear and the car groaned. She wasn't sure she had the confidence to get in and out of such tight spaces without someone to help her. Shit! It was such a drag that she had to think about every stupid little move.

In the end she parked next to a small Volkswagen but drove in crooked. The car stuck out at an extreme angle and she was totally unable to straighten it up. The more she reversed, and seesawed backwards and forwards, the worse it got. Sweating and swearing, she left it as it was, with the rear end sticking out violently to the right side. She'd only be here ten minutes.

She stepped out of the car and looked for the minivan. A different-coloured one was parked up just ahead. She went hesitantly towards the window with some cash to sweeten the deal. As she got nearer, she saw the familiar dark bob and imposing face. Dorcas saw her and narrowed her eyes spitefully.

'Haven't you had your baby yet?' said Dorcas, shaking her head. 'It looks as if it's due.'

*Just ignore her,* Frannie said to herself. She took out the money and handed it to Dorcas without a word. Dorcas fell about with laughter.

'What! You want sex?' She sounded as if she was high. Frannie looked at her as neutrally as she could.

'It's Tomek,' she began, doing her best to use all the right German. 'He went to the club tonight but hasn't come back. He was supposed to meet me at three a.m. So I wondered – this Hans guy, is he…'

'What, dangerous? Aggressive?' said Dorcas tersely.

Frannie didn't know how to put her unease into words. She looked defiantly at the younger woman and, despite her feistiness, Dorcas paled. She shivered in the fresh morning breeze and hugged her knees. It was cold for her talking with the window down in such a skimpy bikini.

'Hans is not what you think,' said Dorcas in a bitter voice. 'Anna got involved with him at the club.' Her eyes looked spacey and she kept sniffing. She looked into Frannie's open face and started talking in a little-girl voice. 'Hans, you know…he's…he makes people do things for him. No, not in that way.' Her voice wound down. 'He just makes you want the same things he does.' She started moving her hands. 'He picks you up, and you're on top of the world… Then…'

She looked away. In the early morning light she looked washed out. Frannie saw that she had cut her lips and wondered how it had happened.

'If I go to the club, will he speak to me?' Frannie asked, stepping closer.

Dorcas jumped up nimbly and got out of the van. 'Don't do that!' she cried, her face visibly shocked. 'You'll make it worse.' She wagged her finger in Frannie's face.

Dorcas's toned legs looked unreal. As before, Frannie found herself mesmerised by the bikini. Today it was blood-red, with little silver pearls stitched on. The waist in between the two parts was just a sliver of taut flesh that dipped in unnervingly.

'Look, nobody knows where Anna is. Even I don't know what happened,' said Dorcas. The two women just stood, sizing each other up. Dorcas absentmindedly took out a cigarette and lit it up. Frannie didn't react.

Dorcas looked at Frannie carefully, as if it was the first time they'd really spoken.

'I've been feeling curious about Anna too,' she said, stroking her arms with her hands. 'I'd like to know where she is.' She was no longer looking at Frannie with animosity. Her eyes seemed drawn to her expansive tummy, as if she wanted to know what the baby inside looked like.

Behind them, the full yellow of the sun was now high in the sky and the sight of it made Frannie feel queasy. Her legs suddenly started to give way. 'Can I just sit down for a minute?' she said, almost forgetting her German. She was used to this. Sometimes heavily pregnant women just conked out.

Dorcas looked horrified, but she opened up the back of the van so that Frannie could climb awkwardly inside. She lay down on the cleverly disguised mattress. Was she going to pass out? She burped. Dorcas's eyebrows shot up. At that moment, their artificial line seemed absurd. Frannie gulped and, before she could stop herself, threw up a bit of clear-coloured bile on to the red blanket. The pungent odour was instant.

'Oh, I'm so sorry,' she said, trying to dab at it with a handkerchief.

'That stinks!' hissed Dorcas, her lips one thinly pressed line of red. 'How am I going to work with customers in here?'

Frannie felt hot and uncomfortable. Miserably, she lay her head back and looked at Dorcas. 'Well, I did pay you, so I am your customer!' she said, grumpily, thinking, *If the silly girl ever gets pregnant herself, then she'll see*. She looked at her watch. It was coming up to five. Bloody hell, she had to get a move on. She tried to stand up, and Dorcas took a hand to steady her.

'Just lie down and rest. I'll get a bottle of water from the garage,' said Dorcas, in a snappy tone, although she obviously meant well.

'Thanks; I just have to get back before my husband finds out I'm gone,' said Frannie trying to push herself up.

Dorcas pushed a card with a startling photo of herself in a burlesque pose. 'This is my mobile number. Call me tomorrow and I'll see what I can find out.'

'Do you really want to help me?' asked Frannie in a surprised voice, attempting to climb down from the minivan.

Dorcas put out a hand to help. 'We're both women, aren't we?' She shrugged her shoulders. They exchanged a shy smile.

'Thank you. I didn't expect much,' said Frannie, trying to find the right words in German.

'What?' said Dorcas sharply.

Frannie tried different words but couldn't quite express the meaning and gave up. 'Look, thank you, sorry about being sick.' And she waved goodbye.

By now the sun was high in the sky and she could see that the *Autobahn* bristled with traffic, which whisked past the service station in frighteningly efficient queues. *Shit*. She'd stayed out too long. She just hoped it was worth it. Thinking of Tomek was the only thing keeping her going.

When she got back to her car, a bigger vehicle had parked next to her, leaving virtually no room. Her head felt hot and tense. It was going to be as tough as hell to get the car out. She could never figure out alone how far to move the wheel. Every time she reversed, she got closer to the other car and then she'd move back into her original position. After five minutes of sliding back and forth it felt as if even the car was on the verge of giving up.

Frannie felt like crying. Now she was exhausted. Kurt needed the car to get to work. Somehow she *had* to reverse out. She got out of the driver's seat and tried to judge the distance. Just millimetres to spare, and from inside the car she could never work out her spatial position. In panic, she decided to pretend to know what she was doing and just hope for the best. She moved the wheel just slightly and let her foot off the clutch.

The car zoomed back and smacked into the car beside it with a dull thud. Frannie's head was jerked back. She put the handbrake on, and, with a horrified feeling in her stomach, went to take a look.

The other car had a ladder hanging at the side, so it was unscathed. But Kurt's Audi had a deep long scratch on the passenger side of the car as if someone had taken a sharp implement to it. In stark daylight, it looked dreadful. Frannie couldn't believe her eyes.

Behind her, Dorcas came up, wearing a dress over her bikini. She examined the damage. 'This your husband's car?' she said, sizing up the situation.

'Yes, and he's going to kill me,' said Frannie, clutching her hand to her neck.

'And he doesn't know about your driving?' said Dorcas, a mischievous smile playing on her lips.

'No, I'm not supposed to drive for medical reasons,' said Frannie, moving her hand to her stomach.

'OK, well, if he thinks you can't, then he'll never guess it was you.' She laughed brightly. 'He won't see it when he gets in to drive it, so later he'll assume someone did it while he was parked.' Dorcas took a manicured finger and felt the depth of the scratch. 'You want me to reverse it out?'

Frannie could have hugged her. Like a pro, Dorcas deftly drove out. They swapped places.

'Let's talk tomorrow,' said Dorcas, giving her a wink.

Frannie gingerly pressed the accelerator and began the journey home. She'd never felt so humiliated in all her life.

🚗

The summer breeze danced through Dorcas's open window. Long, pure white curtains flapped seductively. In a high, antique four-poster bed, she dreamed on. Her dark hair contrasted starkly with the expanse of mahogany silk that draped the bed on all sides. Splashes of rich colour came from the exotic flower collection that plunged the room with rich glorious scents. Dorcas cherished flowers.

She hung in between consciousness and sleep, not wanting to acknowledge the breeze that fanned her with little rushes of energy. She clung on to the slow not-knowingness. Moved her head further under the sheet. Better stay there. In her exquisite bathroom, with its marble-lined floor, she could visualise the candy-red box of the pregnancy test.

It was high up in the cabinet, hidden behind a bottle of a limited edition perfume. It was out of place with the cool, classic lines of everything else. She'd read that the first pee of the day was the best. When she got up, she had to find out. Today, it was possible.

Dorcas always woke up hungry. Her thin body craved. Just a little hit, a magic flash to kick-start the day. But the bag was empty. She usually saved a few lines of coke to snort first thing. Not enough to get high; she just needed to be functional. What she wanted was to catch the buzz without falling into an all-day binge.

She licked her finger and tried to dust off the last remnants, but the bag was done. Perhaps Lars might come over soon with some. He was such a lovely guy. It was a pity she wasn't in love with him.

She lit a cigarette and paced around in her lace nightgown in search of coffee. Sat and tried to convince her body the only hit it needed was nicotine, but her hands were shaking. She was sat hugging her knees, admiring her cute painted toenails and her dainty feet. She loved being dinky and cute. Her bladder was giving her furious signals, but she ignored it, concentrated on making the cigarette last. Once that was gone, she'd need another distraction.

Then she made a full pot of coffee. She decided to hand-grind the beans she'd got as a Christmas present long ago. It was an irksome process. She got bits all over her hands and it didn't taste any the better for it. She went to the bathroom, but before she could even open the cabinet she noticed that the sink badly needed cleaning and set to it with gusto. Lars always said she was a busy bee.

She could wait no more. She reached up for the test and pulled out the stick. Without another thought she sat down on the toilet and urinated on it. She left it on the side of the bath without looking at it and went out to smoke another cigarette. When the cigarette was burned right down to the tip she would go see. Although it was warm she was shivering.

She almost jumped out of her skin when the door buzzer went. She opened the door. A pair of brown twinkly eyes confronted her with a buoyant, 'Dörchen!'

It was Lars, come to the rescue. She was so pleased to see him she gave him a quick hug.

'Hello, darling,' he said patting her on the back. His hands were full of marzipan pastries and bread rolls. He'd also brought some wild peaches and Parma ham. He was generous to a fault. They often had brunch or afternoon tea together.

She pulled him into the living room, which contained dozens of impressive bonsai trees and a bougainvillea flowering plant that was opulently purple.

'I've already got a pot of coffee on,' she said. She looked at him beseechingly, 'But I need you to do something in the bathroom first.' She pulled the packages out of his hands.

'You have a leak?'

'No, not exactly.' She just stared at him with big eyes. 'I just peed on one of those pregnancy sticks.' Her head looked down. 'Can you go and see, and tell me what it says?'

Lars's jaw dropped. He looked as if he'd been punched in the throat. Without a word he headed off to the bathroom and closed the door. For what seemed like minutes Dorcas bit her nails. The door stayed mysteriously shut. She couldn't imagine what he could be doing. Normally he was so cheery.

'Larsey,' she called. She tried to open the door but it was locked. She tried knocking. Why was he being so silent? In desperation she tried to peep through the keyhole. Was he upset?

Eventually, when he opened the door, he was sitting on the side of the bath, trying to make sense of the instructions that he'd taken out of the packet.

'What is it?' she said, clenching her hands into fists.

'Not sure,' he said, shaking his shaved head. 'Look, see, there is a line, but it's so faint it looks nothing like the example on the packet.' They crowded over it, trying to read some meaning into the indicator window. 'Don't know what to say, really.'

'It's faint, but it's something, isn't it?' said Dorcas, her eyes wide with shock. She put her hand to her mouth. 'Oh, shit, shit.'

'Never mind,' he said, patting her shoulder again. 'We can make a proper appointment and get the doc to check it out.' They embraced.

'I can't bear it,' she said. 'I need a line.'

Lars automatically put his hand in his pocket but then stopped. He gazed at her drawn face. 'Drugs and fags ain't exactly the ideal breakfast if you're pregnant,' he said, his beady eyes staring down at her.

Dorcas wrenched herself from him. 'Give me a sodding break.' Her eyes twitched at him. 'I don't think you can have any idea of what it's like to be me.'

Awkwardly, they moved into the kitchen and sat before the laden table.

'You're a big girl, Dorcas, you can handle it,' said Lars, biting into a pastry and sending crumbs everywhere.

'Can I?' She hadn't drawn her eyebrows on and her face looked strangely naked, hostile.

'Yeah, well, they got these pill things you just swallow now, ain't they, it's all nice and straightforward,' said Lars, tucking in.

Dorcas wasn't able to touch a thing. She took in the way that Lars was eating with relish. Ugly frown lines changed her face. This couldn't go on. She'd needed to ask this for a long time. She took a deep breath, bit her lip.

'Just tell me how it is. Do you fuck him too?' Dorcas said, real anger in her voice. 'Or does he fuck you, or how does it work?' She looked at him scornfully.

Dead silence. Lars couldn't look at her; his chin hung down. He looked like a naughty child who had been caught out. All the pleasantness had drained from his face. He put down his bread roll and faced her. For a second she didn't know who he was. This was a taboo subject for them. They normally alluded to Hans rather than talking directly about him.

Lars played with his fingers. When he spoke, it was in a quiet voice as if he was afraid someone else might hear. He was finally letting his guard down.

'We've had sex, many times,' he said carefully, checking her reaction with watchful eyes. 'And he does whatever I want.' He looked defiant. As if he was ready to take anything she could throw at him. She'd never seen him look so odd.

Dorcas blinked furiously. She allowed a single tear to fall on to her nose. At that moment she hated Lars, her life and everyone in it. Her hands and knees shook. Every part of her body seethed and ached. She needed a hit. Now. Couldn't wait; the emotions running through her body were lethal. She had to seriously calm down.

'Fuck, can you *please* give me a line?' she said, sniffing and rubbing her nose. 'I need something.'

Lars plopped the bag on the table. Hurriedly, she opened it up and expertly cut some up with the back of a playing card until she'd got four neat lines. Dorcas handed Lars a straw. She leant over and snorted a line aggressively, as if the sucking up could get rid of all her frustration. She stuck a finger in her glass of mineral water and sniffed it to quell the burning effect. Instantly she felt as if she was being propelled to a cleaner, lighter place, all her worries weightless, as if they could be washed off with a gentle rinse. She allowed her mind to drift.

Dimly, she was aware of the fact of her pregnancy, but it was so far away it could be controlled. Something you could indulge yourself with, if you wished to. Coke did that, it changed your perspective so that you were somehow always on top.

She could hear Lars snorting alongside her. They both sat back, stupefied, taking huge breaths as if recovering from an underwater dive. Lars began talking again; alcohol zonked him out, but drugs always got him talking.

'You're a top girl, Dörchen, you should get away from all this,' said Lars spreading out his hands as if planning a world invasion. 'And, if it's Hans's, get rid of it. He's no good.'

'Why do you say that?' she said, screwing her face up. 'You

seem to think he's fine.' She found herself sinking into melancholy, despite the line.

Lars stuck his chin out and spread his legs. 'You may like the way he looks, but he's not good enough for you,' he said, taking out a cigarette and lighting it with gusto. He puffed at it as if it was something exotic and not an ordinary Marlboro. 'You don't know what he's really like,' he said.

'And you do? Is it about Anna? You know something, don't you?' Dorcas leaned forward. 'Her brother came looking for her; he doesn't know where she is.'

Lars looked away as if he didn't want her to even catch a glimpse of what he was thinking. His cheeks flushed red. He swallowed and gave a little cough. She caught him staring at her neck. It was the first time she'd felt uncomfortable with Lars.

'Someone wanted her gone,' he said, as if he were a little boy confessing some untruth to his mother.

Dorcas stared. 'Who?' she said.

'Hans.' He said the name with a little gasp, as if it hurt to tell it.

'Hans?' said Dorcas, her eyes widening with shock. 'Did he send her away, or did she decide to leave?'

Lars rubbed his hands briskly. Relaying the gossip seemed to perk him up.

'Let's just say that you won't be seeing her again.' His eyes twinkled as if it were all some big joke. The men she loved and trusted weren't what she thought. She shivered. He looked at her as if he could see right into her mind. She tried to brush away her unease. It was her Lars, but his face wore such a strange smile, it gave her the heebie-jeebies.

Evidently he was done talking about Anna. He handed her a straw for the next line. Dorcas's mind was buzzing just trying to work out what was going on.

Dorcas was stupid about some things, but she was no fool. Her paranoia had been activated. Could have been the coke or the pregnancy making her feel off, but she hid her suspicion with drug buddy talk. She got loud and flirty and ridiculous. Acted for all the world like good old Dörchen, slapping his back and making wisecracks the whole time. But, through the haze of cigarette smoke and smears of coke dust, she was scrutinizing Lars. Although he didn't mind talking about Anna's past, he refused to talk about her in the present at all. It was as though he knew something.

Admittedly, although she was fighting it, Dorcas was high. She had the feeling of floating, as if everything was on water or just out of reach. Minutes just seemed to rush by, as if time were speeded up. Her head felt both light and heavy; her body might explode if she put anything more stimulating into it. Thinking about Lars and Hans overwhelmed her. Her brain seemed to be running a story in her mind. But she didn't want to listen any more.

For some hours they went at it, making swift cups of coffee and snorting, occasionally downing schnapps. They made a real mess on the table, their discarded food and drug chaos wildly out of place. Nearly everything in Dorcas's life breathed elegance and order, but, if she hadn't been a coke addict, she wouldn't have done a lot of the things she did.

It looked as though she was going to have to get her ass down the club, find out the score for herself. She was on edge about facing Hans right now, especially with all this Anna palaver hanging up in the air, but she needed to finally know the truth.

🚗

He must have been out of it when they'd come in. Because the metal he was lying on was so hard, it felt as if his spine was pinned like an insect specimen in a case. He seemed to be floating in and out of consciousness. He had no idea how badly his head was hurt, only that it ached so much he could barely move it from side to side.

With one finger he could feel an egg-shaped bump on his crown. Something wet was near to it. Could be blood or sweat. No way to tell. His whole body was one throb of agony. Thoughts of water tormented him. He could no longer tolerate his tongue in his mouth. He kept moving it around. There was no room for it now, he was so parched. He was beginning to wish he had fewer teeth. He just wanted the nagging thirst to stop.

He could hear them moving around the crate, doing something. There were two voices. One was meticulous, softly spoken. The other was brash. They both sounded cruel. He decided not to beg for help this time. If they didn't let him out he was just going to piss himself and get it over and done with. He was fed up of the constant pressure on his bladder. He was almost beyond caring if he soiled himself or not.

There was a grating sound. They were moving something near his head. Suddenly, his world of dark was plunged into horrifying clarity. A white-hot light pierced his senses. It felt as though his eyes had been scorched. He screamed and snapped his eyelids shut. One of them laughed; it seemed they had shone a torch directly into his eyes. His body trapped, he could only wince and moan as they stood over him, laughing. He took it as a bad sign that they made no effort to disguise their faces. He'd just have to see who was worse, the human gorilla or movie-star-face, the crazy one.

The gorilla one took something out of a case. It was a little device with the sharpest blade he'd seen. It was held inches away from his face. It shone wickedly like a diamond. He screamed.

# Chapter Twelve

When Frannie woke up, the full glare of the midday sun was remorseless. She ached from her chest to her feet. If she could stand up straight it would be a miracle. She could taste her tiredness on her teeth. She winced, tried to push herself up. Now she was eight months gone, it was a saga just to get out of bed. She waddled to the bathroom.

When she'd slept it had been fitfully. Every little fly had breached her consciousness. She was being haunted by Tomek. In her mind's eye she saw him speeding along on his bike, talking, holding the photo of his sister keenly in his hands. She'd failed to do anything concrete to find him; just inflicted the long, ugly scratch on Kurt's Audi.

But then Kurt wouldn't even dream she could be responsible. With cars he knew she was a frightened rabbit who couldn't even fuel up. She was racked with guilt, but, because he'd forbidden her to drive, she couldn't explain herself or ask for his help. She kept checking her phone. But there was nothing.

Perfunctorily she went about her morning. She drank tea after tea, wishing it were coffee. While she bathed, her mind obsessed. Although she was tired – *fertig*, as the Germans said – she felt a little gush of excitement thinking about Tomek. She smiled wryly as she soaped her naked body dutifully. He wouldn't be interested in her in this pregnant state. But still, there was no harm in fantasising about him. In her mind's eye they exchanged sensuous words and long, deep kisses. She'd seen him in action on his bike, wanted him to ride her with that cowboy hunger. For a moment she played with her hardened nipples and smiled. Her breasts felt as if they belonged to someone else. They were massive. Her nipples had mysteriously darkened. She sighed: unbelievably, she was horny. She looked hard at a piece of wallpaper near to the ceiling that was falling off.

It was already gone one, but the day passed slowly with a series of little rituals. She put off the boring household chores that needed doing. Told herself she was too shattered, even though she knew she should get everything perfect, as Kurt would be steaming as soon as he found out about his car. Every few minutes her eyes glanced at her mobile, which lay in front of her on the coffee table. Normally she didn't even have it switched on, but she had to know the second Tomek or Dorcas made contact. She'd tried phoning Tomek, but she always got the sound of dead air. Must be broken. She didn't want to think about that, if the phone was *kaputt*, perhaps something violent had happened to him too.

Her thoughts turned to last night's weird encounter. When she thought of the car she gave a little shiver. What she'd done was so terrible. Any second she expected an angry Kurt on the line. Thank God Dorcas had reversed the car out in the end. She was a strange one alright. Turned green at the mention of Hans, was obviously intimate with him, but had offered to help. She was a real looker in a thin, poky sort of way. Frannie was sorry she was a prostitute. She wanted more for her than that.

Frannie whiled away the hours. It was more restful chilling out when Kurt was not there, although she could hear his voice in her ear, nagging. The front room was in need of attention. But she wasn't up to it just now. She was resting, gathering her strength.

She checked her phone again for missed calls and texts. *Nothing.* Finally, she went to Kurt's computer and did a google search for the Moonlights Club. A gothic-looking German language site came up with lots of glossy pages, but she could just about figure it out. The club looked vast, with lots of nooks and crannies. A scene photographer had taken dozens of smiling photos, everybody looking narcissistically chic for the camera. She looked to see if there was a picture of Anna there. There was one with a glamorous blonde in a funny dress who could be her.

What she really wanted to check out was this Hans Grans. She clicked on the staff contacts and found his photo. The second it loaded, she got a tingle of recognition. His face was so exquisite, with his perfect chin and wide cheekbones, that he looked familiar. His youthful face gazed back at her, a mask of serenity.

No wonder Dorcas was mad about him. He was the perfect specimen of an alpha male who scrubbed up well. But, despite his clean-cut looks, one glance at his eyes told her the truth. He looked like a beautiful snake, smooth but treacherous.

From the map it looked as though the club was located just on the outskirts of Hannover. She'd have no choice but to drive on the *Autobahn* to get there. She frowned. She could take the B6 *Schnellstrasse* most of the way, then she'd only have to drive on the *Autobahn* for one junction.

Without realising it, she was planning a route. If she got up earlier, as soon as Kurt was snoring, it was theoretically possible. There was a telephone number on the site. Her hands itched to punch it through. But the image of Dorcas's worried face flashed up. She'd told her to keep away.

But she thought about the way Tomek had flashed around the photo of his sister. Both of them seemed to be missing now. Dorcas seemed to work for Hans too. Could she really trust her?

Her mobile phone started ringing. She rushed to get it, hoping it was Tomek or Dorcas. To her surprise it was her gynaecologist's office.

'Frau Snell? Frau Doktor asked me to call to find out if you are OK. Have you had your baby?' said the receptionist; it sounded like Frau Engel.

'What? Sorry, *nein*.' Frannie was flustered. She'd become so immersed in her fantasy life, she'd forgotten all about her usual schedule.

'It's just that you missed your appointment today. Do you want to come tomorrow at eight a.m.?'

'Eight? Er, do you have something later?'

'Then only next week Thursday, but you have to come twice a week now. It is important that the baby is regularly checked.' The receptionist's voice was firm. 'Since your accident, we have to be more careful with your pregnancy.'

'OK, I'll be there.'

Frannie put down the phone despondently. Her two separate worlds were colliding. Both were important, but she couldn't go to the club if she had to get up at God knew what time to get to her appointment. Shit! She couldn't decide what to do.

Suddenly the door banged open. Kurt was shouting before he was even through the door.

'Fran? *Fran!* FRAN!' he shouted in a voice like thunder. She gave a little shiver. He must know. She composed herself to face him. Quickly she pushed the clutter under the table.

'Someone's scratched my car and done a hit and run,' he shouted, his eyes two dark staring holes of anguish. 'No note, nothing.'

If someone had cut his legs off and stuffed them under his arm sockets, it couldn't have been more personal.

Frannie abstractedly patted his shoulder. 'When did it happen?'

she said, trying not to look red in the face. She often blushed if she tried to lie, and Kurt knew it.

'When?' said Kurt as if it was a stupid question. 'The police don't know. I guess between when I parked it this morning and when I picked it up.'

'The police?' she said in a little voice. She tried not to look too surprised.

'Well, obviously,' said Kurt staring into her face. 'You're meant to report an accident or leave a note on the car.' The muscles in his neck were standing out like wire. 'They could easily have come into the building and got reception to put a message out on the loudspeaker.'

Frannie tried to look sympathetic. 'Can I get you a beer?' she said.

'Don't you want to see the damage?' screamed Kurt. His huge hands slapped his sides as if they wanted to punch someone. 'Or is it just too much hassle to go ten steps?'

Frannie just blinked. It was happening again: the belittling, the strained shouting, his neck getting redder and bigger. He was a bully. She could never do anything right. A little part of her was glad she'd knocked the car. Serve the sod right! He didn't really know what was going on. She shivered. And now she'd scratched his car, what would he do if he found out she was responsible?

She let him take her hand, drag her outside. As if she was in a pantomime, she oohhed over the long scratch, delicately fingered the deep wound in the metal. Kurt spoke at the top of his voice without stopping. She blanked it out. When men turned bad, the thing was to avoid their eyes. The scratch seemed to stare back at her. It was her fault and she was sorry.

She was even sorrier she'd married Kurt in the first place. She'd got to that certain age when all the most interesting guys went for someone younger, and Kurt with his little-kid affection had bowled her over. He had seemed so sweet, but somehow he'd hidden his true nature until he had his feet under the table, and then there was no need to pretend any more.

After thirty minutes of steady moaning, Kurt eventually took a shower.

Frannie ran to the bedroom and closed the door. Quickly, she dialled the number of Moonlights which she'd written down earlier. With bated breath she waited for someone to answer the other end.

'Er, I'd like to speak to Hans Grans, please,' she said in a low, hushed voice that was nearly a whisper.

'Pardon?' said an efficient woman. 'Can you speak up?'

Frannie repeated the words.

'One moment please.' She heard the click of the phone being connected.

The man who answered spoke in a soft, melodious German.

'Is that Herr Grans?' she said.

'It is he,' the wonderful voice answered. Silence, she imagined him inhaling breath.

'I have a friend who came to look for you, a Polish man called Tomek.' Frannie spoke in a little gush. 'He was looking for a blonde girl called Anna who worked for you.'

She stopped. Waited. The voice said nothing.

'He said he went last night; did he find you? A young man, dark hair, a motorcyclist,' said Frannie in the most accurate German she could muster.

He clearly wasn't impressed, because he answered in English. 'Anna is gone. She's working at another club.' The voice stopped. He waited again. There was a lengthy pause. 'She owes me money for her flat, therefore she go in a hurry. I think I never find her again.'

Frannie nervously played with her fingers. Something about the voice unnerved her. The answer was a bit too forced.

'And Tomek, the brother. Did he find you?' she asked. Every part of her focused on analysing his answer.

Again the pause, as if he was trying to think of the right answer. 'No, I don't recall seeing him.' Then the voice became lower, almost haughty. 'But then I do run a nightclub. We have a lot of guests to cater for.'

Frannie pursed her lips. She had to be absolutely sure. 'Do you have CCTV?' she asked.

'Yes.'

'Then I will come tonight to check it myself,' said Frannie.

'What?'

'I need to find out if he was there or not. Please can you help me?' said Frannie in her most persuasive voice.

The voice pondered over it. She could hear tapping, as if he was drumming his fingertips.

Suddenly the bedroom door opened. It was Kurt, a towel wrapped round his tall muscular body. She could have screamed.

'Who you talking to?' he said, with raised eyebrows.

Frannie couldn't hear what the voice on the telephone said. It was too awkward to ask him to repeat it.

'*Mache ich,*' she said in abrupt quickfire German. She put the phone down with a bang, and turned to Kurt, who was still looking sulky.

'What you going to do?' he asked, his corn-blond hair darkened by the water. He looked peeved, but still sexy.

'Ah, that was someone from the birth course; she wants me to bring her a book next time.'

Kurt made a huffing noise and retrieved clean clothes from the drawer. His wet towel lay abandoned on the bed where it fell.

Frannie felt overwhelmed. She lay on the bed, hugging her secret to herself like treasure, her eyes glowing with excitement.

# Chapter Thirteen

Lars was in position. Pole position, he liked to call it. His foot was firmly down on the accelerator, the truck cruising at maximum speed. He had an open road in front of him and all the night and wind that went with it. Normally he'd be in his element. But tonight all the poetry was gone. Even at this speed, he felt the truck was only rumbling along like some giant fucking albatross. And he was stuck to it.

Normally doing a journey excited him. It was the only time he could let his mind roam loose. His body usually went into a trance until it buffered in the wind like transparent paper. Then the weight of his fantasies would creep over him. Often on long stretches he'd get a hard-on, just turning over stuff in his mind.

Tonight there was nothing doing. With no excitement, the dark stretch of the *Autobahn* he was on seemed endless. The wheels were rolling into infinity. He was moving, but it was only an illusion. He'd be stuck in this stinking cab forever, trapped in his thoughts about what had gone wrong. Why it had all turned to shit with Hans, Dorcas and Anna.

However it had started, he knew that Hans had now turned bad. But, every time he saw that boyish face, it brought it all back. The first time. With his victims it was always the last time; he'd forgotten it before it was even over. But with Hans he was perpetually reliving their first scenes, like a broken DVD player stuck on rewind. He remembered the boyish testosterone-fuelled hunk with gigantic lips that he ached to kiss. The strong angle of his forehead and jaw. The way the first time they'd undressed Hans had lain there sulkily like some Greek god. The young muscle on him, lithe and strong. The dark blond sheen of his eyebrows. Hans, absolutely beautiful, corruptible. The monster he'd made him.

It was over. He wished he could just drive away without looking back. But they'd been through too much. Now he was sinking in the mess left behind. They'd been soulmates; Hans had understood his unnatural urges. Perhaps it was he, Lars, who was responsible for tainting him. The thought of that depressed him even more. Despite his predilections, he wanted to be better. Hans had pulled his finer feelings to the surface, made him what he was not.

He looked out of the window. In an open-top Chevrolet, a young man zoomed past like a young colt on his first race. He wore huge sunglasses; it looked as if he was smiling. Lars grinned. What he needed was to take his mind off of all this. He rubbed his crotch mechanically through his jeans. What he needed was a little cruising. A young, hot lover with desperation on his breath, a whole body quickening with life. It was exciting to have that control. And to lose it in the madness of passion.

The hunt. That was why roads were invented; for the chase.

🚗

Inside the club was inky gloom. Dorcas reached out a hand and the wall shuddered to Marilyn Manson. Everything was alive with flickering lights that made the show of naked flesh stand out more. Strobe lights bounced off the audience, bare legs and cleavages illuminated for the tiniest second. It was a neon tease.

Hans always said the dark made things possible. Tonight it was so packed, she could get high just breathing in the energy. On the dance floor, the bodies formed a stomping pit of energy. For a few seconds she let it all wash over her. Enjoyed being a beautiful woman, anonymous, looked at; what she needed, though, was Hans's approval, not the stares of strangers.

She'd taken extra care with her appearance: a striking red dress that fitted just so, elegant thigh-high boots that she walked in with a little swagger. Moving through the throng looking for Hans, she could scent the crowd's excitement. She knew it was what the punters could smell and not what they could see that made the difference.

The smell of sex was everywhere. It fuelled what working girls called 'the promise'. Her nostrils inhaled earthy testosterone, flirty perfume gone flat and the whiffs of a thousand different beauty products. It was overwhelming. The chemical residue of it coated her tongue.

She strutted through the club. Hans was probably in his office. Slowly, deliberately, she walked up the winding staircase to the top floor. The music boomed up from the floor below. In measured stops she went along, no longer just a girlfriend, but an archetypal woman going to tell her lover the most important news of all. Her eyes were bright, her cheeks and neck flushed. Although her hands were cool, she felt hot. Unexpectedly, she was nervous. Since Anna's disappearance and Lars's visit, she wasn't sure she knew Hans as well as she thought. If Anna had simply moved on of her own accord, surely she would have said something?

She knocked at the office door, opened the door a crack and peeped round. Empty. She continued along the corridor. Some rooms were used for storing some of the more expensive drinks; the VIP room was also just round the corner. Perhaps Hans was in there, entertaining the former chancellor.

She tapped gently at the door of the VIP room. Put her ear closer to hear if there was any response. There was a faint murmur, the sound of someone trying to shout out, but the voice was muffled. She knocked again, called, 'Hans, are you in there?' Her tapping seemed to energise the speaker inside, and there were noises and the sound of something banging on the floor, but she couldn't make any of the words out. 'Hans?' she said again. She didn't know the latest code number so she couldn't enter. 'HANS!' she shouted, this time hammering on the door with her fists.

A hand grabbed her from behind. To her surprise it was Hans, his face creased with fury.

'I thought you were inside,' she said, trying to smile, although his hand was gripping her too tightly. It was crucial this conversation went well. She tried to twist out of his embrace.

'Aren't you meant to be working Junction 6 tonight?' said Hans with a frown. Tonight his raw masculinity was pushing away the boyishness in him. He pulled her gently away from the door.

'I had to see you,' she said. Then she pointed to the door. 'There's someone in there. You should go in and check everything's alright.' Hans glowered at her like some Italian mafia boss. It was the first time she'd seen him ruffled.

Then he did it, the confident smile that showcased his regular features. Everything was perfect except for his slightly crooked teeth.

'It's OK, it's Lars with someone he just picked up,' he said, laughing it off. He prised her away from the door. Dorcas knew how Lars liked the boys. She grinned back. He led her back to his office. Again she felt flushed, unable to start the conversation. Perhaps she should just grab a drink, take a few deep breaths. She quickly poured herself an iced tea and sat down on the sofa facing Hans, who was sitting stiffly at his desk.

'So, what's up?' said Hans, pushing the fingers of both hands together in a V shape. He was still nervous, although he was pretending to be chilled. It was odd that he didn't realise how well she knew him.

'Yeah, er, something's come up that I had to tell you about,' she spoke quickly, almost slurring her words in her haste. She watched for Hans's reaction but his face had become impassive again. His eyes were trained on her, but she couldn't be sure he was really watching.

'It's…' Her voice trailed off. He just sat there, immobile. This wasn't going the way she wanted it to. If he was going to sit there all tight like a mannequin she didn't want to lay her vulnerabilities bare. It needed to be right. She went for an easier tack. 'It's this Anna business,' she said almost in a whisper. Her eyebrows were raised. 'People have been asking about her.'

Hans immediately stiffened. He struggled to compose himself. 'Who's been talking?' he said in a contemptuous voice, as if she didn't know what she was talking about.

'Anna's brother came to see me, with an English woman.'

'Impossible!' Hans leapt out of his seat, all sense of style, composure gone. Even his voice was rough. His hands beat at the desk. 'Why did they come to you?'

Those eyes, malevolent, furious: she had his attention now alright.

'Well, I was one of Anna's best friends; she must have spoken to her brother about me.' She found herself on the defensive. She glared at him, unable to understand his reaction. She so badly wanted to tell him she was pregnant, but they were way beyond that now.

'And the woman, what does she have to do with all this?' he said, clenching his hands into fists.

This was all too weird. She ignored him. Some sixth sense urged her to protect Frannie.

'Why has Anna gone?' she insisted, her mouth pressed into a thin, angry line.

Hans banged down both hands on the desk, sending his glass paperweight flying. It shattered into a thousand pieces on the floor. A piece of it flew up and buried itself in her hand. 'Ow!' she said, nursing it and trying to get the glass out. Hans did nothing. His beautiful eyes stared, contemptuous. She suddenly knew absolutely that she could not change him.

'This is a staffing matter,' said Hans, running the words together for emphasis. 'I run the club. I'll decide who works here.' His mouth twisted. 'And I have no personal interest in any of the girls.' Again he smiled, although his eyes didn't change. The closed look on his face frightened her. It was as if he had no soul.

For a moment they just stared at each other. She was afraid that he knew that she knew.

Her breaths started coming in little gasps. Without taking her eyes off him, she backed out of his office, slammed the door and scuttled to the public bathroom to wash the glass shard out of her hand. She had to phone Frannie, in case she got worried not having heard from her as she'd promised and decided to come here.

She locked herself into a cubicle. Her nervous hands dialled the number. She could barely stop shaking. Although she was trying to be sensible, she knew she had to have a little hit. Her entire body was craving it. She stood there with her nostrils twitching as she waited for Frannie to answer and took a little snort out of a silver bullet she kept in her purse.

Because she was so tense, the hit snapped through her like a gunshot. The phone went straight to voicemail. The seconds ticked by absurdly as she waited for the beep.

She almost screamed as she left a message. 'Frannie, it's Dorcas. Stay away from the club, Hans is off his rocker… Call me, OK?' She put her hand on the wall to steady herself. The rush, her panic, it was all too much. Her heartbeat was accelerating at full throttle, slamming hard into her chest. Her beautiful, lithe body struggled to keep control of her sobs. It was over. She never wanted to see Hans again.

# Chapter Fourteen

Because Kurt was upset before he started drinking, Frannie had to be extra-careful. She sat there keeping the emotions from her face. She itched to just jump in the car and zoom off. Now, even though she had her driving licence, she was stuck in her web of lies. She was too scared to call Hans back in case Kurt caught her. She found herself rubbing her hands and tapping her feet. She felt trapped.

The scratched car had made Kurt restless. He drank beer after beer until the smell permeated the living room and made Frannie nauseous. She couldn't go to bed and just let herself fall asleep as usual. Somehow she had to force herself to stay awake. The second Kurt was snoring she would drive over to Moonlights.

The sight of the full moon out of the window eased her nerves. Whatever happened in the day, the night belonged to her. However mad this search for Tomek was, she needed to find him. Meeting him had made her realise how small her world was.

She sat listlessly while her husband downed beer in smacking gulps. He seemed to drink with even more gusto now she had to abstain. Her mind visualised the route to the club. The roads wouldn't be so empty, but they'd still be relatively quiet. She might have to stand in small traffic queues at red lights, but she would drive in the right-hand lane so she could go at a slower pace. She counted down all the traffic lights in her mind: at least six to get through. If it got too much, there were a couple of places where she could turn off and rest a moment. She could try.

It was midnight by the time she got in the car. Because she hadn't been to sleep already, she was tired. But her nerves were taut, her eyes almost glassy with concentration. Slowly she reversed out of the garage. It was no problem going backwards if the car was already straight.

She hadn't figured out what she was going to say to this Hans Grans. Just worrying about getting there was enough.

The B6 was surprisingly busy. Teenagers swerved by with half-opened windows that blared out music. She had to watch the traffic lights like a hawk so that she could accelerate as soon as they turned green. Even in the slow lane, she was being shoved around by boy racers feeling horny. A couple seemed to enjoy driving close to her bumper, forcing her to speed up. She bit her lip. This was tougher than she'd anticipated. She put her foot down even more.

She concentrated on keeping a good stopping distance between her and the next car. Still she was unnerved by a few madmen behind her. She did what her driving instructor Heinrich had told her to do and changed the position of the mirror so she couldn't see what was happening behind her. Let them worry about not going into her.

Another two traffic lights and she'd be able to get on the *Autobahn*. Just anticipating it made the pit of her stomach quiver. Now they were getting close to Hannover, the cars were queuing up with a lot of revving and engine heat. Frannie's heart sank. This was exactly the kind of thing she wanted to avoid.

The muscles in her thigh were aching from all the stop/start action. She hoped to God she wouldn't get an attack of cramp, which was one side effect of being pregnant. That hadn't happened yet while driving, but it freaked Frannie out. Since her accident, though, there had been no more bleeding. Driving seemed to relax her and free her mind. She was sure the baby wasn't affected by her night driving.

Still it was hard to concentrate when she was so tired. She found it peculiar to just inch up gradually behind the other cars. She was used to dramatic movements on an open road with plenty of time to brake and accelerate: all this micro-movement was frustrating.

For once she was glad to see signs for the *Autobahn*. Although no one was behind her, she sped on to the junction for all she was worth. The curve was wilder than she anticipated, the car seemed to wobble, but she held it together. Ah, here it was – from what she'd seen on the internet, the Moonlights club was just a few kilometres down this road. She hoped it would be clearly signposted.

Flanked by two huge tankers, she crawled along in the slow lane. She felt safe between them but it made it difficult for her to look for things coming up. In the night sky she could make out the shape of factories, some lit up brilliantly, others just a blur. This part of Hannover was run-down. She'd never driven on this road before, didn't know what to expect.

Even though it was an *Autobahn*, the road wasn't completely flat. She had anticipated everything being stretched out so she could see the club, but she really had to concentrate to make any sense of the darkness.

She could see another service station coming up. And what looked like a diner. It was all on top of her before she had a chance to react. *Shit*. She'd gone past a turning marked 'Moonlights Discotheque'. She hit her steering wheel with a fist. Now she'd have to loop back and try to find it coming from the other way. Her eyes had registered, though, that the club's car park was ominously full. Perhaps the easiest thing to do would be to park anywhere she could now and walk the last kilometre or so on foot.

On her right she spotted an abandoned factory. Quickly, she indicated and moved off the motorway on to a very old and crumbling road that threatened to collapse into rubble at any minute. There were no lights. Dimly, she could make out the giant roof of a building and a tower, all hidden behind an ancient strip of barbed wire that seemed to hold important secrets. At least there was plenty of space. She parked in a corner, well away from the road. Didn't want to attract attention. Although it was summer, the night was cold. The moon was high in the sky.

It looked as though there was a feeder road that led from the factory back to the club. Carefully, she started to pick her way along it, going as fast as she could in the dark.

Although Frannie always wore flat, comfortable shoes for driving, she hadn't anticipated a hike. Very quickly, her late-stage pregnancy asserted herself. The path was wild and overgrown, and she couldn't really see what she was doing. Her body slowed down, her feet trying blindly to feel the path. It was mainly grass and weeds now, but occasionally glass crunched under her feet.

She was halfway there, practically marooned in the dark. The sounds of some kind of throbbing music carried on the wind. She gave a little shiver. She had been so nervous about simply getting there that she hadn't planned what to say when she did.

The path seemed to be getting wilder. Now, the obstacles weren't just weeds: abandoned chairs and shopping trolleys littered the way. For some reason this forgotten strip had become a dumping ground. Not much further now…she could see the club, all lit up. Loud music blurted out on the wind. Every time someone opened and closed the main door of the club it became louder for a second.

She would do anything to sit down. It occurred to her that if anything happened she'd be a sitting duck. Her mobile wasn't working; she'd had it on so long today it had run down and she'd forgotten to charge it. Another two hundred metres and she'd be there. Then she'd just have to hope that in her hot and bothered state the bouncer would admit her into the club.

By the end, Frannie was limping along. Because of the exertion, her ankles had ballooned and her black trouser suit was dusty. From the car park she could see that business was good. There was a queue of scantily dressed girls waiting to get in. Pockets of men stood around in little jostling groups.

She approached the bouncer at a run. He was a stocky fellow with a crew cut who looked as if he didn't know what to do with his hands.

'Can you please get Herr Grans on the phone?' she asked.

He looked at her twice, trying to understand her accent. She repeated herself slowly, gave him her friendliest smile and stood there holding her stomach. Within fifteen seconds he handed her his mobile.

'Hello?' she said this time in English. He already knew who it was. 'Hans Grans? Can you give me ten minutes?'

'Come up to the VIP room,' he said in an odd voice. He sounded astonished that she'd had the balls to get there. Frannie was looking forward to seeing him in the flesh.

The bouncer opened the door for her and pointed her in the right direction. She made her way into the dark ambience of the club. It was gothic-looking, but incredibly chic, but she had to go away from the crowd to the office upstairs.

She looked as though she was going for a job interview, but these were the only smart clothes that still fitted. She made her way up the spiral staircase. Everybody else was going insane in the basement disco; she felt odd creeping up the red stairs in the dark.

Upstairs she dived into the bathroom. Her face looked hot and shiny in the mirror. She washed her hands briskly, didn't bother drying them. This was the moment of truth. She had to tackle Hans Grans, and despite her language difficulties, find out where Tomek was.

The VIP room looked shiny, ominous. She could see it just there, on the right…

🚗

Inside the club, Dorcas had fled Hans's office and was desperately heading for the exit. One hand attempted to wipe her running nose, the other grasped the wall. In her high heels her feet stuttered. She couldn't walk straight. Her sense of balance was gone. It was as though someone had snapped a nerve in her back.

What was left was trying to scuttle off and hide somewhere in the darkness. Her hands clutched at the air in front of her face as if she'd just witnessed a traffic accident.

When Lars encountered her on the stairs, such was her distress that at first he didn't recognise her. But there was no mistaking the Jimmy Choo boots. He'd helped pick them out for her himself.

'Dörchen?' he said, reaching out and trying to grab her hand. She was on the verge of pitching forward headfirst.

When she saw him, she flinched. A little gasp escaped her mouth. She wouldn't look at him. She rushed down past him. He could swear there were tears in her eyes. The sound of her boots scraping against the metal stairs below him was true horror. He could hear her sharp breaths, smell her fear.

Lars stood there for a minute. His mouth tightened in a way that showed the big solid bones of his face. He knew he was ordinary-looking, that he'd never make hearts race like Hans. But he'd never want to hurt them like that. That bastard! He looked upwards with his face fixed in pure rage. The swine got off on women sobbing their hearts out.

With a little snort, he continued up the stairs, two at a time.

# Chapter Fifteen

Reaching the first floor where she'd been told to go, Frannie recognised Hans as soon as she saw him in the corridor. He looked even better than his website picture. His frame and face suggested vitality, robustness. The way he moved was powerful but refined. Every part of him was thoughtfully put together.

'Frau Snell?' He greeted her with a warm smile, but his charm was so mannered that she found it vampiric. She quickly snatched her hand back after shaking his.

'Please, call me Francesca,' she said. He nodded at her. She was sweating where her blouse clung to her heavily pregnant stomach. Her old business suit was speckled with dust. Some kind of weed was trailing off a trouser leg.

He radiated a languid energy; his lightweight beige suit seemed to glow. There was nothing of the tough man she'd expected. He looked harmless and gave the impression he had nothing better to do than help her out.

Hans led her a little way down the corridor. 'The VIP room is just here,' he said, gesturing. 'I can make you very comfortable in there.' He grinned. She didn't quite understand why he found it so funny. His hand was about to punch in the numbers on the key pad.

The noise of running steps along the corridor distracted them. They were too hurried, the heavy breathing too forced, to ignore.

A stocky man with a shaved head ran up furiously.

'*HANS, du Arschloch!*' he shouted, at the top of his voice. He almost ran into Hans as if he wanted to do him real physical harm. Frannie instinctively flinched. She stepped to the side.

He continued shouting, totally out of control.

'*Was hast du mit Dorcas gemacht? Sie ist schwanger!*' His voice was charged with fury.

'*Was?*' Hans looked surprised. The two men were at each other like dogs. They shouted so fast that Frannie couldn't understand a word of it. *Dorcas*. Could it be her Dorcas they were talking about?

Hans's face had paled. He seemed frightened of the other man. The two men grappled with each other clumsily. Hans seemed to collapse, as if he wanted to embrace the man and not fight him back. His eyes rolled back. The man with the shaved head got Hans's head up so that his neck was exposed. She watched him trace a finger there. Hans blinked. He looked more shocked than if he'd been hit. He turned to Frannie with desperate eyes.

'Lars, Francesca Snell here is looking for someone,' he said, almost squeaking, he had so little voice left.

The shaved head swivelled and turned his deep brown eyes at her. He looked shocked; the only thing interesting about his face was his eyes and they glinted crazily. Frannie felt as if he could slash her throat as look at her. She shivered. He seemed to be taking her in.

'*Englisch?*' he said to Hans. He looked back at her then his face fell. He whispered something to Hans she couldn't hear.

When he took a step towards her, she shrank back.

'I'm sorry,' he said in halting English. 'Don't...' He turned and shouted something in German to Hans. With one more meaningful glance at her, Lars turned and left without another word. Hans stood straight again, tried to straighten his clothes.

'I'm sorry about that. A little personal business, but Lars wanted to say sorry to you. He doesn't really speak English.' He ran a hand though his hair.

'Sorry for what?' said Frannie, her eyebrows raised.

Hans looked awkward again. 'I believe you had a little accident in your car? Lars was the lorry driver.'

Frannie's mouth open and closed. 'That was Lars Steeg…?' she said, not able to pronounce the surname.

'Yes,' said Hans simply, playing with the tips of his fingers. 'I'm sorry for this inconvenience.' He looked at her and then glanced at the steel door of the VIP room. His eyes were expressionless, Frannie felt herself shiver. Despite his good looks, she didn't relish the prospect of being alone with him. Then he suddenly seemed to change his mind about where to take her and led her instead to his office. Somehow, he'd lost his sparkle.

She nodded slowly, trying to take in the information. So that was what Lars looked like close up.

She followed Hans along the corridor. The deep red carpet was plush. Everything about the club was elegant in a grand way, as if it had been a gathering place for centuries. The flickering candles made it seem like a vampire's lair. She had to admit that Hans looked good, but she wasn't going to be bowled over by his fancy looks. She'd already decided not to trust him.

His office was plush and modern. The walls were lined with red brick with a wooden ceiling and broad beams that held the roof high. There were six monitors that showed running CCTV cameras. Frannie quickly ran her eye over them.

'As a member of the public, you're not really meant to be in here, for data protection reasons,' said Hans. He gestured to a comfortable armchair and offered her a fruit juice.

The office buzzed with hi-tech equipment which continually

flashed and clicked; the room seemed to hum with electricity. One camera showed the entrance outside, where the surly-looking bouncer who had let her in waited like an obedient dog. Others showed the main dance floor, an ultra-long bar, a view outside the main toilets; another showed the private booth. Hans turned off the one that showed a couple having sex in some nether region of the club. Another one seemed to be dark. She couldn't really see anything properly.

'What's that one?' she asked.

'Just the VIP room,' he said with an odd glint in his eye. 'There's nothing going on at the moment, but we need to keep an eye on important visitors.' He turned to her again. 'When did your friend visit the club?'

'Yesterday; he was supposed to meet me afterwards at three a.m., but he never showed up.' Frannie tried to keep her voice neutral. Just being in a closed room with him she could feel his magnetism pulling at her. There was something diabolical about his attractiveness, as if it was there just to entice people in. She wanted to get this over quickly and escape.

'Do you have a photo of him?'

'No.'

'Could he have paid by credit card?' said Hans.

'I don't know his full name, but he's the brother of Anna, who worked here, so he's Tomek whatever Anna's last name was.' Frannie was flustered and she knew Hans could see it.

He looked at her carefully. 'You don't know his last name but you're searching for him?'

Frannie refused to look at him. She clenched her lips.

'Look, if you show me last night's footage from the entrance-door camera, I'm sure I will be able to recognise him,' she said. 'And do you know where Anna is now, or have a phone number for her?' This was the question she'd wanted to ask all along.

At the mention of Anna, Hans did a double-take. His eyes seemed to darken, his nose twitched; his whole mood abruptly changed.

'Anna no longer works here,' he practically spat at her. 'And if I knew where she was I'd be able to get the money back she owes me for rent.' He sat there, immobile at his desk, with his youthful face twisted with shadows.

'Well, perhaps we could check if Tomek was here last night?'

He fiddled around with something in his desk. 'You're not really supposed to see the CCTV footage; you're a member of the public. If you gave me a photo, though, I could have someone search it for you.' He looked at her aggressively, as if the meeting was already over.

'I don't have that,' she said, giving him her best smile.

'Then I don't really think I can help you,' he said staring at her. 'If he's missing then it's best to contact the police, although it is rather difficult without a full name.' His eyes seemed to bore into her. At any moment she expected him to jump up and sink his teeth into her neck.

'Perhaps I can tell the police that both Anna and Tomek seem to be missing and their last location was this club,' said Frannie, two red spots visible in her cheeks.

Hans just smiled. 'The last time you went to the police, it didn't really help matters, did it?' he said with a little laugh. He placed his hands flat on the desk.

Frannie gasped. How could he know about that? When he saw her panic, his eyes darkened. It looked as if he was subtly undergoing some change and was enjoying every second of it.

'I'm sorry – thank you for your help anyway,' she said, rising clumsily to her feet. She was desperate to leave. Hans was on his feet in an instant. At first she thought he was going to block the door, but he held it open mock-courteously. Quickly, she mumbled her goodbyes and made her way down the winding stairway. For a pregnant woman, Frannie wasn't slow. Somehow it was clear to her that, if she gave Hans Grans even a second more to delay her, she might not make it out of there at all.

Lars sat in his truck and tried to listen to the pure sounds of the night. To let himself be soothed by the wind moving between the trees. All he heard was irregular beats coming from the club door, which opened and shut with regular monotony. His head ached; the pain was ferocious and made him wince. He should just find somewhere dark and lie down.

But that was impossible; the mood he was in, anyone he encountered was in for it. He had to sit still for a bit and figure this all out. Try to get in touch with something inside him that was a higher force. That didn't *care* how it was all falling apart with Hans.

It was all fucked, and he knew it. If he didn't forget about Hans, he was going to get dragged down by him. The angst of losing Hans's desire got to him. Without him he was ordinary, despicable, a wretch no better than a dog.

And why was this silly English bitch after him? He banged his fists to his forehead. He hadn't meant to cause her any harm. He'd only played with her. Jesus Christ. Everything he did was turning to shit. Maybe if he waited a while, he'd see her come out. He was going to keep his eye on her.

His migraine had got so bad it was like was looking through a red mist. The tension in his head increased, as if he was on a plane about to land and his ears might pop at any second.

The cab echoed with the sound of his maniacal laughter.

He only knew that his mouth was opening and closing. He was fucked up and someone was going to pay.

🚗

Once Frannie had her back turned to Hans, she didn't stop running until she was out of the club and could see the bouncer's legs standing on the safe turf of the car park. Her breathing was rapid and sweaty, every muscle in her legs strained; her stomach was getting more unwieldy by the second. The boom of the music had almost deafened her. It was only coming out that she realised how loud it had been.

She gave a little shiver at the thought of the walk back to the car, the waiting dark. She just wanted to collapse, fall down dead asleep. If only she could drive confidently, she'd have been able to park in the club car park and be able to get into the car in seconds. She hated her fear of driving and the problems it caused her. Her exhaustion was weighing her down.

She made her way round the back of the club. The air was close. The sky had gone a strange metallic colour. The wind was up and rain threatened at any minute. The moon was obscured by scudding clouds that felt spiteful. How desperately she needed that moonlight to find her way! She felt sick to her stomach with tiredness. The path stretched out in front of her, dark and ominous. She gave a shiver. As there were no lights where her car was parked, it felt as though she was leaving civilisation to get back to it.

She gave a little shudder when she thought of Hans. All this way and she'd achieved nothing, although she'd seen for herself what type of man he was. What on earth could she do now to find Tomek? She noted that Hans had neglected to tell her Anna's surname, although he must know it. Whatever he said, he obviously had no interest in helping her.

Now she'd gone on a bit further, the path was completely bleak. She could barely see her own hand. The wind had got up and was busy blowing leaves and foliage into her face. Her feet slipped and stumbled. It was impossible to clearly see what she was stepping on. She tried her best to go faster. It was getting harder to ignore the feeling of dread. Behind her she could hear noises and rustling. Something seemed to be prowling around in the undergrowth. Was it some big animal? But what could it be? Surely no dog owner would choose this path. Urban foxes were normally lithe and sly. Whatever it was, it sounded like trouble.

She was about halfway there. The undergrowth grew so tall that it threatened to cut her off. Her breathing was laboured, hoarse. Her centre of gravity had shifted to the centre point over her cervix. She was like some grotesque round toy with joke legs that wobbled under it.

The rustling noises became more distinct. There was definitely something on the path behind her. She went cold with fear. She was in trouble.

# Chapter Sixteen

Hardly daring to breathe, Frannie paused and listened. It was moving towards her from where she'd come and now it was too late to run back. With a desperate burst of energy, she continued. Her eyes scanned the darkness looking for sticks or a bottle, but she couldn't see anything clearly. From her shoulder bag she took out her keyring and pushed out the car key so that if someone tried to attack her at least she could stick them with something.

Her calves ached from the urgency of her movement. Perhaps she should just find a gap in the undergrowth and wait and hide.

No, from the deliberate movements she could tell now that it was a person, and one who was determined to find her. Perhaps they had a torch or some kind of light. Her only hope was that they wouldn't realise she had a car parked there and she'd be able to drive off before they caught up with her.

She turned round and looked back. She couldn't be sure, but her mind painted for her the figure of an evil man in pursuit. He was gaining on her. It was another two hundred and fifty metres to the car, at least. He'd be upon her in seconds.

Some inner survival instinct seemed to click in. Although she was exhausted, without even seeming to breathe, she hurried her legs into a sprint. Once upon a time she'd competed for her school, specialising in the four hundred metres. As quietly as she could, she ran on, clenching her key tightly in her hand like a talisman.

Behind her the undergrowth seemed to come alive with noise. Her pursuer also began to run, except that he could do it in big loping strides that gained on her every step. Still she ran, moving her legs as quickly as she could make them. The sound of his footsteps getting closer egged her on. If she ran much faster her startled lungs wouldn't be able to function. Her body was being pushed to its limits.

The path was coming to an end. Her car was somewhere in the darkness. She cursed herself for every extra step she had to take to find it.

From behind she heard a scuffle, the sound of an angry man's voice crying out '*Scheisse!*' He'd fallen down. This was her chance.

She bolted into her car and slammed the door so hard she thought the glass would break. It took a few seconds for her shaking hand to slide the key into the ignition. All the time her body sobbed for breath.

Out of the corner of her eye she saw a tall, dark figure approach the car park, limping. She knew that if he hadn't fallen he would have had her. She skidded into reverse, needed two attempts to take the handbrake off. With a little squeal she sped out of the car park, leaving the desolate expanse behind her.

She didn't look to see if she could see anyone. Every part of her was concentrated on exiting. When the car met the road, in her haste she almost drove into a red Jaguar. She had to fight to brake and control the car. Her relief at finally entering the middle lane of the *Autobahn* was overwhelming. All she could think about was putting her foot down as hard as she could and making it home at twice the normal speed.

Lars laughed out loud. His knee was bleeding where he'd fallen. And clambering around through all that undergrowth he'd scratched his arms to pieces. A bloody pregnant woman had outrun him! Just went to show how unfit he was.

It seemed a long time since he'd been in active service with the army. Of course, if he hadn't fallen it would have been easy. He could have watched the look of fear in her eyes. Not that he would have hurt her. He didn't kill women. There was only that time with Anna, and what a shitstorm that had unleashed.

He didn't kill women.

He didn't kill for killing's sake.

He only got excited, and then he wasn't responsible for what happened.

But still he needed to warn this woman off. In his pocket, his hand searched for his mobile. He phoned Inspector Koch so often he was like a friend. They did things for each other, whether out of duty or respect, he had no idea. What he was sure of was that Koch would help him out.

Frannie was no longer a slow driver. She was shooting up the fast lane, pushing the other traffic to the middle lane. The car was as swift as an arrow, and it hummed faintly as it raced along. The empty bottles that Kurt had forgotten to take for recycling rattled in the boot. Even though it was illogical, she wanted to put as much distance as possible between herself and the man she'd left behind on foot.

Signs flashed past. Frannie found her way back fairly easily.

Now that she had the protection of the car, everything felt easy. Within minutes she was exiting on to the B6. She forgot to come down in gear and the car nearly stalled.

After the exhilaration of being able to drive as fast as the car could go, it was a drag doing seventy. As there were few other cars she went faster, eating up the kilometres. She was looking forward to getting home and collapsing into bed.

She was just about to turn right at Burger King when the flashing blue light of a police car dazzled her. She froze, slowing down drastically, not sure what to do. The police car fixed itself firmly to her bumper. She decided to stop and pull over. She groaned. A wrangle with the police was the last thing she needed.

It seemed to take ages before the policeman tapped at her window. He had steel-grey hair and a hard face. Even his brilliant blue eyes looked shocked, as if it was hard to live with his own temper.

She wound the window down. He said something unintelligible. She thought she heard him say *Führerschein* so she looked in her purse on the passenger seat and dug out her driving licence. It was a struggle to find everything, and all the time the policeman looked at her as if she was guilty of something terrible.

'Registration papers?' he barked at her. His eyes flashed. Her face dropped. They were in her husband's wallet, although in theory they should be carried at all times.

'My husband has them,' she said in her best German. She pointed again to her driving licence. 'I live just five minutes away.'

It was not sufficient. The policeman told her she didn't have the correct paperwork. Shit! It wasn't Deutschland but paper land. Bureaucracy was everywhere.

'You need to come down to the station,' said the policeman. She was forced to follow him, away from the twinkling lights of the road home. By now Frannie was just too tired to do anything than mechanically go through the motions. Kurt was going to find out everything. It occurred to her that ten minutes ago she would have done anything for proximity to a police officer. Now all she wanted was sleep.

The station was the Garbsen one, a stone's throw from the minimall that was small beans compared to English ones. She hoped that her German would be good enough to get her through the interview.

They took her to a big room with a table that could have sat twenty. She was given a cup of water with an ice cube in it. The man who brought her the drink was nice and friendly. Good cop, bad cop, she thought. Should she tell them about Anna and Tomek, about the man who had chased her? But she'd never even caught a glimpse of the man's face. And perhaps she'd been trespassing when she'd gone on the path? Whatever she did, she didn't want to make things worse.

Her blood pressure must be up; it felt as though her heart was going to pump itself out of her chest.

A man came in. 'Frau Snell?' he said, indicating that she should sit again. He explained that she had been caught speeding on the B6. She licked her lips and tried to look scared. Although it occurred to her she should have been nervous, she was so freaked out by the night's events that she was mentally shutting down.

'Have you been drinking?' he said in a stern voice.

She looked down pointedly at her pregnant bump. 'No,' she said.

'Although you were at a discotheque?' he replied.

Even through the tiredness, Frannie felt something in her mind click.

'I didn't say where I was,' she said. Her face was puzzled.

'Oh, I guessed you were at a club. Where else does one go at this time in the morning?' said the policeman hastily. He turned to his paperwork.

Frannie stared at him. Another man came into the room and the two men whispered ridiculously loudly. What could they possibly be talking about? She was starting to feel increasingly agitated. Her tongue was a piece of dumb cloth in her mouth. No matter how she sat, her legs ached. Something was going to give if she had to stay there much longer.

The younger of them turned to her. 'We need to see the vehicle's registration papers. Is there anyone we can call to bring them?'

Frannie sighed. The second she phoned Kurt, he'd know all about her nocturnal adventures and that she'd scratched his car. Acid crept up sneakily from the pit of her stomach. She could feel the nausea rising like tendrils stretching out. There was no putting it off. She had to throw up. It had been one hell of a night and it wasn't over yet.

Dorcas burst out of the taxi before the driver could properly stop. She thrust the fare into his hands and ran up the steps to her flat two at a time. When she was through the front door, she locked and bolted it from the inside and leaned against it.

Her heart thudded frantically. She allowed her body to slump down until she was on the floor in a heap, rasping out deep painful breaths. Her mind raced so hard that her eyes must have looked crossed. The only meaningful thing she could do was to take off her shoes, which had been rubbing her heels. When she wiped her face with her fingers they were covered with mascara. She had openly wept in the taxi whilst the driver had stared dead ahead.

Tonight the elegant ambience of the flat was *egal*. Her lovely face was creased with pain. She reached for a cigarette, needed to sit and think. Her shoulders quivered. The decision had to be made, and quick.

Lars had finally confessed to sleeping with Hans. Anna was missing. She hadn't even been able to tell Hans she was pregnant. And after their fight, if she didn't work for him how would she pay the rent, and for coke? Perhaps it was time to just pack a bag and go. But she still had to decide. One hand strayed to her stomach.

She checked her mobile. No messages or missed calls. Hans hadn't even bothered to check that her bleeding hand was alright. *Bastard*. Her face tightened. She carried on nursing her cigarette. She'd turned a blind eye to his drug dealing, but if he was involved in people-trafficking, or worse… Whatever she did for a living, she knew right from wrong.

Nothing made sense any more.

Despite her misery, her heart-shaped face was resolute. In this chaos she was certain of one thing. If Hans had hurt Anna, she didn't want to carry his child. It was a knee-jerk reaction.

Dorcas took out another cigarette. She didn't know what to do, but she couldn't stand living in this twilight world any more; had to find out the truth. She rose to her feet. She wasn't going to be blind to Hans's criminal life. Restlessly, she fingered her beloved plants as her mind worked overtime…

Dorcas was carefully pruning her bonsais when the buzzer went. It was gone one a.m. She wasn't expecting anyone. Her concave cutter dropped and clattered on the floor. Now she couldn't pretend she wasn't home. The voice on the other end of the buzzer shouted a muted, 'Dörchen.' It was Lars, but he sounded odd.

'I was just going to bed.'

Lars refused to be put off. In the strangest voice he said, 'I'm bleeding...' There was a long pause, and she could hear the sound of him breathing heavily. 'Can I just clean up?'

Reluctantly, she opened the door. She didn't want to face him right now, but needed to know what was going on. In the dim hallway, for a second he stood in bulky profile like the bogeyman. His hands were twisted into fists, and his broad, shiny full-moon face was covered in dark stuff. When he got closer she saw it was blood. An open cheek-wound was bleeding profusely, and it was going all down his shirt. Inwardly she shuddered.

She led him to the bathroom and attended to him with her first-aid kit. He sat down on the edge of the bath like an old man. Lars had also hurt his knee, and a graze, filthy with debris, was sticking out of a hole in his jeans. She was burning with questions, but Lars had to keep his face still while she cleaned him up. She began to worry about who could have caused the injuries.

'What happened?' she said, trying to get all the blood off his ear.

'I had to chase a customer and managed to fall down on the bloody derelict path out back,' Lars said with a sardonic grin. It sounded lame. He was probably lying through his teeth. From the smell of him he needed a date with a shower pretty bad.

'Did you call the police?' she said, her hands rubbing away at his skin removing dried blood and dirt.

Lars grinned. 'Well, I called Koch, and they'll make some trouble, don't you worry.' He noticed the plaster on her hand. 'Someone else has been in the wars, I see!'

Dorcas snatched her hand away. 'Hans broke a paperweight and a shard grazed my hand,' she said.

'How did he take it?' Lars looked at her intensely.

'What?' Her eyebrows were raised.

'When you said you were pregnant?'

'I didn't,' she said, bending down to concentrate on his knee, her movements, as ever, efficient. 'Wasn't the right time.'

'Oh, shit!' said Lars, wiping his cleaned face with filthy hands. 'After I saw you on the stairs, I gave him a piece of my mind.'

'He knows?' Dorcas turned on him. Her face was incredulous.

'Well, I thought that was why you were running away – 'cos he'd given you the knock-back.' Lars's eyes were downcast.

Dorcas lost it. She dropped the cotton wool she was holding and swiftly slapped him round the face. She did it so hard that the plaster she'd just put on his face turned crimson as the cut started bleeding again and seeping through it.

'Stay away from him!' she shouted, her eyes blazing with anger.

Lars, shocked to his core, just sat there. Blood was now seeping down on to his shirt. Dorcas knelt on the floor, sobbing. Lars placed an arm around her shoulder, but she pushed it off. Then she looked up at him, her eyes full of pleading. She couldn't stand a minute more of this.

'Please Lars, I need to know,' she said, wiping her eyes with her fingers.

'Know what?' He just looked shocked.

'What did Hans do to Anna?' she was still on her knees, big tears falling down her cheeks. The floor was getting into a fine mess.

Lars wiped the blood off his cheek.

'If you really knew Hans,' he said in an even voice, 'you wouldn't want him.' His eyes seemed to stare through her.

'Spit it out, you swine,' shouted Dorcas, rising to her feet. Her voice had become hard and bitter. Lars was sitting hunched on the bath. She was never going to let him in again. Never.

'There are some things you shouldn't even tell God,' said Lars. She couldn't tell if he'd gone potty or was being a sarcastic arsehole.

Dorcas lashed out again, beating him with one of her good towels. The cloth whipped him pretty damn good. Lars wrenched it away. He stood then, facing her, eyes blazing. His face looked theatrically scary with his staring eyes and the bleeding cut. He took a threatening step towards her. In his hands the towel became an offensive weapon.

'Lars!' she said, begging, trying to reach that part of him that knew her. He loomed over her, a bogeyman poised to strike. She screamed as loudly as she could.

One minute the towel was stretched taut between two hands, as if he was going to tighten it around her neck. The next, the blaze in his eyes had diminished and without another word he took off. He casually dropped the towel, which was now stained with blood. He'd done nothing, but she'd seen the malevolent glint in his eyes.

The door slammed. She exhaled slowly. She'd didn't want to think about what would have happened if he hadn't gone of his own accord.

Dorcas began to spill out anguished tears, until her eyes were puffy-ugly. Her Lars, whom she'd known for two years, looked as if he could be capable of just about anything. She'd seen him lose control more than once, but in defence of her, not against her. But she couldn't do a thing. With no proof, she had to be careful. He was a police informer, and the police looked after their own.

She tried to concentrate on slowing her breathing. She felt terrible. And she had an inclination, deep in her belly, that everything was even worse than she could imagine. She couldn't leave until she'd found out what the little shits had actually done. And, to top it all, Hans knew more than he was letting on about Anna. She reached for another cigarette. Her hands were shaking so much she nearly burnt herself trying to light up.

When Frannie finally got up and asked to use the bathroom, it was too late. All the evening's stress reared up in one nauseating wave. She opened her mouth and a viscous gruel splattered all over the floor in front of her. There was no stopping it. Her stomach emptied itself four, five times with frightening efficiency. Before she'd finished she was already gagging at the smell.

The young policeman looked at her aghast. Her head felt as if it was about to burst. She tottered where she stood. The room felt too hot and the lights sharpened to pinpoints as the world went black.

The policeman rushed back towards her, but Frannie was already falling backwards into a dead faint.

The young policeman tinkered with his radio; his voice loud, crisp.

'An ambulance please: a pregnant woman has collapsed, and she's about ready to pop, I'd say.' Frannie's condition brought running footsteps into the room. Minutes passed as they waited for the ambulance to arrive.

They were covering her with a blanket just as Inspector Koch came in with a well-muscled, tall guy with lanky blond hair. It was Kurt. He didn't look as if he appreciated being woken in the middle of the night and having to take a taxi because his wife was out with his car. But, when he saw the men bending over Frannie, his sulkiness turned to panic. He rushed over and knelt by his wife's side. His hands were outstretched, as if he could make everything better by laying them on her.

'That's my wife,' he said, in a furious voice. His muscled body looked awkward, as if he only knew how to push weights. 'What have you done to her?' In his haste, he'd stepped in the sick.

The young policeman gave him a look of dislike. 'She was sick and then she fainted. Why was she out at a discotheque in her condition?'

Kurt just stared.

'My wife?' he said. He looked confused. With his tall bulk he had all the physicality of an alpha male, but psychologically something deadened him. He stood there, clueless. He was still staring when they carried her out on a stretcher.

# Chapter Seventeen

Frannie was trapped in a thick fever dream, with a face as pale as her pillow. Her hands clenched restlessly. Although physically she was lying down, in her mind she was driving fast on an open road. Because her parents hadn't owned a car, there would always be something magical about the freedom of being about to jump in a vehicle and shoot off like the clappers. In her dreams she was always driving. But this time she was stuck. The car she was driving was broken. *Kaputt.* And her arm felt funny when she tried to do something about it.

She opened her eyes, felt down her arm, to find some kind of strange device that was peculiarly fixed to it. The pressure of it was painful. She screamed and tried to get her bearings.

The first thing she noticed was the agonising white of the walls, with bright lights that bounced off the surfaces until you winced. The atmosphere was dominated by an antiseptic smell and the strange hum of the equipment. It was Neustadt Krankenhaus, the hospital where she was due to give birth. Another brash, impersonal medical institute she felt uncomfortable in.

When she looked down, her arm was attached to a drip and she wore a blood pressure cuff. She was still wearing her own clothes, but they'd put some kind of stockings on her legs.

One of the machines beeped and a nurse came running up. She spoke so rapidly that Frannie couldn't make out one word.

'*Noch mal, bitte?*' said Frannie, hoping she'd understand the second time round. The nurse spoke rapidly, using words she couldn't understand. Whatever was wrong, the specifics were beyond her conversational German. She lay back weakly and waited. At some point, Kurt would come and explain everything in English.

*Kurt.* She gave a little groan. The police must have told him by now. What the hell should she say to him? This was all so unfair. If the moody sod hadn't banned her from driving, she wouldn't have had to night-drive in secret. She pursed her lips. The baby was kicking fiercely.

A nurse came and measured her blood pressure. As usual, she hated the vicious squeeze of the cuff; it felt as if a python had wound itself round her arm.

'A hundred and ninety over one hundred and forty. *Meine Güte!*' said the nurse, shaking her head in disbelief at the numbers. 'I will fetch a doctor, *sofort!*' She hurried away, her starched uniform swishing.

It was her highest reading yet. Frannie rubbed her arm. Pressure from the cuff had imprinted lines on her skin. From experience she knew that, if she thought about her blood pressure, the worry would make it rise and it would be even higher when the doctor came to check it personally.

The door opened with a little whine. It was Kurt. For a second he hesitated, his handsome face a mess of emotions. He practically ran to her bedside. She winced, afraid he might be angry, but instead he flung his arms awkwardly around her.

'*Schatz!*' he said, stroking her blonde hair which was spread all over the pillow. 'What's going on? Are you OK?'

'I don't know,' she said, looking at him with big, pleading eyes. 'The nurse said something, but I couldn't understand.'

'Just lie back, I will sort out everything,' he said, his tall figure confident, protective. 'As long as the baby's OK,' he said, placing a hand on her tummy.

'What about me?' The resentment rushed into her voice before she could stop it.

'Well, the two things are the same, aren't they? If you're OK, the baby's OK.' He looked at her puzzled. His perfectly oval face had a well-defined forehead that made him look super-intelligent at first glance. But when he raised his blond piglet eyebrows they were so pale they disappeared, making him look odd.

She snorted with disbelief. He looked at her with edgy eyes. She could see all the confusion about last night turning nasty. His fingers started twitching. Another few minutes and he'd be off on one. She knew the signs and lately the smallest things enraged him. Nervously, she bit her lip.

At that moment a doctor came in. He was older, and did everything deliberately slowly, as if he was not going to let anything get in the way of obtaining a correct diagnosis.

'*Guten Tag, Frau Snell,*' he said, shaking her hand crisply. When he discovered she was English he instantly asked a series of questions in her language about her existing blood pressure condition. Kurt just stood there. The doctor, who seemed to have sensed the tension in the room when he came in, steadfastly ignored him. Kurt hated that. He was used to being her translator and general helper in his home country. It was as though he thought, if she could understand everything and didn't need him, then she would love him less.

'And you were at the police station last night?' said the doctor, with a keen appraisal of her chart.

'Yes, they did a routine check on my car and I didn't have the registration papers.' Frannie kept her voice even.

'Was there some emergency you had to get to, to be out so late?' said the doctor, genuinely trying to understand what had happened.

Frannie looked at Kurt who was standing there, his face glowering. 'No, I just got my *Führerschein* and I wanted to practise when the streets were quiet.' She stared defiantly at the doctor, who was looking slightly surprised. 'I need to be able to drive to get nappies and stuff for my son when he's born.' She looked pointedly at Kurt. 'We live in a village, so it's hard to walk to the shops.' Her face was flushed. Neither of the men could understand it, the terrible need to cope.

'Aha,' said the doctor. He nodded, measured her blood pressure again. This time it was two hundred over one hundred and fifty. 'That is very high,' he said in a slow voice. He rubbed his chin pensively. 'The problem is that it is normal for all women to get higher blood pressure at the end of their pregnancy. And because you have an existing condition, yours will be higher, *natürlich.*' He paused for a second, as if he were talking to an audience. 'So we do not know if this is normal for you, or a possible problem. Eclampsia is a dangerous condition.'

'So what can you do?' said Kurt, stepping forward clumsily as if he was about to do a rugby tackle.

'For now we will remain calm and try to keep the patient comfortable,' said the doctor pointedly, fixing her chart back on to her bed. He looked only in her direction. 'Frau Snell, we will keep you in for twenty-four hours and observe you.' He left briskly without even looking at Kurt.

Frannie looked at her husband. She tried to smile, relax, but it was difficult when he looked so awkward, as if some conjuring trick were being played on him. His hands were stuffed into his pockets. He obviously wanted to know about last night, but he didn't know whether to ask outright. When he was suspicious he got riled up, and some part of his brain closed down.

The longer they stared at each other, the more the tension built. Their relationship was routinely stormy, but now the air felt supercharged, as if a tornado was about to slam into the hospital and tear it to shreds.

'You were just out driving?' he asked, almost in a whisper.

She nodded, although her eyes burned and her cheeks, she was sure, were flushed a brilliant red. It was too awkward to try to explain, especially as she wasn't sure herself what had happened to Tomek or who had chased her. *There's a sodding time and place*, she thought. More than anybody, he knew how badly her pregnancy was affected by stress.

Kurt looked at her with half-closed eyes, as if he didn't quite believe her. She waited with bated breath. His eyes, now they knew they'd got her attention, widened. He stared at her as if he'd never seen her before.

'You did it,' he said pointing a finger at her. His eyes burned into her, his mouth was one furious snarl.

'What?'

Kurt's fists clenched. 'It was *you* who scratched the car.' He was as repulsed as if she'd committed murder.

She didn't answer, didn't need to. He could see it in her face. She could feel her cheeks burning up.

He stood up, put his face near hers and said in such a low voice it came out like a hiss, '*I don't do liars.*' His finger jabbed into her breastbone. She shied away from his touch. Then she pushed him away with her free hand and flung her head back.

'If you weren't such a bloody control freak, I wouldn't have to sneak out at three a.m.' She glared at him with eyes like daggers.

'We'd go out in the evening like a normal couple, eat something, and you'd sit there all supportive while I drove us home.' She turned her face pointedly to the wall.

'Don't you get tired thinking about yourself constantly?' said Kurt, in that mocking voice she hated so much.

'I'm already tired of you.' It slipped out with such honesty, it was impossible to take back. The very core of their relationship was crumbling in front of them.

Kurt's face darkened. 'If you ever do that again, then we're finished,' said Kurt in a slow voice, every muscle in his face clenched. He forced himself to hide his restless fists behind his back. 'You should be thinking of our baby, not your sodding self.'

Frannie gasped. It was shocking to be confronted like that, especially in a hospital bed.

Something on the machine beeped, alarmingly, and the nurse ran back in. 'Frau Snell, your blood pressure is getting higher,' she said, looking at Kurt with disgust. 'You need to relax, avoid stress.'

'My husband likes to get me when I'm down,' said Frannie viciously, her teeth fixed in a snarl. Kurt took a few steps back.

The nurse stepped towards him. 'Visiting time is now over,' she said firmly. With both hands she escorted him towards the door. When he was gone she turned to Frannie. 'Whatever's going on between you two, you need to think about your baby.' She gave a smug look, turned and left.

Frannie lay back, exhausted, her mouth downturned. She never cried, but if she were the kind of person who squeezed out tears when she hit a sticky patch she'd do it now. She looked down at her bulging belly with distaste. She couldn't imagine continuing like this. And while she was laid flat out, feeling sorry for herself, Tomek was out there, helpless.

She got her mobile, which one of the nurses had charged for her, and found Dorcas's number. This time, the silly cow had to come over, and quick. She'd sort out Kurt once she'd found Tomek.

A man was driving an old pick-up truck that was so battered no one could tell what colour it had been. Maybe it had started off sky blue, but now the lacquer was mostly rubbed off to a faded turquoise worn down to the metal in places. Lena, as he called her, had been old when she'd belonged to his father. Since he'd got back from Afghanistan in March, one of his few pleasures was riding round in it. He'd first driven her illicitly at fourteen and wouldn't have parted with her for the world. Chugging obscenely along on the *Autobahn*, next to much newer cars, he stuck out like a sore thumb.

He'd also inherited the farm, but what good was that, now the supermarkets were in control of farm production? Every week he was selling off perfectly good cows and pigs that he didn't have the heart to keep locked up in little pens. If he'd had more field space he could have maybe hung on to them.

That was the irony of his farm: although it was surrounded by a vast expanse of forest and scrubland, it was a snare of a place with limited ground. It was off all main roads, and the dirt track that led to it was so overgrown you'd never dream there was a house down there. Not ideal for farming, but its hidden location was perfect for him. Even though he was hogging the slow lane, a stupid woman was driving up his arse. He grinned, slowed down even more.

If he was honest he hated humans as much as he hated modern farming. If he visited any of the neighbours to borrow anything he'd get into a row about animal welfare. Most farmers didn't bother to muck out properly. They let an overhead shower hose away the worst of the dung but standing on metal floors was harsh on hooves. The cows got infections. They didn't like standing in their own shit. Most farmers did less than the bare minimum. So many things that were done routinely to animals, like milking, were institutionalised torture.

Since he'd done his tour of active duty, the transient nature of life in a war zone had shocked him. Now he found himself doing everything *sofort*, just in case. He couldn't make a cup of tea without instantly washing it up and putting it away as soon as it was drunk.

He'd been dismissed as a field medic when he'd administered too much morphine to a dying man. A mercy dose, there was only so much suffering he could stomach, but the attending doctor hadn't seen it that way. But then, he'd come on the scene later, after the soldier had stopped screaming. Those cries were still reverberating in his ear, high-pitched like a pig squealing.

Stefan didn't do appearances. He seemed to live in old jeans and boots that never looked washed. His young face was spoiled by scars and a perpetual gloom that hung his lower lip a fraction lower than it should have done. He looked thin and vicious, like a starving dog. After the army, he'd been seeking a purpose, some higher guidance. Now he'd found it. He turned on to the road that Hugo had drawn on the map and indicated right for the Moonlights Club.

The Animal Liberation Front didn't do leaders and strategy or force you to stand in a line. What they did was action: covert, undercover. Anything, as long as it got a result. He was going to make sure that Wrexin Pharmaceuticals could no longer use animals for profit. Once he had the money together, the group could infiltrate and gather evidence.

The irony was that, to make the money to save hundreds of animal lives, he had to take one lousy human life. Although even then that slippery Hans had estimated that about ten to twenty stupid human lives could be saved with all the transplants. He just had to look after the body until they found a surgeon to carve out the organs in a secure, sterile environment. If you did the maths, it was a win-win situation.

His eyes blazed over the steering wheel. He was sure he was doing the right thing, but he could only maintain control of himself by not letting himself think about it, even for a second. It was like being on patrol all over again: the perpetual readiness; the mind waiting in turmoil, body just physically going through the motions.

Although he was going to do it, he was dreading this job. He sighed and put his foot down. All he had to do was pick up the victim.

He figured he could just about cope with someone who was virtually unconscious.

# Chapter Eighteen

After he'd nearly lost it at Dorcas's, Lars stood on the landing outside her door unable to think straight with his hands rolled up into fists. The pain in his head had got so bad he thought he was going insane. He could not walk straight, never mind drive; the migraine attack was forcing him to temporarily shut down for a few hours until the pain receded. It hadn't been this bad since he was in military service, but they'd said the headaches and the epileptic fits would increase as he got older. He didn't want to suffer a fully-fledged attack, but he would rather cut his own leg off than order a taxi.

He moved downstairs with difficulty, holding the rail all the way, and forced himself to negotiate the garden. He climbed into the fancy hammock that hung outside all summer long and closed his eyes. It wasn't sleep as such, but his head felt calmer, soothed by the night air.

He became aware of a spider making its curious way over his hand, but let it be. The possibilities of the open space whispered in his ear. He thought about going on the hunt, finding some faceless guy to take his frustration out on, but he had to ease his migraine first. He sighed and screwed his eyes up a lot. The garden was small, but he was hidden under a shady apple tree. Dorcas wouldn't see him unless she was looking for him.

Even though he'd blown it, he wanted to be close to her. Dorcas wasn't just his best friend, she was what he could have had if he did women rather than men. Sometimes he hated his fucking *Pimmel*. Automatically his hand went to his crotch. It stiffened, absurdly, at the slightest touch. His whole life was dominated by pleasing it, feeding its unspeakable desires.

Things ran through his head, images he'd rather not think about. He wished he could just lay his head down on the same pillow as Dorcas and be at ease. Instead he was always thinking about forcing himself on some youth, tasting the blood. It wasn't that thinking of these things turned him on, actually they sent acid tendrils into his mouth, but in spite of that he couldn't stop.

He'd never been able to say why he did what he did. All he concentrated on was covering it up and craving more. Whenever he'd stayed over, cradling Dorcas in his arms, he'd been unable to get rid of the searing images of lovers that plagued his mind. That was the funny thing. It took just minutes to kill them and then they stayed with him forever, tormenting him. There would be no release until death. He shivered and tried to squeeze his eyes shut, but it was all there in his head like a video he couldn't turn off.

It was no good trying to persuade Dorcas he was sorry on the phone. He'd have to go after her when she came out. If he had to, he'd get down on his knees and beg her not to turn her back on him. Without Hans he was a lost soul, but without Dorcas he was finished. Because there was no actual sex between them, even though she was a prostitute, she was the only decent thing in his life.

🚗

At the first throbbing tweet of her mobile ring tone, Dorcas practically fell off the bed with fear. After Lars's outburst, she'd spent hours lying fully clothed with all the lights on without managing to shut her eyes properly. Her body was coiled as if under attack from a giant snake that might strike in any direction.

She was surprised to find it was the soft-spoken English woman, Frannie, and that she was calling at six a.m. The weariness in her voice immediately put her on edge.

'What?' said Dorcas, tiredness making her voice quicken with impatience.

'I'm calling from the hospital,' said Frannie, in a subdued tone. She'd lost her usual sass. 'I did it – went to the club and met him, your Hans – and I'm sure he knows something.'

Dorcas frowned. 'I know,' she said, in a voice so low it came out as a whisper. 'I went there and he freaked out, I tried to call, to warn you, but you didn't answer your phone…' Frantically, she ran her free hand through her hair. 'Are you hurt?'

'I got picked up by the police for speeding,' said Frannie in a little-girl voice, 'and it was such a shock I fainted!' She started to laugh hysterically. It was infectious, Dorcas startled giggling too. They both laughed together in full-throated rasps. Dorcas felt almost giddy with relief. She wiped away a tear of mirth from the corner of her eye. They were tittering like schoolgirls.

'We need to meet up, to make a plan,' said Frannie, with a note of urgency. 'While I'm lying here, I'm sure something bad is going down with Tomek and Anna. Oh, and do you know Anna's surname?'

Dorcas hesitated for a second at the mention of her rival. 'It's a good Polish name – Kalinowski,' she said, mock-slurring the words.

'Thanks,' said Frannie. 'So can you come over?'

Before she'd had a chance to think about what she was doing, Dorcas had agreed to meet Frannie at Neustadt Krankenhaus. And not just in a regular ward, but the maternity wing. The thought of encountering other women with just-born babies made Dorcas feel peculiar. Everything was so upside down, she'd had no time to decide about her pregnancy. There was still no sign of swelling, nor did she feel sick, but she was consumed with a tiredness that engulfed her, threatened to drag her down to the depths. She had to find out what the hell Hans was up to so she could decide. Frannie was her only ally now.

Dorcas was frighteningly quick at turning herself into a glamour puss. There was something driven about everything she did. In the bathroom her two hands worked like programmed robot arms as she completed her morning ritual. Though she'd decided to wear sunglasses to cover her puffy eyes, she still carefully drew on eyebrows with black kohl, and highlighted her eyes. Her hair was moussed into a jaunty bob that matched the tight black silk dress that clung to her thin frame. It made little swishing noises with every step. She added layers of neo-gothic black bead jewellery that contrasted with her pale skin. By the time she left the house she looked like an animated mannequin, all shiny black silk and ruby-red lips; something between a femme fatale and an Angel of Death. Anyone seeing her would have thought she was slinking off from an all-night bender.

Outside, within seconds she was belted into her little Polo and driving off. She was too preoccupied to clock that Lars was waiting for her, like a man possessed.

🚗

Sharp eyes followed her as her car disappeared down the street. Lars was stunned at how fast she moved so early in the morning, and how good she looked despite being a broken doll only hours before. He bent his face into a cracked grimace that hurt his cut cheek. Women! They had something men lacked: a curious rubbery firmness that shielded them, enabled them to bounce back. And Dorcas always bounced back. She was resilient, always cheerful.

Fabulous girl, she was, a real *Schatz*. He strode quickly to his waiting car and started the engine. He'd gone through confusion, anger and grief at the thought of losing her. Now, with a new dawn already high in the sky, he knew he had to go after her, do his best to make it right. With a hooligan's touch his car screeched forward. He was doing what he did best: moving in hot pursuit.

# Chapter Nineteen

During the drive Dorcas kept stealing little glances at herself in her wing mirror. Again and again the sight of her fully made-up face calmed her. She worked hard to look good and took comfort in that fact. She sighed. Her strong cheekbones and sleek figure were the only things she could rely on. When she got scared she piled on the lippie and winged it.

Her mobile phone was right there on the passenger seat but Hans, the swine, still hadn't even texted her. Her rouged lips grimaced. That bastard! Leading her on, forcing her to work out of the minivans to help set up the business. And what did she get for it? All of it had been just talk. She tried to blank out the word 'prostitute'. But it was easy money and gave her an enviable lifestyle.

Her tiredness and irritability made her drive more recklessly than usual. Even though her car was small, she had more nerve than most of the drivers on the road.

She thought she was OK when she got out of the lift. The newborn babies were so small and crumpled you couldn't really see their faces. They could have been puppies or tiny monkeys being wheeled around. Mostly what was visible was their blankets, and their mothers' tired eyes.

She was alright until she saw someone bringing flowers. Her favourite ones: gorgeous sweet peas, in vivid pinks and lilacs, bursting with the smell of innocence. At that she broke down and shut herself behind a toilet door.

The thought of something blameless growing inside her, which she was somehow going to screw up, was more than she could bear.

🚗

Frannie tried not to let a surge of despair get her down. Her arm had been pinched consistently by the cuff that viciously took her blood pressure every fifteen minutes. She was trying to remain calm, but Dorcas, goddamn her, was taking her time. She was tired of being pinned to the bed by all this machinery, having to call a nurse every time she needed to pee. She sighed. Being here only made her feel more stressed. She flung her head back on the pillows.

Outside, she caught a glimpse of a startlingly sleek figure all got up in black wearing her hair in an exaggeratedly short bob. It must be her. Nobody else would dress like that in a maternity unit. The door opened and a wry face, all fringe and eyebrows, laughed at her from behind dark sunglasses.

When she saw her slumped out on pillows, Dorcas seemed to smirk. Frannie couldn't decide whether she'd come dressed for a nightclub or a funeral. Frannie flung up one hand in an exasperated wave by way of a greeting. They eyed each other awkwardly.

'Hey, you're pretty blown?' Dorcas sashayed up to her, like some exotica geisha. Frannie winced. Dorcas's vivid red lipstick looked absurd so early. It was not yet seven a.m.

'Do you know someone called Lars Steeg…?' Frannie tried to sit up higher without ripping the cuff off her arm. 'I can't say the last name.'

Dorcas paled. She looked at Frannie as if she wanted to slap her. 'It's Stiglegger. Lars Stiglegger.' She sat down with a ramrod-straight back and pushed her face nearer to Frannie's. 'How do you know that name?'

'At the club, while I was talking to Hans, this Lars came up and started shouting about a Dorcas,' said Frannie, pausing in mid-sentence. 'Actually, it got really mad. Were they arguing about you?'

Dorcas's eyebrows arched even higher. Her brown eyes filled with emotion. At that moment it was hard to work out if she was actually ugly or absurdly beautiful. Her face was pinched, as if her smile had been stolen. She looked at some particular spot on the floor. 'He was my best friend, then he betrayed me. Last night he turned up bleeding, with a cut leg and face,' she said in a low voice. Her words trailed off. 'It got pretty nasty.' She abruptly crossed her legs.

'So he was a *friend* of yours?' said Frannie sarcastically. She flicked her head impatiently. 'Oh, that's nice. He was the one who caused my car accident. That's why I'm in here right now.' She lay fidgeting, unable to get comfy.

Dorcas looked as if she'd been shot. 'What?' she said repeatedly, like a parrot who only had one word. She shook her fringe and rubbed her face with her hands. 'I thought I knew them,' she said. Finally she'd taken off the glasses, and Frannie could see the bags under her eyes; a brittleness that suggested another blow would snap her in two.

'And another thing,' said Frannie, relieved to be piecing things together at last. 'Hans knew all about the fact that I reported the accident to the police.' She tried to raise herself more upright. 'I mean, how is that possible?'

Dorcas laughed and shot her a cynical look. 'That's easy, Lars is a *Spitzel.*'

'A what?' said Frannie frowning.

Dorcas shrugged her shoulders. 'How you say it – police informer?' she said, brushing an imaginary hair off her dress. 'He gives them tip-offs and they turn a blind eye to some of his activities.'

Frannie looked aghast. 'So that's why they were so odd at the police station.' She opened and closed her eyes with indignation like an angry doll. 'But that means…'

Dorcas just nodded at her.

'If we don't have real goddamn proof,' said Frannie slowly, banging her hands on the table in front of her.

'Then we ain't got a leg to stand on,' said Dorcas.

The both looked at each other gloomily.

'Did Hans do anything to you?' said Dorcas carefully, hardly daring to look Frannie in the eyes.

'No, but he looked as if he wanted to,' said Frannie, frowning. 'I was too scared to park outside the nightclub without you there to reverse out for me!' Both of them giggled knowingly. 'I went on foot from the abandoned factory next door and someone followed me.'

Dorcas groaned and banged her hands against her forehead. She seemed to be ageing as the conversation progressed. 'The person who followed you – why didn't they catch you?' she said. 'No offence, but…'

'Yep, I am a big fat blimp, you don't have to remind me,' said Frannie irritably. 'He would have caught me, but he fell.'

Dorcas covered her face with her hands. 'I think that was Lars. He came to me all bleeding on the cheek and knee,' she said, hardly able to take in the news. Her Lars, who had been like the big brother she'd never had.

'And he also said he got Inspector Koch to go after the person he chased.' Frannie cringed. One hand strayed to her stomach. 'I can't remember any of the policemen's names,' she said, shaking her head. 'This means it's something really serious. Why would he come after me?' She felt sick.

'You were looking for Tomek and Tomek was looking for Anna,' said Dorcas slowly.

Frannie rolled her eyes and looked at the clock. Something caught her eye. Outside her window a burly man was staring in with maddened eyes. His face was bruised and covered with crusted blood. She'd only seen him up once close-up, but she recognised him instantly. The machine on her arm started beeping, trapping her arm in its panicky embrace.

'Dorcas,' she whispered, her eyes widening. 'Don't look behind you, but it's him. Lars is standing right outside.'

# Chapter Twenty

When Dorcas had driven in the direction of the hospital, Lars had assumed she was going for an abortion. He licked his lips nervously. Now he was here, it didn't feel right. He'd told her, hadn't he, to get rid of it? And here she was.

It brought stuff up he hadn't thought about in a long time – Erna, the girl he'd tried to be normal with. He grunted to himself. He'd been, what, twenty? Still, she'd got wind of him, his real sexual desires, then got rid of it. He puffed out his lips. It was funny to think of a world with his child and Dorcas' child in it. Big feelings welled up in his chest. *Carpe diem*. He had a good feeling about today. The sun was already high in the sky painting everything with golden warmth like magic fucking Technicolor.

He should do it. Go right in to Dorcas and tell her he'd take care of her and the baby. Take this chance to start again. He wouldn't have the big Hans, but he'd have the little Hans, make sure that Dorcas had nothing to do with the crafty bastard. He smiled at that: little Hans on his knee.

When he saw Dorcas bolt into a toilet he'd thought he was already too late, that she was in there slamming the pills down her throat, but then she'd gone right in the room as if she was expected, and when he'd looked she was talking to that English bitch. Hans must have sent her to talk about the accident he'd caused. Hans said if she lost her baby then it would be manslaughter and they'd send him back to the loony bin. He felt goose bumps sneak all up his spine just at the thought of it.

'*Scheisse!*' Still he could not believe what he was seeing. Dorcas, his *Engel*, turning like that. The warm, throaty feeling he'd felt in his chest evaporated. He felt cold fingers of betrayal nudging his ribs; the familiar worry-headache starting up again.

'Fucking bitch!' he said to no one in particular. People kept giving him odd glances. He badly needed a shower, his body odour was rank. But he had to get to Hans right now, before the swine caused him more grief.

He was about to go when Frannie clocked him. Dorcas whirled round and he saw the demon-fury in her face. Her eyes were so scary, he had to look away. He headed quickly for the lift. It seemed to take forever before the mechanism responded and the steel door shielded him. Then the shakes got him, and he couldn't sit still till he was behind the wheel again. Hans had gone too far this time. He had to get him whilst he had the chance.

🚗

Lars was used to driving trucks, so being in a car felt like skateboarding. He zig-zagged his way through the traffic, at one point mounting the pavement in order to access a junction quicker. He ignored the other drivers' honking horns; when he saw fear in their faces, he laughed out loud.

He screeched up to Moonlights with his tyres singing, nearly giving himself whiplash when he slammed on the brakes roughly.

An old blue pick-up truck was parked in his usual spot out back. Two men were carrying the coffin-shaped 'toy box' as if it was really heavy, with Hans directing everything in one of his fancy suits.

He narrowed his eyes. It couldn't be.

He got a good look at the beat-up dude who was manhandling the box with that dirty sod Hugo. The crate was all being knocked about. Jesus! They were trying to get it in the back of a van that was too small. Could Hans have found someone else to do his dirty work so quickly?

Lars frowned. He felt a sharp inner pain as if the bastard had taken a knife and stabbed him between the ribs. He didn't hesitate. He reversed so forcefully the tyres squealed, and neatly boxed in the blue van. Everybody stopped what they were doing and looked. He jumped out like an agitated gorilla and waited for one of them to say something.

Hans stepped forward with his usual smile. He looked immaculate, but he was beyond taking any notice of that.

'Lars, how are you? This is Stefan; he's doing some transportation for us,' said Hans.

'I know what he's doing,' said Lars, taking a step forward. Stefan just stood his ground and grunted. There was something about him that bothered Lars. Even though he was a bit ragged around the edges, he stood ramrod-straight, his fingers cocked as if accustomed to cradling a gun. Gotcha: ex-military – looked like he'd been in the wars a bit. Lars read his eyes. No real killer, although he'd probably had to bump someone off in conflict. Capable, but didn't enjoy it. Lars frowned. What the hell was Hans up to?

Hans walked up to him, grabbed his sleeve and took him to one side.

'I've got business orders to fulfil. Stefan will bring the crate back, once...the contents have been emptied,' said Hans. He kept his voice light and melodious, but he was rattled. Lars could tell by the way he was pursing up his lips. He smiled. About time he got one over on the smug little bastard.

'Thing is, before this here Stefan pops off, I think I left something in the crate last time; can I just check?' said Lars in a high falsetto voice that made him sound like an old woman. In front of the others they were careful with their talk.

Hans frowned. Hugo gave Lars a shifty look; he was also in a suit, but it fitted so badly it made him look like a bear.

'I can assure you, it was empty. I helped load it myself,' said Hans in a slow drawl.

Lars stepped towards the crate and put his hands on the opening. 'Well, see, it would put my mind at rest if I just checked it myself,' he said. Before anyone could stop him he'd forced the lock and jerked it up.

There was a muted gasp. Inside was a man, hog-tied and bleeding, who at the first glimpse of sunlight shuddered as though he'd been struck. The victim led out a loud groan. He was desperately dirty, his face smeared with dried blood, but he was smooth-skinned and light-haired; on a good day he would have done very nicely, thank you. Although worse for wear, he was very much alive.

Lars couldn't make head or tail of it. He shut the crate with a bang and turned on Hans. 'What the fuck?' he said, taking an angry step towards him. The other men looked on. At first no one was saying anything. Lars started to shake, and his lips began to mutter. It felt as though his head was on fire and about to blow.

'How could you do this to me, Hans?' said Lars, his voice slightly less than firm.

Hugo moved closer to Hans, tittered. All the men were sneering at his show of emotion. The three men had Lars surrounded now and in a manic burst of anger he screeched out something wordlessly and went to grab Hans. Hugo and Stefan pushed him back and he fell flat on his back. He felt the whack as his helpless body slapped on to the concrete. His funny bone almost doubled-up in shock.

Hugo turned to Stefan and laughed. 'Larsey used to know Hans before he was a gentleman,' he said. Hans raised his eyebrows. Stefan just looked ahead but Hugo gave a dirty laugh. 'Hans swings both ways when it suits him,' he said in a mocking tone.

Hans acted as if he'd heard nothing and held up his hands calmly as if he was about to give a speech. 'We told you about the new business model; you weren't interested,' he said, as if he'd just changed suppliers.

Lars just felt confused. His wide mouth was open. 'You what?' he asked. His voice was getting louder.

In two strides Stefan was facing him. They stared each other out.

'He's going to be organ-harvested, brother; he's worth more alive than dead,' said Stefan in a worn-out voice as if he was already an old 'un.

Lars blinked furiously. 'You're going ahead with that shit?' he screamed, looking at Hans.

As usual, Hans wouldn't even bloody look at him. He'd gone into officious mode again. 'You weren't interested, so I'm sorting it,' he said with a wide smile. 'Drugs is getting too dangerous; whores is a mug's game. Someone's got to have a rational head, keep the money coming in.' He stood there, pleased with himself, as if he'd just won an award.

Lars seethed at the cheek of the guy. Caught red-handed and still giving it all that. He stood there with twisted shoulders, in turmoil. At that moment he was not capable of rational thought. Then a sly thought came into his head, and his whole body seemed to unravel and straighten itself up again. His hand brushed against his crotch. He was full of himself again. Now he was grinning at

Hans with a foolish grin like a child blackmailing for yet another sweet.

'Do you know where I just saw Dorcas?' he said. His head moved from side to side like a blackbird's.

Hans said nothing, just thrust his hands into his pockets. Lars's face was shining in the sunlight. Beads of sweat broke out on his brow.

'She was with that Snell woman, the English bitch,' said Lars smugly.

Hans's features visibly tensed, as if his whole form had been struck by a giant bolt of lightning. He seemed to shrink inside his suit like a frightened little boy. Now he didn't look arrogant. It looked as if he was afraid Lars would get up and leave.

'Come upstairs and see me,' he said almost in a whisper. He waved his hand at Hugo and Stefan to get on with the loading, got closer to Lars. 'You know, you've taught me everything I know,' he said, flashing his eyes that were an unreal mixture of blue and *crème de menthe*.

Lars felt his emotions tugging at him. He knew he couldn't trust Hans any more, but he had such glowing, vivid skin, that ridiculously soft pursed-up mouth. The memories of their passion together seared him, had imprinted part of Hans on to his soul. Their bodies had fevered their way into each other. He was stood there, trying to make up his mind what to do.

Hans smiled and went to walk off, then looking over one shoulder he turned and said, dead casually, 'I'll be waiting, but move the car first, eh.'

🚗

Frannie froze, but Dorcas sprang into action. She pressed the automated bell that prompted a nurse and started to empty Frannie's things into her night case, which was set neatly next to the table.

'What are you doing?' said Frannie, too shocked to intervene.

'Now that he's seen us, we've got to get you out of here,' shouted Dorcas. 'If he tells Hans, he could get to you in here.'

With her dexterous fingers she packed all Frannie's things and had her going-home clothes waiting on the chair before the nurse arrived.

Dorcas spoke in rapid-fire German to Krankenschwester Bonn. There were raised voices and commotion. A doctor came in and out twice and shook his hands in exasperation. He shouted at Frannie in heavily accented English, 'Think about your baby!' But Dorcas was unstoppable. Finally, she got what she wanted.

'Here, sign this,' she said, brandishing a pen. An official-looking document Frannie couldn't read lay on the table.

'What is it?'

'*A Schwarzer Peter*; it means you refuse treatment,' said Dorcas. She tapped the chair when Frannie paused. Much as Frannie wanted to escape her penalising cuff and the endless intrusions, the thought of potentially putting the baby at risk made her hesitate. But Lars had been here, outside the door. She couldn't take the chance and stay here; trapped in her bed, hooked up to a drip, she was a sitting duck.

She bit her lip, her hand hovering with the pen in mid-air, but Dorcas guided it to the right line and pressed. Frannie signed. The doctor came in as Dorcas was ushering her out of the door and looked her directly in the eyes.

'If anything happens to your baby, it will be on your head,' he said. Dorcas banged the door shut and pulled Frannie outside.

# Chapter Twenty-One

Lars stood outside Hans's office. He'd been in there hundreds of times, but it didn't feel right coming back to the place he'd spent the most time with his lover. *Déjà vu* and all that. The things they'd done on that sofa, it was a wonder it was still in one piece! The relationship was *kaputt*. But he knew that Hans would push him, do anything to get what he wanted. And he always wanted something.

They'd met when Hans was a twenty-something prostitute: gawkily good-looking, surreally submissive. He'd lie down like a puppy dog, let Lars do anything he wanted. And somehow, after he'd taken him under his wing, it was as though he'd given him a magic potion but pushed him in the wrong direction.

Sadism energised Hans. Instead of being a vampire himself, he looked on greedily while others drank. Now look at him: a regular bloody gangster. Always wanting to hurt, destroy. And all the bloody women loved him.

Lars still couldn't get his head around Hans's dodgy mates, the terrible money-making schemes, the way he treated everyone like shit. Just looking at him now, he was all worked up, couldn't deal with the dangerous thoughts in his head. His headache banging so hard he thought it might crack.

There was killing: quick, so swift it was practically painless. It sure was ugly, but it was a release. He only killed those he liked.

But this keeping 'em alive in little boxes, making them suffer. Nah. He couldn't be doing with that. Proper sick, that was. Hans had given him a knowing look, thought he could just wriggle under his skin again. But there was a line – with everything there had to be a line. And Hans had crossed it.

Lars liked to think he had something of the wolf in his genes: the right to hunt, to seek out and press his teeth down on an inviting neck. There was a name for people like him, but most people couldn't get it. 'Swift like an arrow,' he said to himself, thinking of warm, tantalising flesh.

His head and face was throbbing again, but he made himself knock, sauntered in with sagging knees. He couldn't believe his eyes. Hans was outstretched on the sofa, naked to the waist, a big fat cigar in one hand. His fancy suit pants were held up with shiny braces that looked erotic strapped over his naked shoulders.

He looked absurdly camp, like he was a roaring homo from 1930s Berlin about to pop his cherry. The air buzzed with a haze of thick cigar smoke, and Hans just lay there, smiling, sunbeams winking on his naked upper torso. Jesus, what was he trying to do to him?

Hans laid his head back provocatively, giving Lars a good view of the delicate skin underneath his neck. There was a little dent just under his Adam's apple that moved every time he spoke.

Lars felt himself stiffen, bit his lip. He could just imagine kissing that dent, licking it, going further; going mad right there on the black leather sofa. He didn't know why the boy was taunting him. A bitter taste welled up in his mouth. He wished he could spit all his badness out. But he wasn't going to be tempted by Hans. No. No. No.

'You can start by putting some clothes on,' he said roughly. He went to the fridge and took out a can of Red Bull; instead of drinking it, he held the coolness of it against his head.

Hans looked surprised. His eyes appraised him. 'Headaches getting you down again?' he said softly. He gave a diabolical smile. 'It's all the bad things you've done coming out of you.' He carried on looking into Lars's face. '*Ya'll better come here right now. I just killed a man!*' he screeched in a mock-serious voice. He was doing the serial killer shit again. Lars couldn't remember which one it was, but it was one of the American ones. Hans loved to throw odd quotes about.

Lars fidgeted with his hands, looked at the mosaic pattern of the marble on the floor. The antique feel of the place had always unsettled him. It had given Hans a chance to wallow in his 'true crime' obsession. And being the boss only made him more narcissistic. Once upon a time he'd just been a shag, a potential, and now he thought he was calling the shots. He had to ask him.

'Did you send Dorcas after that English bitch?'

Hans paled visibly. For a moment he stopped smoking his cigar. 'No. She came here looking for Anna's brother, and I managed to fob her off.' He played with the lit cigar, made his voice high like a little kid's. '*I didn't want to hurt them, I only wanted to kill them,*' he screamed. He kicked his legs out on the sofa, slapped his own bum. '*He won't let me stop killing until he gets his fill of blood,*' he screeched. Then he added, 'That's the Son of Sam talking about his neighbour's dog.' He threw back his head and laughed.

'But Dorcas was with her today at the bloody hospital,' said Lars, his voice getting louder as vented his frustration. 'You telling me that's nothing to do with you?'

Hans's shoulders stiffened, as if someone had snapped his braces. '*The first good-looking girl I see tonight is going to die!*' he screamed.

Lars sighed. He was always like this, talking in riddles.

Hans sat up. 'I didn't know Dorcas even knew this English

bitch. I mean Dorcas and Anna were hardly pals,' he said with a little smile. 'You know, it would be easier if you hadn't got rid of Anna. This mess keeps getting bigger.' He stopped for a moment then carried on. 'Even when she was dead, she was still bitching at me. I couldn't get her to shut up!'

Something buzzed in Lars's head. His hands bunched into clumsy fists. In this elegant, air-conditioned room with the old-fashioned fancy furniture, he felt like microwaved shit. The dark red wash of the walls was hypnotic. The heavy, ornate furniture made him claustrophobic.

That last time, in the VIP room, he couldn't even remember killing Anna. What he recalled, vividly, was Hans's voice whispering to him that he'd done it, that he wouldn't tell. That seductive voice calling his name over and over until it washed over him and soothed him. Hans fed his lusts then made him feel bad for indulging in them. What did the fucker actually want now?

'Do you get off on trapping that guy in the crate?' he said, sitting down on the little chair opposite Hans. It was the first time he'd questioned him like this. Normally between them it was a given that he was the Killer, the One, and Hans lapped it up along with his books and murderabilia material. He was a true crime freak.

Hans laughed lazily. 'You heard of Dennis Radar the BTK killer?'

'No. BTK?'

'Just three little words: Bind. Torture. Kill,' said Hans wickedly. 'He wanted to kill an Anna, but she escaped him.' His eyes glazed over and he began to quote mechanically, '*You don't understand these things because you are not under the influence of factor X. There is no help, no cure, except death or being caught and put away.*' Hans stopped and gazed at Lars's sweating face. 'That could be you speaking.' He stopped and took a little breath to check his reaction. 'If they find you they'll put you back in the loony bin.'

'No, not that,' said Lars, flinching at the mention of the asylum.

'What's wrong, Lars, you think you're not suitable for treatment?' said Hans with a sly grin.

'Is that how you think?' said Lars. 'That I'm some sort of living crime library for you to explore?'

Hans blinked and sat up. When he didn't get constant attention, he suffered. All the fight had gone out of his shoulders and his head hung down, all dejected. His eyes stared into Lars's as if they could kill him as soon as look at him. Lars didn't know whether to feel sorry for him or afraid of him.

'After all we've been through together, it would be smart to be nice to me,' said Hans, making the big eyes again. His face was perfect in any profile. That was one of the problems with Hans: no matter what nasty stuff came out of his mouth, he always looked so bloody legit, nobody paid attention to what the fucker actually said. The women all got off on his eyes, which were neither blue or green and constantly changed colour. This time, he wanted to nail the bastard.

'The one who loves you is Dorcas – you know, the broad who's knocked up with your kid?' said Lars with a sneer. He walked up to the sofa and threw the can of Red Bull at Hans and it hit his ribs with a clang. Hans cried out and the can exploded as it hit the floor. A squirting plume of foam shot out. Its savage hiss deepened the tension between them.

'I can do it with woman, but they don't do it for me,' said Hans in a monotone voice. He lay there lazily, puffing away. His bare chest was splattered with foam. He went off on one again. '*I would loved to have raped them, but not having any experience at all…* That's Edmund Kemper, the necrophile,' he said, puffing out his chest with pride at his own cleverness.

Lars felt like a father with a disobedient son.

'Sometimes I even have to fake orgasm,' said Hans. He continued puffing his cigar and looked at him. 'Never had to do that with you.'

'What about what Dorcas wants? Lars tried to get him to look in his eyes but Hans was out of it. He'd probably popped a pill or something worse. Lars couldn't believe the things that kids got down their necks these days.

'What does do it for you, then?' said Lars, genuinely puzzled. Hans turned to him with a little grin, took out a remote control from his pocket and turned one of the TV screens on. The office was lined with a bank of overhead TVs that could be used to monitor the CCTV system, or something else. A machine somewhere whirred into life, a TV flickered on and grainy footage started to play.

Lars stared. Wasn't that the bookcase in the VIP suite? He could count the fancy bottles even. And the guy sitting there, didn't he do him about four months ago? He recalled the fancy shirt; it was one of the things that had first made him consider him as a potential.

Then he saw himself on camera. It was the oddest feeling watching yourself, seeing all your little faults and not being able to shield your ego from the fat belly, broad face, the slight stoop in the shoulders. With bated breath he watched himself advance on the boy – Joe, he'd called himself.

All he'd wanted was to mutually wank. But the boy knew what was coming. There was a series of high-pitched screams as the sharp blade made contact with the flesh, the terrible searing sound as it grazed off the bone, dug right in and then the artery disintegrated into slivers.

Lars tried to cover his face with his hands, but still the boy's screams reverberated around the room. That one had been a bit of a bodge job, taken ages to bleed out with him pleading every second. He hadn't enjoyed that. There was something hideous about the way he finally crawled like an insect across the floor, all squirming shoulders.

Lars turned to Hans to tell him to turn it off and was horrified to find him furiously wanking, trousers undone, openly playing with himself as if he didn't have a care in the world. *Schweinehund!* Lars watched as Hans continued to pleasure himself. 'Hans, what are you doing?' he asked, in a squawk of indignation, rising to his feet.

'You asked me what I like,' said Hans, with a crude wink. 'Well, you can see for yourself. It's been like a dream getting you to kill to order. My custom-made killer in my own club.' He lay back laughing, the cigar clenched between his teeth.

Lars flinched. He knew about the security cameras, of course; he partly owned the club after all. But this? This was what turned Hans on? All the colour drained out of his cheeks. He'd been a bloody puppet for a sicko all along! He stared at the recording with alarm, and saw Hans's face go through the mock-agonies of climax. He turned away, lost for words, and slumped down in the chair, absolutely gobsmacked. Hans had been pushing him too hard for months, always wanting a bit more, but he'd never even imagined this.

Hans cleaned himself up and got dressed. With a clean suit on he was on his high horse again. And when he'd come he had always been unbearable. Lars sat with his face in his hands and groaned. Now his headache was really kicking in; he couldn't take much more. He flinched at the touch of Hans's hand on his shoulder, let out a sob.

'Thing is, Larsy, with this Anna thing we're in trouble. It would be best if you got this Frannie in here and did her in,' said Hans in a sly voice, patting Lars as if talking to a very small child. 'And you can use the VIP room again, like old times. If you're going to do something, do it well, and leave something witchy – that's what Charlie Manson says.'

Lars trembled under Hans's half-hearted embrace. There was a time when Hans had meant everything to him, when he'd assumed that the bloody boy had accepted the fact that he killed because he was in love with him. Hans's tireless organisation, the way he'd comfort him afterwards, it had all been a sham. The fucker was getting his rocks off all along!

He couldn't be doing with this any longer. He slapped Hans's hand away, screaming, 'Murderer!' loudly in his face before turning and running heavily through the room.

As he left Hans seemed in another world. He went into one of his serial poses again. '*I had no other thrill or happiness…*' he said with hands outstretched.

Lars got out of there. His mind was a mass of emotions. He had to go quickly, before he lost all control and lashed out. With his mind tired but half-crazed, the only thing he could think of was getting a kill, fresh blood running into his mouth. With a moan he ran through the crowded club, barely seeing the dancing bodies he had to push through forcibly to get out.

🚗

Dorcas had done the decent thing and dropped Frannie off, although the stroppy cow was so emotional that she had had to agree to go in there with her in order to get her out of the car. Her house was in a large, imposing street but it was unkempt. The windows badly needed a clean and the garden was full of weeds. Inside Dorcas wrinkled her nose at the general state of disorder, although she admired the spacious grace of the house. The things she could do with it if she lived there!

A wedding photo on the mantelpiece revealed a much thinner Frannie and a giant of a man with brooding good looks. He was so tall he hulked over his bride and would have been a bit of alright if a sullen look hadn't ruined his looks. When she looked at the plump English woman with a rump like a well-fattened cow, Dorcas wondered how women like her managed to keep hold of their men. Just as well she didn't work in the sex industry. Wouldn't last two minutes! She smoothed down her dress, tried to find a way to leave.

'I'll phone you tomorrow,' said Frannie after the last bag was deposited in the messy hall. On every surface a layer of clutter was strewn as if nothing was ever put in its place. Frannie looked as if she didn't really want to her to leave, but Dorcas breathed a sigh of relief as she walked out into the fresh air. This was a bloody nice neighbourhood, she thought, looking at the well-tended gardens in the street. Of course, she liked her little flat, and kept it immaculate, but nice to have a bit of space. She pursed her lips. Even if she had the bloody kid, she wouldn't let herself go or live in chaos like that. She gave a little shudder. She didn't do mess or disorder. Couldn't abide it. As a child her mother had let the house run itself and the dogs used to shit in the bath. She could never go back to that. And she'd rather sell it than put up with the bums her mother had dated. One day she'd find a good bloke, grab her own slice of the good life. She waved goodbye and headed back to her car.

Once on the road, Dorcas couldn't shake off a feeling of dread. What possible reason had Lars to follow her? And what would Hans do now? She closed her eyes for a second, and a horn from the right-hand side pipped furiously as she wavered too close to the next lane. 'Get a grip!' she shouted to herself, slapping both hands on the wheel. When she was angry, she drove at her best.

She drove home like a road hog, cutting everybody up, cursing every red light. She was all energy, purpose, but, once her little car was parked, she had no idea what to do with herself next.

🚗

Lars awoke from a stony sleep. Although he'd been flat out for hours, his head still pounded. Less intense, but he preferred his pain sharp. That way he knew exactly where it was coming from. He rubbed his eyes. He couldn't shake off the gritty feeling, the need. When it got like this, if he couldn't stand up without feeling every vein in his body pulsing, then it was time.

The throbbing pulsated mostly in his groin: his penis had become so horny it it had a life of its own. The feeling radiated out in a crude V down his legs, even washed up into his belly in little waves so he could barely walk straight. Sometimes he swore his nipples were on fire. The need prickled his senses, maddened him, until he wanted to scratch himself from the inside out. Sometimes he could satiate it for a few moments by getting off on violent porn, but then afterwards it only made it worse.

When he got horny, his whole body was wired to his sexual senses, anticipating payload. In his perfectly normal flat decorated in soothing sky blue, his desire could not be contained. He could put on his favourite DVD, cook a nice meal, smoke to try and calm his nerves, but it made no difference. He wouldn't be able to sleep or do anything without being consumed with the fierceness. Of course, he wanked off, three times a day sometimes. But it did no good. Not against the hunger. He knew what he had to do.

Dusk was coming, just a hint of greyness that at first seemed inadequate to block out the glare of the brilliant sunset. It had been a spectacular summer day. But as he watched out of the open window; in the time it had taken to smoke a cigarette, the cloak of dusk had dropped. The wind blew more strongly, although it was still mild, a cooling-off period that anticipated his vivid handiwork. He smiled. The birds startled. Soon it would be hunting time. Everything seemed to happen at night.

In an hour or so he'd get in his truck and start on the deliveries. He supplied fancy drinks to clubs and restaurants, not the regular stuff like beer and coke, but all the special orders where they had to call a specialist retailer to deliver the goods. It meant he was always in and out of Hannover, carrying crates up little allies, having a laugh with the bar staff.

Good opportunity to shift a bit of coke here and there, find out what was going on. And hanging out in all these back streets was perfect for meeting strangers. The people he knew! He had a better social life just doing his job than most people did who paid to go out. He grinned. Now he would smile and turn into good ol' Onkel Fritz!

He did being the dead ordinary bloke really well. All you had to do was get 'em to laugh, slap a big fat easy smile on your face and you were in there. People liked him, trusted him; he fooled them every time.

Lars headed to the bathroom. He was going to take a slow, sweet shower and rinse away his headache before he took off. His cheek still looked shite, and he didn't want to look too closely in the mirror, but it wouldn't hold him back. Cheerfully scrubbing himself with shower gel he sang like a teenage girl with two hours to get ready for a disco. The scent of Claire Fisher milk and honey gel seeped into the neat shower room. The water felt good on his aching body. He allowed some of the water to run up his nose. Sometimes he even enjoyed this more, the getting ready-ness.

It was his way of getting into the zone.

# Chapter Twenty-Two

Kurt was still doing it: that thing where he clicked his tongue impatiently every few minutes. It was a harsh, abrupt tick, something between a *tsk* and a dog signal. Frannie looked at his regular features made ugly by temper and wished he would lighten up. Smile occasionally. He'd been pacing up and down since he got back, leaving black tread-marks on the living room floor. His fine blond hair was spread all over his face. Since he'd found out she'd discharged herself, he kept running his hands through it.

He couldn't stand the fact that she'd managed to escape without him. Frankly, he couldn't believe she had managed it.

'You signed a *Schwarzer Peter*?' he said, his eyebrows raised so high they'd disappeared somewhere under his hair.

'I think so,' she said neutrally, trying to keep her tone light. 'I've got the paperwork somewhere. I just really needed to come home.' She was propped up on the armchair, with her swollen feet on the foot stool. The doctors had told her to rest, or else. She looked at him, tried to smile. 'I'd rather be with you,' she added hastily. She shut her mouth. That didn't sound convincing, even to her.

Kurt circled her, his hands outstretched.

'Do you know what this means?' he said, shaking his head. 'You refused treatment! It could mean your health insurance refuses to pay for the rest of the pregnancy.' He stood in front of her and bent down to shout in her face. 'We could have to pay out thousands if anything goes wrong!' He sat down on the sofa opposite her with his head in his hands.

Frannie sat frozen in her chair. Since she'd become pregnant his mood swings had got progressively worse. She hardly recognised him any more. And he was always texting his old army pals on his phone. She waited for him to stop shouting and exclaiming, his words the incoherent rant of a madman.

For the fiftieth time, he ran his hands through his hair. Frannie wondered what she had ever found sexy about it, even though she liked blond men.

'I know you don't know everything, it being a foreign country and all,' he said, his voice trailing off, 'but this just isn't working.' He slumped forward with his head in his hands. His whole being was sad.

Frannie could have kicked him. Instead of having sex, he shouted, then, in between bouts of fury, he turned into this apathetic, self-pitying fool. If he'd ever been like this *once* when they were dating, she would have dumped him instantly. When they'd met she'd been bowled over by his good looks and charm. He'd had a dry humour, but she'd thought he was alright underneath. But these bitter moods threw her completely. You never knew someone until she lived with them, she thought. She was fated to end up alone. Her last boyfriend had littered the house with his dope ends and lived in artistic chaos. Kurt had seemed, clean, decent and into positive living. But now he'd turned into someone else.

Despite the warm, balmy evening, she shuddered. She coughed and raised herself up from her armchair.

'I was stressed out in there and needed to come home,' she repeated in a steady voice. Her hands twitched in her lap. She looked at him and smiled. 'And I need you to support me. Please.'

She tried to hold his smile, make eye contact, but Kurt just looked back at the floor. His face wore a permanent woebegone look, as if he had the troubles of the world on his shoulders. And the bloody baby wasn't even there yet! Frannie bit her lips in despair. She'd put on some make-up, tried to fancy up her hair, but it had done no good. Kurt would rather sit about moping and fretting than be happy. Add sleepless nights and a tetchy baby to the mix, and they'd be at each other's throats.

Of course, she couldn't tell Kurt the real reason she'd left the hospital. She longed to call Dorcas, plan her next move, but she had to wait until Kurt went out or fell asleep. My God, Dorcas might be in danger now! She swallowed, tried to slow her breathing so her blood pressure would not soar out of control. At least for the minute she was safe. Lars didn't know where she lived.

Kurt poured himself a beer. He didn't ask her if she wanted anything. Just sat there, slurping it down in front of her. Now he'd got the football on, he'd be preoccupied for a bit, unless they started losing and then he'd start shouting the odds. Frannie appeared to be right there, watching the match with him, but her mind was very much elsewhere.

🚗

At first Dorcas had packed a little suitcase neatly, then she made herself a coffee and unpacked it again. She smoked a cigarette, checked the empty inbox on her mobile phone. There had been no communication from Lars or Hans.

If they were going to do something to her, she thought, they would have done it already. Hans had bouncers and all kinds of rough types to do his dirty work for him. If she was going to find out anything about Anna and Tomek she just had to sit tight, play it cool. She exhaled smoothly. Time to be seductive; it was one of the things she did best.

She was busy most of the day. Her whole flat smelled freshly polished and scrubbed and was fragrant with the smell of French cooking. Not one thing was out of place. The high windows were all open, white curtains billowing in the deliciously cool evening breeze. She'd been to the fruit and veg stall over the road and made Hans's favourite, a pepper quiche with brie, which was cooling on the wooden kitchen table. A generous salad stood next to it, the dressing already assembled, waiting in the fridge.

The living room smelt of girl; she'd bought big fat pink roses that had scent falling out of them. She couldn't stop inhaling the gorgeous aroma. On the opulent four-poster bed were freshly laundered sheets and sprigs of lavender under the pillows. A few innocuous rose petals were scattered on the bedspread. She lit some aromatherapy candles.

Now she'd got everything perfect, it was time to run herself a luxurious bath. What she knew from her job was that it was getting the basics right that counted: linen, aroma and ambience.

She sent a simple text to Hans – *Come to dinner if u want, luv Dorcas xxx* – and smiled to herself. In her bathroom cabinet there was an orgy of expensive cosmetics and bath products, all neatly arranged. She picked out one of her favourite bath foams, L'Occitane Harvest, and shook most of the contents into the tub. It turned the water into fragrant froth.

She reapplied her make-up before reclining in the bath and started reading a magazine as if she didn't have a care in the world. The suds clung to her, giving her naked body an air of mystery. She didn't look at the clock. Dorcas was not one of life's worriers. She'd learnt pretty early on that what you actually wanted didn't count for much so there was no point agonising about everything. Once she'd made a decision, she didn't dither over it. She was reading the third article in the magazine when she heard a sound at the door. It must be Hans; he had his own key.

Dorcas played it cool. She carried on soaking in the bath. Hans had to shout her name a good four times before he got an answer.

'*Ich bins!*' he said with a dazzling smile. He bent to kiss her on the cheek. He was acting as though absolutely nothing had happened, although she knew he had the ability to deceive.

'Can you stay to dinner?' she said, looking the picture of serenity outstretched in the bath. 'There's quiche and salad, it'll take just a second.'

Hans smiled. 'For you, anything,' he said, casually taking out a cigarette out of his Gucci suit pocket. He was wearing cream pants with a matching waistcoat and a bright claret silk shirt that had most of the buttons open so that you could see his perfectly tanned chest. The exposed skin looked tantalising. As the summer progressed he was dressing more exotically. It occurred to Dorcas that the more stressed he was, the more he fussed over his appearance.

Hans went to smoke his cigarette on the little terrace outside the living room.

In just minutes Dorcas calmly appeared in a grey bathrobe edged with lace, looking fresh and natural. She arranged generous slices of quiche and tossed the salad, opened a bottle of French white wine and carried everything out to the little terrace. With ivy growing up the wall and a treasure trove of potted flowers in glorious multi-colours all in bloom, it had all the ingredients for a delightful late supper. She smiled as she poured the wine. *Let's see what the bastard has to say for himself.*

Hans pointedly ignored the plaster covering her wounded hand, although he had plenty of opportunity to see it as she served the food. He devoured over half the quiche with his bare hands. For all his grooming, deep at heart he was a slob. He sat back licking his fingers while Dorcas picked at her salad. Dorcas could feel his eyes burning into her, tried to act casual as she ate her supper.

'You had a bit of a falling-out with Lars?' said Hans suddenly, as if he couldn't wait any longer to ask her about it. He took out a cigarette and lit it.

Dorcas shrugged her shoulders, smiled again. 'Hans, I'm so sorry,' she said in a little girl voice, clasping her hands together. 'Lars happened to be here when I did the pregnancy test. He told you, before I had a chance, and…well, I was very pissed off.'

'That's it?' said Hans hypnotically in a subdued voice. Dorcas was on full alert: when he got quiet he was at his most unpredictable.

'And he even followed me today. I don't know why,' she said pushing back her little fringe. She had to be very persuasive to get him to back off. 'I mean, I visited a friend in hospital, big deal.'

'You really went to see Francesca Snell?' said Hans, almost knocking over his wine. His aquamarine eyes darkened until they looked almost black.

'Yes. I met her at the gynaecologist's the other day,' said Dorcas, also lighting up. 'She's a foreigner here, hardly knows anyone, so when she had medical problems she asked for my help.' She sipped her wine and casually slipped out, 'How do you know her?'

Hans reclined back in his chair. 'Lars had a run-in with her, police reckoned he caused her to have an accident – dangerous driving. Then she came to the club chasing after a guy she fancied. Didn't even know his bloody name!' He laughed, but it came out flat. '*The demons wanted my penis!*' he screeched in a fake high voice.

Dorcas felt as if sometimes he only talked as a chance to drop out serial killer quotes. He had his mouth open, laughing, but his eyes were guarded, tight. He was rattled, she could see it. Night was descending around them, giving the glowing candles on the table more focus.

'And so the pregnancy?' said Dorcas with a little nod of her head. 'Like, you know now, right?' She sat there, waiting, playing with the table napkin.

Hans tapped his fingers on the table. He smirked at her. '*I like children – they are tasty,*' he recited with a laugh. 'Just ask Albert Fish.'

'C'mon, Hans, be serious for once.'

'*I can't stand a bitchy chick,*' he said provocatively, hissing. Now he was giggling. He puffed a smoke ring at her. 'Know that one? Gerald Stano, little-known serial killer, probably didn't do it. He was so badly neglected by his birth mother at six months that he survived by eating his own shit.' He frowned, stared at her. 'I hope you'll do a better job.'

'Hans!' shouted Dorcas. 'Enough!' She had to stop him or he'd be on about it all night. He had a photographic memory and spent all his free time obsessively poring over books on serial killers.

'You're twenty-four,' said Hans carefully, as if he was talking a bank manager into granting him a huge loan. 'You really want the whole family thing right now?' He sat very straight, and she found herself mesmerised by his red silk shirt.

'I'm not sure,' she said in a little rush, her little shoulders shivering. 'But I'm going to stop the coke anyway, get clean.' Looking at her cigarette, she stubbed it out and bit her lip. 'And I want to work behind the bar, rather than out of vans. I've had enough of the sex trade.'

She waited for an angry reaction – initially he'd found it a turn-on that she fucked other men – but he carried on.

'*I believe the only way to reform people is to kill them.*' He let out another sarcastic laugh. He was doing it again, the deadpan voice, quote after quote. He could go on all night.

Hang on. Her stomach dipped as if she'd dropped several floors in a lift. Was that another quote, or was it a threat?

Then she remembered. 'Carl Panzram,' she said, laughing. 'You use that one a lot.' She shook her head. 'You'll be running out soon.'

'*I have several children who I'm turning into killers. Wait till they grow up,*' quipped Hans sticking his feet out. He laughed at her earnest face. 'That's why I'm making my own.'

Dorcas quickly inhaled. Now was her chance. She had to convince him she still wanted him if she was going to get any information out of him.

'What about making a go of it, being properly together?' She sat hugging her arms, waiting for his response.

He didn't even blink. He looked at her with a wine in one hand and a cigarette in the other. 'Expectant mothers usually don't smoke or do coke, or other things,' he said drily. 'Charles Manson said you make your children what they are.'

Dorcas blinked. She couldn't believe such an important event was being brushed off. She rushed her words out so they all came out together. 'But what about you? You're a sex addict, and you know it.'

Hans carried on smoking, tapping the chair with his foot. '*Total paranoia is just total awareness,*' he said.

'But you were seeing Anna!' she said angrily, reaching defiantly for another cigarette. 'The whole club knew you were carrying on. How could you do that, when I worked there too?' Her trembling fingers took two attempts to light up. If she got him to think she was just jealous about Anna, then he wouldn't suspect she knew more.

Hans's face betrayed nothing. He was wearing his solemn poker face. Most of the time she had no idea what he was thinking.

'Well, I'm glad the bitch has gone,' she said, scraping back her chair and leaving the terrace abruptly in an apparent huff. She made her way to the bedroom and flung herself on the bed.

Outside, a thoughtful look passed over Hans's face. '*See you in Disneyland!*' he said with a bitter laugh and stepped inside. He followed her into the bedroom, banged the door. He didn't so much walk as prowl over to the bed. Dorcas had the feeling he didn't even notice the petals, all the little details. He unzipped and was instantly ready, as if he'd been sitting there with a rock on the whole time. He'd probably only eaten to work up the energy.

After kissing and fondling her neck for about ten seconds, he was already trying to mount her. Dorcas cried out. Lately he'd got more and more forceful. Once upon a time he'd been a thoughtful lover who had revelled languidly in her sexual experience, but the more sex *he* had, the rougher he wanted it. She tried to slow him down, get him to wait until she was ready, but he ignored her pleas. Dorcas smelt the odour of sweat, her own fear, and tried not to wince. He pistoned into her as forcefully as he could, his hands clawing at her, all the time moaning in a deep, guttural tone that was barely human. After five minutes of solid pumping, he came fiercely, grunting in pleasure. His back and forehead were coated with sweat. He was oblivious to her lack of sexual release. When he was done he threw himself down by her side and let out a huge sigh.

Dorcas lay there, fingering the ruined rose petals, with no expression on her face.

'I don't care,' she said. If she could only persuade him to trust her, pretend, then he might open a clink of the darkness inside him. Let her see. 'I don't even care what happened to Anna, as long as I've got you all to myself.' She flung herself on him. There'd be time later to work on his defences.

Hans let out a little snort of laughter and gave her the first kiss of the evening.

# Chapter Twenty-Three

Lars was so wired it had stopped being work. He was swimming it, throwing the crates round as though they were nothing. In between stops, he was really hitting the coke. Bloody nose would not stop running. He was in and out of the truck constantly; the lights from the various clubs burned into his eyes as he scurried in and out of the dark.

He'd show him! Hans thought he'd got this thing sewn up, but he was nothing but a jumped-up kid playing gangster. Let him dream. It was he, Lars, who had it, the power, the demon inside him. Now it was snapping, straining to get out. He felt so strong, nothing could stop it. The power was mightier than any mere man. And you couldn't reason with it. It just kept on and on, consuming you till you had to act. There was no choice. He'd never had any goddamn say in it.

He kept moving, constantly alert for a sign of someone standing outside the crowd. Before he could spring, unleash it, first he had to pick someone up. The more he concentrated on his work, the more the idea burned in his brain. *Tonight's the night!* he thought to himself, with a smirk. He wiped his nose with his sleeve and laughed out loud to no one in particular in the dark tunnel that led to the car park. Behind all the fancy buildings it was nearly always a run-down mess to get the drinks in. No one about!

He climbed back into his truck, reached into the glove compartment. My God, was the bag already nearly empty? It was good that he wasn't with Hans. Wanker always disapproved of 'consuming the merchandise'. *Und?* He was having a beautiful fucking night, had finished the deliveries in record time, and now he was going to cruise round a bit, enjoy it.

Although it was dark, twinkling stars lit up the sky. It was hot. Pitch black and still twenty degrees. Lars was running round in just a T-shirt, praying for the heat to drop, a bit of wind. He wiped the sweat off his brow and smoked a quick cigarette to slow him down. But his mind was racing like a speeding engine. He wanted the voice in his head to stop. But he was a long way from that.

What he enjoyed most was the zone. The time when he could do whatever he liked in his truck. He did some work for private companies. Lorry drivers worked alone, seemed to be masters of their own destiny, but they were always at the mercy of some computer system that worked out their routes, gave them a mileage and time for each destination, with no time for idling. If they ran into treacherous weather conditions or traffic snarl-ups, too bad. No, sir, they were constantly under pressure to perform, and, whatever problem cropped up, they had to make it up in their own time. He'd grown to hate car drivers. They were careless, and no professional could work without taking the right precautions.

Now his work was done, he was free to go. The truck was freedom; steady, throbbing movement. Sheer motion was progress, even when he was going nowhere. He got behind the wheel. Although his body was physically tired, he was too high to care. Deftly, he manoeuvred the truck out of the clogged-up city streets, escaped a long series of red lights. Now he was free!

With an almighty roar he entered the slipstream to the waiting *Autobahn*. As he picked up speed, the white lines either side of him turned into an endless flicker.

He whooped – 'The zone, man! Fucking A!' – put his foot down hard on the gas and the truck hurtled into the darkness. Ol' whore wanted to ride it hard tonight. She was practically empty, and when she rattled around like an empty tin can she was much faster going through the gears.

Now he was prowling along, practically on autopilot in the slow lane, keeping his options open. His truck seemed to will him on. He patted the side of her white-painted frame. For the first time in days he didn't have a headache.

His kept his eyes peeled for drivers to the left of him pulling over to his lane. These were the ones who might make a turn-off to the waiting lay-bys and petrol stations. If there was someone alone in a car who'd just pulled in somewhere, chances were that no one knew where they were. That was the time to get 'em, when they were mid-pee with their trousers open or just having a little smoke.

Nobody paid attention to a truck driver when he was off the road. They became invisible, part of a sub-human species that parked all over, no questions asked. Folks campaigned against gypsies, but truckers they didn't even see.

It hadn't been like this since he was first discharged from the Bundeswehr. He'd killed once before he hooked up with Hans, and then, after they got the club, he'd had the VIP room; his own private kill zone. How many had it been now? Over twenty? Lars licked his lips with his parched tongue. Thinking about that was like trying to remember how many sexual partners you'd had. After the first few you started to get 'em all mixed up.

When he thought of them at all, what he remembered was the light going out of their eyes, like TV screens being switched off.

You got to see them ghosting out; not alive, but not yet consciously dead. That bit he enjoyed the most.

He rubbed his chin. Where was everyone? The dawn was getting up and that unnerved him. Everything seemed easier in the dark. Alright, he'd admit it: he was goddamn nervous. Hans had made it too easy for him. Bin fuckin' spoiled. He slipped the last bit of coke on to his finger and waggled it around his gums to keep himself awake. He drove round remorselessly, his initial eagerness fading. It was a slow night. No one seemed to be out. He thought about crashing into someone and staging a small accident but rejected the idea. What he wanted was to mingle among them, catch them unawares. It was a form of seduction. Hans had never understood how he relaxed into a kill.

Indicating right, he went on to the B6, decided to hit civilisation again. There was nothing lonelier than a deserted *Autobahn* when you were cruising. He had to laugh: most of the time he wanted the *Autobahn* clear when he was working.

He pulled into a petrol station on the B6. If he was going to go any further he needed a coffee and a piss first. It was nearly five a.m. and the sun was slowly streaking through the sky. Through the windows he saw the wide, flat streets connecting the city like a spinal chord. This was the industrial bit, heading off west to Berenbostel with its giant multi-coloured shops, Möbel Hesse, Kibek and Baumarkt, that attracted shoppers like flies.

He thought about Dorcas: she'd probably be asleep now. And Hans was probably in somebody else's bed. He squeezed his eyes shut. *Don't think about that now.*

He ordered a triple espresso and drank it in one hot gulp. The bitterness made him gasp. Now he was thirsty. He'd get a juice to go, from the machine. First he needed the john. He was having a serious come-down from the coke. He'd done so much he didn't think he could get it up anyway. There was always tomorrow.

He went to the men's, which was outside the main building. Lorry drivers knew all the conveniences and best places to park.

On the way to the john he saw someone standing around. Not a day over twenty. Hoody on, with his jeans halfway down his arse, seemed to be unsure, like he was planning his next move and hadn't worked it out himself yet. The face was dark, intelligent, with wiry hair dark as black molasses. Turkish most likely, or Algerian. Lars walked by without saying anything but left his face open. The easiest way to pick up folks was just to look agreeable.

The boy turned around and came after him. Lars relaxed, made all his movements very deliberate. He was standing there having a piss when the bathroom door opened and closed. The boy approached hesitantly, still had the bloody hood on. Lars tapped out the last few drops and zipped himself up. He made to go to the sink to wash his hands, then with lightning speed turned and grabbed the boy and, before he could struggle, banged his head viciously against the plain white-tiled wall.

There was a sickening crack, a wail, and the boy fell into his arms. Lars felt as though it was divine deliverance. He stood there, sweating. He'd forgotten the arm-pulling dead weight of a body. Holding him, he had to grit his teeth. Being this close to the boy's beating warmth... He was like a dog who'd unexpectedly caught a rabbit.

In a vice-like grip Lars dragged the boy towards the door, and peered round. His truck was just about ten metres away. He hesitated, breathing in deep, laboured breaths. He couldn't hold up much longer. There was no one in sight. Should he risk it?

He half-dragged the boy to the truck and threw him in the back. The body flopped like a fish and fell with a sickening thud. He turned on the lights, jumped in and locked them both in, nearly gagging on the stuffy trapped air, which smelt like a sauna for the homeless. If he could keep the boy quiet he could work undisturbed.

The boy lay on his back like a wounded bird. A bruise was already coming out on his forehead. Lars ran his fingers over the delicate, well-tanned face like a sculptor admiring his work. He liked 'em young – the symmetry was just right. After twenty, twenty-five, gravity set in, distorting all the proportions until a face was all nose. Even Hans was changing. But this way he got to keep them just right.

He bent down to kiss the lips and the boy murmured. The smell and sight of him defenceless in front of him was too much and he cried out. Immediately he worried someone might have heard. Now he longed for the confines of the kill room, which was soundproofed, private. The kill room allowed him to be intimate about it. Here he was cramped, kneeling painfully on the uneven metal of the truck floor.

He breathed in dust as took off the boy's navy hood and put a hand under his neck so that he had full access to the naked throat. The boy was wearing a black T-shirt with some kind of graffiti pattern on it that made no sense to Lars. The skin was musky when he licked it, as if slightly smoked. With one hand licking at the exposed neck, he opened his trousers. The feeling was electric as he touched himself. He had been fully erect ever since he'd had the body in his arms. He groaned again, trying to muffle his sounds.

He wanted to turn the boy over and take him from behind, but it was too much hassle to get the jeans off. Normally he took willing participants: they'd have the sex first and then if he got too aroused he wouldn't be able to help himself and the kill would follow. He sighed. This was hard work. He tried to figure out a way to get himself going. Repeatedly he slapped the boy's face but there was no response. He'd cracked the boy's skull too hard, probably done internal damage. *Scheisse!* Desperately, he furiously wanked, but it was no good. Lars was panting, nearly spent. This could not be happening!

As a last resort he opened the guy's trousers. He liked oral sex, both giving and receiving. The guy was wearing no pants. Lars put his face close and just smelled. A young body smelt different to an older one, as if they sweated sugar and talcum powder. The boy was circumcised, clean.

Even though the guy was hurt, in just seconds he felt him stiffen as he worked on him vigorously. The boy was starting to murmur out, jerking his head. Lars carried on sucking whilst at the same time furiously masturbating. It was hard to relax in these surroundings, but if he could just carry on at this tempo for another five minutes…

The boy was fully erect now, but, as he stirred into consciousness, he started to scream, huge, ear-splitting wails. The inside of the truck seemed to vibrate. Lars was not sure if it was his sexual actions or the pain of his head injury that were making him so loud. He put his hand over the guy's mouth and sat back. '*Was ist los?*' he said, and hovered over him, deftly masturbating. The sweaty closeness of him was thrilling. Nearly there, oohh!

But the boy couldn't bloody lie still; kept getting in the way. Lars could have stabbed him with frustration. And he continued to shout out. His loud, frantic cries were disturbing, even for Lars. Normally, he took them when they were already ecstatic; that was why the pain of him sliding in the knife was only like a nick: a little piece of love all in one piece.

The boy was out of control now. Lars stood up to find something to shut him up, frustrated. *Bloody hell, all this hassle for nothing.* He grabbed one of the thick blankets he sometimes used for packing. It was made from rough, grey material; just holding it dried out your hands. He chucked it over the boy's face and started to smother him with it. He held on to him as the body furiously struggled. Lars was being bruised, his bare knees scraped, just trying to keep his grip. Clouds of dust were rising up from the blanket that he nearly choked on. He was so tired by this point, he had half a mind to just the kick the boy out and drive home, but he'd gone too far already. Once he'd smacked the head on the tiles he'd crossed a line. And the boy had seen his face.

The boy was young and strong. Lars had to grit his teeth as he held him down. But after a long, grasping struggle, the boy was still. Jesus, he hadn't even been able to watch his eyes. Lars pulled the blanket off, looked in disgust at the now obviously dead face, purple from lack of oxygen, smeary with dust. Now he'd have to dispose of the body as well. The boy's shirt had come half-undone in the struggle and Lars suddenly found his erection at full-mast again as he leant over the body inspecting his handiwork.

He sucked in the stale air. Whatever he did, it had to be quick. He took the knife out of his pocket and carefully felt for the vein. He was only just dead. With trembling hands he carefully made an incision. If it was too big, it would make too much mess.

He cut a little hole right over the jugular vein as best he could and got ready to suck. As soon the crimson seeping started, he swallowed it. The blood was like warm liquid energy. He felt his own body relax and transform as it entered his body. He only had a few minutes, had to relish every second.

With the blood filling his mouth, Lars instantly wanted to come, and after all the frustrations he let go and came like a rocket. His orgasm seemed to stab itself out of him. For a second he felt god-like, as if there was nothing he could not do. His body felt as if it had been shot with bright white light.

Afterwards, he sat back on his haunches and looked at what he'd done. He'd managed to come on the floor of his own truck. The boy's neck was still bleeding out and he had to get it out of here before the vein completely disintegrated. Lars didn't understand these things exactly, but he knew DNA could be traced in blood and semen. He'd clean up the van later, but he had to get the body out now.

Normally Hans sorted this out. It scared Lars, how difficult every little thing was. He thought about burning the body but didn't know where to go to do it undisturbed. He rubbed his eyes. Of course, his body now craved rest.

He quickly pulled his trousers up and opened the back of the van. He was deafened by birdsong. It was now full daylight. No other cars had parked nearby. *Clear*. Fuck it, he was gonna risk it. He shoved a cap over his face and dragged the body to the edge of the truck. Jumped down, looked again. He picked the body up over one shoulder and tried to run back to the toilets. Jesus, it felt as if every bone in his body was going to collapse, but his fear of being caught was so strong that he was able to stagger the few steps back to the public toilet.

There was one stall. He sat the body awkwardly on the toilet and locked the door. The body already slumped, it would probably fall down soon, but for now he could escape detection until the toilet was checked.

With trembling hands he got on his stomach and crawled back out underneath the stall, gasping at the dirtiness of the floor. He reckoned the body might remain undiscovered for an hour or so. He didn't know about DNA whatsit, but he had no opportunity to clean up anyway.

Now it was over, his body was close to collapse. You got such an adrenaline thrill from it that it practically knocked you out. He could barely walk back to the truck. He exhaled, started up the engine and got the hell out of there. Within seconds he was back on the B6 heading towards Hannover.

He started to relax, but felt black depression descend on him. Normally he felt elated after a kill, but that had been sordid. For the first time in his life he felt like a killer.

It was hard for him to admit, but if this was what it was going to be like on his own perhaps he should get back in with Hans. He took out a beer and started drinking it to take the taste out of his mouth. The little fucker was rotten, but when Hans wanted to please him, he knew exactly what to do.

Hans groaned. His hair was matted with sweat, his eyes dark with exhaustion. He lay prone in the bed, huge rings under his eyes. Still she would not stop. She touched the hard muscle of his stomach, teased him with her fingers, moved further down. He let out a little moan. After his forceful, unsatisfactory lovemaking, she'd decided to mellow him. And it was possible, but she needed to spend hours being intimate with him in order to draw him out. He was a difficult lover, but worth it once you got to the inner him.

'Please, I am in hell, help me.' He threw his head back, waited for her to start over. Dorcas giggled, ran her hand through her dark, lustrous bob. Despite everything, it was still there, the chemistry between them, when he chose to see it. Because he was a sex addict, the trick was to keep his desire revving through mutual masturbation that could last for hours until one of them fell into an exhausted sleep. Once she'd got him in the mood, they could not stop touching each other. And if she didn't let him penetrate her, then she could spend hours riding his fingers, licking, teasing, allowing him to play with himself, but every time he came that way it just made him want her more.

With a cool, professional eye, she appraised him. If he was going to talk she had to get him into a state of frenzy. Or beyond.

'*Schatz!*' he moaned in her ear, kissing her like a drowning man. He was desperate to possess her, but when they were in role-play he allowed her to dominate, got off on being sweetly submissive. The shadows made her thin body look almost voluptuous. Dorcas knew her face was all eyebrows and sharp angular bones in this light. She exuded sexual power, possible cruelty.

Hans was insecure, that was why he felt compelled to stick his dick into everyone. You had to get past the first layer of his sexual consciousness, the usual macho bullshit, to reach him. He'd made her into a slut, and now she revelled in it, used it torment him. She could handle multiple partners so much better than him.

She slapped him across the face, hard. 'Where is Anna, you little bitch?' she said as dominating as she could muster.

He smirked. '*I just view things as objects: people, animals, trees, cars; they're all the same to me,*' he said. 'That's John Hughes.'

Dorcas gave a little laugh. 'Bitches are all animals to me,' she said, picking up a candle and tipping a bit of the hot wax gleefully onto his chest.

'Aaaargghh!' he cried, but there was an ironic smile on his face. He was closing his eyes, grimacing, becoming undone.

'Promise me she won't work at the club again,' commanded Dorcas.

'She'll never work anywhere again,' said Hans with a laugh. He spoke slowly, as though he was out of breath. 'She's…gone.'

There was something final about the way he said it. Dorcas felt as if someone was walking over her grave. She made herself carry on smiling. Then he made his voice high, shrill. *'We all go a little mad sometimes!'*

'I'm sure you had to get rid of her,' said Dorcas in the same shrill tone, as if she was role-playing too. Then she threw in her own quote in the same high, false voice. *'I didn't want to hurt them, I only want to kill them.'*

Hans opened his eyes and looked at her as if he was seeing her for the very first time.

# Chapter
# Twenty-Four

As soon as they left the doctor's office he started. Just from the way he quizzically raised his eyebrows, before he even opened his mouth, she knew he was going to be loud.

'Are you happy now?' shouted Kurt as they walked back to the car. It was a gorgeous day, Germany was enjoying warmer temperatures than the Med, but Frannie couldn't enjoy it.

Her check-up at Dr Kanton's had been a nightmare. She's missed the one she was supposed to go to yesterday because she was in hospital, but they had fitted her in as an emergency this morning. Everyone was blaming her. She was hobbling slowly, trying to concentrate on making it back to the car. The heat had swollen up her ankles so that it was difficult to put weight on them.

'Did you understand all that?' said Kurt, shaking his head. Dr Kanton had mostly spoken in rapid, excited German. 'Your blood pressure's sky-high and it's affected your placenta. Presumably the baby's getting less nutrients, but you discharged yourself! But of course, you know best!' They walked in silence. He opened the driver's door. 'Here. Why don't you drive back, have a practice right now, seeing as driving means so much to you.' He stood there with his arms folded, waiting.

Frannie shook her head. 'I can't in all this traffic. You know that. You drive, please.' They were parallel-parked on a busy side street.

She doubted she could even drive out.

With a grunt he got in. He seemed satisfied that he'd proved his point. His long, bulky body seemed to fold to fit into the car. Wearily she fastened her seatbelt.

'Perhaps it would be best if you went back to hospital and stayed there for the rest of the pregnancy,' said Kurt, swerving to avoid roadworks. He swore under his breath. The city traffic was getting busy; the commuters were all going home. Carefully he manoeuvred the car into the afternoon rush-hour traffic.

Frannie looked at the newly filled-in pages in her *Mutterpass*. Since her last visit, every reading had got worse. Even her iron levels were low.

'That only makes my blood pressure go up,' said Frannie timidly. 'All this interference just stresses me out. I wish everybody would just leave me alone.' She closed her *Mutterpass* and looked out of the window.

'I expect our *baby* would like to be left alone too, to develop. You have to stop running around, this night-driving.' They'd only been en route for a few minutes, but all the traffic on the B6 was at a standstill. Kurt's tense face looked into hers. Outside people were honking horns; angry faces stared out of windows. 'You're about to be a mother. Racing around in cars is not part of the job description.'

'I was only trying to get my confidence so I could be a proper mother,' she said.

He looked at her with eyes of stone. 'Is it worth risking the baby's health?'

Frannie slumped miserably in her chair. Dr Kanton had taken pleasure in going through every negative number on her results: blood pressure, bacteria in urine, ECG. Even the baby's heartbeat had been a bit erratic, although it was too soon to draw any conclusions.

Frannie felt as if her body had been put through a wash cycle. If she could barely get out of bed in the morning, how could she look for Tomek? She couldn't carry on fighting any more. She felt sick thinking about it.

The baby kicked, a series of hard thuds. She put a guilty hand to her stomach. He had certainly been making his presence felt, the past few days. She sighed, closed her eyes. Perhaps Kurt was right, she should be concentrating on the baby.

Her hand seemed to settle the baby's frantic kicks. If she spent most of the day lying down, stopped worrying about what had happened to Tomek, or what Lars and Hans could do to her, everything would be alright again. It was such a bright, sunny day. If she just sat out in the garden, under the cherry tree, perhaps the sun could make it all go away.

She tried to push all thoughts of Tomek out of her mind: his lithe, boyish frame, the way he said his sister's name. She concentrated on the view out of the window. Streets and shops sprawled in long, straight lines. The transport system seemed to have been planned before there were people to use it. From somewhere behind them she could hear the sound of sirens bouncing off the queue of waiting cars, getting closer.

'*Scheisse!*' Kurt abruptly turned his head, tried to move further to the right lane to make room for the police car to pass. All the cars were snarled up, engines revving. The police car crawled up, forcing confused motorists to scatter. They were temporarily deafened by its siren. Then it zoomed ahead and the cars closed ranks again.

Kurt twiddled the knob on the car radio and finally found a local news channel on Radio 21. A female voice was speaking in well-enunciated German. Frannie zoned it out. Her window was wound down and she tapped her hand against the side of the car.

The traffic was totally at a standstill. If she left her hand out much longer it was going to get sunburned. Kurt turned the radio up louder.

'Did you hear that?' said Kurt, for a moment forgetting his anger.

'What?' said Frannie, looking round for another emergency vehicle.

'On the news they said someone has been murdered, just over there. Can you see the police presence?' Kurt pointed to the right. 'A young man had his throat cut and was dumped in that gas station.' He sounded amazed. The BP petrol station was right on the road in front of them.

Frannie stared out of the window. 'My God!' she said, her eyes wide. In the distance she could see a line of police cars, both the old green ones and the new, more masculine blue ones, parked outside on the forecourt. Their siren lights flashed like angry wasps about to sting. Police tape had been put up to stop customers driving in. There must be four, five police cars there. She felt as if she couldn't swallow any more. A horrible feeling of *déjà vu* came over her. *A murder*. She couldn't believe it. Could it be Tomek? The thought of him dead, casually dumped there made her want to howl. But it could be… It had been days since she'd last spoken to him.

She tried to suppress the tear that started trickling down her face.

Instinctively she wanted to call Dorcas, but that was impossible with Kurt sitting next to her, angrily banging his hand on the steering wheel. She rubbed her forehead, tried to pull herself together. They might not know where Frannie lived, but what if poor Dorcas was next? A cold fear gripped her. It might be an unrelated killing, but she could no longer contain her anxiety. For the first time in front of Kurt she allowed herself to openly cry.

'I'm sorry, Kurt,' she cried, taking the opportunity to just let it all out and sob for all she was worth. 'I've let you and the baby down.' She carried on sobbing, praying she would get a chance to talk to Dorcas soon. Let Kurt assume she was crying over her negative check-up results. 'Did they...say who it was?' she said. She let out a little sob.

Kurt at looked her and she covered her face. 'No,' he said with a little laugh. 'It wasn't you, was it?'

'I drove past that station a few times,' she said, sniffing into her handkerchief.

'Well, there's another reason for you not to night-drive,' said Kurt with a grim smile. 'Apart from the fact that our baby might die, and that I'll leave you if you do it again, now there's a killer on the loose. That's pretty compelling.' He gave her an unpleasant grin and turned his attention to the road again.

Frannie felt as if she'd been punched in the stomach.

In her mouth she could taste acid. It was hopeless to try to talk to him. Kurt didn't understand, and, worse, he didn't want to. *I can't go on*, she thought to herself. With red eyes, she sighed, and continued staring dully out of the window.

In first gear, the car continued its slow, miserable journey.

🚗

If she was lucky, she had twenty minutes. She waved goodbye to Kurt nervously. He was only going to get a newspaper.

She had to get hold of Dorcas, find out if she was OK. It was so hot her clothes were sticking to her, and it felt as if her breasts were forcing themselves out of her bra. She was even having problems putting on shoes. This call was the last thing she was going to do in the doomed quest to find Tomek.

Quickly she took out her phone and dialled the number. There was no answer. Perhaps Dorcas was working. She sent a text. Nervously, she went to the kitchen. She sat there, jiggling her foot, trying not to feel so tense.

Her mobile rang. It was Dorcas. 'What?' she whispered, as if she'd smoked a full packet of fags first. 'I'm with someone right now.' Frannie imagined the prone body of some man lying next to her.

'It's Frannie,' she said quickly. 'Did you hear about the murder? A body's been found on the B6.' She peered out of the window so that she'd know the second Kurt's car pulled back into the driveway.

'What?' said Dorcas again, for once shocked. 'Hang on…oh, it's alright, he's sleeping. I'll go in the bathroom with my laptop.' There was a long silence, Frannie could hear clicking sounds, but was left waiting. After a few minutes she began to get anxious. Who was there with her?

'Dorcas?' she said, anxiety making her voice louder than she'd planned. 'DORCAS?'

After what seemed ages, Dorcas was back, talking so quietly she was still practically whispering. 'It's OK, just had to get the MacBook working. There's an article in the *HAZ.*'

'Hats…?'

'Hannover's daily paper. They don't name the victim but they say he was dark-skinned, so it doesn't sound like Tomek,' said Dorcas in a brisk tone. 'But it goes on about other things…' Her voice trailed off as if she didn't want to discuss it further. After a long pause she continued. 'It's probably a journalist looking for a good story, but apparently ten men have gone missing from Hannover in the last eighteen months. Some of them were openly gay.'

Frannie frowned. 'They think there's a gay-killer out there?' She tapped her fingers on the window sill. 'But Anna was female, so that can't be anything to do with it.'

'It's being compared to the notorious Fritz Haarmann case.'

'The what?'

'Hannover's most famous serial killer from the 1920s. They're comparing these disappearances to his case.'

'So?' said Frannie, trying hard to understand the German.

'Well he had an accomplice apparently...someone called...Hans Grans.' Dorcas's voice was so low Frannie could barely hear her.

'What?'

'I said Hans Grans,' said Dorcas. She sounded as if she was in shock.

Frannie exhaled sharply. She felt suddenly like throwing up. 'That can't be a coincidence, can it?' she said incredulously. 'Is it a common name in Germany?'

'No,' said Dorcas tersely. And what she said next made shivers run down Frannie's spine. 'Actually, he's here right now.'

'Dorcas! You can't be alone with him, it's too dangerous,' pleaded Frannie. She could feel her face going red. She'd meant to tell Dorcas she couldn't carry on with the search for Tomek, but she couldn't leave it like this.

'Dangerous is kind of in my job description,' said Dorcas with a bitter laugh. 'Trust me, I know what I'm doing.'

'Dorcas...'

'Drop it. I'll phone at midnight tonight. Just go for a piss or something, and take your phone; that's what you're always doing, right?'

Frannie nodded. Dorcas was coarse to the point of being rude, but she had the exasperating knack of being able to put her finger on everything in seconds.

'I'm gonna do a little research,' said Dorcas.

'But wasn't Anna one of your co-workers?' said Frannie, trying to muster the courage to speak up, protect her new friend.

'So I'm motivated to find out what happened to her just in case it happens to me, right?' Dorcas sounded shaken-up; perhaps she wasn't as tough as she thought she was. Frannie closed her eyes. She couldn't stand the thought of Dorcas alone with that animal.

'Why did you even let him through the door?' she said.

'Someone like you could never understand.' Dorcas practically spat the words out and then she hung up. Frannie put her face in her hands. Actually, she did get how you could be obsessed with someone's physical presence, the idea of them. How it was possible to be excited by a forceful personality – or an imagined one – in a beautiful shell. Kurt looked like a caricature of a Nazi poster boy, with his tall blondness, that pink, creamy skin, but in reality there was nothing pretty about him on the inside, he was empty. And what did it say about her, that she had been so bowled over by his appearance and charm that she had forgotten to check if he had a personality underneath? But people lied and hid their true selves. She knew that from bitter experience.

And now what should she do? It was an impossible position. She didn't want to compromise her baby's health, but what if Dorcas ended up killed? After all, she, Frannie, had dragged her into all this.

She wiped her eyes. She wouldn't have a moment's peace until she knew Dorcas was safe. As long as Hans was with her in her apartment, she couldn't rest.

Dorcas went straight back to the bedroom. Hans's Gucci suit jacket was hung up on the chair. Even though it was early afternoon, he was still sleeping. She smirked: he should be, she'd kept him up most of the night. But, even though she'd skillfully worked to make him vulnerable, what she'd learned was precisely nothing. Some of her clients thought her practically psychic because she could read their thoughts so well.

Asleep, he had the look of a child, a sulky, spoiled one who you knew wouldn't do as he was told, but who looked unbearably cute with his eyes closed. She looked at him closely. Could he really be involved with all these missing men? She touched her stomach. She needed to know what kind of man he was. If she was going to be a single mum, she didn't want to bring up a monster.

Carefully, she reached into the neatly hung jacket and her deft fingers found his wallet. She flicked through various cards until she spied the white rim of the identity card. His real name would be on it. A much younger Hans stared out at her, the features softened by extreme youth. But the name staring at her was 'Gunnar Liss'.

*Gotcha.* Her mind was whirling as if she'd drunk too much coffee. He'd been lying to her from the start. She took the card and went to her terrace with her laptop. In a trance she did a Google search for Gunnar Liss but came up with nothing in particular.

The historic Hans Grans was another story. In some reports he was executed, in others sentenced to twelve years and then, after he did the time, ended up in a death camp. He'd lived in a tiny room, sharing a single bed with a serial killer who had hacked up the bodies of his victims afterwards, but he had claimed to know nothing about it. The relationship between him and Haarmann was ambiguous. In addition, Hans Grans also had three girlfriends who worked for him as prostitutes. Her lover would probably know all the ins and out of it. She pondered, lit a cigarette.

Why would he take that name? 'Fritz' she would have understood, but 'Hans'? She looked at the picture of Fritz Haarmann again, the broad, slightly simple face, and it reminded her of someone.

It was just coming to her when a hand touched her shoulder.

# Chapter Twenty-Five

Hans stood there frowning, taking in everything she was doing. He'd already clocked his real ID card on the table and seen the page she was looking at online.

'Who *are* you?' said Dorcas. Her voice was hesistant; she couldn't imagine her next move.

Hans's face darkened and Dorcas thought about making a run for it, but then he smiled and casually took out a cigarette.

'You know my predilections,' he said, as if going under a false name was like donning sunglasses. 'Nosy cow, aren't you?' He grabbed his ID card, gave her a sharp look. 'You're becoming a liability.' The tip of his nose was going white, a sign she knew meant he was close to losing it. She froze, but she was determined to find out more.

'But why Hans Grans?' she said.

Hans took out a cigarette and lit up. 'I'm a "true crime" fan,' he said exhaling slowly. 'And they're the local legends.' Nothing was going to stop him enjoying the first nicotine hit of the day. 'But ol' Fritz was a bit crude – too ugly.' His sharp eyes seemed to see right through her.

Dorcas tried to look relaxed. 'There was an article in the *HAZ* about Haarmann,' she said, closing her laptop.

Hans looked out of the terrace balcony and puffed away. Then, looking over his shoulder he said, 'This pregnancy's making you hysterical. He was executed in 1925.' Hans made a chopping motion at his neck and laughed. 'I think you're safe!'

Dorcas felt cold inside at the rebuke, but she laughed it off. Hans was standing there in his underwear, languidly smoking, but he was getting quiet. The less he said, the more nervous she felt. She'd tried, but now she had to save herself.

'I'm going away for a few weeks,' she said hesitantly turning to stand next to him. She casually put her arm around his shoulder. 'There's a rehab programme in the Harz mountains that starts tomorrow.'

Hans smiled. 'But you like smoking coke, Dorcas, it's what makes you tick.'

Dorcas shrugged her shoulders. 'It's paid by the *Krankenkasse.*' Instead of looking at him, she stared at the grand flats on the opposite side of the street. There were lilac trees in full bloom. When she spoke her voice was wistful, 'I've got four weeks to make up my mind whether to have an abortion or not.'

Hans just laughed and carried on smoking. 'So it's a toss-up between a kid or coke?' In a high-pitched voice he quipped, '*Isn't it funny how once you become convicted you immediately become combustible.*'

Dorcas stared at him, her lips a thin line. These bloody quotes!

Then his voice hardened. 'Getting knocked up was never part of the equation. Stay away from the club for now.' He walked back into the flat. Dorcas defiantly stared at him. He turned around and seemed to look through her. 'I mean it! I don't want you working in this state or upsetting the other girls.'

His moody eyes flashed at her and Dorcas recoiled. There would be time for her to get her own back, but she knew better than to go against him when he was in a mood. And God, did he look mad. She heard the sound of furious movements as he gathered his things.

She sat there like a mouse until she was sure he had left the flat. When she saw him getting into his car outside, she picked up her phone and called Elli: the one person left who could maybe find something out at the club. Better not tell her too much, though. It was getting too dangerous to tell anyone else her suspicions out loud.

At midnight, Frannie was waiting in her bathroom, her phone clenched in her hand. Although she was only wearing short cotton maternity pyjamas, she was sweating.

Dorcas called on the dot. Frannie was so nervous she could barely press the green button to answer. And Dorcas sounded even more agitated. Frannie could immediately tell something was up.

'Has he gone?' said Frannie, whispering to make sure Kurt couldn't hear upstairs.

'Yes. And I found out his real name – it's Gunnar Liss,' said Dorcas, getting straight to the point.

Frannie gasped. 'Did he say why?' she said.

'No. He's, like, a "true crime" nut, and this duo are Hannover's answer to Jack the Ripper. He thought Hans was cooler than Haarmann the butcher. And yes, it's weird, but we can't go to the police with that.'

'So nothing's changed?' said Frannie, disappointment souring her voice. She noted that her bathroom urgently needed cleaning. The demands of the real world were constantly closing in on her.

'Well, I called Elli – another working girl from the club – and she's trying now to have a sneaky look in Hans's office. But when I spoke to her she reminded me of something I forgot.'

NIGHT DRIVER

'What?' said Frannie, interest animating her pale features.

'Anna apparently sent an email to her, about something she saw on Hans's laptop. But Elli never got it. Or thought she didn't.'

'You mean maybe it went to her spam filter or something?'

'Could be. The thing is, I've told Hans I'm going on a rehab course…'

'Rehab?' interjected Frannie, forgetting to whisper. The more she found out about Dorcas, the scarier it all got.

'Just for coke, nothing serious,' laughed Dorcas.

Frannie winced. 'You take…cocaine?' she said, falteringly.

'Yes, Mum!' said Dorcas laughing. 'And Hans has told me in no uncertain terms to stay away from the club. He caught me looking at his ID card with the bloody stuff on Hans Grans on my laptop. So I can do nothing directly.' Dorcas hesitated, then her voice hardened, 'So it has to be you who meets Elli to try and retrieve this email.'

Frannie spluttered, feeling felt sick to her stomach. 'I can't!' she said. 'My pregnancy's not going well, Kurt's threatened to leave me if I drive again—'

Dorcas cut in savagely. 'It could be me next!' she said in a voice filled with unbearable tension. There was a crackling noise, as if she'd knocked something down. 'Look, it's just one drive. You don't have to go in the club. Just go to the car park and phone me. I'll tell Elli you're there and she'll come out to you. You can look at her laptop in the car.' She hesitated, 'Then come here and we can go to the police together and it will be over.'

Frannie shuddered. Dorcas was out of her mind with worry and she'd put her in that position. With disbelief, she heard herself reluctantly agree. It was late, she was tired. There were a thousand reasons for not going. But she'd got Dorcas into this. Now she had to get her out of it again.

She'd already laid out a full set of clothes in the bathroom. Although she'd told herself they were for tomorrow, subconsciously she'd known it would come to this. Before, she'd always been nervous about the actual driving, and then that Kurt would find out. But now – if Hans caught her at the club, something much, much worse could happen. She shuddered, tried to press that thought to the back of her mind.

She dressed quickly and decided to disguise herself a little. She put on a silly hat with fake red hair sticking out and added shades. Even if she was only going to sit in the car, it was worth trying not to be so obvious. Her pregnancy bump was too pronounced to hide, but she had on a baggy top she hoped would cover everything up.

Just before she left, her tense, hard stomach seemed to lurch, and she vomited into the sink. The sight of it made her want to retch again. This drive was going to be tougher now her blood pressure was elevated. She cleaned up and popped a mint into her mouth. Her face in the mirror was so drawn that she didn't even bother to put make-up on.

Kurt had forgotten to put the car into the garage so she only had to reverse it off the drive. Guiltily she closed the front door, but on this sultry night it felt wonderful to be out with the grass singing in the breeze. The keys in her hand felt like magic; after all the tension of waiting, getting into the car felt like actually doing something.

Normally she night-drove later, after a solid stint of sleep, but tonight she'd been too nervous to attempt that. As soon as she got behind the wheel, she felt different. It must be tiredness; in her driving theory lessons she'd learnt that was as bad as being drunk. She tried to compensate by driving faster – after all, no one was about – but the car made a groaning noise as she shoved too quickly into the higher gears. After a brief struggle, the car went smoothly and she tried to concentrate.

Even though the car had air-conditioning, she decided to open the roof so that the rush of air would help keep her awake. The invigorating blast was a distraction, though, and as she turned a corner she came upon a hedgehog scampering in the headlights. Before she could blink, there was a sickening thud. Her heart sank, but she just pushed her foot down further. With acid pooling in her mouth, she carefully forged her way along the minor roads to the B6.

It was just after twelve, so there was still some late traffic going to and fro from the city but luck was with her tonight. Most of the traffic lights hit green as she approached them and none of the other cars bothered her as she trundled along in the slow lane. She was already panicking about parking in the nightclub car park, which would probably be full.

All this detective work was pushing her out of her comfort zone. She resolved to drive around the car park slowly, and then to assess the situation. If all else failed, she could ask someone to park for her.

She'd started off the journey in a buoyant mood, pleased to be chasing a real clue, but halfway through her energy levels slumped. It was as if she was in a dream, imagining the drive rather than sitting there doing it. She drove right up to the sign for the *Autobahn* without registering until the last second that she had to turn right. Shit. She squealed into the lane without indicating, her whole body flushed with sweat. She swallowed uneasily. The fuel in the car was low; if she got stuck on the *Autobahn*, she wasn't sure she could actually tank up herself at a petrol station. And was it diesel or petrol that the car needed? She didn't even know which direction

Osterwald was on the motorway. There were so many things she had to learn before she could drive without thinking about it.

It was a relief when the neon-lit signs for the Moonlights Club came up. Slowly, she turned into the car park. It was busy, but evidently many customers would come later, and she spied two spaces together that she decided to nab. It was upfront, near the entrance and she could reverse in, so that she would then be able to drive forward if she needed to get out quickly. She straddled the middle of the two spaces; it was the best she could do. Anyway, she didn't plan on staying long.

Now she was here it didn't feel real. She was no computer expert, but she'd worked for five years as a PA to a magazine publisher and was used to troubleshooting the Xerox machine. Being physically outside the club, though, was scary. Last time she'd walked right in there like a sitting duck. The thought of Lars and Hans sitting somewhere behind those walls chilled her to the bone. It was hard to resist the temptation to just scarper.

With trembling fingers she dialled Dorcas's number.

Dorcas tried to play it cool, but the hoarseness in her voice betrayed her anxiety, 'Don't tell Elli anything when you see her,' she said roughly.

'Why?' said Frannie. Wasn't this Elli on their side?

'Because it's safer for her not to know. We have to think about everybody we involve in this.'

Frannie winced and sat and waited. Dorcas assured her that Elli would be out in five minutes with her emails already loaded on her laptop. She only had to check through the spam filter from about a month before. *Come on!* she thought to herself, chewing on a piece of gum, trying not to let her stomach tie itself in knots. She'd reached that part of the pregnancy where it was uncomfortable to sit upright for too long. Just breathing was exhausting.

She wound down the windows. There was a long queue of kids all dolled up waiting to get in the club. There was a lot of shouting, but Frannie's eyes never left the front entrance. Every second being here was torture. As usual her bladder had started aching. She tapped her feet impatiently. 'Come on,' she said out loud.

Something told her she should just get the hell out of there, but she'd promised Dorcas, so she'd have to hold out.

Only seconds after she'd spoken to Frannie, her phone rang again. Dorcas groaned. She felt so guilty that she'd sent Frannie in there instead of doing it herself, and the slightest disturbance made her jump. She was itching with nerves. What she really needed was a goddamn line to straighten her out. That was the problem with falling out with your boyfriend and best mate all at the same time: she'd cut off her supply chain. If she left it too long she'd be too desperate to get a good deal with a street dealer. When the girls were humming with need they clocked it in seconds. And then they put the price up.

'Hello?' said Dorcas, suspiciously.

'Is that…Dorcas?' said a male voice she didn't recognise. 'I found your card in my wife's things.' He spoke in the grammatically correct German of the Hannover region, but stumbled over his words.

'I am she,' said Dorcas archly. Perhaps it was one of her old clients.

'My wife is missing,' continued the voice, 'and I found your… details…' He stopped, as if he'd run out of words.

Dorcas gave a horrified snort. That must be the husband! *Scheisse!* Frannie had said if he found her out driving again he'd end the relationship. Trust a bloody man to give out ultimatums. As if they didn't have enough to worry about.

'Frannie's meeting someone for me,' she said, desperately trying to placate him, anything to make him go away.

'A client?' said Kurt fiercely. 'I mean…you are…?' He couldn't even say the word out loud. This one was no diplomat for sure.

Dorcas swept her eyes around her immaculate room and gave one of her low little laughs. 'Nothing like that,' she said, 'She's doing me a favour, helping me check a friend's laptop.' Her voice was light and high, as if it was the littlest thing.

'That is not possible!' shouted Kurt. 'My wife, out in the middle of the night!' Dorcas grinned. She'd seen his photo on Frannie's mantelpiece. His type she could read like a book. All verbal tetchiness and then they fudged on the job. The moodiness was compensation for passions that should have been directed elsewhere. She grinned. He needed professional help. When his sort had good sex it made them feel like real people again.

'Look – Kurt, isn't it?' she said, deciding to take the matter in hand. Frannie should have the email soon anyway, then they could go to the police together. Maybe this Kurt guy could help translate.

'Yes?' He seemed surprised that she knew his name.

'I'm expecting Frannie here in around half an hour. Perhaps you should come over; she might need you.'

'Need me for what?' said Kurt, deeply confused.

'I'll tell you when you get here,' said Dorcas, giving out her address languidly as if it was an invitation to an exclusive party.

'I'm going to have to take my old motorbike,' said Kurt, making it sound as if he was going to have to walk the whole distance by foot. 'Since my wife has run off with my car again…'

She knew it was her as soon as she came out of the club. Elli was tall, with honey-blonde hair that fell in voluminous waves to her shoulders. If a professional had spent an hour with her hands on it, it couldn't have looked better. But when she moved she looked like a dead woman walking, and up close the eyes were vacant.

Her face was still pretty, but the skin looked odd, as if it were too stretched, making it impossible to tell how old she was. Although her youth was all there, she had a look about her that made her seem off, as if she was ill or had a spectacular hangover. Dorcas had told her she'd been hitting the meth.

Frannie tried not to let her concern show in her eyes.

'Are you Dani?' said Elli as she approached the open car window.

Frannie nodded. Dorcas had insisted on a pseudonym. She was being frighteningly efficient about keeping her distance.

When Elli got into the passenger seat, her skirt was so short she inadvertently flashed her knickers, but she handed over her MacBook as promised. The screen showed her inbox. She had the same type of email account as Frannie, which made it easier for her to log into. Frannie frowned, tried to concentrate, she had to get this over with. If Kurt found out she was gone, she was done for.

'Every day I get one message about spam, but I can never get to it,' said Elli. She spoke in a nasal whine, as if something was up her nose. A peculiar sweet smell came off her in waves that made Frannie feel nauseous. She reeked of vodka and vomit with a bit of talcum powder thrown in for good measure.

Frannie needed to access the spam folder, but the wi-fi network evidently did not extend to the car park. She clicked furiously, but all that happened was that the little arrow bounced all over the page and the laptop made annoying pinging noises. All this bloody way for nothing! But she couldn't just give up.

'We need to log on again. Does the club have wi-fi access?' said Frannie trying to keep the urgency out of her voice. She badly wanted to leave, but if she was honest her desire to pee was stronger.

'I don't know,' said Elli, looking around distractedly, 'do we need it?' Then after a long pause she said, 'Well I go online at the club, right?' She spoke slowly as if she'd just woken up.

Frannie felt a prickle of horrified fascination as she saw a line of clear snot oozing out of one of Elli's nostrils. Going inside was the last thing she wanted to do, but she just had to go a hundred metres to get this thing to work. Her lips were pressed in a thin, straight line. And while she was in there she could use the bathroom.

Silently she cursed Dorcas. She was going to have to take a risk again. In the car mirror she inspected her 'disguise'. She looked like shit, and the heat was making the cap stick to her head, but it was all she'd got.

'I'm barred from the club,' she said, pulling her cap lower down, 'so make it quick.'

As they approached the neon outline of the Moonlights sign, Frannie felt awkward that she was wearing saggy maternity clothes. Elli had on high heels, teamed with the skimpiest top and skirt Frannie had ever seen. From the back, she could have been on a Vogue photo shoot. She got them both through the door with a nod to the bouncer. Frannie nervously stepped inside, trying to keep her cool, concentrating on breathing.

Once inside, the innards of the club swallowed them in. It was like entering another world. The decor of the club was almost-black, with playful strobe lights that broke through the gloom like streaks of wild lightning. The crowd was shrieking and dancing. Frannie was deafened by the boom of angry, throbbing music that thickened the air. Or maybe it was the smoke and the humidity.

On this warm night, the place steamed like a jungle. Her heart started to race. She followed Elli's tight denim-encased rear and swishing locks, wishing she looked half as good as her.

Elli quickly led her through the mayhem to a discreet lift and ushered her inside. It was nothing more than a dank metal box that smelled as though no one had used it for some time. Frannie shivered. Her fear seemed to come on like an attack of chickenpox. In the car she could have driven off at any time, but away from the crowds she felt trapped.

The lift was old and descended creakily, as if it might give way at any minute. Abruptly, the doors opened to a room painted in such a featureless grey that it could have been the underworld. The walls were dense so the music from above bounced off it like an echo, but everything vibrated with intensity. Frannie found her knees quivering.

'These are the original bank vaults,' said Elli.

'Nice to know,' said Frannie drily. 'Is there a toilet anywhere or is it just a hole in the floor?'

'Yeah, here's where the girls get ready. We can surf in there too.' Elli led her to a dressing room with adjacent shower and toilet facilities. Six big mirrors surrounded by fairy lights lined the long room. On each little table were baskets crammed with cosmetics and hair brushes. Costumes and every type of beauty paraphernalia filled the room. Frannie found herself choking on the chemical residue of the used cosmetics.

'I'll just use the loo,' she gasped, coughing.

As she locked herself in the stall she wondered if she could trust Elli. The other girl had whisked her so quickly away from the public area. If Hans and Lars wanted to nab her, this would be a good place. Above her the din of the party going on was muffled. No one would hear her if she screamed.

Elli had already managed to load her webmail page when she got back. Quickly, Frannie found the button for spam mail and started to scroll her way through. As Elli hadn't deleted any emails in twelve months, presumably from the time from when the account was set up, the programme had to upload over two thousand items. The laptop whined and groaned as it frantically tried to process the data.

Frannie found herself tapping on the table in impatience. Any of the other girls could come in, and she stuck out like a sore thumb. 'Come on, come on,' she said out loud. Elli was sat touching up her make-up as if she didn't care either way.

'When did Anna say she sent the email?' said Frannie.

'It was so long ago, I dunno,' said Elli.

'OK what's her email address?'

'AnnaK@gmx.de,' said Elli. 'I always called her Special K.' She looked at her strangely. She seemed to be appraising her bump.

Frannie was biting her nails. She couldn't believe how long this was taking. She looked at her watch; she'd been here ten minutes already. Elli meticulously curled her eyelashes with a special curler and reapplied her mascara. Frannie wondered why she didn't just stick on fake ones and be done with it.

'You didn't read the email?' asked Frannie.

'It didn't come into my inbox! Is it something important?' asked Elli.

Frannie just nodded, tried to force herself to relax. 'Anything's important if Dorcas wants it,' she said with a forced laugh. God, she was getting desperate here with this excruciating small talk.

Another flash and some groans, and the spam folder opened. She listed the files alphabetically; at least "A" should be near the beginning. She could feel her heart thudding in her chest as she waited for it to come up. Here it was: an email forwarded from

Anna which had been evidently sent from Hans's laptop. The frightening thing was that it was in English. It read:

FW: New Business Venture: Hearts and Minds
Dear Hans,
We have a medical expert who is prepared to 'babysit' them until the right circumstances can be arranged. Flight transfers are no problem. Please ask Stefan to send blood samples in each case as soon as possible so we can begin the work of finding suitable matches.
Yours,
Leonard

Frannie scanned it quickly then leaned back in her chair. What the hell did that mean? In just a second she'd forward it to her Hotmail account that couldn't be traced back to her so easily.

Elli was looking over her shoulder. 'It's in English,' she said with a note of distaste, 'That why you're here?' Her face suddenly soured. Frannie nodded, her mind mulling over the message. Elli snapped the lid back on her mascara. She was up on her heels in a flash with her hand aggressively touching Frannie's belly. Her thin, over-manicured fingers raked at her bump. It hurt, and Frannie recoiled.

'You got a bun in there love?' Now the fingers were digging in.

'What?' Frannie was so shocked she could barely speak, tried to push her away.

Elli lifted her head back and let out a huge laugh. 'Now I know who you are!' she said, her eyes suddenly glittering with deviousness as if she wanted to rip Frannie's head off. 'You're what Hans calls the English bitch. I heard him talking about you and getting someone up the duff!' She eyed up Frannie from head to toe, laughed again. 'Must have been drunk when he did it!'

Frannie gasped. How could Elli think she had anything to do with Hans? In her embarrassment, she stumbled over her German. 'I'm married,' she gasped out, backing away as a furious Elli approached, all long-legged, banging down her heels forcefully with each step. The laptop was still in her hand, but now she'd have no chance to forward the email; she was too busy trying to save her skin. Frannie knew she must be blushing down to the roots of her hair. Presumably that only made her look more guilty.

Elli's dull eyes had flickered into life at last. She looked pure bile. Frannie backed carefully out of the room. 'Thank you for your time,' she said, trying to duck gracefully out of the situation, but it was no good. Elli was on to her like a spiteful cat. Frannie made it to the lift, but then Elli lunged at her.

'You bitch!' she screamed. 'Keep away from Hans!' Her pupils had dilated to pinpricks; she projected pure rage. She pushed Frannie hard against the wall as if she wanted to knock her through it. There was a sickening thud. Elli's hard beautiful eyes appraised her gleefully.

# Chapter
# Twenty-Six

Frannie gasped and put a hand up pleadingly. In her panic it was hard to grope for the right German words. 'I only met him once,' she said, trying to push Elli off, 'and believe me that was enough.'

Although Elli was stick-thin, she possessed a manic strength. Must be the bleeding drugs. The situation was so far from what she'd thought would be the danger in coming here that Frannie wanted to laugh.

'You're going nowhere till I've got some answers,' screamed Elli, pushing Frannie hard against the wall. Her head bounced off the hard brick. Frantically she jabbed at the button to call the lift. Elli was too busy screaming incoherently to pay attention to the creaking noise as it descended. Frannie closed her eyes and acted defenceless. The only way for her to escape Elli was to act dumb and then suddenly make a run for it. Elli was all noise and big make-up, and clearly had no idea what was really going on here.

When the lift opened she shoved Elli off and ran into it blindly. Her frantic hands attempted to close the door but a screeching Elli was already in like a demon. In her pocket Frannie had her only weapon, an open car key, and she thrust it with all her might into Elli's forehead.

Frannie had expected Elli to back away, but she'd come even closer, and the tip of the key made a little sucking noise as it made contact. There was a horrified gasp, and to her surprise the key actually penetrated the skin a little way and she had to tug at it savagely to retrieve it. She pushed Elli backwards and the girl fell flat on the floor. A tiny trickle of blood was beginning to seep out of her wound. Frannie paled. She didn't think it was a serious injury, but she shouldn't stay in the club a second more than she needed to be. Dorcas was going to be furious with her as well. Why couldn't this sodding lift be a bit quicker?

Finally the door closed and the lift lurched into life. It seemed to take forever to get back to the main floor. When it opened, Frannie forgot about any thoughts of acting incognito and ran for all she was worth through the crowds to the main entrance door. The punters stared at her in surprise; she even got a few wolf whistles. The bouncer looked at her, alarmed. At first she thought he was going to detain her. She couldn't have that. Not so close to freedom.

'*Baby kommt!*' she shouted, clutching her stomach.

All men were worried about seeing a baby pop out right in front of them. Hastily, the bouncer stepped back as if she had a contagious disease and held the door open for her.

She rushed out into the cool night air and legged it for all she was worth back to the car. Thank God she'd parked near the front this time. Elli would be after her any minute. Probably bring down the wrath of all the club staff with her. She slammed her car door shut. Her breaths were coming so fast there was virtually no space between them. She had a stitch and a sudden agonising attack of cramp in her right foot. So much for letting the baby rest!

'Goddamn it!' she shouted loudly to no one in particular. She was sweating but elated. She'd made it out, and not one of the men she was afraid of had apprehended her. She wound down the windows to let in some fresh air and the balmy night breeze felt good on her skin. There was no time to call Dorcas; she had to get out of there.

🚗

After a kill he always slept like a baby, needed a good twelve hours to recover. Must be all that adrenaline. You got wound up really tight. It was like doing a bungee jump. With murder everyone thought about the victim, but the *Täter* also had to suffer a little bit. Nearly gave themselves heart attacks doing the dirty. Killers had to take absurd risks. Afterwards you needed to cool-down; the chance to catch a breath.

When he got up the 'B6 murder' was all over the news. Lars smiled at that: his handiwork on display for all and sundry to see. But every time he thought about Hans he grimaced. If he was honest with himself, he'd left the scene a bit of a mess. He should have got rid of the body properly, burned it or something. He didn't have a criminal record so they didn't have his DNA on file, but still.

With any luck Hans would never find out it was him. He wouldn't understand. Everything Hans did had to be fussed over. For all his fucking idolisation of serial killers, he didn't get it, the overwhelming urge. He didn't therefore really understand what really made serial killers tick. Hans just saw the killing as an extra taboo button on a remote control. But then he didn't do spontaneity. Couldn't even shit without planning it in his diary.

Since Lars had got up, though, he'd been thinking about getting back in with Hans. Although he didn't want to admit it, after the débâcle of last night he had to admit it was easier having the kill room to do his dirty work in. That swine, twisted as he was, certainly made his existence as a killer easier. Deep in his gut Lars knew he couldn't go it alone these days. He was like a prisoner who had become so institutionalised that he couldn't face life on the outside. The fractured feelings he had for Hans frightened him. In one way the young 'un accepted him as no other human being could, but there was a terrible price to pay for it. Hans was just too damn manipulative, and he couldn't keep his cock in his pocket. But...

So now he was sitting outside the Moonlights Club in his van, trying to work out his next move. He'd already delivered their drinks order right on schedule. The night was young and he was feeling pretty much up for anything. He really didn't want to kill the English bitch – Hans knew he didn't do women, for fuck's sake – but maybe it was a test.

He was just contemplating going into the club for a good whisky when he was distracted by a commotion. A fat bird was legging it for all she was worth out of the club and the bouncer on the door – Wittmann, was it? – looked as if he didn't have a clue what was going in. Hang about, was the bird preggers too?

Every sense in Lars's body moved to high alert. Could it be? Then her baseball cap fell off and he saw the mass of pale blonde hair. The fucking English bitch! Here she was, served up to him on a plate, and no one had even seen him directly speak to her. All he had to do was drive after her, do the business, and for Hans he'd be a cat bringing back a mouse.

He didn't relish the thought of killing her, but when he turned the engine he was already feeling high. Party time!

🚗

Dorcas desperately wanted a cup of strong coffee, but Frannie might be there any minute and she knew that pregnant women didn't do coffee or couldn't stand the smell of it or something. Then she smiled, laughed at herself. Now she was one of those women, although her sense of smell hadn't changed yet. She was in denial about her pregnancy until she decided whether or not to have a termination. Nonetheless, there were three pots of different fruit teas sitting nice and hot on the table when the doorbell rang.

'About time...' said Dorcas, expecting Frannie, but instead it was The Husband, tall and gawky-looking, and so edgy he looked as if he might rearrange her face if she put out the wrong biscuits. *Mein Gott!* She smiled exquisitely and ushered him in, hoping Frannie would get there before she had to do the talking.

Kurt strode in, his legs and arms so aggressively muscled he could barely walk in a straight line. He was broad-boned; even his hips were wide. He turned his head from side to side, evidently looking for Frannie. He seemed surprised by the lavish calm of Dorcas's apartment: the unexpected beauty of her flower collection. After seeing the squalor Frannie lived in, that was no surprise. Dorcas smiled.

'She's not here yet!' she said brightly.

The man looked through her rather than at her. He seemed as uncomfortable with himself as with the situation and she instantly recognised his type. She'd seen it so many times before. He was gay, wasn't he, but he probably loathed himself for it and spent his life trying to shoehorn himself into what he thought of as 'normal' relationships with women. And hated them for it.

After long pauses he blurted out, 'How do you know my wife?' without even attempting to blend it into the conversation.

Inwardly she winced, but she maintained her professional smile, noticing how innately attractive he was. She stared at him provocatively.

'I helped Frannie to reverse out once when she was night-driving, and she's helping me find a missing friend,' said Dorcas with a little laugh. 'At three a.m. every driver is significant on a *Rastplatz*.' She stared at him. 'We're a *community*.' She whispered the last bit, as if she was letting him in on a secret. She appraised him with an experienced eye. She knew how to give a closet gay the kind of sex he wanted, without challenging his view of himself as a straight-as-a-die Neanderthal.

'Night-driving?' He looked at her as if she was mad.

'Yeah, Frannie does it in the early hours when she's awake anyway, when the roads are practically empty. Makes sense.' He looked uncomfortable every time she mentioned his wife.

Dorcas pushed a plate of assorted cookies at him and he took one. Even his hands were massive. Part of her longed to rouse his sexuality, which seemed to be lying under the surface of him like a second skin he longed to peel off. If she had enough time she could do so much with him. Long minutes passed. Dorcas kept stealing glances at her antique clock to check the time. 'Frannie's at the Moonlights Club trying to find an email that never made it into someone's inbox,' she volunteered.

Kurt looked like thunder.

'She's coming here once she's finished,' she said.

Kurt gave an animal nod of recognition and simply drank tea and ate all the cookies by himself until they were gone. When he'd been there for an hour, the tension between them was palpable. Kurt had taken to tapping his feet. No one was reachable by mobile. Dorcas flung her phone on the coffee table so hard that it nearly cracked. She assumed Frannie had decided to go home after all and that Elli was off her head somewhere.

So what the hell was she supposed to do with Kurt? She couldn't maintain her smiley face much longer. This had gone on longer than a john session. What people didn't realise was how much acting and role-play sex workers had to engage in. Most of the time the sex was nothing more than an afterthought like the full stop at the end of a sentence.

Dorcas was half-lying on the sofa, playing with a stress ball that she deftly caught in her fingers. Although she was intent on a steady rhythm of throw and catch, she could feel Kurt's gaze as his eyes burned into her. It was hard for her not to laugh out loud. He was so repressed, he was like a thirteen-year-old with a crush on a teacher. It would be so easy; she knew exactly how to edge her way into his deepest fantasies while still being enough of a woman to not frighten him off. And maybe she'd be doing Frannie a favour. Maybe a bit of fulfilment would blunt that edge of suppressed violence in him, send him home less stressed.

She closed her eyes. *Don't*, she told herself. But it was hard. Here she was in close proximity with a man whose sexual desperation was virtually screaming at her. She just wanted something to numb the nagging noise at the back of her brain, even if only momentarily.

Kurt seemed to be mellowing now he had a full belly. Dorcas tried a final time to reach Frannie and Elli, but only got answering machines. She couldn't call Moonlights and risk drawing attention to herself. Better just to wait with Kurt. Get him to relax a bit. After making Frannie do this drive, she owed her that much.

'So, you work on the *Rastplatz*, then?' asked Kurt suddenly.

'Yeah,' said Dorcas, lighting up a cigarette. 'And sometimes at the club – you know, lap dancing, private customers, that sort of thing.'

She leaned closer and blew smoke provocatively in his face. His sullenness thawed and she saw the little boy in him, the smile his mother must have seen the day he was born. She was within a whisper of his soul.

The air between them seemed to be vibrating. All it took was one lingering look and it happened. Their bodies fell together. She kissed him full on the lips and he responded with an anguished groan. She kissed him forcefully, as a man would have, taking control. Already his body was reacting. Her dress was hiked up and she turned her back to him and bent provocatively forward. His toned, dense body was trembling, that musky testosterone smell all over him. 'Surrender, Dorothy!' she thought, and closed her eyes.

# Chapter Twenty-Seven

Frannie roared out of the Moonlights car park in third gear. She guessed Elli would raise the alarm, that the security men in their bulky black outfits would lose no time in getting in a bit of excitement and coming after her. She almost drove into the side of a car in her haste to exit the car park but managed to turn the wheel at the last minute.

With shaking hands, she hit the turn to the *Autobahn*. Her hands were sweating and she badly needed a drink. There were some cars about but she ignored them. As far as she was concerned, she was the only driver that mattered tonight. This time she sped into the fast lane with glee and put her foot down as hard as she could. It was no time to be cautious.

It was around quarter past twelve, so there were not many cars. It was the lull when most people had got to their destination, and too early for them to be coming back. It was a perfect summer night, the sky barely dark. Frannie felt mesmerised by the scary pull of the wheel which was vibrating with energy. The faster she went, the more it hummed. She stopped looking at the speedometer. Just drive straight, she thought. One false move and everything would be lost. If they caught up with her she was finished.

Once the truck lumbered into action, Lars's anxiety vanished. The steady, smooth acceleration of the truck eased him. His mother had always said that it was better to travel than to arrive, and my God, she was right. Motion always felt like progress.

He turned on to the *Autobahn*. The section here was flat but he couldn't see the English bitch's Audi. *You're sure shiftin' it tonight, honey!* He laughed out loud. No matter. He knew where this road ran to, just as he knew all the roads in and out of Hannover; they were like his own arteries. He knew roughly where she lived, too – that there was only one exit she could take.

He couldn't push the truck as fast as Frannie was driving, but he'd played chase games with cars before. The bastards who cut him up and drove past rudely usually got a surprise. No matter how you speeded on the *Autobahn*, once you got to city traffic lights everything evened out. He'd be up her arse at the next red light. Or the one after it.

He grinned, humming a tune to himself. Tonight he'd showered twice and was freshly shaven. When he finally met up with Hans, everything was going to be coming up roses again. Good ol' Onkel Fritz still had it. He didn't know yet how he was going to kill her, but he wasn't going to plan it as such. All he had to do was concentrate on moving towards his target. Once he'd got her, his natural instincts would take over.

He tried not to think about the fact that she was pregnant. That put everything into a different dimension. But he was good at staring at the road ahead and thinking of nothing but fulfilling his own desires. It was painful to acknowledge, but he badly wanted to get back with Hans again, and she was his ticket.

In the end that was what it was all about – being a killer, being anything – it was the absolute realisation of your goal. And what he loved most of all on this fine clear night was that he practically had the road to himself. With a smile, he roared towards the B6.

🚗

When she got off the *Autobahn* exit near home and saw familiar surroundings, Frannie began to relax. And, when she did, the tiredness her body had been fighting came back with a vengeance. She blinked fiercely to keep her eyes open. Her pregnancy bump was wedged up against the steering wheel and her back felt as if it was on fire. What she wanted to do most was to lie down flat. If she stopped at a red light now, she was in danger of falling asleep.

The B6 was lit up with orange lights, but the brightness of them made her eyes run. This section was all traffic lights. And, being so tired, she was in a worse state than a drunk driver. All she wanted was to get home, hit the sack. She put her foot down recklessly on the gas. The quicker she got there, the better.

Frannie sometimes forgot she was an inexperienced driver. When a car in front of her slowed, she nearly smacked into the back of it. She'd got used to the bland swiftness of *Autobahn* tempo and couldn't get into the stop-start pace. She slammed on the brakes but had to swerve into the next lane to avoid hitting the car. The other driver hooted and drove on. Frannie braked too hard and the car stalled. And when it did her hands were so jittery she could barely turn the ignition key. *Shit*.

Carefully, she eased the car into first gear and resolved to go slower. It would be stupid to have an accident on her freaking doorstep. She'd nearly made it.

Burger King was coming up. Just a few more miles and she'd be home. As the lights hit red, she slowed. In her mirror she noticed a lorry trundling up behind her. She winced. Even before her accident she had hated anything bigger than her on the road; they were steel bullies that could barge into her. This one was driving right up her arse.

She nudged the car forward just over the dotted line. Still the truck kept coming. She tutted. This wasn't right. Hang on…those red and white markings, she'd seen them before, hadn't she? As the truck closed in on her like a bad dream, it came to her.

Jesus, it was Lars!

She drove frantically on through the red light, almost colliding with the car coming right that she should have given way to. There was a screech of brakes and the driver savagely sounded his horn. He was probably swearing in the privacy of his car. But Frannie was long gone, with Lars in hot pursuit, his fender virtually pressed against her bumper.

It was insane. She should turn off to go home at the next light, but she couldn't outrun Lars now and she didn't want to lead him back to where she lived. If she'd gone right she could have raised the alarm at Burger King, and to the left she might have made it to the police station in Garbsen. But on the road ahead, the only thing waiting for her were open fields.

🚗

His truck was just centimetres away from Frannie's bumper. No matter how fast she drove, he kept a steady tail. He had the bitch right where he wanted her. With one push he could have shoved her car to smithereens, but there were other drivers around. He had to wait for the right moment. There was a lay-by just ahead; perhaps he could force her to stop there, take her out without damaging his own truck. Not that he had a problem pushing her off the road. In the zone he was invincible. Nothing else mattered.

Just from the stiff way she was sitting he could tell she was terrified. They were frantically speeding and her car was shaking from side to side, as though she could barely keep hold of the wheel. On her back window the windscreen wipers were desperately swishing at the dry window. But she didn't turn them off. She was rattled, a wild animal running blind.

He drove closer still until both vehicles were within a whisker of touching. Still she outran him dead ahead. He laughed. She had pluck, alright. Never mind, the B6 ended temporarily just ahead. She was gonna end up crashed-up strawberry jam if she didn't slow down.

'Chasey, chasey!' he said, shrieking with laughter. On a whim, he let her speed off ahead for a bit, to give her the illusion of escape. His face was flushed, jovial. He loved this cat-and-mouse business.

🚗

The noise of the back window windscreen wiper scraping blithely set her teeth on edge. In this car she didn't know how to turn them off. She was pushing the car to its maximum and had temporarily left Lars behind. His truck couldn't go as fast as her, although this road was coming to an end soon. But her home was coming up, if only she could get out at the next lay-by and run over the bridge quickly enough. Or she could make a dash for it through the sparse traffic of the B6. He wouldn't be expecting that.

Because she was moving so much quicker than normal, the *Rastplatz* was on her before she expected. She had to brake heavily and the car spun in a skid that jerked the car out of the allotted parking spaces. With a screech of gravel, her car got wedged on the bicycle path that took you all the way to Frielingen. Her head bounced back and she felt winded. She didn't feel like running now.

This June had been a hot one and the long tendrils of golden corn waved high and proud in front of her. She stared at it. Perhaps there was another way. If she drove round the corner of the field and dared to drive right into the corn, her car might be hidden from view. Lars wouldn't be able to fit his truck through the gap. He might not see the trail her car had taken. Or he'd think she'd driven round on to the road and look for her elsewhere.

She drove quickly, without any lights, down the farm path. She hoped to God there were no late-night walkers out. She could hardly see a thing as she drove in the blackness. When she was out of sight of the road, she roughly turned the car and began to plough through the billowing strands of corn.

It was hard work. The car shuddered on the uneven surface. All she could hear was the steady thud of corn stalks hitting her windows. Soon a fine powder had completely coated her windscreen. She didn't dare look back, just kept going, praying to God that her desperate act would not send her up in flames. Heinrich had stressed how dangerous it was to drive through undergrowth in case the catalyser got hot and created a spark. She didn't want to set herself and the whole field alight.

Still she drove, until the only thing she could see in any direction was squashed stems of golden corn. They cocooned the car. Lars wouldn't be able to drive in here. If he realised what she'd done he'd have to come on foot. She turned off the engine, slid all the windows open and just listened, every one of her senses strained for Lars's approach.

In the dark, she waited. Her stomach was so hard and tense she felt it might crack open. If she waited it out, she'd still have a chance to drive away if he came after her, although she could barely see over the high, waving corn.

She tried her mobile, but there was no signal in the fields. She sat panting, her mouth dry, with the feeling that dawn was never going to come.

Half a minute later, with a hiss of brakes, Lars's truck rolled into the Rastplatz. His whole body was filled with tension: the anticipation, simply being in the zone, better than any drug. The whole time he was chasing someone he experienced a massive high and an almighty hard-on. Killing was his favourite sexual activity.

But the car park was virtually empty. No sign of the bitch's car. What the hell?

Lars jumped frantically out of his truck, leaving the engine running. This rest stop was nothing more than a dozen parking places with a picnic table and a portable toilet. There was one other truck parked here, probably got his head down now for the night, but everything else was clear.

His head jerked round, panicky. But he'd seen her pull into the side road with his own eyes. Perhaps the crafty cow had driven straight to Frielingen without actually stopping, which meant she'd come out near a crossroads. Why had he let her get a head start? He was dumbstruck at not finding her here, cowering in her car. Now she could be anywhere.

He ran quickly to the edge of the path that led to the fields and sniffed the air. Nothing. Could she have taken the little field road and driven off that way? He didn't think so. It was no place for a woman with a killer on her back. All he could see was the whispering stems of the cornfield billowing in the wind.

He sighed. His body was so wired he was practically shaking. Now he was going to have to drive round till he found her. He supposed he could let it go: she had nothing on him really, not enough to go to the police. If she did, he'd just say he thought the traffic lights were broken and had followed her lead when she rolled on red. But Onkel Fritz didn't just give up. There was more than one way to skin a cat.

He jumped back in his truck and roared back on to the B6. There wasn't much traffic, so he could see the stretch of road ahead. But there was no Audi in sight; the trail had gone cold. He rammed his fist down on the dashboard.

The B6 ended abruptly and Lars turned left into the village of Frielingen. He drove up and down, struggling to turn his vehicle on the tight bends, but it was a dead end. He lit a cigarette and tapped his fingers on the dashboard. She must live near here somewhere. Perhaps if he just drove round in a rough circle she might double back. He'd find her parked somewhere like a frightened rabbit, trembling, with her eyes all big and her blood pulsing, ready to jump out of her veins.

But the back roads were deserted. Lars felt incredibly visible edging round them in his truck. He was used to doing the "A" roads, riding with his foot down on the *Autobahn*. Not driving in a straight line felt pretty weird. The only folks who drove this road were the suckers who lived there. He was driving in a rage, becoming more exasperated with every turn on the endless deserted country road. His headache was extending from the back of his skull to his crown until the road in front of him narrowed through his maddened eyes. He stopped giving way at junctions and hogged both lanes when he took curves. A few times he stopped, turned the engine off, and rolled both windows down to listen. At night you could hear for over a kilometre. Perhaps he could track her by sound. All he got was the exotic insect sounds of the night; restless crickets. The intense movements in the darkness excited him further.

He could sense her fear – that she was out there somewhere. But the bitch had bolted. He'd tried all the local roads, and now he didn't know what to do. Stupid interfering cow! He started smashing his hand down on the dashboard. He couldn't believe she had escaped him again.

🚗

After being chased, the hardest thing was waiting. Every sense tremulous, Frannie was sitting in the trampled corn-hide of her car. Her breathing was jagged and her blue eyes darted in her pale face. Her heart was beating so hard, all she could hear was its monotonous beat. *Duh duh duh.* She put a hand on her chest as if it were a frightened rabbit she could soothe. Her bump felt more conspicuous than ever. The baby kicked intermittently. She was on her own and her mobile was dead. Dorcas would be going out of her mind by now.

Frannie sat with all the windows rolled down, doing her best to strain all her senses for anyone coming. She was parched, but there was no water or liquid in the car. She had mown down so much corn in her frenzy to hide and now the dry powder dust was making her skin itch. The windscreen and inside of the car were covered in a fine layer of corn dust.

She mustn't sneeze or make any sound, though. It was important to keep still. More than anything she wanted to drink. But she could only torment herself with thoughts of refreshment in the hot and sticky dark.

At first she'd been glad of the night because it had swallowed up the outline of the car where the corn didn't quite cover it, but after some minutes she found the darkness weighed on her. There was a big moon tonight, but what light it offered made things worse; she gasped at the suggestive shadows it cast. Her eyes kept playing tricks with the waving corn ears dancing in the breeze. She couldn't stop her mind from conjuring up terrifying shapes. Sometimes she fancied that the battered corn wanted to wreak its revenge on the car that had mangled it. That, if Lars didn't come, something worse would.

She had no clear way of seeing if Lars came on foot, but her fear of him made it feel as though he was everywhere. There was no way she could run out of this. Her only hope was that if he came after her she could drive off at the last minute. Home was only half a mile away, but she couldn't risk getting out of the car until first light.

It was only 1.35 a.m. Hours to go until dawn. She didn't like to think about the eternal waiting, but nothing would persuade her to leave the relative safety of her hiding place.

She was sticky with sweat and bits of corn were stuck all over her. The car was unforgivably messed up. Where her hands fiercely gripped the steering wheel, her knuckles were white. Beads of sweat had broken out on her brow. The baby kicked its frustration, she felt it dully in her womb. She was trapped and dared not relax, not even for a second.

Lars kept smoking with the windows down. Because he was so tense, the nicotine was hitting him hard, although he couldn't get much enjoyment out of it, felt like throwing up. But he kept going. He'd got a scent of her fear, and his need hung low and heavy on him. Because she'd evaded him he felt flat. He would never amount to anything. Hans was never going to take him back. All the good feelings he had had about their reunion was slipping away.

He was staring at his own tiredness when a sports car out of nowhere overtook him.

The sight of the speeding yellow vehicle galvanised him. He felt a sudden surge in his erection that made his senses quicken. It was a welcome distraction. Inside that sort of car, inevitably there'd be the type of solidly built man that would look good with his shirt off. It was too late for a shift worker to be going to work. What Lars knew was that in the grey hours before dawn few people ventured out.

Lars could not keep his eyes off the car's retreating bumper. He smiled, licked his lips and pushed his foot down hard on the accelerator.

# Chapter
# Twenty-Eight

In the dressing room at the Moonlights Club, Elli touched her forehead, appalled. Had that really happened? She felt like screaming. Her appearance, especially her face, was everything.

The hole was not deep, but its position in the centre of her forehead made it stand out more. It was hideous. Elli stared at it with her mouth open. She had washed it with some cotton wool and waited for the bleeding to stop, which had taken forever, but it had got bigger the more she looked at it. She was deformed.

Hans was already complaining the drugs were wasting her looks. She was already fearful of looking at herself in the mirror. Her knockout good locks were slowly being eroded. No matter what she did, the bones in her face were coming to the surface. And she didn't like what she saw.

This might finish things off; make him decide he didn't want her in his bed any more.

Wincing, she took some foundation and tried to fill it in with make-up. It was painful doing it, but she persevered. But, when it was partially covered, it only drew more attention to it. She could have wailed. That cow!

Seventeen-year-old Nel came in with her big fawn eyes and slanted cheekbones. A look of alarm came over her when she saw Elli there, with good reason. Elli wiped her face quickly with a tissue. Nel was dressed in a bikini with a hipster skirt, and she noticed right away that part of the appliquéd-on jewellery had come off her bikini top.

'What shit is this?' said Elli aggressively. She grabbed Nel by the hair and forced her to sit down. 'You want to look a mess for the customers?' Pretty, dark-skinned Nel was from Cambodia. She'd been sold at thirteen by her parents for the chance of a better life and had been working in brothels around Europe ever since. She was one of the new girls that Hans had bought recently in a bid to hike up profits. She didn't get any pay; they only had to feed her and pay for basic necessities.

'Sorry, boss,' said Nel in her lilting voice, and lowered her head. Her humble apology just made Elli madder. She viciously slapped the girl around the face three times each side until her cheeks were bright pink. Then she lit a cigarette and blew the smoke spitefully in her face.

Still Nel said nothing. Her honey-toned complexion was radiant; her form graceful and petite. Elli felt a stab of jealousy. She pushed Nel roughly to the side.

She felt as if a dark void was about to consume her. The weariness imprisoned her. When she was rock-bottom it was lethargic city. She badly needed meth.

If she wanted a hit perhaps she should see Hans and tell him all about her little encounter meeting his fat bitch. She felt the tension rise to her head. She should have known better – once upon a time she'd have been loyal to Dorcas without a thought, all of them in it together – but being given the responsibility for looking after the new girls had changed her. She liked the power, but it filled her with an uneasy pleasure.

Filled with a brittle self-righteousness, Elli strutted off angrily to Hans's office. With her long legs she ground her heels into the floor with every step. She'd show him what she was made of. When she knocked at his office door and he answered, she swept in. Her mood seemed to shake the very ground.

She'd meant to be reasonable, but when she opened her mouth it all spilled out of her.

'Why didn't you tell me you'd got her knocked up?' she said. 'That fat old slapper.' She practically spat the words out.

Hans sat there in a cream Gucci suit, looking faintly displeased. He touched his fingertips together.

'Who are you talking about?' he said slowly. His eyes bored into hers uncomfortably.

'The English bitch, Dani, whatever her name is. She just came in, wanted me to find an email and then she stuck me with her bloody key! Look!'

Elli pulled her hair back and showed him the dent.

A watchful look came over him. 'Was she heavily pregnant, blonde, English?' he said.

'That's it,' said Elli, nodding. 'Said her name was Dani, that Dorcas sent her.'

'Dorcas?' Hans was hunched over his desk now.

'Yeah, she came to find an email Anna sent that wound up in my spam folder. Dani found it, but it was in English so I still don't know shit,' said Elli.

As she finished her sentence she realised her mistake. The light in her eyes went out. Hans was now standing, his eyes so dark they looked like reptilian slits. His hands were bunched up into fists. Elli froze where she stood. She felt as if she was being sucked into a shadow. She had to have meth now before her whole body went into a spin. She shuddered, her mouth open and shut like a fish.

'Hans please, give me some Tina,' she pleaded. She tried to stop the tears.

Hans just sat aloof as if he hadn't heard her. 'An email from Anna?' he said carefully. 'Dorcas was trying to find an email Anna sent to you?' He stood up. Elli seemed to shrink into the carpet.

She just nodded. Her body felt as if it were dropping in freefall. He was frowning, and she imagined she could see evil thoughts written over his face. She shivered. Jesus, she was shaking so bad! There was usually some in the cabinet by the whiskies. If she could just get a taste, maybe she could deal with this shit.

With an animal cry, she ran to the drinks cabinet and clumsily pulled out the hidden drawer. Everything fell on to the floor.

'*NEIN!*' shouted Hans. Now he was really steaming. The floor was littered with little plastic and foil wraps, the drawer had hit her knee, but she didn't care. She was on her knees, rifling through the merchandise with a smile on her face. Now he was coming up behind her, shouting, but she wasn't listening. Got one! It was in her goddamn hand; she could already taste it in her mouth.

Suddenly there was a whack, like the stormy sound of a train being swallowed by a tunnel that she heard long after she'd fallen unconscious to the darkest place she'd ever known.

# Chapter Twenty-Nine

Because Hans didn't really feel, it was hard for him to respond to others normally. Other people did it automatically, but he had to mimic, constantly fake it. When the girls smiled, he showed his teeth back. What they took for contemplation was simply him planning his next move. If he hadn't have been so good-looking, they would have seen right away that he was a phony. He wasn't a serial killer, but he shared the trait of lack of empathy. And after months of maintaining a calm exterior, when Elli said the wrong thing he'd seized the baseball bat that he kept hidden under his desk and all the angst inside him about the latest kills had rushed out.

He'd cornered the stupid bitch and whacked her. She hadn't even seen it coming. The bat had been light and easy in his hand. It was nothing. He had brought it down on the back of her head until his arms were exhausted and he was breathing so hard he could barely stand.

He was still holding the red-stained bat. The back of Elli's head was matted with blood and she was flat out on her stomach. He tried to calm himself. *People are like maggots, small, blind and worthless.* But he couldn't push away the fact that a second prostitute going missing in his own club was bound to blow up in his face.

Calmly, he poured himself the most expensive whisky in a special glass. That was why he needed Lars. Somehow the guy had the proper proportion. He had his belief, nurtured calculatedly by himself, that he was the reincarnation of Fritz Haarmann and his own ideology of what was the right way: his earthy, hunter's right to eliminate.

Even if he didn't exactly feel sorry, at least Lars *felt*. And killing was, for him, a blessed release, something sacred. The guy actually killed as an act of love. But Hans felt absolutely nothing. Whether he farted or nearly killed someone, he had the same reaction. He wished he could make sense of it. Without Lars he would degenerate into madness.

He looked down at Elli, found a pulse. She was still going strong, even though the back of her was all bashed in. Should he finish her off, get her medical attention or what? *I had a compulsion to do it*. But that was wrong. He didn't feel compulsions; very little registered with him. It was getting harder to maintain the lie. He couldn't access the emotions he should have been able to. Everything had the same weight.

He took out his mobile and called Hugo. It wasn't a good idea, but he had no one else to turn to. Once he would have gone to Lars, but Lars didn't do women. He'd do his nut if he found out.

'It's like a nightmare; I am in a movie,' he said dramatically. Hugo, drunk somewhere, shouted something meaningless. No, mate, this was no drunken boy's talk. Hans sat up very straight.

'Hugo, can you come over to my office, right now? There's a situation,' he said, hoping he wouldn't have to spell it out.

He didn't like to think about all the things Hugo might do with Elli. He needed to check his email account, but he had to admit that it was harder to concentrate now Elli was cluttering the place up. The nearly-dead were so goddamn *ugly*.

After ninety minutes in the cornfield, Frannie could bear it no longer. Her bladder was ready to burst. But Lars knew she was pregnant, might be waiting for this.

With difficulty she removed her panties while still sitting in the driver's seat. Cautiously she stepped out of the car, crouched and began to urinate, holding on to the car door. Her heartbeat was going mad. She was shaking so badly that half of it went down one leg. If Lars came, she'd sit back down, whether she'd finished or not, drive off. But as she finished emptying her bladder there was only endless waving corn whispering in the darkness.

For hours she'd fought off drowsiness with her fear. But when the sky turned grey she couldn't stop her eyes from closing. She was too exhausted to remain alert. It was time to go home.

She stepped outside the car, crouched down and looked carefully in all directions. Nothing. Dawn was coming. Surely Lars had gone by now? It occurred to her that the farmer would be in the field soon and he'd be furious with her for wrecking his corn. Best to move fast.

Frannie got back into the car and tried to shut the door without making a noise. Shit, she thought. This is it. She had to get out of the field without sending herself up in flames. Her fingers hesitated on the key. As long as she didn't remain stationary for too long she'd be alright, but she had to reverse first and turn around fast, a hard feat on such an uneven surface. If Lars was still out there, he'd hear her as soon as she started the engine.

She counted to three, then forced herself to turn the ignition key. She reversed so quickly the car skidded and she had to fight to keep control of it, steady her breathing.

Now she was moving. The easiest thing was to follow the path she'd mown down on the way in. Swiftly she turned, trying to follow her earlier trail, and drove back to the farm path. But it was hard work over the rough earth. The engine seemed to groan more than usual but she made her way raggedly back and went the other way to the road.

She'd be home in three minutes. The car was battered by its ordeal, but she'd made it.

She drove slowly up the lane, still holding her breath. Even from the inside the car looked battered and filthy. There was no way she could get away with a secret night-drive. What would Kurt say? Her lower lip trembled. *All this for nothing.*

When she pulled into her drive, her heart sank. Although it wasn't yet five a.m., the lights were on downstairs. She'd been hoping for an hour or so to wash, do something with the car, but he must have noticed her absence. As she waddled into the house, it occurred to her she still didn't have any knickers on.

Nervously, she opened the door. She sneaked into the kitchen and began drinking a litre bottle of Evian water as fast as she could. She was still slugging it when Kurt appeared with shadows under his eyes, as though he hadn't slept either. He did a double-take at her frazzled appearance.

'What the hell, Frannie?' said Kurt in such a broken voice she didn't know how to react.

'I know you told me not to drive,' said Frannie hesitantly, pushing her untidy hair off her face. 'But it was an emergency. I had to help a friend and then I got chased...' She broke off, rubbed her tired eyes with her hands. 'For hours I've waited in the cornfield out back, Kurt.'

'You drove into a *cornfield* in my car?' said Kurt in such a tone of horror that Frannie flinched.

She nodded. Kurt gave a roar and ran outside. When he saw the state of the car he jumped up and down on the spot with anger.

'Who would do that?' he shouted to himself. He fingered the many scratches on the paintwork and put his fingers sorrowfully in the dust marks. Frannie stood behind him, silent, still drinking the water. Kurt carried on ranting about the state of his car. The neighbours were going to be woken up again.

'You stupid cow!' he said. He glared at her as if he hated her. Frannie felt deflated. All he was bothered about was the car. He hadn't even asked who had chased her. 'I suppose your fancy friend with her cute-ass bob made you do this!' shouted Kurt.

Frannie looked at him as if she couldn't believe her ears. 'How do you know what she looks like?'

Kurt suddenly stopped carrying on, wouldn't look in her eye. He rubbed his hand absently through his hair. He no longer looked sullen, but guilty. She sucked in her breath. She had no idea what could have caused this change.

'When you went, I looked in your things and found a card,' said Kurt slowly, with nervous hands. He had a downcast mouth and haunted eyes. She didn't quite want to hear what he was going to say next. 'I phoned the number and she told me to come over, that you would be heading there.' He was talking as if he'd learned it by rote. All his anger, the sullenness was gone. 'You know what she is, Frannie?' he said in a meek voice.

Frannie bit her lip. She knew what was coming.

'I…' His voice trailed off, then he covered his face with his hands, started to sob. Frannie was gobsmacked.

'You *slept* with her?' she asked in a low voice. She was so horrified it was hard to say it out loud. She hoped none of the neighbours was hearing this.

'Not sex, not like we have.' Kurt was sniffing, wiping his eyes. Frannie's stomach lurched. She felt nauseous.

'What then, Kurt?'

'Everything else,' he said.

The betrayal soaked into her like squirts of lime. 'How could you?' she screamed. Almost instantly, she felt a wave of nausea hit her. She ran back into the house and rushed to the bathroom. She retched until there was nothing in her stomach. She sat on the edge of the bath and washed her face and hands. How could they do this to her? Dorcas had forced her to put herself in danger and this was the thanks she got. And her husband was only worried about his precious car.

She sat on the edge of the bath, her mind racing. Her heartbeat seemed to be running out of control. She clenched her hands into fists. This was the worst night of her life. She looked up at her reflection in the bathroom mirror and looked with disgust at her tired, bloated face. Bits of corn were stuck in her long blonde hair. Even she was amazed at how frightful she looked. Since falling pregnant she seemed to have aged ten years. Perhaps that was why Kurt had lost interest. She sighed heavily.

Her husband suddenly appeared in the doorway, his face all tense and messed up.

'This thing you were doing,' he said, being surprisingly careful how he phrased it. 'Is it about a *man*?'

Frannie felt a rush of emotions sweep through her. She frowned and he leapt at her hesitancy, nodded as if she was the guilty one. 'I see,' he said tersely.

'It's not what you think,' she said quickly, her indignation making her blush.

He bit his lips. 'IT IS A MAN!' he shouted aggressively, but he wasn't up for a fight. Without a word he turned away from her and got ready for work.

'Kurt, that's not it...' said Frannie angrily, going after him. She was about to tell him everything, but he pushed her away.

'I've said all I've got to say,' he said forcefully. 'When I do shit, at least I tell it to you straight.' What scared her was his almost polite, detached tone as if he no longer cared what she did or thought. *We have gone beyond sarcasm*, she thought. 'I'm taking this,' he said, grabbing his car key. 'You're never driving that car again.'

He flounced out. Frannie heard the roar as he drove up the lane. She made her way up to bed, showered quickly and pulled a nightdress on. She was in shock, exhausted, at her wits' end. Later she could think about this whole mess. She lay in bed and hoped for oblivion.

But she was too messed up. It felt as if she'd been hit sideways by a tornado. The tears just wouldn't stop. Bitterly, she cried herself to sleep.

# Chapter Thirty

For all Stefan's training, it had been hard getting the man out of the box. Hugo had helped him. They'd worked together enough in Afghanistan and were accustomed to scraping up shit: bomb victims, acid attacks, obstructed fistulas from the local women, all kinds of crazy stuff. Hugo had been a top-rate nurse, absolutely dedicated. But the war had changed him, had changed *them*; the hideous meanness of dirty fighting, so many lives pointlessly ruined. Now Stefan didn't know what he was doing. *Times change,* he thought.

Stefan knew stuff from the wallet. That Tomek was Polish, twenty-four, O Rh. negative, allergic to penicillin, and he'd suffered so badly lying untended in the hard metal box that he'd managed to get first-degree pressure sores around his spine. The skin was permanently red, wouldn't go white when prodded. Didn't look serious at first glance, but he'd seen what could happen to untreated bed sores.

He closed his eyes. Around the fleshy genital region, where the guy had urinated and lay trapped in his own shit, it had advanced to the second stage. He'd ignored the superficial head injuries, the cigarette burns on his tongue, but he'd grimaced when he got out the PVC gloves and cleaned him up. It hurt Tomek to be touched on his buttocks even with baby wipes; ulcers had already formed.

Stefan's face had darkened at the sight of the maltreatment.

'Who cares?' Hugo had said roughly, 'he's going be harvested anyway. This patient is destined to die.'

Stefan had ground his teeth at that. Hugo had changed so much that he didn't know who he was any more. What they were doing was terrible, but he'd expected high-tech drips, to administer saline, change the occasional adult nappy. Tomek was being treated as badly as a neglected lab animal. And he was so out of it, he couldn't speak up for himself.

Stefan had carefully showered the man down with lukewarm water, placed him in clean cotton and made him comfortable on a makeshift bed in the old machine room. Every two hours, without fail, he carefully changed the man's position, rubbed in special lotion to improve the skin texture and packed foam around the injuries to rest them as much as possible. He also inserted a saline drip and a catheter tube and neatly bandaged the man's facial wounds.

It was exhausting. Most of the time Stefan longed to call an ambulance. There were times his every action seemed pointless. The patient would only be alive until enough donors had been matched for the major organs. It ran counter to all his training.

But, he told himself, if the pressures sores advanced to the fourth and final stage the organs would be compromised. The patient could get septicemia, gangrene, or renal failure. He could die before his organs could be utilised.

Whatever the outcome, it was his responsibility to keep the man healthy, for now. If he told himself that often enough, maybe he'd begin to believe it.

🚗

Hugo came quickly to Hans's office. Although he acted the wild party boy, in reality he was sharp and ruthlessly efficient.

Hans observed with distaste Hugo's sagging jeans, the T-shirt stained with beer. But as soon as he came in and saw Elli on the floor he sobered up. The efficient nurse in him sized up the situation.

'Annoyed you, did she?' he said impassively. He had an uncanny way of reading a situation. He bent down, felt her wrist to determine her pulse, examined the wound and shone a torch into her eyes.

Hans watched everything he did with tolerance. Most of the time he saw the world without colour; it was hard for him to understand why other people got so emotional about so little. He could relate to Hugo's genius for rational thinking. Neither of them had time for trivialities.

'How long has she been out?' asked Hugo. He didn't seem interested in who had struck her.

Hans looked carefully at his watch. 'I hit her thirty-seven minutes ago. She went out like a light.'

'She's got concussion,' said Hugo, looking carefully at the wound. 'The problem is that she's been hit right at the back of the neck, where the brain stem is.'

'But it's not bleeding much, is it?' said Hans, with a little yawn. 'She'll be able to recover if I leave her outside a hospital?' His face was stiff; he spoke like a robot just learning to talk. With Hugo he didn't need to mimic; he'd sussed out his condition the first time they'd met.

'It would be better actually if she had an open fracture,' said Hugo neutrally. 'The skull is hard and brittle, so it can't expand to repair the damage. And there's no room for extra blood if she's got a bleed.' He closed her eyes manually and turned to Hans. 'If you want her to live she needs a hospital: CT scan, the works.' His face was serious. 'And if she wakes up and identifies you as her assailant then you're in big trouble.' He looked pointedly at Hans. 'Make up your mind quickly.' He smiled and raised his eyebrows expectantly.

'Shit!' said Hans, drinking a gulp of whisky. 'I don't need this right now.'

'The organs of addicts are less attractive,' said Hugo, kneeling next to Elli's body. 'And if blood tests show she has hepatitis or HIV they're of no use at all.' He looked down at her as if she were already a corpse. His voice was neutral. 'But most likely we'll be able to make money from her.'

Hans frowned. He played with his fingers pensively like a piano player warming up.

Hugo looked at him. 'It's not as if there's going to be any hard feelings, is there? You don't give a shit about anything.'

Hans still said nothing.

'I'll take that as a yes, then, shall I?' said Hugo. He was clumsy, but effective at getting what he wanted. The speed at which he and Hugo had started doing business was startling. Hugo sold people: live ones for work, and soon-to-be-dead ones for organs. He didn't mess about getting poor people to sell a kidney; the bastard wanted the lot.

Hans felt a twinge, as if he'd just eaten something that disagreed with him. Elli had annoyed him, but he'd only wanted to teach her a lesson, hadn't meant to whack her that hard. The thought of her body, which he'd enjoyed, being cut up and sold was startling. He felt like a small grain of sand facing the merciless force of an oncoming storm. Should he just succumb to the inevitable ruthlessness? When he closed his eyes he felt the rush of the wind, the spray from the roaring waves. This was real life. The weak were nothing but prey.

He couldn't work out which option was less trouble. 'Could she recover?'

Hugo shrugged his shoulders. 'Without a CT scan it's impossible to say, but she's been out a while and one pupil's blown so there's definitely a bleed in there.' He stood up, poured himself a whisky. 'Don't think of the girl, think of her organs. There's a lot of money lying there,' said Hugo with a shrug of his shoulders.

Hans frowned. It was unsettling meeting someone who gave less of a shit than he did. He was used to being the sociopath without empathy. Hugo was going to make him a shedload of money, but he was so calculated he made Hans feel almost human. The guy would sell his grandmother for a pair of new shoelaces.

'And there's another problem,' said Hugo slowly, sipping his drink. 'This gay-killer in the papers. You realise that could be Lars, right? I read they're taking DNA samples from lorry drivers. If they catch him, it will lead the police straight to us.' Hugo smiled. 'Looks like you're going to have to lose your rag again.'

Hans paled. 'Leave Lars out of this!' he said in an angry voice. Hugo stood up and rubbed his hands. He gave Hans a funny look. Hans ignored him. Could Lars have already become a disorganised killer on the outside? He couldn't afford to have police sniffing around, not now! He bit his lip in frustration. He couldn't explain it to Hugo, but he still needed Lars. He didn't want to get rid of him…couldn't. Hugo would never understand.

He sighed. Hugo was the one who'd introduced him to human trafficking. The margins were much higher than dealing in drugs or prostitution. But Hugo was a cocky fuck. He wasn't loyal like Lars. Sooner or later he'd become a problem like a ripple far out at sea that eventually becomes a huge wave that will knock you off your feet.

He could feel the burn of the whisky as it went down into his stomach; imagined his whole body being tossed around in a stormy ocean. Part of him longed to be swept away, to finally feel something other than his pithy bond with Lars.

'Phone Stefan,' said Hans finally. 'See if he'll take her.'

'Another one for the fire,' said Hugo.

Hans didn't have a clue what he was talking about. But that didn't worry him.

The thing inside Lars had evaporated. All the funny tingling had gone from his legs. Now he just wanted to sleep, but he had something to do first. The English bitch had outrun him, but he'd show her.

He turned back in the direction of the B6 and shot off towards Garbsen. He decided to make an impromptu drop-in on Inspector Koch. Not only could he see if they had any leads on the gas station murder, he wanted to wangle Frannie's address out of him. Although Koch was police, he was a good 'un. And he had to admit he was curious to know how close they were to his trail.

He smiled, licked his lips. His brown eyes shone brightly. They couldn't do without him, and good ol' Onkel Fritz knew a lot about the latest murder. Ha ha. He laughed, wiped his mouth. Softly, softly does it. Mustn't let his tongue run away with him.

Inspector Koch was grey-haired but energetic and instantly offered him a coffee and a filled *brötchen* when he arrived. When the other officer had gone out of the room he put a generous slug of whisky into Lars's drink. They grinned. Both of them drank heavily on the job.

'So I heard about this so-called gay-killer?' said Lars, taking out a cigarette.

'Yeah, we've had a lot of missing men in a certain age range, and some of them a confirmed type, if you know what I mean,' said Koch, with a sly grin. He made a slack hand signal, then stopped himself. 'No offence, eh?'

Lars grinned like a pup having its tummy tickled. 'So you got any evidence? Going to making any arrests soon?'

Koch twirled himself in his swivel chair. 'There was something. One of the CCTV cameras at the gas station recorded a lorry parked up around the estimated time of death.'

Lars tried not to flinch, to keep the smile on his face broad. 'Aha,' he said with a flourish.

'We sent it off to a special lab in Hamburg, got to have it enhanced and shit. But it's a significant clue.'

'So why do you think this guy's doing it?' said Lars, hoping his voice didn't sound too strained.

'*Lustmord*. The guy gets off on it. This was a crime of passion, if you like that kind of thing,' said Koch with a sly grin. 'But it's early days yet.' He looked down at the floor. 'Actually, we're collecting DNA samples from all known lorry drivers to eliminate people. Would you mind letting me scrape your cheek while you're here?'

Lars laughed and drank his coffee in one slurp. 'Not at all, mate,' he said grinning from ear to ear. 'Be my guest.'

Koch took out the necessary kit. Swiftly he took the sample and put it in the mail tray to be sent off to the lab.

Inwardly Lars was reeling. He knew his DNA would be all over the guy they'd found. It was only a matter of time. He felt his head go tight, as if a migraine was going to spring itself on him.

So, now he had nothing to lose.

'You know that English woman that had an accident because of me?' Lars broached the subject lightly. His eyes looked soft, as if he couldn't hurt a fly. 'I've been feeling bad about it – could you give me her address? I want to send her some flowers or something.'

Koch's prematurely lined face grinned and he tapped on his keyboard. 'And they say the age of chivalry is dead.'

Lars made himself give a little smile, but inside his rage was screeching at full volume. He'd show the bitch not to play games with him. Before he was done with her she was going to be very sorry indeed. He'd show her she had no hiding place.

# Chapter
# Thirty-One

Frannie woke up to the blazing heat of mid-afternoon. Although she'd slept over eight hours, she still felt exhausted. The memory of last night hung heavy on her. Kurt's betrayal still stung. Her stomach felt volatile, as if it might erupt. The physical after-effects of her night in the field were kicking in. Even though she'd drunk nearly a litre of Evian it still felt as though she'd eaten sand. Her whole body was one big ache, and she found her ankles had swollen cruelly in the heat. She'd be lucky if she had a pair of shoes in the house that fitted.

On the way to the bathroom she had to kick her way through the unwashed clothes piled up on the floor. Her personal items were fighting for space with Kurt's on every flat surface. She sighed, rubbed a hand over her face. She was fat with his child and he was more distant than ever. All around her was evidence of their crumbling relationship. And now he'd been with Dorcas. She grimaced.

In the night she'd fantasised about taking a hammer to his car, cutting up all his clothes with scissors. But if she did these things he'd only feel sorrow for his mangled objects. What she wanted, what she needed, was for him to care about hurting her. That was the problem with Kurt: he made a fetish of his possessions but somehow hurt feelings didn't count. He worried about how she'd damaged his car, but not at her terror of being in the cornfield.

Frannie had just finished dressing when the doorbell rang. A young dark-haired man stood on the doorstep grasping a bunch of flowers. There were beautiful red gerberas and pretty pink carnations. Frannie smiled.

'Frau Snell?' the young man said with a smile.

Frannie nodded.

'For you,' he said, 'I hope you enjoy them.'

Frannie took the flowers into the kitchen. Perhaps Kurt did care after all. Maybe this was his way of saying sorry with a gesture. When she was putting them in a vase she noticed the little Interflora card. She opened it and read:

Dear Frau Snell,
I wanted to apologise for causing you to have a car accident.
With best wishes,
Lars Stiglegger

Frannie's eyes widened in alarm, and she let out an anguished howl. He knew where she lived! He could be outside right now. And because he'd sent her a nice note with flowers, she could hardly complain to the police. He was letting her know he was on to her. The bastard knew what he was doing.

With trembling fingers she punched in Dorcas's number. She'd been putting it off, but now she had no choice.

Dorcas picked it up after one ring.

'Where the hell have you been?' said Dorcas, angrily. 'I've been up half the night waiting for you.'

Frannie was taken aback by the venom in her voice; she'd been expecting an apology. All her terror and fury from last night surged up in her. She could strangle the bitch.

'You've been with my husband! What the hell have you done?' screamed Frannie. If Dorcas had been there she would have slapped her.

'I'm a sex worker, Frannie, it's what I do,' said Dorcas in a weary voice. 'I didn't charge him, and we didn't do anything you'd be interested in.'

'You didn't treat him like a client! What is he, your new lover?' Frannie's eyes filled with tears. Her hand holding the phone was shaking uncontrollably.

'I think Anna and Tomek are dead. That I might be next!' said Dorcas in such a desperate voice it chilled Frannie to the bone. 'I was in such a bad place, I would have done anything to get out of it.'

'But why Kurt?' asked Frannie. She spoke in such a hurt voice that even Dorcas started getting upset.

'I'm sorry,' said Dorcas. Her voice broke off. 'I was vulnerable and he was frustrated… it just happened.' Her voice trailed off, as if she was trying to hide further details.

Frannie didn't want to listen any more, had to resist the urge to slam the phone down. But they had Hans and Lars on their backs. She coughed, tried to put it aside and make her voice neutral.

'We've got stuff to talk about,' she said, strained. 'At the club I didn't get a copy of the email. I read it, but Elli went mental so I couldn't forward it, and then Lars…' Her voice broke off for a second, she let out a sob. 'He was waiting outside in the car park.' She stopped, burst into tears. 'He followed me and I had to drive into a cornfield and hide. I was there the whole night.' Reliving her ordeal, she couldn't stop herself from crying. She was shaking, with her head in her hands.

Dorcas made little noises of comfort. 'Are you alright?' she said, eventually.

'Yes. I tried to phone you but there was no signal and when I came back, Kurt...' Frannie broke off and Dorcas tutted.

'Frannie, I'm so sorry. I didn't mean that to happen. I asked him to come over because you were meant to be coming here.'

Frannie took a deep breath. At this moment she hated Dorcas for what she had done. She swallowed. It was taking all her willpower just to speak to her.

'There's more,' said Frannie, her voice rising. 'Lars just sent me flowers through Interflora.'

Dorcas spluttered her trademark, 'What? You have to get out of there,' she went on, her tone urgent. 'Just pack a bag and drive to me. Lars or Hans could attack us at any time.'

'I have no car.' Frannie started trembling.

'Call a taxi, then. Just do it!'

Frannie had to sit down suddenly. Her heart was racing furiously.

'Just get here as fast as you can,' said Dorcas, 'I'm going to start packing now. We both have to get away.'

'What shall I tell Kurt?' said Frannie, still hesitant.

'Nothing,' said Dorcas. 'It's safer that way.'

Frannie swallowed.

'It would be no great surprise to him if you left now anyway, right?' said Dorcas.

Frannie squirmed. In her mind's eye she imagined Kurt kissing Dorcas's thin, glamorous face, tried to block it out. Her knowledge of the betrayal was like drinking agonising poison. The more she thought about it, the worse it hurt.

Mechanically she put together her things. She felt incapable of rational thought. Her mind was endlessly playing images of Dorcas and Kurt: kissing, touching, being intimate. She was sick of torturing herself with the imagined details of their passion. She didn't want to, but now she knew about it she couldn't stop herself. And the worst of it was, she understood perfectly why he would prefer Dorcas to her.

🚗

Frannie already had her hospital bag ready, so she only needed to add some extra clothes, but she had no idea how long she'd be gone for. In the end she packed a large suitcase. *I'm practically moving out*, she thought. Perhaps Kurt would get the message.

She was exhausted and the baby kicked her for all he was worth, but there was no time to lose. She rang a taxi. Her life had been so humdrum; now she was running away into the unknown.

She barely breathed on the thirty-minute cab-drive to Dorcas's. The busy city streets were chock-full of traffic. Again and again the taxi driver swore under his breath and the cars could only crawl as they waited behind endless red lights. Frannie was glad she wasn't driving.

The taxi stopped in a pleasant, tree-lined street. Dorcas lived in an apartment on the second floor. With difficulty Frannie made her way up the stairs carrying her heavy suitcase. When she rang the doorbell she was out of breath and sweating heavily. She was dreading seeing Dorcas again after what had gone on with Kurt. Her husband had always been too handsome for her, making her nervous around pretty women.

The door opened. Dorcas stood there like a rock star, immaculately dressed in a dark purple silk top and skirt that showed off her slimness to perfection. Some fancy gothic bead jewellery completed the look. Frannie felt her jealousy flare. She staggered back. Perhaps she couldn't do this.

Dorcas looked at her with surprise.

'Why didn't you phone me? I would have helped you with your things!' said Dorcas with a frown, looking at her heavy luggage. She virtually pulled Frannie inside and gave her a hug. Frannie flinched and half-pushed her off impatiently. Dorcas said nothing, but there was a hurt look on her face. Frannie tried to compose herself.

It was the first time she'd been to Dorcas's. It wasn't what she'd expected. She was almost blinded by the all-white minimalist décor of the long rooms with their graceful high ceilings. Everything was neatly organised; the rooms seemed to breathe energy and efficiency. And, just to add a bit of colour, Dorcas had a riot of flowers growing everywhere in pots. Frannie looked around in wonder. She had a feeling of instant serenity just being there.

Then she thought of Kurt, and how this was another reason he would prefer Dorcas. The vision soured.

'I just need a few minutes and then we can go,' said Dorcas.

Frannie sat down. 'Where are we going?'

'The Dreams Hotel,' said Dorcas. 'It's a spa as well. It's close by, but I don't think anyone would dream of looking for us there.' She slipped on a pair of improbably high heels. 'Wait here,' she said, 'I'll load the car.'

Frannie was trying to imagine how Kurt would have felt in this flat; presumably a damn sight better than at home. She felt the ghost of their sexual encounter mocking her, imagined them writhing together on the white leather sofa. She couldn't look at Dorcas now without feverishly wondering what exactly she'd done with her husband.

She rubbed a hand over her eyes. Their sex life had never been all that great. He had seemed to want her so much that until they'd married she hadn't realised there wasn't enough between them. Then she thought of all the kinky tricks Dorcas would know. She was torturing herself again. She had to fight not to burst into tears. Her insides were churning as if she'd swallowed bleach.

Every second she stayed there, it just got worse.

According to the satnav it was a twelve-minute drive to the hotel, but, by driving through amber lights and cutting everyone up, Dorcas did it eight minutes. Frannie was so shaken by the experience that she could barely stand when she got out of the car.

'I used to live in Berlin,' said Dorcas by way of explanation. 'You'll never get anywhere if you don't use a bit of push.'

'Is that what you did with Kurt?' said Frannie crossly.

Dorcas frowned. 'It just happened, damn it!' she snapped, throwing the suitcases onto the ground. 'When you met me I was sitting in my van waiting for customers to turn up. Sex is my job.' She slammed the car boot and carried everything into the lobby area.

Frannie bit her lip. How on earth was she going to get through this? The idea of staying with Dorcas repulsed her.

The hotel faced a big lake, the Maschsee, which had been constructed by unemployed labourers under Hitler's regime. There was water as far as the eye could see, and the lake was lined with thickly wooded forest. The hotel was a long, low building overlooking the water. Although they were still in the centre of Hannover, with the top of the majestic town hall sticking out to prove it, it felt as if they were in the middle of nowhere.

'How are we going to do this?' said Frannie, an awkward look on her face.

'I'll pay a few nights, cash in advance,' said Dorcas. 'That way we can't be traced.'

Dorcas booked a double room. Most German hotels had two single beds pushed together, but when they got to the room there was only the one big bed. *Shit.* She'd have to lie next to her. Frannie felt sick. It was humiliating having to do that.

She sprawled on the bed and watched while Dorcas neatly unpacked. She didn't feel like doing anything; after all the upset she was feeling downright peculiar. She pressed a hand to her stomach; to her surprise a hard jerk, like an electric shock, radiated out from her uterus.

'Ow,' she said, clutching her stomach.

'What?' said Dorcas.

'Something really weird just happened. A hard pain,' said Frannie, pressing her stomach. She felt hot and faint. 'Oh, God, I hope that wasn't a contraction.'

Dorcas hurriedly got her a drink of water and made her gulp it down.

'It's just all a bit much,' said Frannie weakly. The patterns on the floral wallpaper in the room seemed to be swirling. She'd missed several gynaecology appointments, and presumably her blood pressure was sky-high. Nervously, she held her stomach. Dorcas sat next to her on the bed.

'So what about this email, then?' said Dorcas. Her face was impassive under her smooth bob as Frannie told her everything that had happened.

'Elli thought you were pregnant with Hans's child?' said Dorcas incredulously. Frannie looked at her suspiciously. 'I don't know where she got that idea from.'

'But what do you think it means?' said Frannie. 'They're going to fly people away to operate on them? Why?'

'I overheard something,' said Dorcas playing with the beads on her necklace. 'Hans was involved with a bit of crime – selling drugs, knock-off goods, that sort of thing – and then this guy Hugo arrived.' She, touched her chin, took a deep breath. 'I think Hugo sells people. Some girls came into the club and I don't think they earned.'

Frannie sat up. 'You mean sex slaves?' Her voice was breathy with emotion. 'And you never did anything?'

'It was just a suspicion,' said Dorcas stiffly. 'But most of the girls are in it for the lifestyle. Some go under because of drugs, or the customers get too much.' She grimaced and her face creased with worry. 'But I can tell when someone is broken.'

Frannie gasped. She'd gone in there with no inkling of what she was getting into.

'But what does this have to do with operations?' asked Frannie. She hadn't been able to figure out the email.

'I'm not sure I even want to think about that,' said Dorcas.

Frannie stared. Her blonde hair was sticking up all over the place. Dorcas's brown eyes looked scared. She looked at the wall as if she didn't dare confront Frannie with it directly.

'The fastest-growing crime in the world is organ trafficking. You can make hundreds of thousands of euros from one single body if you harvest the organs. I read about it in the *HAZ*.'

Frannie sat up. Her abdomen twitched again. She fell back on her pillow. When the pain passed, she turned to Dorcas in panic. 'Let's get out of Hannover. We can't help Tomek or Anna if they've been cut up. It's too late.'

'That's just it,' said Dorcas in a gentle voice. 'First they have to match the donor to the recipients, then they fly everyone to a hospital somewhere foreign, and do the operations all together so the organs are fresh.'

'You mean Anna and Tomek could be still alive, waiting?' whispered Frannie, stunned.

'Yeah, so we have to find this Stefan guy, the one who was babysitting them in the email,' said Dorcas. They stared at each other. Frannie felt terrified.

'You mean we're not just going to lie low?' she asked, quietly.

'Afraid not. Stefan must be a contact of Hugo's. If we stake out the club, follow him, maybe he'll lead us there.' Dorcas had never looked so dramatic.

Frannie flinched. 'You're going to do that?' she said. 'I don't have a car here.'

'Hugo knows me,' said Dorcas energetically, as though she was planning a war. 'You're going to have to take my car. I'll hide in the back seat.'

Frannie collapsed back onto the pillows and stared mournfully at the ceiling. Her face was wet with tears. 'I can't,' she said. When Dorcas moved closer to her she pushed her off, hysterical. For five minutes Frannie screamed and cried and punched the pillow repeatedly. She wailed out her despair with a sorrow that was beyond words.

Eventually she collapsed. Dorcas took Frannie in her arms and rocked her. 'Shhh, shhh,' she whispered, stroking her hair.

Frannie went limp. She didn't want to leave the room, or to have any more adventures. She just wanted to lie down. It was only the afternoon, but she fell into a feverish sleep.

Her uterus continued to spasm periodically, but she was too far gone to notice.

# Chapter Thirty-Two

During the hot and stifling afternoon, Frannie slept fitfully. The bed was hard, the shiny fabric of the cover pressed into her skin. The curtains were drawn to give a fake darkness, which only seemed to emphasise the glaring sun outside. She was hot and fed up, too tired to do anything but doze.

Dorcas stayed with her. Frannie was conscious of her rapid movements like a little bird. For hours she was in and out of the bathroom. Frannie couldn't imagine what she was doing. When her mobile rang she shut herself in the bathroom and talked extra quietly.

*I hope I can trust her!* With her connection to both Lars and Hans, she wondered where Dorcas's true loyalties lay. And there was something different about her, perhaps the shape of her face, a mysterious quality she couldn't quite put her finger on…

She woke up when Dorcas lit up. The sharp unmistakable smell of cigarette smoke cut through the fetid air. Frannie nearly gagged. She heaved herself out of bed, muttering crossly, and pushed the bathroom door open.

Frannie gasped. Dorcas was holding a cosmetic mirror which had three neat lines of white powder cut onto it. Her index finger elegantly pressed one nostril closed as she held a rolled bill to the other one. A lit cigarette burned in an ashtray. Even when Frannie came in, she carried on snorting with great efficiency.

Frannie stared. 'What you doing?' she said, the heat making her temper rise.

Dorcas gave her an indolent smile. 'Just a few lines of really good coke. Nothing for you to worry about.' Dorcas did another line and threw her head back. Her features softened as a look of wonderment washed over her face. Frannie clenched her teeth. The bitch looked as if she'd just come. She had no bloody shame!

Frannie wrenched the mirror out of her hands and threw the powder down the sink.

'*NEIN!*' shrieked Dorcas. Her good mood vanished. She fought with Frannie to stop her from turning the tap on, but it was no good. Frannie grimly washed every last speck away.

'You're not doing that shit here with me.' Frannie seemed to grow inches taller as she confronted Dorcas. She handed her back the dripping mirror.

Dorcas looked at it in horror. '*Scheisse!*' she shouted. She scrabbled like a rabbit digging a hole for any last traces. But it was gone. She turned angrily to Frannie; her sharp eyes vicious. 'If you had ever been normal, ever had any fun, you would think nothing of this!' shouted Dorcas. She held a hand to her face, wiped the residue of powder from her nose. 'And I paid for the room!' Dorcas stood there sizing her up.

'So what? I've left my husband, everything,' shouted Frannie. 'Do you think I'm going to let you mess it up with this shit?'

She'd been itching to punish the hussy. Her anger reared up. *I'll show her*. She couldn't stop herself. Her hands pushed Dorcas roughly and she yelped. Frannie felt of surge of satisfaction. She gave her another shove. This time Dorcas's legs gave way and, with a squeal, she landed in the bath.

'What, you're going to send me on a mission whilst you're high? Think again!' Frannie spat out the last word. She leaned over her, her face flushed, her hair falling onto Dorcas's face. She surprised herself with her ferocity.

Dorcas was a sight sitting in the bath. Her heavy eye make-up was smudged like a one-eyed panda. Inwardly Frannie rejoiced.

But then her womb hurt as if someone had struck her from within. She clutched a hand to her stomach. She let go of the shower attachment and it clunked in the bath.

'Ow!' screamed Dorcas, her hands rushing to her forehead. 'That hit me on the head.'

'Fuck you,' said Frannie, but there was no conviction in her voice. She waddled slowly to the bed and tried to lie back down, find a comfortable spot, but the pain continued. It was like nothing she'd felt before. She could feel the blood rushing to her head and had no idea what to do. Maybe this was normal at the end of a pregnancy.

She watched Dorcas climb out of the bath like a long-legged spider extracting itself. She walked slowly to the bed. Frannie noticed again how fine-boned she was; the way she practically glided across the floor. The other woman's presence maddened her. Dorcas stood there with her hands on her hips.

'If we find out where Stefan lives, we'll get the evidence,' said Dorcas. Her hard face was resolute. 'Then everything goes back to normal.'

'I've left my husband,' said Frannie sarcastically. 'I've left normal.'

'And I've left Hans,' said Dorcas with a smirk.

'So what?' shouted Frannie, 'He's just a pimp!'

'We're more alike than you think,' said Dorcas archly. She pointed her face at Frannie. The gloom accentuated her pointed features. She'd smoothed out her bob.

Frannie glared at her helplessly. Why did Dorcas always look so bloody invincible? She was constantly pushing, needing something from her. And, being heavily pregnant, she wasn't exactly up for a fight. She tensed as the next spasm kicked in.

'When you were asleep I called a bouncer at Moonlights,' said Dorcas. The coke had done something to her: she couldn't stop pacing around, doing things with her hands. 'He's going to text me the second Hugo arrives.'

'And you've got no idea when that's going to be?'

''Fraid not,' said Dorcas, who, after running out of things to do, had started unpacking Frannie's things.

'Fabulous,' said Frannie sarcastically. She lay back on the pillow. The thought of having to follow someone without being caught, and drive at the same time, in a strange car, filled her with horror. It was harder for her to concentrate when she didn't know where she was going. She blinked, tried not to crack up. Dorcas was watching her like a hawk.

Even though compared to her experience in the cornfield, she had a bed, a toilet and all the water she could drink, once again she was trapped.

🚗

Eventually they'd put her on the floor behind the sofa. Elli was not moving much or saying anything. Most of the time she just had her eyes closed. Idly, Hans wondered if a coma was like sleep. Maybe she was having one long dazzling dream, a little vacation for the brain. Jeffrey Dahmer had tried to turn his victims into zombies by drilling holes into their skulls and injecting hydrochloric acid.

But her neatly bandaged head only looked ridiculous. It looked as though damaging their heads was a waste of time. They didn't turn into zombies or sex slaves; they were just broken. *Kaputt.* Elli's plight irritated him.

Dahmer – now there was a serial killer. Handsome, blended in, killed over an astonishingly long period until he let the darkness take over. Hans walked over to Elli's limp body and spoke as if he was addressing a conference.

*'I don't even know if I have the capacity for normal emotions or not because I haven't cried in a long time. You just stifle them for so long that maybe you lose them, partially at least.* That's Jeffrey, one of the best.'

He eyed her. Every few hours she got paler. Hugo had gone to sort something out, but he was taking his time. He wasn't sure what was going on. It didn't make much odds to him, apart from the question of the money, but there was some kind of problem with Stefan. The whole lynchpin of their operation was having a tantrum; objected, apparently, to the victims being maltreated. Idiot! He laughed to himself. These bleeding-heart types. Once you'd decided to kill someone you'd already done the worst thing you could to them. He thought of the Crossbow Cannibal: *The path of the righteous man is beset on all sides.* But people didn't see that rationally. When it had just been Lars and him, things had been simpler. It was easier killing strangers.

He peered again over the edge of the sofa. Elli just lay still. He frowned. He wondered whether she was capable of feeling anything. He went to the side and crouched down. With a light hand he tapped her head. 'Knock, knock. Anyone in there?' he shouted. Nothing. He laughed, wiped his mouth. An odd look came over his face, as if he was about to do something bad. With curious fingers he pinched her arm hard, to see if she reacted. There was no cry, or attempt to move away.

When nothing happened instantly, he looked at his watch. He'd do it for two minutes. He kept annoying the skin. Still her face was lifeless.

He carefully chose a cigar from his humidor, sat back again on the sofa and prepared to smoke it. He wanted to chill out before Hugo came back. He'd better come soon. Elli was in the way. If he'd known Hugo was going to be so long he would have asked him to help get her to the VIP room. That was the place for bodies, dead or alive.

Another one for the fire.

Frannie sat and watched the sky darken outside. The brilliant glare of the pink sunset was beautiful over the lake. She wished she could relax. Her stomach growled. She'd barely eaten today. They'd ordered room service but she couldn't swallow properly. Her body was fiercely telling her 'Leave me alone!' She was sick of being her own worst enemy.

One hand rested perpetually on her stomach. The pain was not regular so it couldn't be contractions, she'd learnt about all that on her prenatal course. Her waters hadn't broken either, yet still she felt weird, as if her body had changed. Once this was over she would go straight to hospital and check herself in. Just one more night, she told herself.

Dorcas was in the bathroom again. She was running in and out of there constantly. Perhaps the bitch had more drugs on her. Around each other they were twitchy. Even though the hotel boasted a spa, they were too anxious to try it out. They'd spent all afternoon cooped up in the room, staring at the walls, waiting for the bouncer's call.

Kurt had not rung her mobile although he must be back from work by now. She'd bitten her nails down to stubs wondering about him. Perhaps that was why she hadn't been able to eat. She sighed. He was no bloody good for her. Let's face it: if she hadn't been stuck in a foreign country and pregnant she would have got out months ago. She climbed back on to the bed where Dorcas sat watching German television in some kind of yoga position.

Dorcas checked her phone for the twentieth time.

'*Gar nichts!*' she said, her eyebrows shooting up into her fringe. 'Let's get some kip.'

Frannie murmured. They decided to sleep in their clothes so that when the call came they could drive straight off. Awkwardly, they took it in turns to brush their teeth in the bathroom and lay down on top of the bed together under a cotton sheet. Frannie couldn't get comfortable. The bed wasn't that big, and she couldn't seem to move without knocking into the stick-thin Dorcas; getting close to her was like touching a skeleton. Frannie kept excusing herself, trying to quash her resentment.

But Dorcas's scent: something between musk and an Indian bazaar, was overpowering. Even when their bodies weren't touching, she could feel her presence, kept imagining what she'd done with her husband. She rubbed her forehead. She'd battled with horrible visions of Dorcas and Kurt through the torturous afternoon. Trying to understand, to conjure up how it'd been.

What was this? The relentless desire to know was tearing at her, even though she knew it would do her no good. Finally, she could take it no more.

'What happened?' said Frannie breaking the silence, 'With Kurt?' They were two shadows lying in the dark.

Dorcas clicked her lips then turned to Frannie. 'Icebreaker,' she said.

'What do you mean?' Frannie thought she'd misunderstood the German.

'When a man waits a long time with a strange woman, he gets nervous…doesn't know where to put his hands. He eats, drinks, and tension builds up…'

'Go on,' Frannie couldn't stop herself.

'And so because the mind is uncertain, the body takes over, becomes primal. You start to feel a mutual attraction which is little more than tension. And then it's easier to get to the turning point when someone tips over and becomes sexual.'

Frannie tried to take this in.

'Icebreaker?'

'That's an English word, isn't it? To break the ice.'

'And so you touched first, or what?' Frannie's voice got louder. She pushed herself awkwardly into a sitting position.

Dorcas sighed. '*Nicht fragen*,' she said wearily, turning away.

'I can't stop thinking about it,' said Frannie in a hopeless voice. Her long hair hung limply over her face. She wanted the whole narrative like it was an erotic story, but Dorcas was reluctant. What was she hiding? Frannie needled her.

'There was no intercourse, OK? That's all you need to know.' She turned away from Frannie.

Frannie felt like getting up, going to the hotel reception and getting some fresh air. But then Dorcas's mobile rang. Frannie froze. She wasn't sure she could trust her. 'Put it on speakerphone,' she said, 'let me hear.'

It must be the call. Frannie felt her throat tightening, the pressure of the baby squeezing everything in. But when the man spoke she gasped. She'd recognise that voice anywhere.

'Dorcas? It's Kurt. Alright, are you? Look, I'd like to see you as soon as possible. Finish where we left off.' He let out a rude laugh.

Frannie groaned and rushed into the bathroom. She banged the door shut, and slapped cold water over her face.

In seconds Dorcas was behind her. 'I'm sorry, Frannie,' she said simply.

Frannie broke out in huge sobs hunched over the sink as Dorcas tried to comfort her.

'I told him no,' said Dorcas.

'I don't care. The relationship's over. *Kaputt*,' sobbed Frannie. It hurt to bend, but she was too distressed to move. 'I should have seen it coming,' she said.

Dorcas hugged her. 'You want to know something, girlfriend? I'm also pregnant,' she said in a little girl voice. She squeezed Frannie again.

'What?' Frannie turned to Dorcas, her eyes wild and staring.

'It's early days yet, but yes,' said Dorcas with a wistful smile on her face.

Frannie gave her a horrified look. 'You know, and yet you smoke and put that shit up your nose?' She pushed Dorcas away. She wanted to slap the stupid cow. 'Do you plan to keep the baby?' asked Frannie, her eyes glaring at Dorcas.

'I haven't made up my mind,' said Dorcas, her head hung low.

Frannie felt as if she'd been punched in the stomach. This was incomprehensible to her. She stormed out of the bathroom, shaking her head. This new revelation turned everything upside down. Maybe Dorcas didn't care because she planned to harvest the organs from her baby. It was probably Hans's, which meant she couldn't be neutral in all this. And why had she never once mentioned before that she was pregnant?

Frannie slumped on the bed with her head in her hands. She felt as if she'd been wrenched into a million pieces. Maybe they wanted her baby as well, for some terrible plan. Perhaps this Tomek business had been nothing but a ruse to hook her in. She started to tremble, and a low, sour pain gripped her innards. She cried out. At that moment, she couldn't stand being with Dorcas a second more. She had to get out, leave now before anything else happened. She stood up, put on the light and was just about to pack her things when an excited Dorcas charged out of the bathroom.

'I got the call,' she said, quickly putting on her shoes. 'Hugo's just turned up at the club.'

# Chapter Thirty-Three

Hans was still enjoying the cigar when Hugo barged into his office without knocking. Hans raised his eyebrows. The dude looked rough. Hugo was sweating and looked like shit in his expensive clothes. He had the body of a fat gorilla; no designer gear could put that right.

Hans smiled.

Hugo marched over to where Elli was hidden, behind the sofa. He had a bag full of syringes in his hand.

'Stefan's not happy,' said Hugo as he swiftly put a tourniquet around Elli's arm and started the tedious process of drawing blood. 'If the blood samples show she's hepatitis-free and HIV-negative, he'll take her. But he wants to be sure first.' He glared at Hans. 'You do know she's a meth-head, right?'

Hans frowned, shrugged his shoulders. 'Who put him in charge?' he asked in a smooth voice that betrayed nothing.

'He's on his own,' said Hugo, who looked exhausted as he sat back on his knees collecting the blood. 'That Polish guy's got bedsores and he's moving him every two hours. He's good, is Stefan, but he's a perfectionist.'

Hans carried on smoking his cigar as if everything was just dandy. Hugo, out of breath and in severe need of a wash, seemed to take forever filling the vials. Finally he stood up and turned to go. 'I'll get these to the lab.'

'What about Sleeping Beauty here?' said Hans, with a smirk. He was tired of being inconvenienced.

'She's out of it, no one will be any the wiser.'

Hans sighed. '*The desire to inflict pain, that is all that is uppermost*: Albert Fish,' he said.

Hugo gave an irritated laugh. 'Well it's not for Stefan,' said Hugo tersely. 'He can see the big picture as long as it's sterile, know what I mean?'

Hans grinned. Hugo had never looked so damned ugly. He wondered if he was doing all this so he could finally get a woman. Birds liked dosh.

'Go straight there, yeah?' said Hans annoyed that the matter of Elli was taking so long to resolve. 'I want to get the results as soon as possible.'

He wanted to get out of here. He had some vacancies in his staffing and needed to test-drive some potentials so he could rectify that as soon as possible. He stroked his chin. That was one part of his job that he genuinely enjoyed.

And he always felt, as Lars did, that if you'd fucked someone it was one step closer to killing them.

🚗

Lars hesitantly got out of his truck. He'd parked in his usual spot at Moonlights, but the familiarity of the place only reminded him of what he'd lost. Being here was like *déjà vu*; the recognition prickled at him, but he knew damn well why he felt odd about the place. He'd been able to kill there, let himself go, and now he could not.

His *Lustmord* had got the better of him. It was only a matter of time before he was arrested. Hans was going to do his nut, but he had to let the young 'un know, give him a chance to destroy evidence. It made no odds to him if he went down for killing two or twenty, but he didn't want Hans dragged into it. Much as he resented the cheeky beggar for what he had become, his loyalty to the young Hans, the boy first met, was still there. He remembered the adoring, brilliant eyes. He licked his lips.

Hans had aroused his finer feelings and he didn't want him touched. Or perhaps he wanted to protect the part of Hans that overlapped with him like a Venn diagram; their past. He, Fritz, had unfolded as a bird opens its wings, and his darkest desires had been accepted with relish. He smarted at the memory. He didn't want to get too Onkel Sigmund about it, but he was doing his best to protect the little sod. With heavy steps he made his way to Hans's office.

When he knocked and walked in, the young 'un went white, as if he'd seen a ghost.

'Hans…' began Lars, not sure how to proceed. Hans just stared at him. His eyes like two bits of coal. The girls always said when he was moody they changed colour and now he saw it right in front of his eyes.

'I've killed again,' said Lars, almost slurring in his haste to get the words out. 'The lad at the gas station on the B6 – you probably saw it on the news.'

Hans seemed to shrink inside his clothes like a pricked balloon. 'A disorganised kill?' he said hesitantly, as if he couldn't believe he was hearing this.

'I screwed up,' said Lars sadly, rubbing his hands together in a shaking movement. 'And I had sex with him, came inside him. The cops are taking DNA samples of all known truck drivers.'

'They've taken yours?' whispered Hans, leaning forward. He looked close to collapse.

'Last night. I visited Koch and he asked me; what could I say?' Lars made a face like a four-year-old. Slowly he sat down in an armchair and exhaled sorrowfully. 'You need to get rid of any evidence, CCTV footage, anything. And get that kill room steam-cleaned.'

Hans looked into the distance. '*You got the darkness coming down,*' said Hans. 'That's what Jeffrey Dahmer said – *I think in some way I wanted it to end, even if it meant my own destruction.*' Hans's expression was subdued. Lars felt as if he couldn't bear to be separated from him. The wistfulness in his face made him want to hold on to him.

'You'll have about a week,' said Hans hopelessly. 'How will I manage, without you?

He seemed in shock. Lars was shocked to see real tears forming behind his eyelids. It was the first time he'd seen Hans upset. He had cared after all.

'I'm not going to say anything,' said Lars. His hands were bunched awkwardly in front of him. He leaned forward. 'I'm done with all this. I can hack it, but you need to be free.'

Hans looked at him wonderingly. He tipped his head to one side. 'Aren't you afraid, Lars?'

'I'm tired of fighting the compulsion. Inside it'll have to stop.'

Lars felt suddenly completely calm. He thought he'd lost him, but the young 'un was weeping. Good God, the tears were running down his face.

He got up and pulled Hans to his feet. With one swoop he roughly embraced him. They pressed cheeks. He felt as if the huge engine of his desire was roaring at full speed. When things were good with Hans it was like being constantly in the pure burn of the zone. The fierceness of his feelings astonished him. He looked into his eyes and they began to kiss, passionately. Lars felt euphoric and his mood lightened his constant headache. He didn't even care about going to prison; he just wanted this moment to last forever. He closed his eyes and rocked his body along Hans's. The dark red walls of the room were spinning and he was waltzing passionately without a care. He was so incredibly goddamn high he was about to fall off the earth.

Then he heard it: a low, unmistakable groan. He stopped. He stared around the room in disbelief. It came again. The noise was low down. Someone was there alright, behind the sofa.

Grimly he peered over the leather edge. He saw Elli shoved there like a broken doll, propped up against the wall. Her face had the sick, slack colour of runny vanilla ice. At first he thought he was seeing things. But when he bent down he saw the bandage, that she was *not right.*

The sight of her shameful injuries activated the rage in him; he wanted to bellow like a bull. Elli was trying to move her head. Her lips were moving faintly, but she was too far gone to actually speak. All she could manage was an animal wail, like a cow that knows it's to be slaughtered.

'Hans?' exclaimed Lars, still crouched down. His hands were clenched; he wanted to rip Hans's fucking head off. He'd thought he could not get worse, but he was wrong. And somehow he, Lars, had activated this senseless sadism in him. He felt a tremor run through himself. This was his mess, and now he had to put things right.

He turned around and faced the young 'un.

Now he'd been caught, Hans's face was blank, like an unplugged robot. Lars wanted to stick needles in him, he was desperate to get a reaction, but Hans seemed unable to register what he'd done. The realisation hit Lars that Hans was also a *Täter,* that this could not be the first time. His head burned trying to take it all in. Anna was dead, Elli was bashed in, so that left only Dorcas from the original three prostitutes Hans had hired when they had opened Moonlights. She could be next. The young 'un had lost it, he was totally out of control.

Anna. It hurt to think about her murder. It was his one regret. Fritz didn't do women. He only killed men that he fancied, the ones he really liked.

But when he recalled her final struggles, it felt wrong, as if the picture he was seeing wasn't properly in focus. He hated thinking about it. He advanced on Hans, stuck his face aggressively near to his.

'That wasn't the first time, was it?' Lars's eyes blazed with anger.

Hans shrugged. '*It's just like a big chunk of me has been ripped out and I'm not quite whole,*' he quipped.

'Stop that shit!' shouted Lars, his neck turning an angry red. He stood in Hans's face. 'Answer me.'

Hans laughed, knowing he was winding him up, pushing him over the edge, but he became increasingly melodramatic.

'*I was completely swept along by my own compulsion. It didn't satisfy me completely so maybe I was thinking another one will.*' He laughed again.

*Schweinehund!* Lars's breathing was getting laboured; he was bristling with frustration. The telephone rang. Hans turned towards it, off-guard for a second. Lars seized his chance. That smug bastard! He'd show him.

Lars punched Hans in the kidneys solidly from behind; with that one blow he was down. Quickly, Lars sat on his back and pushed both Hans's arms up past his body as far as they would go. He jerked at the extended arms, forcing them to rock in their sockets. Hans screamed. It was painful, easy and effective.

'Who killed Anna?' said Lars, still keeping his grip on the shoulders.

'*Me!*' screamed Hans. His head was twirling from side to side as he fought against the pain.

Lars winced, but he felt instant relief. He wasn't such a sick fuck after all then. 'Why did you make me think I did it?'

Hans was just screaming now. Spittle was coming out of his mouth and running on to the wooden floor. Lars relaxed his grip a fraction.

'To confuse you. I needed you on board the organ-trafficking scheme. If you thought you were only a gay serial killer it was so fucking restrictive. You couldn't be *used* as effectively.' Hans's words were bitter; he was full of hate. Now he was beyond desperate. Lars pushed his arms even deeper, and Hans's screams got higher.

'And Dorcas – what about her?' said Lars in an odd voice. He could barely bring himself to broach the subject. It was painful to realise that he *had to know*. He relaxed his grip to give Hans a chance to speak.

'She was the best of them, but we had no future… She was only a woman.' Hans managed an ironic laugh.

At that, Lars pushed him away in disgust. Hans lay screaming, trying to move his badly dislocated shoulder joints. Lars bent down and pushed Hans's head up to show him Hugo performing on camera 6. He was naked with the Vietnam chick in the Blue Room. Hans's eyes widened.

'That the logical alternative, is it? Lars whispered in his ear. 'This the way you do business?'

Hans's face squirmed. It felt as though Lars was torturing a rabbit. Just the threat of the pain was making Hans jittery.

'Where are you taking them? The folks to be harvested?' Lars was completely in control now.

'On a f-f-farm west from Barsinghausen: Müllers Hof.' Hans was wriggling, his face screwed up in pain. He looked like a butterfly which had lost one of its wings. *Not so fucking clever now are you?* Lars's rage was making him hot-blooded. He felt completely justified in stopping Hans. Maybe he could do one last favour for Koch and get this trafficking ring closed down. But he had to move fast, before they captured him. There were so many loose ends and he didn't care what methods he used.

He held Hans fast in a deadly grip. There was no way he was letting him walk out of here alive. He couldn't take the chance that he would do a deal with the police. As much as he hated to admit it, Hans was a danger to others. He had to take care of it. Now.

He took out his knife and put it ritualistically in his right hand. Although Hans couldn't see what he was doing, he sensed it and fought back with renewed strength. The tendons in his neck flexed like a python, but Lars overpowered him, showing his superior strength. He forced Hans's neck to the side to get a good view of the delicate vein.

Almost lying on Hans, he pressed the neck taut as if he was going to apply a wax strip and swiftly stabbed the jugular vein where he could see it flickering. The blood spurted out in a wondrous arc but the sound of it only sickened him. Hans gasped and blood came out of his nose. His face went grey, he tried to utter a final gurgle, but the exertion only speeded his loss of blood.

Lars stood over the crazy scene like an executioner surveying his handiwork. He wasn't aroused and made no attempt to taste the blood. A pool of it formed around the body and Lars had to move to avoid being totally splattered. He shuddered. *Eklig!*

The speed of Hans's passing stunned Lars. Perhaps because it was in real time as opposed to the high of orgasm, where a millisecond of euphoria left its presence for hours. He realised for the first time how ridiculous it all was. It was only the sexual feelings around it that had made it make sense. In truth, it was a nauseating business.

Lars looked dispassionately at the blood. He couldn't put into words what he felt, but somehow it was like seeing his own blood running out. He felt as if he'd committed suicide and was watching his prone body from above.

They'd had a bizarre relationship, but they'd been two broken shards of the same whole. Now he was broken. *Kaputt.*

# Chapter
# Thirty-Four

When Dorcas's car roared into the car park, it was dark. The huge Moonlights neon sign had come to life. Just looking at it, Frannie started to shake. It reminded her of too much. She was sitting in the passenger seat, afraid of everything, including losing control of her bladder.

Every ten to twenty minutes her uterus rocked with a force that took her breath away. When she stood up it felt as if gravity was affecting somewhere it shouldn't, like the time when a newly inserted coil had worked its way out. It was painful and humiliating. There was no way she could sit upright for long. The tension was obviously getting to her. But her waters hadn't broken, so nothing was happening yet.

What she wanted was to lie down, make the pain go away. Not to have to drive Dorcas's piece-of-shit car. She'd never even sat in a Polo before.

'We need to swap,' said Dorcas, unfastening her seat belt briskly.

'I don't think I can drive this.' Frannie looked blankly at the gear stick. The reverse gear was in a different position and she'd have to overcome that to even move the car. Using anything technical, from lights to windscreen wipers, filled her with anxiety. Never in her life had she pipped a horn.

'I'll be in the back seat to give you any instructions you need, don't worry about that.' Dorcas gave her a quick smile. '*Alles in Ordnung.*' She got out and lay down in the back seat with her head looking out of the window. Frannie half-slid awkwardly into the front. She had to put the seat back completely to get in, which earned her a fierce *tsk*.

Dorcas shoved her head through the gap and confronted her with a picture on her mobile phone.

'Introducing Hugo. He's fat, always sweating. You can't miss him. We all try to avoid him.' Dorcas gave a sarcastic laugh. 'If you see him, follow him. Perhaps he'll lead us to this Stefan.'

The man in the picture was dark and swarthy and gave the impression of not washing properly. His sallowness looked cruel. He seemed a complete rogue; a man to avoid, not chase after. Her mouth dropped. *Great!*

Frannie hesitated. Something did not feel right. She tried to speak without sounding fearful.

'Are you sure we should do this?'

Dorcas looked at her quizzically, her eyes beady like a hungry bird's. She was a woman used to taking what she wanted. 'Do you want to spend the rest of your life looking over your shoulder?' She tapped on the headrest.

'But every time we go after them it makes things worse. I mean, you should have seen the way Elli attacked me…' said Frannie. She promptly shut up. Two rosy spots formed on her cheeks. Dorcas was sprawled on the back seat. Not one bit of her showed anxiety.

'She was pissed, but you weren't in danger.' She dismissed her fears with a wave of her hand.

Frannie glared at her angrily. 'You and your so-called friends! Lars chased me *twice* and Elli attacked me. I had to push my key into her forehead,' said Frannie banging her hand on the wheel. *Zicke*. She was tired of this sniping.

'You did what?' Dorcas was practically clambering over the seat.

'What else could I do? It's not like I carry a bleeding gun.' Frannie brushed her hair out of her eyes impatiently. She purposely hadn't told her that before. In the mirror she saw Dorcas rise up like an animated corpse; her expressive eyes filled with malice. Frannie shuddered.

'What are you, a trainee psychopath or something?' shouted Dorcas with a snort. 'How hard did you hit her?' She glared at Frannie. Both women seemed to hold their breath.

'The key went in…just a bit…honestly, it was nothing,' stammered Frannie. 'There was hardly any blood.'

Dorcas exclaimed, and bent over her mobile, presumably trying to reach Elli. When there was no answer she jumped out of the car. Frannie flinched as the door slammed.

'I'd better go see what's up. After all, I set up your little date,' she said, striding off forcefully. Then she turned around. 'And if Hugo comes out, just put your foot down. Driving a car is like riding fellas – they're all the fucking same in the end.'

Frannie sank into the seat with her head in her hands. She felt like weeping uncontrollably, just letting go. But she had to stay alert. God knew what Dorcas was really up to. Even the follow-that-car scenario could be staged.

The only way to cope was to be prepared for absolutely anything; and that meant being able to drive this thing. Meticulously, she looked down at the gears and checked the indicator panel to familiarise herself where everything was. When she had to react, it was going to have to be fast.

🚗

Frannie was scanning the entrance to Moonlights so hard she couldn't stop blinking. Most of the crowd were going in, but the bouncers were obsessively checking each customer for drugs, so she had to constantly squint over their shoulders. In just minutes she saw a tall, fat man coming near the open doors. He chatted amiably with the bouncers as if he worked there.

Her chest tightened. She'd been here less than five minutes. It was awfully convenient that she'd spotted him so soon. Could it be a trap? Dorcas had just gone in. But she couldn't, could she? She frowned. *Shit*. She banged the dashboard frantically. But he was already coming out. Frannie could barely breathe.

She watched as Hugo, despite his bulk, walked swiftly to a black Mercedes 4x4 parked over two parking spaces. In a few seconds he'd be heading out of the car park. His car was high and squat, like a tank. Inevitably he'd outrun her. With shaking fingers she turned the ignition key. At least she was going to goddamn try. As long as she stayed in the car, she'd be relatively safe.

The engine of Dorcas's car sounded totally different from Kurt's A4. Dorcas had left it in first, and, when she put the gear stick to the left where the 'R' was indicated, nothing happened. Frantically, she pushed on the clutch, but the car remained stationary. The handbrake was off, and she couldn't figure it out. Red-faced, desperate, she checked again.

There was a ring on the gear. She experimented with pulling it up. Ah, that worked. But her foot was still clamped on the clutch. The car shot backwards at full speed before she could react and knocked into the car behind her. She heard the tinkle of broken glass.

Frannie put her head in her hands. My God! She turned the car nervously, looked back. It was just a broken light. She blinked, tried to steady her breathing. No one had been hurt; she could deal with this later. She just hoped Dorcas's car was still functional.

Taking a deep breath, she drove out of the car park lot as fast as she could manage.

Hugo was already far in front when she hit the *Autobahn*. His hefty black car stood out. Its bulk and profile seemed intensely masculine. Frannie felt angry every time she looked at it.

If he'd gone at top speed she'd have had no chance, but Hugo drove steadily in the middle lane. Frannie pushed the little Polo as fast as it would go in the fast lane to catch up. When she drew near she had to swerve dangerously into the middle lane to nip in two cars behind. She almost collided with a silver Volvo. But she'd got him in her sights.

Because his car was so high, she could still see it. She didn't want to tail him too obviously. Hugo's car was so clean the paintwork reflected all the street lights like a mirror. Frannie just hoped he was going to Stefan's, that this would not all be for nothing.

Once she was driving along a straight road, and didn't have to concentrate so hard on driving, she became aware that the pains in her stomach were getting worse. She was operating mainly on adrenaline; every time her tension eased, her stomach seemed to hurt more. As she had no idea where Hugo was going, her mind had to race to keep on top of the situation. The constant stress was making her dizzy.

Before, she must have been in shock, her guilt at having another car accident began to pull at her. Every car she borrowed got damaged. And if she pushed herself to take risks, as she'd have to, it was likely Dorcas's car would end up battered beyond recognition, too. She gripped the wheel. *It was down to the line.*

It was hard work keeping up the chase. Cars kept cutting her up and forcing their way into her lane. She had to fight to keep her place and ended up driving up the tail of the car in front of her. The overhead lights stung her eyes, making it harder to concentrate in the dark. And she had to look ahead, as well as checking the traffic flow on both lanes either side of her. Beads of perspiration formed on her brow, but she kept her foot down hard on the accelerator. This was no time for cop-out driving, taking the easiest route. She had no idea what roads were coming up ahead.

Abruptly, Hugo turned right and went off at a junction. Frannie saw him go at the last minute and frantically blinked to get over into the slow lane, but there was a solid line of trucks blocking her path. If she didn't go now, she'd miss the junction.

She closed her eyes and nudged the car sharply right, hoped for the best. Her actions forced a truck to slam on his brakes. She heard the high-pitched squeal as his tyres slid, the fury of his horn.

But Frannie was preoccupied driving the precarious circular route that took her left again over the *Autobahn*. It was like being on a fairground ride you had to negotiate yourself. The curve didn't seem to end.

The second she turned the corner she saw Hugo driving away, but she knew where he'd turned off; a *Schnellstrasse* in the direction of Gehrden. The name meant nothing to her, but they were moving west away from the city.

She set off in pursuit, her chin clenched. This city street was full with traffic. Just the kind of start/stop flow she dreaded. To keep up with him, if she didn't take risks and cut everyone up like Dorcas, she might as well pull over now.

She sighed and pushed the car into fourth gear. She had to step up, get this over and done with.

🚗

Dorcas pursed her lips as she got to the entrance of Moonlights. Her instinct was to run. She'd only stormed out of the car because

Frannie was getting on her tits. Being constantly with a heavily pregnant woman made it impossible to blank out her own situation. Now her black silk skirt was digging in at the waist, and when she smoked she felt sick. Everything was falling apart and she'd hurt her one ally. She frowned. Why did she do this shit?

She nodded to Marcus, her favourite bouncer, and entered the club. The boom of the music led her into the frenetic darkness. She gritted her teeth. Hans could not find out she was here. She'd learned the hard way to be wary of disobeying him.

She made her way in the cranking lift down to the staff changing rooms. If she was quick, she could check on Elli, or ask someone if she was OK, and leave without Hans finding out. Although there were CCTV cameras everywhere, most of the time they weren't monitored.

The club was air-conditioned, but Dorcas felt flushed, as if she had a fever. It hurt her to admit it, but this peculiar nervous feeling was fear. When she pushed open the door, the new girls Nel and Candice were there.

'Have you seen Elli?' said Dorcas. The Vietnamese one, Nel, looked at her nervously. Dorcas thought she was always going to look like someone's kid sister. She had that innocent look no one could fake.

'I haven't seen her since yesterday,' said Nel. She looked lost, as if she had no idea what she was doing there. 'She went off somewhere, didn't come back. Her things are still here, look.'

Dorcas nodded. Elli had left her purse, even her mobile phone. She frowned and exited, mumbling her thanks. Nel looked as if she'd had all the fight kicked out of her. She clenched her fists. She didn't like to think Hans's little empire included forced labour. As a prostitute she'd learned to turn down the volume of her anxiety. You had to get it to a manageable level and overlook the drugs, the petty crime. But this was a step too far. So much of her past had been a mistake. She was realising that now.

She was on her way to the lift when a hand clapped on her shoulder.

Dorcas instinctively hit out at the person. It was Lars, and in the dark corridor he loomed over her. There were new lines on his face and his breath stank.

Dorcas refused to tremble. She stared at him.

Lars was agitated. He went from staring at her with a tender smile to nervousness. He was also carrying a briefcase, something she'd never seen him with before. She shrank back, but he flung his arms round her and hugged her.

'Dörchen,' he whispered, pulling her to him. 'I just saw you on the cameras and ran down to fetch you. Everything's nearly ready.' He whirled her round as if she was a little girl.

'To fetch me?' said Dorcas with a frown. 'What do you mean?'

'I can't tell you the details,' said Lars, 'but I have to go away and I'm sorting things out.' Now he was laughing, as if nothing had happened between them. 'I've got a surprise for you.' Dorcas looked at him with misgiving. Did he have amnesia or what?

'I only have two minutes,' said Dorcas, trying to extract herself. 'I just came in to find Elli.'

'Don't worry about that, it's being taken care of,' said Lars, 'She's sitting in my truck right now. You can help me. *Komm mit.*' Dorcas exhaled sharply and followed Lars. He led her out to the car park, practically pulling her by her hand. She wondered if Frannie was watching this.

Dorcas climbed into Lars's truck. When she opened the door, she gasped. Elli was sprawled lifeless on the seat. Only her seatbelt was keeping her in place. She was breathing and her eyes were moving, but that was about it.

'What have you done?' screamed Dorcas, kicking to get down. But Lars was too strong. He threw her back on the seat. The door slammed shut. She banged her fist, but she was locked in. Desperately she looked closer at Elli. There was dried blood from a head wound that looked deep and vivid bruises around her forehead. When she held her hand it was cold. She could barely feel a pulse. Dorcas felt as if she could fall into a dead faint. Too much was happening. Had Lars hurt Elli? It couldn't be true. Part of Dorcas's mind seemed to close itself down. First Anna, now Elli. Was she next? And what about poor Frannie waiting for her outside?

Lars got in with a little whistle and got the truck moving. He seemed in a world of his own. Dorcas begged him to let her and Elli go, or to call an ambulance, but when she got her mobile out Lars grabbed it and put it in his pocket.

'Don't bother. I'm dropping her off in about ten minutes at the Friederikenstift Krankenhaus. You can help me get her to the entrance.'

'Why did you move her? Why didn't you call an ambulance?' screamed Dorcas, clasping her hands. 'She's got a head injury, for God's sake.' It could be her turn next. Maybe he was driving them somewhere to get rid of them.

Lars grinned like an imbecile and wiped his mouth. 'If I'd called an ambulance there would have been too many questions. I've got to stop them first, Dörchen,' he said in the strangest voice. 'You won't believe it, but it's for the greater good.'

'What are you on about?' said Dorcas crossly. She was perched on the edge of her seat, holding Elli's hand. Even though she knew she could do nothing for her, it made her feel better. Lars glanced sideways at her and licked his lips. He swallowed a few times as if preparing to make a speech.

'In the army I was paid to kill, if necessary. But I also kill for kicks. Funny how you're a hero and the other you're scum,' said Lars. He spoke in a neutral tone, as if explaining how to make an Italian pasta sauce. Although his voice was tense, he seemed relieved to be talking about it. He took a deep breath.

'I'm a gay serial killer,' he said. He paused, looked briefly at Dorcas. 'All those missing men reported in the *HAZ* – I killed them, and the recent one you probably heard about on the news.' He spoke with a curious calm. His manner and the actual words he was saying didn't add up.

Dorcas couldn't get her head round this, so she used her drug reflexes. Even though she wasn't high, she remembered how it felt. She floated to the top of her thoughts, distanced herself. She was aware of the seriousness of what Lars was saying to her, that in telling her he'd probably have to get rid of her too. But it just wouldn't sink in. She couldn't accept it.

It was impossible. Her Lars, a *serial* killer? He was playing some ridiculous joke. In fact she was pissed he'd told her. It was like finding out a fundamental fact was wrong, like that Germany was actually part of the African continent instead of being in northern Europe; it made everything else she'd ever been told into a potential lie. She wanted to smack him.

'Why?' she said, raising her eyebrows.

'If I knew that, it wouldn't be a compulsion,' said Lars softly. Then he looked at her knowingly. His voice became a sick whisper. 'I get an incredible high at the moment of death. It's addictive.'

Dorcas exhaled, clapped her hand over her mouth. She was wrestling with the unthinkable. 'And Anna, and Tomek – and Elli?' she said quietly. He might as well give her the lot now.

'That was Hans. He used me, Dorcas.' He turned to face her. 'He let me use the VIP room to do the kills and then sold the bodies to a medical institute. I got my kicks and he got money for it.' Lars started to break down, his face seemed to fold. 'I had a compulsion, but that little fuck *enjoyed* it. Do you understand?'

He had to wipe a tear from his eye. Dorcas sat absolutely still. It was as though she was turned into stone. She was listening, but she didn't want to know what she was hearing.

But Lars wasn't finished yet. He mechanically drove as he spoke.

'And then he got greedy. There was more money in organ trafficking, but I didn't hold with that. He killed Anna and he's got her brother in some farmhouse waiting to be cut up.'

Dorcas gasped. She took out a cigarette with trembling fingers. Lars lit it for her. 'You're still smoking, are you?' he said, looking at her disapprovingly.

'What the fuck? You're a *serial* killer and I can't smoke?' Dorcas's pencil-thin eyebrows rose high into her hair-line. Although her mouth was dry with terror, she couldn't mask her essential assertiveness. She scowled at him and carried on smoking regardless. She wished she could pretend this were all a joke, but Elli's lifeless body bumped into hers every time Lars turned a corner.

'So if you're a *gay* serial killer, why did you chase Frannie? And send her that threat with the flowers?' Dorcas looked at him questioningly. Lars rubbed his chin, gave a deep belly laugh.

'Oh, yes, your little mate?' He stared at her sarcastically. 'That was what Hans wanted. He'd made the mistake of killing Anna, someone he knew. Frannie asked too many questions, and she was a squealer.' A dark look came over his face. 'She complained about me to the police, stupid cow.'

Dorcas's eyebrows shot up, but the mention of Frannie roused Lars's anger. In a thick, vicious tone he said, 'It's because of that interfering bitch that I'll be caught. Hans stopped me from using the VIP room because I *didn't* kill her.' His mouth smirked at the irony. 'On the outside I made too much mess, and now they've got my DNA.' His eyes were hooded, his face and neck bright red. He turned again to Dorcas. 'So the bitch is going to have to pay.' He banged his fist on the wheel and let out a guttural roar.

Dorcas shrank back. She was finding it hard to swallow. Outside, the scenery flashed by as Lars's truck rumbled around the city streets. They were going at a hell of a pace. There was no way she could try to break the window or get out.

Lars opened up a new packet of cigarettes. He could talk and drive and smoke without thinking about it.

'OK, first we drop off Elli, then I'm going to this Stefan geezer to release anyone they've got. After that you get your surprise and then I'm done.' He laughed at that and nudged her in the leg.

Dorcas had to resist letting out a scream. If Hugo had come out and was going there, he'd lead Frannie right into Lars's path. She'd put Frannie in the thick of it again. She sat on her hands to stop them from shaking. There was no doubt that she would be next. She wanted to moan, lose control of her senses, but she did not.

She concentrated on breathing, on filling her mind with pure, white calm. She thought of her flowers, the *Ordnung* of her apartment. Although it was the last thing she should be thinking about, she couldn't stand the thought of dying without dignity.

# Chapter Thirty-Five

It was going so easy that he felt light-headed. He'd got Dorcas here with him. Now her unborn child was fatherless he'd make sure she was looked after, good and proper. He smiled; at least they were friends again. His hand patted her abstractedly on her knee. He was looking forward to showing her the surprise.

But first he had loose ends. There was this Stefan to sort out. He didn't hold with torture, sadism. He dismissed instantly the possibility that any of his victims had suffered lasting pain. That had been love - okay, lust - but not *sadism*.

And then there was the English bitch, the one responsible for his darkness coming down. He sighed. It was all such a mess. Every time he thought about her being pregnant, the dull ache in his head notched up a bit. He didn't like to think of her unborn child. And he didn't do women!

But it was only a matter of time before he would be caught. He rubbed his hands over his eyes. Before, he only came into his own when he was in the zone. Now he had nothing to lose. Until they caught him good and proper, he had to take care of all the loose ends.

Frannie found it much harder to tail Hugo on the city streets. Once she had to wait at a red traffic light Hugo had already passed. She drove like a madwoman to catch him up, but on all sides she was hemmed in by slow-moving cars. She only managed it by overtaking dangerously.

It was harder operating an inferior car. The brakes were slow to react, she had to really step on them to get any effect, which meant she nearly gave herself whiplash every time she had to stop. When the traffic went down to walking speed, she found it impossible to keep up with the flow. She was either too slow, or virtually colliding with the other vehicles. The more she concentrated, the more her swollen feet slipped on the pedals. She cursed, but Hugo's car kept moving relentlessly ahead.

She was hot and her tummy hurt like hell. Eventually they left the city behind and headed out to an almost deserted road in the direction of Barsinghausen. The streets curved and were tree-lined. The challenge was to keep out of sight without losing him. She kept a generous stopping distance and if another car came along, pulled over and followed again with another vehicle between them. Hugo wouldn't be able to see more than one car behind.

Still he went further. There were no other cars and she had no choice but to follow him openly, hoping that he would not notice she was constantly on his tail. She drove after him through the dark, winding streets. Surely he would stop soon; there was nothing out here. If he parked, she'd drive on ahead then double back. As soon as she got an address she'd phone Dorcas.

But Hugo didn't stop. She gritted her teeth and concentrated on trying to remain as invisible as possible.

Then the road got narrower, and there were no street lights. They were in deepest countryside, going in the direction of country park Weserbergland Schaumburg-Hameln. Or perhaps they were driving through the park already. It felt like driving in a tunnel under the earth. There was no light, only country fields and lone trees each side, and she found herself driving closer to Hugo for the view of his tail lights. Although she considered herself a night-driver, she was used to the B6, which was lit up like a funfair day and night.

Hugo continued, his black car almost invisible, his tail-lights little amber specks. The lane got smaller and the bushes either side got more overgrown until both sides nearly met in the middle. Frannie felt prickles of fear touch her scalp. Maybe he was on to her and had led her to this remote spot to kill her.

She pulled back so that her car was out of sight and drove with parking lights so she was less visible. It limited her vision, though, and she cursed as the path got wilder.

The road unexpectedly became steep. Hugo disappeared over the brow of a hill and Frannie tried to stop herself from racing on ahead to catch up with him. All she could see was the ghostly outline of trees, so if there was a house or building here, it would be easy to find. There probably wasn't another place for miles.

Suddenly his tail-lights disappeared. She drove after him hesitantly, then stopped with her windows wound down, listening. There was a willow tree hanging low on the path; it was hard to believe that his car had gone that way.

Briefly she switched on her headlights. There was a path, little more than a dirt-track. Because of the thick undergrowth she'd never have found it alone. She looked carefully for any sign of civilisation. On the left, there was a faded wooden sign, Müllers Hof. There must be a farmyard ahead. She shivered. It was barely a farm track.

For long minutes she sat there with no idea what to do. If she drove after him, anyone there would notice her car pulling up instantly. On the other hand, she didn't want a long walk in the dark. She dithered, one hand trying to soothe her heaving stomach, terrified of being caught.

Finally, she reversed three hundred metres or so until she was on the lane again. She parked near to a bush that partially hid the car. With shaking feet she got out. Now she was out of the car, her stomach seemed to be palpitating more. She felt like lying down on the moist earth, but the fresh night air revitalised her. The exotic bird and insect sounds spurred her on.

It wouldn't hurt to take a look. She could scope out the area under cover of darkness, see if she could see anything – a name, something in the postbox, anything. She checked her mobile; she still had reception. She hesitated. Perhaps it was better not to tell Dorcas yet. If she was in any way involved, she was not going to hand her ammunition.

Her back suddenly tipped in agony. She felt as if she had humungous period pain. Simultaneously her bowels contracted fiercely. She dismissed, it, kept walking shakily in the direction of the farm. Her waters hadn't broken, so labour couldn't have started. It must be just the stress. She'd follow the track and see where she ended up. If she was quiet and really careful, she could hide behind the trees and have a quick scout of the place. She was so close now.

It felt as if she was twelve years old, doing something she shouldn't. There was a dense wood to the left of the farmhouse. Frannie slipped behind the treeline and began to make her way closer.

# Chapter Thirty-Six

At first the moon was cloaked by cloud, and under the thick dark of the branches Frannie couldn't make out the exact position of the trunks. Like someone blind, she reached out with her hands to feel them. The wood felt rotten to touch; it was old and gnarled, and bits of bark kept falling off. She shivered. Her hair kept getting snagged on low-hanging branches. At times the trees were too close together for her to comfortably move between. She cursed, felt fat and hot.

After inching her way along the treeline, she saw the outline of an old farm, complete with barn and stables. She crept closer. In a field she saw the dark shapes of cows lying down. They seemed to sense her presence. One of them mooed. The unexpected sound made her jump.

'Sshh,' whispered Frannie. No one must see her. She had no weapon, and they could easily outrun her. The only thing going for her was the element of surprise. If they had a dog she could give up now. She frowned. Didn't farms always have a dog? She chewed her lower lip. If it was there, it would move on her soon.

She moved even closer and hid behind a large apple tree. There were lights on in the farmyard and the windows were all wide open on this close night. Above the constant chirp of crickets, she could hear two men talking round the back. Slowly, she tiptoed closer.

They were talking in a primitive kitchen. It looked like something her grandmother might have cooked in. The red check curtains at the window were stained and torn. She crouched down and made her way to the wall of the barn to get a closer look, pressed herself into a doorframe and watched.

Her stomach was gassy; periodically it blipped, as if it had hiccups. She held a hand over her mouth. If she so much as burped or coughed, it could bring them out.

The man speaking must be Hugo. His beer belly looked even more massive sitting down. They seemed to be in the middle of an argument. The other man, who looked even rougher, kept banging his hand on the table, but Frannie didn't trust her judgement; she often thought people talking at full speed in German were having an argument, when it was just the hard, guttural sounds of the language.

For a few tense minutes she listened, but she could barely understand more than the odd word. In a foreign language she was like someone deaf: she needed to be able to see the person speaking to properly understand. She cursed her inexperience, her endless floundering in this bloody language. If only Dorcas had stayed with her; *she* would have had a handle on the situation in seconds. There was no point listening further. She might as well snoop round.

The door of the barn didn't quite shut. She used the light on her mobile phone to peer in. There was the ghostly outline of a tractor that looked fit only for junk, and a few tools. She wondered if the farm was really functional. It looked as if it had had its heart ripped out long ago.

There was a half-rotting stable and a shed behind the house. As she padded through the darkness she sensed a presence. As she got closer she could hear little snorts and deep breathing. When she looked in and flashed the light from her phone, about fifty pigs jumped up with one communal snort. Frannie leapt back in fright. She could hear the sound of their frantic scurrying hooves, smell the heady waft of manure. The pigs were agitated, squealing and jumping about in panic. She had to get away before their angst alerted the men.

Frannie tried to run quickly to the next building, but she could barely waddle. Her stomach looked ridiculous and twinged every time she moved. The pains were still coming on and off, but she was so hyped up on adrenaline that she was able to keep going.

There was a utility room attached to the farm. Quietly, she crept in. It was unlocked, and someone had left a light on. She saw instantly that it was another dumping ground for unused machinery. Bits of twisted-up engine and old farm tools were stacked everywhere. The hallway had a white tiled floor which was caked with bits of straw, dry mud and general debris. This section was attached to the main house, but with the men inside there she didn't dare go in. There were another few doors in the outhouse section. She steeled herself to check each one.

She listened behind the first door for some seconds, slowly turned the handle and silently peered in. In the dark the first thing she noticed was the acrid antiseptic smell, as if it had been scrubbed recently with disinfectant. She clicked her mobile light on for a few seconds and gulped. This room was spotless. It contained an orderly collection of medical supplies: stands for drips, bags marked 'saline' and plastic sheeting. She turned on the electric light. In a cupboard she found medication and bandages and a bag of adult nappies. Nothing in the room seemed appropriate for animal use.

She let out a stifled cry and clapped a hand to her mouth. Before, they'd suspected Hans of being an organ trafficker, but seeing for herself the paraphernalia of their sick operation made her feel nauseous. She steadied herself against a wall. In the small room she was conscious of her rapid breathing. If they caught her, she didn't want to think about what they would do with a pregnant woman. Nervously she put a hand on her stomach, tried to reassure her baby. Swiftly she took three pictures of the room on her mobile phone. Finally, some evidence. Then she noticed that in the corner there was another door.

It was a badly made alteration, all cracked and disjointed, so she hadn't seen it at first. The smaller door was locked with a giant, old-fashioned key. She put her hands over her face, tried to breathe smoothly. If all the medical equipment was here, Tomek must be close. Her instinct was to flee, to run back to the woods and call the police, but – she scanned the equipment in the room again – none of the medical gear was illegal. She needed more compelling images: a body, evidence of kidnapping; something. With shaking steps she moved towards the door.

First she listened with her ear to the door, but all she heard was her own thudding heartbeat. Slowly she turned the key. Sweat broke out on her upper lip as she painstakingly opened the door, trying not to make a sound.

At once she saw a man lying asleep on what looked like an old hospital bed. A small red-shaded lamp gave the windowless room a warm glow. It had evidently once been some kind of machine room, pieces of old hefty equipment were still in one corner, but someone had cleaned it up, used it as a place to keep the man confined. His lower legs were covered in bandages. One arm was tied to the metal frame of the bed with string. But all the restraints were unnecessary. It didn't look as though he was going anywhere.

Frannie bit her lip. This man looked bad. She had to photograph this before she got emotional. It was imperative she had evidence.

She gulped, stepped closer. Could it really be him?

Lying down, he looked different. His youthful grace was gone; even in sleep this man was tense with pain. He was pale and had lost a lot of weight, but it was Tomek.

With a cry, she rushed to his side.

'Tomek!' she said, crouching down awkwardly by his side. 'It's Frannie, I've come for you.' She stroked his hair.

Tomek's eyes flickered open. Rather than speaking, at first he seemed to gurgle at her. She jumped back. His eyes blinked rapidly as if he was seeing a ghost. When he spoke, she had to bend near his face to hear him.

'Soon, Stefan's coming back soon. Go, now.' Tomek's face turned slack at the effort and he lay back exhausted on the pillow.

Frantically Frannie untied his hand, tried to drag him to his feet. But every time she bent and put any weight on her stomach it hurt so badly she felt as if she was being cut in half. She could have sobbed with frustration. There was no way she could carry Tomek even a few steps, never mind the whole distance back to the car. She banged her head with desperation. What had they done to him?

Tomek tried to sit up, but, although his face tensed with effort, he was too weak. His hair was lank and matted. He licked his lips, tried to speak.

'Frannie, go now, call the police. It's the… *Druckwunde*…' Seeing her blank face he grasped for the English words. 'Push sores?' he said, smiling shyly. Frannie, red-faced and panting, frowned. When she realised what he meant, she gave a nervous titter.

'Oh, pressure sores?'

Tomek nodded. 'He comes to move me every two hours. You have to leave before he find you. Go, hide. Call the *Polizei*.' He looked grateful but waved his hands at her. 'Go, go.'

Trembling, Frannie squeezed his hand. 'I'll get help, I promise,' she said. She tied his hand back up again so that his captor would not get suspicious and ran out of the room.

Frantically she scanned the outhouse. Nothing. She bolted for the exit, and pressed herself against the building, her heart beating furiously. On tiptoe she crept against the side of the farmhouse. Through the lighted window she could see the men, more agitated now. While she watched, Hugo roughly pushed the other one and he reacted angrily back. Frannie trembled at the crude violence. She couldn't stand being here another minute.

She bolted into the woods as fast as she could, banging into trees in her haste. The pigs startled in her wake again, and she heard their throaty squeals of alarm long after she was out of sight.

In the woods her hands got battered and scratched. She was probably making too much noise, but she didn't slow down. She was panting and her sides were heaving. Her belly was on fire with pain. Even with her fear, she could not run much more. All her reserves of energy were spent.

She ran to a little clearing, crouched down and grabbed her mobile. She had to call the police right away. Swiftly she dialled 110. She sat, panting, as she waited for them to answer. Although she could see nothing in the dark woods, she kept all her senses trained in the direction of the farmhouse. The animal commotion might bring them out.

A man answered and spoke to her in polite German.

'*Polizei, was kann ich für Sie tun?*'

Frannie panicked. She could barely breathe through her stomach and back pain. Hesitantly she gave her name and address. When he asked her to spell out the letters of her name, she couldn't do so efficiently. Desperately, she tried to describe her location.

'Where is this *Müllers Hof?*' said the policeman.

'It's on a small country road west from Barsinghausen, near the country park…' Frannie hesitated. 'Weserberg-something… Schaum-something-Hameln.' She struggled to remember the full name. The policeman gave a snort. She had no street names and was sure her pronunciation was off. It was one thing to sound cute at dinner parties because she couldn't say *ich* properly, but when it really mattered she was screwed.

'*Wie bitte?*' said the policeman. She could have cried with frustration. In panic, she spoke more quickly, '*Müllers Hof*, west from Barsinghausen. There's a huge park, names together.' The more she tried, the worse her German got. She tried to explain about the organ trafficking, but as she didn't know the word for trafficking. It was impossible. He asked her questions she couldn't follow. Frannie felt her cheeks furiously blushing.

'They have Anna and Tomek Kalinowski…' She didn't know the word for 'prisoner', so she used 'prison' and hoped it would make sense. The tone in the policeman's voice was changing. She could feel him beginning to tune out. The men could turn up at any minute and she was getting nowhere.

'Is there someone who can speak English?' she said. She should have said that at the beginning. Sweat and tears were trickling down her face. The policeman laughed, and she couldn't tell if he was being sarcastic or not.

'*Kleinen Moment, bitte,*' he said and put her on hold. She felt relieved – she'd be able to make herself understood in a minute. She looked in the direction of the farmhouse. Nothing. It was nearly over.

With a nervous smile, she waited patiently, still trying to catch her breath, but after a few minutes the tone changed. ZZZzzz. She'd been cut off. 'No, no, NO!' she shouted. Once again she'd failed to get help from the police. Despite the humidity, she shivered. If she started feeling the full force of the fear that had been creeping up on her, she'd crumble.

'Ow!' A weird stitch started in one side. She massaged it. Then it happened: the contractions that had been twinging on and off and which she'd been ignoring were suddenly closer together, and the pain was unimaginable. She threw her head back and screamed. It felt as if a whole tribe of little people were inside banging their way out. There was no doubt labour had started. She groaned. With both hands she clutched her tummy. She tried to stand, but the pain was too intense. She slid down. There was no way she could get back to the car. She should have listened to her body before.

Frantically, she dialled home. It was after eleven. Kurt should be asleep in bed. If she told him everything in English, he could phone the police for her. She just had to make one phone call, then wait. She got a dialling tone. 'Come on, pick up!' she shouted to the trees. But it was no good. She tried his mobile which he always left by the bed in case work called. But he was not there or chose to ignore her. She didn't know which option was worse. Alone in the dark, she realised she hated him.

The next contraction smashed into her like a tidal wave. She was whimpering now.

She dialled Dorcas's phone. She started gabbling her distress as soon as the phone was picked up.

'Dorcas, it's Frannie, I'm at *Müllers Hof*, west of Barsinghausen. They've got Tomek here. Phone the police, send help, DORCAS. *SCHNELL! SCHNELL!*' She paused for breath, waited. She had to resist screaming, she shouted again, 'Dorcas?'

But a man answered who spoke thickly as if he was talking through his nose. In a nanosecond she was on to him. *Lars.*

'*Ich komme!*'

'NO!' She let out a shrill scream.

She tried to get to her feet. If she had to, she'd crawl back to the car. But suddenly, she felt a gulp, like the moment when all the bathwater gets sucked out the bath. Her waters broke and gushed copiously over her shoes.

Sobbing, she collapsed on the grass. She was in the worst situation possible and it was all her fault!

# Chapter Thirty-Seven

She'd expected it to feel like intense period pain, but each wave kneaded her stomach with a giant's touch. She was shaking, crying, shocked. Why had no one said anything, prepared her? All those times she'd gone to Dr Kanton's for check-ups and she'd said nothing, zilch, about this, the most important bit: the end. *Bitch.* She shrieked again.

She needed a doctor, midwife, anyone. As usual she was parched. She could have downed a pitcher of beer in seconds. In the ridiculous dark, she couldn't even see properly. A part of her she didn't recognise was taking over. She removed her pants, hitched up her skirt and sprawled out her legs so she was bare to the night air. She didn't care. Her quest for Tomek, her fear of the men, was forgotten. Nature was taking over.

She tensed and screamed again. It was like being summoned by a higher power, some merciless god that took you over. Perhaps it was hell. She closed her eyes and breathed into her screams. Whether this was pushing or not, she had no idea. Being in darkness made it worse. She couldn't even see if she was bleeding. It felt like dying a thousand deaths. All she wanted was for this goddamn, motherfucking torture, the unbelievable insanity, to be over.

When they shone the torch into her face, she was barely capable of speech. She grunted as the two men she'd seen in the farmhouse grabbed her by her hands and feet. Hugo took her legs. He was stronger and held her feet higher than her trunk. She couldn't stand that, cried out. She needed gravity to help push. Viciously, she kicked at him and he dropped her.

She needed water, light, and a comfortable place to lie down. She attempted to move towards the farmhouse to get them. She was half-carried and dragged back to the farmhouse over the other man's shoulder. When they got near a gate Frannie squatted down with her back to the men and held on to the rail.

Her screams were unearthly now; full-throated cries of agony. All the animals were snorting or mooing in unison. As she crouched she tried to remember that her mother, grandmother, everybody before her had been through this too. It didn't help.

'Water,' she said loudly. In a voice like a demon she demanded it, over and over.

The two men were arguing again. She didn't know what they were saying; every German word she ever knew was gone. All she wanted was the goddamn water.

'Water! WATER.' The other guy, Stefan it must be, ran and brought her a litre bottle. When Hugo saw him he grabbed it and emptied it in front of her on the grass. Stefan just stood there with his mouth open. He looked as though he wanted to help but was frightened of Hugo's reaction.

Hugo walked up to her and pulled her by the hair, twisting her head, so she could see his fat face. Frannie screamed, her fear penetrating even her primal directive.

'You stupid interfering bitch!' he said in broken English. 'Why the hell you come sniffing around? Now we can't let you go.' He kicked her brutally in the back. She slammed into the fence with full force on her swollen stomach, and the pain, both in her kidneys and stomach, was agonising. For a second everything went dark.

She thought she would pass out.

She clutched at her back and wailed so loudly it reverberated down the whole valley. It was a struggle for her just to breathe. Frannie sobbed. Everything had ended in failure, and now her innocent baby was paying the price. She put a hand on her tummy. It was over. She couldn't push any more, or focus. Her body seemed to collapse on itself.

She was so wrapped up in her own private agony that she'd stopped paying attention to the men. But she looked up when one of them approached. Hugo stood over her with a pitchfork held threateningly in his hand. She looked at him blankly, her eyes glassy. When he raised the implement high, his T-shirt pulled up and she saw his bloated stomach spill over his jeans. She could smell his sweat, his nastiness. The spikes were pointed directly at her head.

'Time to go to sleep, bitch,' he said. His eyes looked small in his overfed face. Frannie closed her eyes, too horrified to even cry. She did the only thing there was left to do and prayed silently.

# Chapter
# Thirty-Eight

She lay there waiting, all still like an injured bird that knows its time is up. Any second her world would go blank. She anticipated the pain, wondered whether it would be so quick it would be like turning off a TV. *Ping. You're dead.* There was a dull roaring noise that she was not sure she was imagining. The sound came closer.

Then – BOOM! A big truck raced towards them, blindly crashing through a fence in the process. It screeched noisily to a halt. Frannie opened her eyes, saw Lars getting out, advancing at a run. She almost wanted to laugh. What could be worse than death? *Oh shit, oh shit, oh shit.* Here he was, her nemesis.

She rolled hastily to the side. Hugo stood frozen, the pitchfork still ready to strike. Lars was almost upon her. The bastard wanted to finish her off himself! She yelled as another contraction struck. The last few seconds she saw in slow motion. This was it – she was about to die.

But Lars seemed to change his mind. Like a charging bull he knocked Hugo to the ground, seized the pitchfork and used the wooden handle to knock him unconscious. Frannie flinched at the sickening blow.

Stefan's eyes darted nervously like a frightened rabbit. Lars pushed him in the direction of Frannie. She didn't understand what he said exactly, but it was something like, 'Medic, do your job.'

Stefan rushed over and put his hand on her belly. He got her to lie down with her legs up. He put on a latex glove and inserted a finger. He nodded, spoke to her but she shook her head.

'How many?' she asked in English.

He put up eight fingers. She fell back, groaned. He held her hand and made little panting noises. Expertly he examined her and gave her the thumbs-up. Out of the truck she saw Dorcas rushing up with a bottle of water.

'Frannie, you poor thing! I'm sorry I left you!' said Dorcas, her face tense with worry. Frannie grabbed the water thankfully, sucked it greedily down.

Lars turned to Stefan. 'How many you got here?'

'One,' said Stefan, he pointed in the direction of the outhouse. Within minutes Lars was wheeling a disorientated Tomek out on his hospital bed and untying his hand. Tomek stretched himself out, smiled.

Lars pulled out his mobile and quickly ordered two ambulances.

'*Danke schön*,' said Tomek weakly. '*Danke schön*.'

Frannie held Dorcas's hand tightly. She was still in agony but felt safe at last and somehow eased into her pain, cursing every contraction. With Dorcas teasing her, now and then, she was even able to smile.

'Wait till it's your fucking turn!' said Frannie.

# Chapter
# Thirty-Nine

When he'd driven up to Stefan's shithole of a farmhouse he'd been up for it, in the zone. But when he raced up, saw that dick Hugo holding a pitchfork over a woman about to drop, well, it brought it all back. Erna, the pregnancy she'd aborted. The fact that Dorcas was up the duff. Women – they were essential. *And he didn't fucking do women.*

He could have killed Hugo out of anger. But he didn't want to waste his time. Better to let him rot in jail and let the other inmates show him a thing or two. Once he'd done the rescue bit, he went back to his truck. He had something very important to do, and he had to get his shit together before the emergency services arrived. He grinned and rubbed his hands.

He took out a piece of cleanish paper, found a well-chewed pen and began to write. At the top he wrote grandly *Last Will and Testament* in confident strokes. He left everything to Dorcas. That made him chuckle. He had more money than he cared to think about. She'd have so many flowers she wouldn't be able to breathe.

He put it in an old envelope and tossed in the key to a safe deposit box he had at the Volksbank that was stuffed with cash. He wrote the location on a separate piece of paper. Then he opened the dashboard, which was stuffed with brown envelopes bulging with hundred-euro notes. He put everything together in the briefcase and snapped it shut. He was looking forward to seeing her face. *Who's the Daddy now, then?*

He leaned out of the window. 'Dörchen, come here a minute, I have a surprise for you,' he shouted.

She was crouched on the ground, holding on to the English woman for dear life. It looked as though they were stuck together.

She frowned. 'Lars, can't it wait?'

'Just a few minutes and then I'm gone,' he said airily, as if he'd be seeing her around as usual.

She stood up and came to him, her dark eyes wary. 'What?' she said, her eyebrows shooting up.

'You'll need this,' he said, putting the briefcase solidly in her hands.

She opened it and gasped. He explained about his shares in his club, the whereabouts of the safe deposit box and told her to keep all the paperwork safe. 'You know what the officials are like,' he said with a wink.

'But, Lars…?' she said, still not getting it.

'I don't need it where I'm going,' he said with a smile. Then he frowned, licked his lips. *Might as well get it over and done with.*

'I killed Hans, back at the club,' he said quietly with downcast eyes.

Dorcas put a hand to her mouth and made wide eyes. This was the bit he'd been dreading.

'I'm sorry, but it was necessary,' said Lars, 'He would have carried on doing it – this. And worse, probably. And now your child has no father, so this is compensation.'

She looked at him dazed and he could see the pure woman in her. She'd never looked so beautiful. He leaned forward and she fell into his arms. He embraced her tightly and felt soothed by the wafts of her exotic perfume. Gently, he gave her a kiss on the cheek.

'I think someone needs you,' he said, pushing her towards Frannie, whose breathing was now frantic.

'Sorry,' he called to Frannie in a low voice. She turned her head and smiled at him wearily.

He wound up the window and roared off in seconds. As always, he felt more at ease when the truck was moving. He dialled Inspector Koch. He had a few things to get off his chest; there was nothing he would leave out. When he wanted to, he could be as meticulous as any pen-pusher.

'Koch,' he said, 'I have a confession to make. This will be the making of your career, so make sure you bloody record this…'

# Chapter Forty

Dorcas could not believe the things that Frannie's body was doing. But the Englishwoman was stoic, kept at it, despite everything she'd been through. Dorcas gripped her hand and made every pant with her. Stefan said it was important to carry on breathing otherwise you'd run out of strength. It felt as though she was about to give birth as well.

Stefan seemed happier now he'd decided to give himself up. He was guiding Frannie through the process every step of the way. He didn't think he should have ever got involved in the organ-trafficking shit. He'd told them that he'd tried to get out of it, but apparently Hugo had threatened to kill him.

She didn't like to think of Hans's murder. Nor why Lars had done it. Now she'd got at the truth she was still confused about what to do – about the baby, about her life. Her head was in such a mess, she didn't know what to do with her thoughts. Frannie's grunts were now animal-like and she was gripping so hard it was like being pinched. It felt as though some force was melding them together.

🚗

Now she had water to stave off her aching thirst, Frannie felt that she could keep pace with the contractions without going under.

As long as she remembered to relax between every contraction, and steady her ragged breaths, she could keep going. But it was like surfing: you had the knowledge that at any point a huge wave could knock you down and then you'd go under. She didn't want to think about whining helplessly in agony with no resolve to fight back.

The fresh scent of the night invigorated her. She kept looking at the outline of what must be a hunter's moon. It blinked back at her, constant. She gazed at the expanse of sky, trembled at the infinity of nature that made her great struggle seem of no consequence. But Dorcas was at her side, and so she rallied and gathered all the resources she could muster for that last agonising push. *This must be the ring of fire.*

🚙

At one fifty-five a.m., Frannie let out a long scream. With a little slip, the baby burst out of her all covered in goo and blood. Frannie's back arched monstrously. But then he was on her chest, a perfect baby boy, making little squalling noises.

Dorcas felt as if her heart would burst. She touched his foot, just marvelled.

Frannie gave her a tired but contented smile.

'Why don't you move in with me for a while?' said Dorcas suddenly. It felt like the right thing. And this time Frannie's grin was heartfelt.

Two ambulances drove up. Even Tomek was smiling now that rescue was imminent.

'I'm going to call him Tom, OK?' she said.

🚙

The ambulance personnel were horrified to find a third injured person, Hugo, still conked out.

'Let the police deal with him,' said Dorcas to them abrasively. 'Or I could get a bucket of cold water.' She climbed into the ambulance. She held Frannie's hand.

'I'll have to tell Kurt,' said Frannie. 'He has a right to know, and to visit his son as he grows up.' She looked wistful. But then she started to smile. 'But I'm not going back to him. You and I should stick together.'

'Alright,' said Dorcas casually. 'There goes my *Ordnung!*' They both started to laugh. For the first time in months, Frannie finally felt everything was going to turn out well. Her beautiful new baby boy was just perfect, snuggled up in her arms. A sense of euphoria enveloped her. Now her real life could begin.

# Epilogue

Finally, Lars was where he felt most at ease, on a strip of empty *Autobahn*. The road opened out for him like the unfolding of his dreams. He had the radio turned on full, shouting the song out into the night through the open windows. The truck was going as fast as it could. He was exhilarated, happy as he had ever been. It was like being in the zone, but he was calmer; this was the Zen mode.

He went even faster. Damn, this was good. The high hum of the engine sang as he abruptly changed course and forced the truck at full throttle towards a massive concrete post. The wind seemed to propel him towards it and he knew he had been waiting for this moment his whole life.

The eager rush to meet his maker......

# Acknowledgements

Dear Reader, thanks for picking up my debut novel! It has only been possible thanks to my amazing editor Matthew Smith who gave me the chance to get my story out there when so many editors found it too dark. The process of writing a novel is never a solitary one, and I am indebted to the many individuals who helped by providing encouragement or gave many hours of their time answering questions for research.

Firstly thanks to editor Maxim Jakubowski who persuaded me to try writing a thriller novel. Creative writing tutor Dennis Foley of writers.com was instrumental in getting me to write more words per day. Kevin Mullins spent many hours listening to me talk about the characters as if they were real people. Author and creative writing tutor Ashley Lister looked at an early draft of the beginning and showed me how to make it sparkle.

For advice on police procedure, thanks to Scotty, a retired police officer from the Midlands. Security advice was given by John Carter, a security officer who once worked in a haunted shopping centre. The low-down on driving was provided by Worcester taxi driver and lorry driver Ted Morris. US professional barman Dennis Miles revealed what goes on behind closed doors at exclusive nightclubs and former veterinary practitioner Steve Jones and Dr William Burke made sure any scenes involving bloodletting were accurate. My thanks to Joffer, who provided background information on Afghanistan and on working conditions for soldiers on the front line. All the usage of German language was thoroughly checked by lawyer and academic Professor Veith Mehde of Leibniz University.

My old friend veteran designer Mark Cox did the stunning cover design. Guido Schicksnus made the promotional video and Tanja Schicknus handed out hundreds of promotional postcards in Germany. My chiropractor Malte Mittermeier and old friends Chris Brock and David Johnson were supportive in my path to publication.

Finally, thanks to my US agent, Don Fehr, who was interested in Night Driver when it was just a partial. Thanks to my husband Ingo for his support and my son Eric for being understanding. However, this novel would never have even got started if my daughter Scarlet hadn't slept so well as a baby, thus giving me the time and energy to begin....

Marcelle Perks is a British author and journalist living in Germany. She specializes in writing sexually-themed guide books, but also writes short stories.

As a film journalist, she has contributed to such publications as British Horror Cinema, Fangoria, The Guardian and Kamera.

*Night Driver* is her debut novel.

You can find out more about Marcelle on her author website - **marcelleperks.com**

URBANE

Urbane Publications is dedicated to
developing new author voices, and publishing
fiction and non-fiction that challenges, thrills and
fascinates.

From page-turning novels to innovative
reference books, our goal is to publish what
YOU want to read.

Find out more at
**urbanepublications.com**